W9-CNO-614

PRAISE FOR *I'LL STOP THE WORLD*

"Lauren Thoman's *I'll Stop the World* is a whip-smart mystery with a vibrant cast of characters that gives off great eighties vibes. I was absolutely dazzled by this unputdownable genre-bending novel that's equal parts coming-of-age suspense and an emotional tale of forgiveness and second chances."

—Mindy Kaling

"Thoman's sweeping debut defies categorization. A multigenerational mystery, a compulsively readable love story, an intricately woven sci-fi—whatever it is, *I'll Stop the World* is the mind-bendy time-travel eighties romp we all need right now. I'm obsessed with this book."

—David Arnold, *New York Times* bestselling author

"*I'll Stop the World* layers mystery upon mystery, from the everyday secrets in the lives of teens coming of age in a small town now to the dark shock waves still radiating out from deaths that took place decades before. Lauren Thoman's debut novel is a time-bending page-turner packed with twists no one will see coming. This is a story that continues to resonate long after you finish."

—Gwenda Bond, *New York Times* bestselling author of
Stranger Things: Suspicious Minds

"In this standout debut, Lauren Thoman takes the reader on a wild ride, deftly wrapping a coming-of-age story with a clever mystery, sprinkled with eighties nostalgia that'll have you reaching for your Bubble Yum. As I tore through the pages, I fell in love with the cast of flawed and funny characters, who felt as real as the friends I grew up with. Best of all, Thoman delivers an impossibly satisfying ending in a way only the very best time-travel storytellers can. This one should go at the top of everyone's must-read list!"

—Brianna Labuskes, *Wall Street Journal* bestselling author

I'LL STOP THE WORLD

I'LL STOP THE WORLD

A NOVEL

LAUREN THOMAN

MINDY'S BOOK STUDIO

Published by Mindy's Book Studio, New York

www.apub.com

Amazon, the Amazon logo, and Mindy's Book Studio are trademarks of Amazon.com, Inc., or its affiliates.

ISBN-13: 9781662509971 (hardcover)
ISBN-13: 9781662509964 (paperback)
ISBN-13: 9781662509957 (digital)

Cover design by Jarrod Taylor

Cover images: ©Karina Vegas / ArcAngel; ©Bipsun / Shutterstock

Printed in the United States of America

First edition

For my children.
I'd bend the universe for you.

A NOTE FROM MINDY KALING

Who knew a fast-paced mystery could make me choke up? Considering this novel has serious *Back to the Future* vibes, it's not surprising the story had me in my feelings.

Lauren Thoman's *I'll Stop the World* is an incredible coming-of-age mystery that takes place across two lifetimes, and two timelines, as a young man is given an unexpected chance to save his grandparents from their impending murder.

The novel has an amazing cast of characters, but I found myself rooting for the two heroes: Justin Warren, a lost kid who life dealt a crappy hand, and Rose Yin, a perfectionist who feels like an outsider in her own life.

I couldn't hold back the tears as I watched Justin and Rose race against time. This genre-bending book is much more than just a mystery. It had me thinking about fate, the nature of existence, the power of forgiveness, and second chances. I gasped at the twists and reveals! I had to turn back the pages and reread, looking for all the hints along the way. At Mindy's Book Studio, I am all about publishing books that are fun and entertaining, and this one will blow you away.

PROLOGUE

The rain was blinding, sweeping down in angry sheets. She clutched her umbrella with both hands as she made her way across the bridge, but it was no use. Like wearing a raincoat in a swimming pool.

Too late, too late, too late, her heart seemed to beat in time with her sneakers as they slapped against the pavement. Tendrils of sopping hair whipped against her neck and into her eyes as water dripped from her nose, her chin, her eyelashes.

She paused, her breathing coming in ragged gasps, holding tight to the bucking umbrella. It was no use. She couldn't see anything. He'd said it would be raining, but she had never thought it would be like *this.*

Hunching her shoulders against the relentless onslaught of water, she squinted at her watch, straining to make out the hands of the dial. She tilted her wrist this way and that, trying to catch a glint of moonlight, but the moon was gone, swallowed by heavy clouds.

Not that it mattered. She knew what it would say—that it was over. Everything. And she'd missed it all. Today of all days, how had everything gone so wrong?

Her eyes grew hot, tears mixing with raindrops. Clenching her teeth, she started to run again, ducking her head and fighting to keep her eyes open against the stinging rain. She trailed one hand along the cold metal railing, trusting it to keep her moving in a straight line. It was as good as using her eyes—better, even, in this weather.

A loud squeal, like a hundred jagged fingernails being dragged over a chalkboard.

She froze, her fingers still on the railing, her eyes snapping open. Her breath caught in her throat, and her heart thudded to a stop.

Both hands came up in front of her face, though she knew they wouldn't—couldn't—help.

All at once, she was washed in light.

FRIDAY

Chapter One

JUSTIN

"Everyone shut up and pay attention," Mr. Shaw growls as he passes by our row. He sounds menacing—dude looks like a grizzly and has a voice like an auger, so pretty much everything he does is menacing—but then he plops down at the end of a row and pulls out his phone, firing up a game of Candy Crush, so he clearly doesn't actually care.

I roll my eyes as the cacophony around us dims just enough to sort of hear our student body president, Taylor Strickland, introduce our guest speaker from a podium on the stage.

"As you all know, Mayor Rothman won this award back when he was a senior at this very school," she chirps into the microphone, tossing her blonde curls like she thinks she's in a Target ad.

"*Whocares,*" Dave Derrin coughs loudly from the seat in front of me. I kick the back of his seat, not because *I* care, but just because it's Dave and why not.

He spins around and waves his middle finger in my face; I, in turn, make a show of dropping my head onto Alyssa's shoulder. I'm not tired, but that doesn't seem like a good reason to pass up an opportunity to piss Dave off. Alyssa's thick black curls tickle the side of my face, and I reach up to tuck a glossy coil behind her ear, holding eye contact with Dave the whole time.

He's had a thing for Alyssa since sophomore year, and it kills him that she'd rather hang out with me than him.

Even if Alyssa and I are agonizingly platonic, it's still more than *they* are.

That does it. Dave pantomimes gagging, sticking his finger down his throat, but then turns back around and slumps in his seat.

Point, me.

"Get off," Alyssa mutters, shrugging my head from her shoulder and shaking her hair back into place as she continues adding detail to the page in her sketchbook where my profile is gradually being revealed in gray lines and smudged shadows. Her eyes flit to me, then back to her paper. She fills in the hair falling across my forehead with quick, light strokes.

I wish they meant more, these sketches she does. In a movie, it would mean something that the pages she holds are filled with images of me. My face in charcoals. My hands in pastels. My hunched shoulders; my ratty sneakers; my shaggy hair rendered in careful colored-pencil strokes depicting its current state of night-marish orange-red, the faded remnants of a rainy-day experiment in Dollar Tree hair dye a few weeks ago.

But all it means—to her, anyway—is that she is an artist, and I am a willing subject, and she needs the practice.

One day, she's going to be famous; I'm sure of it.

And I will still be here. Alone.

Onstage, the mayor steps up to the microphone. "It's good to be back here at Warren High, although it had a different name back when I walked these halls," he says with a smile. "Looked different, too. Did you know the layout is reversed from what it used to be? In my day, this was the administrative wing, and the auditorium was on the other side of the school. But although much has changed over the years, there's one thing that hasn't, and that's the high standards we set for our students. Which is why I'm so proud of each of the applicants for this year's Buford County Citizenship Award. As you know, we receive applications from all over the county . . ."

He drones on, building up to the ultimate announcement of who's won this year's citizenship award, this giant scholarship the county gives out every year, always to the same type of kid: honor roll, student council, lots of extracurriculars, community service, blah blah blah. The type of kid who doesn't really *need* a leg up, because they've already got so many, but they keep sprouting more anyway, like some sort of overachieving mutant spider.

I slouch in my seat, tuning him out.

"Why does the whole school have to be here for this?" I grumble, closing my eyes. "Why not just email them or something?"

"Shhh," Alyssa hisses, one of the only kids around us taking Shaw's *shut up* command seriously. "It's a big deal," she whispers, her voice barely louder than a breath. "Besides, it's getting us out of Government."

"But Government is where I nap."

"You and most of Washington," she says with zero humor. Alyssa is one of those people who registered to vote the second she turned eighteen, and not just because the school was giving out homework passes for anyone who could produce a valid voter registration. She literally has an election countdown in all her social media profiles that she updates every day.

She made me register, too, although honestly, I mostly did it for the homework pass. It's not that I don't care about my civic duty or whatever; it's just that it feels a little like getting excited about a glass of water while the whole building burns.

Alyssa pokes me in the arm with the back of her charcoal pencil. "Sit up. You're messing up my angle."

I oblige, trying to find the same position I was in at the beginning of the assembly. Alyssa and I have been friends since her family first moved here freshman year and she was seated in front of me in every class. Our last names—*Vizcaino* and *Warren*, respectively—function as the alphabetical equivalent of an arranged marriage, constantly smashed up against one another on the attendance sheet through no action of our own.

As opposed to my relationship with Alyssa in real life, which is regrettably, tragically, platonic.

"But seriously, I don't think it's *that* big a deal," I say, trying to hold as still as possible. "It's just a stupid scholarship." I'm not sure who I'm trying to convince more, me or her.

Alyssa smiles, but it's an empty one. The kind you give a stranger who tells you to *have a blessed day,* or when you happen to run into your mailman at the grocery store. On the paper, Alyssa's pencil traces the curve of my ear. "You don't have to make me feel better, Justin. I'm okay."

I turn to face her, trying to get a better look at her to gauge whether she's telling the truth, but she frowns and pivots my head forward again with her hand, the tip of her pencil scratching my ear. "Stop *moving* so much." Her touch sends a shiver down my spine that I hope she doesn't notice.

"Next time, maybe you should pick a model who isn't so ADHD."

"Next time, maybe my model should take his medication."

"I'm out again."

Alyssa sighs, but knows better than to say anything more. I try to make my one-month prescriptions last as long as possible, but they always run out eventually. I managed to stretch the last one for nearly three months, hoping Mom might have managed to save up the hundred bucks needed to refill it by then. I should've known better.

Mr. Jensen in the guidance office has been telling me for years that I could do better in school "if we could all just sit down and figure out the right accommodations," but that would require a mom who can regularly afford the medication, or who would ever bother to show up to a parent-teacher conference.

Besides, it's my senior year. Seems like a waste of time to change things up *now*. All I've got to do is make it through the next eight months without flunking out of school, and I'm golden—if by *golden*,

I mean I will live at home and work at the Dollar Tree until I die, which I guess is a pretty narrow definition, but you know. It is what it is.

Onstage, Mayor Rothman introduces the entirely predictable winner of the citizenship award, who struts across the stage like a self-important turkey, beaming as he shakes the mayor's hand. Keeping with tradition, he will now be insufferable for the rest of the school year.

Even though the Buford County Citizenship Award is a scholarship, they always present it in the fall, since they like having the winner do things like throw the first pitch at Little League games and flip on the lights for the town Christmas tree, and these things are kind of hard to do if the winner is away at college.

Two years ago, Alyssa's brother, Devon, won. He's now at MIT, and will probably go on to work at NASA or cure cancer or something.

Alyssa wasn't eligible to apply for this year's award. You have to declare your intention to attend a four-year college to qualify for the scholarship, and Alyssa opted for a two-year art school in New York. Her parents have not been thrilled. It was a whole Thing.

I, on the other hand, disappointed exactly no one by not applying for the award, because no one in my life is dumb enough to think I will ever win anything more significant than Employee of the Month at the Dollar Tree.

I mean, I haven't won *yet*, but I feel like my time is coming. Pete Arnold can't win *every* month, can he?

Also, I'm not going to college. When I told Mr. Jensen, he just shrugged and said, "I figured."

I couldn't decide whether that was unprofessional or just realistic. On the one hand, isn't it supposed to be his job to encourage me to follow my dreams or whatever? But on the other, if he *didn't* arrive at that conclusion, he'd be really bad at his job. After all, he's supposed to get to know the kids at this school, and anyone who's met me for more than three seconds can tell you I'm not college material.

So it's a draw, is what I'm saying.

"You *sure* you're okay?" I ask Alyssa, trying my best not to move, which only makes the task seem more daunting. From the waist up, I think I'm doing a decent enough job, but from the waist down, my leg jitters to a silent beat, determinedly signaling the *H* in *ADHD* to the rest of our row like a manic cheerleader. I catch dirty looks from the kids on either side of us. Stupid conjoined seats.

Alyssa shrugs. "Sure, whatever." Which is Alyssa-speak for *let's not talk about it.* "Are we going to the pep rally tomorrow?"

I recognize a pointed subject change when I hear one, but that doesn't stop me from groaning. "It's at *Dave's* house. I don't want to give up my Saturday night to go to Dave's."

It's my own fault for speaking too loudly, but Dave swivels in his seat again and glares at me. "You're not invited, *Bore*-en."

I ignore Dave's stupid play on my last name, Warren, which has been following me around with varying degrees of popularity since sixth grade, despite being painfully unclever.

"*Everyone's* invited, Dave. It's a school event."

Town safety codes wisely prohibit the setting of giant fires on school grounds, but instead of doing the reasonable thing and, you know, *not* having a massive bonfire, the Buford County School Board has been skirting the code for decades by hosting the fall pep rally on private property instead of at the school.

I have a hard time believing that this isn't *also* violating some sort of code, but it would appear that as long as it's not technically on government property, no one cares. Plus, I guess the optics of having a massive inferno on the front lawn of a school that's named after a couple who burned to death *in* that school—making me, their grandson, a morbidly twisted version of Buford County royalty—are not great.

Anyway, tomorrow night, Dave Derrin's family is hosting the Warren Memorial High School pep rally on their massive estate just north of Stone River, as they have every fall since before I was born.

Coincidentally, tomorrow night, I plan to be violently ill for a period of time that may or may not precisely coincide with the duration of the bonfire. But Dave doesn't have to know that.

"I probably *should* go," I say, feigning thoughtfulness, "since the school's named after me and all."

"It's not named after *you*, crotchstain. Just your dead grandparents. Besides, it's not like there's anything special about frying to a crisp. Anyone can do that."

You'd think that insulting someone's dead grandparents would be off-limits for most of civilized society, but that's what makes Dave special.

You know. Like how an abnormally large hemorrhoid is special.

"Ew," says Alyssa, wrinkling her nose at Dave. "Did you really just say that?"

I can see the wheels in Dave's head turning, trying to figure out a way to walk back the offensive comment enough to win Alyssa's approval, but without having to apologize to me.

I put an arm around Alyssa's shoulders, hoping she'll wait until Dave isn't looking to tell me to knock it off.

"I didn't mean it like that," he mutters, narrowing his eyes at my arm like he's trying to light it on fire.

"It's okay, Dave," I say magnanimously. "I forgive you. I know you really do want *us* at your party." I emphasize the *us*.

I feel more than see Alyssa roll her eyes; she's turned her attention back to her sketch, but her shoulders give a slight shake and her chin twitches, which translates roughly to *Justin, you are so full of crap.*

Fortunately, Dave does not speak fluent Alyssa, and therefore does not realize that she's only barely tolerating me right now. Based on the look he shoots at me, if you could give a person gonorrhea through sheer force of will, I'd be covered in warts by now.

Or, you know, whatever the actual symptoms of gonorrhea are. I don't know; I just imagine it's gross.

As if on cue, the winner wraps up his speech onstage, and Taylor Strickland skips back to the microphone, dismissing us to class with a reminder that *everyone's invited!* to the pep rally tomorrow night.

I grin at Dave as I rise to my feet, keeping one hand on the back of Alyssa's chair. "So I guess we'll see you there?" I say cheerily as she packs up her sketchbook.

"Whatever," he grunts, shrugging on his backpack and shoving his way out of his row.

"Single file, Mr. Derrin," Mr. Shaw calls after him, sounding bored.

Even though he wasn't talking to her, Alyssa jumps up, following the person beside her out of our row and grabbing my wrist to make sure I'm doing the same.

The wrist-grabbing isn't necessary; I'd follow her off a bridge. But I'm hardly going to complain about it.

Once we're back in class, Alyssa pulls out her sketchbook again, swapping her charcoals for colored pencils, but has barely started shading in my eyes when Shaw lumbers into the room, dropping a thick stack of papers on his desk with a sound like a door slamming.

"Okay, rabble," he rumbles as we all startle to alertness. He picks up the papers he just put down, clacking the edges against the desktop like an exclamation point. "One last thing before you scurry out of here for the weekend." He begins to distribute them, dividing the stack into chunks that he drops on the front desk of every row.

As we send stapled packets from hand to hand like the well-oiled machine we are, Shaw explains, "As the mayor mentioned at the assembly, applications for the internship at city hall need to be turned in to the front office by next Wednesday. These internships will last through the end of the school year, and can earn you college credit. While the mayor will only be accepting a handful of interns, anyone who completes an application will get a homework pass."

Shaw keeps talking, something about civic responsibility and the unfortunate work ethic of our generation, but I stop paying attention as I scan the application form, my eyes blurring on rows of questions I can't answer.

What are your college plans?

Which accomplishment(s) are you proudest of during your time at Warren Memorial High School?

Describe a time you demonstrated leadership among your peers.

Where do you see yourself in ten years?

What is your greatest wish for the future, and what are you doing now to make it a reality?

Alyssa is already hard at work filling out her form, pinning down her dreams and aspirations with her pen like she's afraid they might fly away.

I stare at mine, trying to come up with an answer to even one question, but they're all about achievements and ambitions, future plans and career goals.

This application wasn't written for someone like me.

The bell rings, and the room fills with the sounds of sneakers hitting the floor, papers rustling into folders, backpacks zipping closed. Alyssa sighs and slides her application into her sketchbook, half of the page already dark with her handwriting.

As we all cluster at the front of the room to shuffle out the door, I glance around to make sure no one is looking, then drop my application in the trash.

Chapter Two

ROSE

"Hi, would you like to donate a dollar to help—"

"Not interested, thanks."

Rose Yin let the hand holding the coffee can drop to her side as the woman shouldered past her, not even pausing to glance at the signs she'd spent all night creating.

FIRE DESTROYS LIFETIME OF TREASURED MEMORIES, one read in bold black marker. Rose had pasted newspaper clippings underneath, detailing the story of the fire that had destroyed Mrs. Hanley's garage and nearly burned down her house. The Buford County Sheriff's Department had ruled the circumstances "suspicious," but wouldn't commit to calling it arson.

"We're looking into it," officers said any time Mrs. Hanley or Noah's parents called the police station. "Just be patient."

Somehow, Rose doubted there was any definition of *patience* that would work out in Mrs. Hanley's favor. Meanwhile, the charred husk of the garage languished behind her house, neglected and forgotten.

HELP HER REBUILD, the other sign said in glittery pink letters over an enlarged photo of the elderly woman's face. The Xerox machine had turned Mrs. Hanley's warm-brown skin black and grainy, and her carefully arranged gray curls seemed to merge with the top of her head. They hadn't had many photos to pick from; she'd moved most of her albums to the detached garage after her husband died, so they were destroyed in the fire. This one had been plucked from a box underneath Rose's bed, taken on Noah's seventeenth birthday last year.

Noah had pushed for her not to use it. "Nope," he said the second she slid the enlargement out of the Kinko's envelope. "You can't show this to people. Gran will hate it."

"It's a good photo!" Rose insisted, tilting her head sideways.

"Not when you copy it in black and white and blow it up to twenty times its size."

"It has to be big for the posters."

"Just put a photo of the house on the posters."

"People don't want to give money to a house. They want to give it to a *person*."

Noah smiled ruefully. "I don't think they're going to want to give money at all, but I appreciate the effort."

"Sure, they will," Rose said confidently. She flipped the photo toward him, holding it up so her nose brushed against the back of the paper. "Who could say no to this face?"

As it turned out, lots of people.

Rose tapped the coffee can against the side of her leg, listening to its meager contents jangle against its tin sides. They'd been stationed in front of the Food Mart ever since school got out and had barely collected anything, despite the bustling Friday foot traffic.

She arched up onto her tiptoes, shading her eyes as she scanned the parking lot for the hundredth time.

"I don't think she's coming," Noah said from the lawn chair beside her, fanning himself with one of the dozens of flyers they'd had printed. His skin glistened like burnished copper in the unseasonable heat. Technically, summer had ended the week before, but it would seem that no one had remembered to tell the weather.

"She said she'd be here."

"If she was going to be here, she'd be here."

13

Rose bit the inside of her cheek, torn between loyalty to her sister and the truth in Noah's words. But before she could admit defeat, she brightened, recognizing a figure in the distance.

"Ha!" she exclaimed, pointing. "Told you."

"Hate to break it to you, but that's not Lisa."

"Shut up," she said, waving at Shawn as he made his way toward them through the parking lot.

"Well, if it isn't the finest citizen in Buford County," Noah said loudly. He took off his glasses, which had fogged up with sweat, and used his shirt to clean the lenses as Shawn jogged the last few steps to reach them. "Thanks for gracing us with your presence, your highness."

Shawn swept his arms to the side and bowed theatrically. "At your service," he said, flashing them one of his perfect, dazzling smiles. Just that afternoon, he'd been announced as the winner of the Buford County Citizenship Award, not that it was a surprise to anyone who knew him.

"Did you tell your dad yet? What did he say?" Rose asked.

Shawn shook his head. "Sorry I'm late," he said, ignoring her question. "How's it going so far?"

"Great. We've earned a whole fifteen bucks, plus these Cokes," Noah said, holding up what was left of the six-pack the Food Mart manager, Mr. Rushkin, had given them when they arrived. "I guess he's a big fan of Diane's," he said, referring to Rose's stepmother. When Mr. Rushkin had spotted the VOTE FOR DIANE pin on Noah's backpack, he'd practically forced the sodas into their hands.

Shawn grinned at Rose. "Hey, look at that, Rosie, you're famous!"

Rose and Noah exchanged glances, sharing a small laugh. "Actually," Noah said, "he thought *I* was Diane's kid."

Shawn wrinkled his nose. "But all Diane's kids are girls."

Noah shrugged, tossing Rose a knowing look. "I think we're all interchangeable to some people," he said, gesturing to his deep-brown skin.

"Oh." Shawn's smile flickered for a second before settling back in place. "Well, hey, a vote's a vote, right? Plus, free drinks!" He pulled one of the remaining Coke cans from its plastic ring and cracked it open, taking a long swig.

Noah looked at Rose with raised eyebrows. *Yikes,* he mouthed, a slight smirk playing on his lips.

She stifled a giggle. *Free drinks!* she mouthed back, and he grinned.

Shawn lowered the can, turning to Noah. "Where's Steph?"

Reality came crashing back over Rose at the mention of Noah's new girlfriend, washing away the warmth that had been rising in her cheeks. Suddenly, she became very interested in her nail beds.

"She had to work. Where's Lisa?"

Shawn finished his Coke in a second long gulp, wiping his mouth on the back of his hand. "At Charlene's," he said, his eyes surveying the parking lot. "Bonfire prep, you know."

Rose's shoulders fell at the nonchalant way he said it. As if this had always been the plan. As if Lisa hadn't told her earlier that *same day* that she would be there, to make up for missing the last two fundraisers.

Shawn was still talking. "She said she was sorry she couldn't—hold on a sec," he said, swiping the coffee can from her hand.

Shawn approached a woman with a baby on her hip who was struggling to push a cartful of grocery bags out of the store. Rose couldn't hear what he said to her, but a few seconds later, Shawn was steering the cart and the woman was trailing behind him, finger-combing her hair and attempting to surreptitiously straighten her blouse without dropping the baby.

"It's like he has some sort of superpower," Noah marveled as they watched the woman dig through her purse while Shawn loaded groceries into her car. He glanced at Rose, then tilted his head. "What's with your face?"

Rose gave him a pointed look, and Noah sighed. "Rosie, I'm sure Lisa didn't mean it personally. She probably just thought Charlene needed her help more than we did."

15

"But this was *important*."

"Maybe she thought that was important, too," he said, unfolding himself from the chair. He gave her a small smile, patting her on the shoulder. "I'm glad *you're* here, okay? It means a lot."

Rose's heart gave a happy flutter, then promptly dropped into her stomach. They were only doing this because his grandmother had lost everything, yet here Rose was, practically giddy at his touch.

What was *wrong* with her?

"She gave me twenty bucks!" Shawn said, holding up the coffee can in triumph as he jogged back.

Noah laughed. "You just doubled our take for the entire afternoon, and you've been here for five minutes."

"Just good timing, I guess," Shawn said, shrugging as the woman's car pulled out of its parking space. As she drove past them, she slowed the car down to smile at Shawn. He waved back, and Rose could see the woman's cheeks flush even through the tinted windows.

"Good *something*." Noah grinned, punching Shawn in the arm.

Shawn shook his head, blushing slightly. With his high cheekbones and athletic build, he looked like a fiery-haired Matt Dillon in *The Outsiders*. Lisa liked to joke that the only reason they were dating was because she was the only girl in Stone Lake who could form a complete sentence around him.

"Here," Shawn said, handing Noah the coffee can as the automatic doors of the Food Mart hissed open to spit out yet another frazzled-looking young mom trailed by kids. "Just do what I did."

Noah shook his head. "No way is that gonna work for me."

"Sure, it will. Just be friendly."

"We've been friendly all afternoon. It won't—"

"I'll bet you five bucks that you're wrong."

Noah sighed. "Show me."

Shawn flipped open his wallet, revealing a crisp green bill.

Noah rolled his eyes, then fixed a cheery smile on his face to approach the woman. "Hello, ma'am, would you like—"

"No, thank you," the woman said, skirting around him with her elbows tucked in close to her sides, like she was afraid she might be poisoned at the slightest touch.

Noah looked back at the two of them and shrugged, but Shawn made a shooing motion with his hands, indicating that he should follow her.

Rose frowned. "Shawn, I don't think—"

"*Shhh*, just watch, he'll get her," Shawn whispered insistently.

Rose remained unconvinced, but Noah trudged ahead, keeping his smile plastered on.

The woman's car was parked at the front of the lot, close to where they were sitting, so he reached her car right as she finished loading her kids into the back seat. With his free hand, he gestured toward her groceries. "Would you like some help—"

"Don't touch that," the woman said brusquely, stuffing the bag closest to Noah into the open trunk, as if fearful he'd try to swipe it. She gave him a quick once-over, her eyes taking in his tight black curls, neatly tucked-in shirt, and wire-rimmed glasses, before coming to rest on the coffee can. "Maybe if you got a *job*, you wouldn't have to beg for *my* money," she sniffed.

Rose's chest tightened, the air in her lungs as thick as soot. Beside her, she felt Shawn stiffen, but she grabbed his arm before he could make things worse. *Just walk away,* her stepmother always said about people like this woman. *They're looking for a fight, but you don't have to let them find one.*

But now, Rose wanted to fight. She wanted to tell the woman how wrong she was about Noah, how smart and kind and hardworking he was, how special he was. She wanted the woman to know she was small, and that she would always be small because her mind was small, but that Noah would be big because his heart was big.

Instead, she stayed where she was, her hand on Shawn's arm, and said nothing. Like she was supposed to.

17

For a second, Noah stood completely still, his hand still pointing to her cart. Slowly, he dropped his arm to his side, his smile gone. "Sorry to bother you, ma'am."

He walked back with his jaw clenched as the woman hurried to load her groceries into her car, her eyes tracking Noah as if she were afraid he'd come running back to steal her boxes of Kraft Mac and Cheese and Lean Cuisine.

"Dude, I'm sorry," Shawn said once Noah reached them. "I didn't think—"

"It's fine, man," Noah said quietly. "Just leave it alone." He kept his back to the parking lot, hands shoved deep in his pockets. No one spoke as they waited for the woman to leave, Shawn stealing glances toward her car while Noah kept his eyes on the ground and Rose kept hers on Noah. When the woman finally pulled out of her space, it seemed to Rose as though she drove by them at a laborious crawl, maybe to gawk at them one last time. Rose didn't give her the satisfaction of looking.

Once she was gone, Noah surveyed the lawn chairs and posters, then sighed. "I'm gonna call it a day, guys. Thanks for trying."

"Noah," Rose started to say, but he patted her shoulder, causing gooseflesh to prickle up her arms.

"It was a nice thought, Rosie. Thank you." He looked at the coffee can and smiled slightly. "I'm going to take this over to Gran. Brighten her day a bit."

Rose doubted that their paltry efforts would be all that day-brightening, but she didn't bother to point that out. She knew the can contained exactly forty-three dollars and twenty-nine cents, including the five dollars in ones and change she'd put in at the beginning of the afternoon so that the can wouldn't be empty. She'd been adding it up in her head every time someone dropped a few coins or bills into the can.

Five fundraisers in the past two months, and all they had to show for it was a little more than $300. At this rate, Noah would have kids of his own before they raised enough to replace what his grandmother had lost.

"Wait." Shawn's wallet was still in his hand. He took out the five-dollar bill and stuffed it through the slit in the lid of the can, giving Noah a small smile. "Fair's fair, right?"

"Sure. Thanks, man."

"You want me to come with you?" Rose offered.

"Nah," Noah said. "I'll see you later, Rosie. Bye, Shawn."

Shawn and Rose stood side by side as Noah walked off, the can dangling limply from his hand. Once he was out of earshot, Shawn muttered, "I should've said something."

"He didn't want you to."

"But maybe if I—"

"Shawn. Let it go," Rose said firmly. Shawn was a smart guy, but he didn't seem to get that some things couldn't be fixed with a winning smile and a clever joke. Some things were bigger than that.

Shawn sighed, looking down at the posters and chairs. "I guess we should pack up."

After loading everything into her car—or rather, her dad's car, a brown Ford Escort that coughed and wheezed like a lifelong chain smoker—Rose offered Shawn a ride home. His house wasn't far, only a few streets over from hers, and they spent most of the drive in silence.

"You okay?" Shawn asked as she pulled into his driveway.

Sure is what she meant to say, but what came out was, "I don't know."

He paused, his fingers on the door handle. "You know they're not going to be together forever, right?"

"What?" Rose blinked, unsure what he was talking about.

"Noah and Steph. I mean, she's a nice girl, but . . . he's going to figure it out eventually."

"Figure *what* out?"

He gestured vaguely toward her. "That there's . . . a better . . . option," he trailed off weakly.

"Oh. *Oh.* Shawn, I wasn't—I mean, that's not what I was thinking about." Rose's cheeks grew warm, and she sank down into the driver's seat, wishing she could disappear.

"Oh." Shawn's face flushed, too, rapidly approaching the color of his hair. "Sorry, it's just, I thought—anyway, what did *you* mean?"

Rose made a mental note to have a serious talk with Lisa about which topics were and were absolutely *not* okay to discuss with her boyfriend. "I just hate that I can't do anything to help Mrs. Hanley," she said, determined to change the subject.

"You did do something!" Shawn protested, but Rose made a face at him.

"Forty dollars isn't going to get her garage repaired, Shawn. It's not going to make the police care about figuring out who did it, or replace any of the stuff she lost." She sighed. "I just feel so useless sometimes, you know? Like everything I do is just like . . ." She flicked her fingers wide and blew a raspberry, pantomiming an explosion.

"That's not true," Shawn said.

She glanced sideways at him. "Shawn, I can't even get my own sister to make time for me anymore. And I'm pretty sure Noah was only there because he felt sorry for me, even though Mrs. Hanley is *his* grandmother. Everyone has somewhere they'd rather be than with me."

"Not me." Shawn flashed her one of his kilowatt grins.

"You're telling me you wouldn't rather be with Lisa right now than with me?"

He shrugged, his smile flickering. "I like being with you," he said. "You're my friend."

She noticed he hadn't answered the question, but he didn't have to. She knew what she was to him, to everyone. A footnote in other people's stories.

"Anyway, I better get inside," Shawn said, jolting her out of the awkward silence that had arisen between them. "Thanks for the ride," he said, unfolding himself from the passenger seat and climbing out of the car. "And hang in there, okay? I'm sure next time will be better."

Rose gave him a tight smile as he closed the door. "Sure. Next time."

Chapter Three

Lisa

Lisa shut the fridge, a Tupperware container of last night's leftovers in her hand, to find Rose gaping at her from the garage doorway.

"What are you doing here?"

"I . . . live here?" Lisa stammered.

"I thought you were at Charlene's."

Lisa's heart sank at the note of accusation in Rose's tone. She'd hoped that Shawn would've explained *why* she needed to go to Charlene's instead of the fundraiser, but from the hurt in her stepsister's voice, she could tell he hadn't. Or at least, not very well. "I was," she said carefully. "It was a last-minute thing. The whole planning committee bailed, and Char was freaking out, and—"

"So you decided to bail on me instead." Rose kicked off her shoes and placed them by the door, keeping her eyes downcast.

"I'm sorry, Rosie. I tried to find you after school, but you and Noah had already left, so I asked Shawn to explain." Lisa frowned, wishing Rose would put herself in *her* shoes for once. Did she really think that Lisa had just changed her mind on a whim? Lisa *wished* she had the luxury of acting frivolously and doing whatever she wanted, but she wasn't that lucky. "I just thought there would be more of you guys at the Food Mart, so you wouldn't need me as much."

"Why were you so *needed* setting up for the stupid bonfire, anyway? Isn't it just dumping a bunch of firewood in a pile?"

Heat flooded Lisa's face. Charlene was Rose's friend, too. Shouldn't Rose care that the rest of the planning committee had just ditched her without any notice? Rose could have planned her fundraiser for any day, but she'd chosen the day before the bonfire, when she knew Charlene would be up to her ears in preparation. Yet somehow it was *Lisa's* fault that she'd gone to help her best friend? "There's a lot more to it than dumping wood in a pile. You can see it for yourself tomorrow."

"I'm not going."

Lisa tossed up her hands. "Why not?"

Rose still wouldn't meet her eyes. "I just . . . don't feel like it." There was a slight tremor in her voice.

Lisa sighed, working to swallow her frustration as she studied Rose's face. Despite her stepsister's valiant effort not to make eye contact, her cheeks were obviously flushed, her eyes glossy. Something was up, and it wasn't just Lisa's absence from the fundraiser.

"Come here," Lisa said, pulling out one of the chairs at the kitchen table and patting the seat. It would be easy to stay annoyed with Rose, but that would also mean Rose would stay annoyed with *her*, a possibility that made Lisa's stomach ache.

Besides, if there was something bigger on Rose's mind, something weighing on her that she was reluctant to talk about . . . well, Lisa could relate to that.

Rose flopped into the chair as Lisa spooned leftovers onto a plate and stuck it in the microwave. When the timer went off, she brought it to the table with two forks and set the plate between them. "What's going on with you?" she asked, scooping up a forkful of creamy noodles and popping them in her mouth. "Why don't you want to go tomorrow?"

Rose sighed, picking up her own fork to flick peas over to Lisa's side of the plate. "Everything is just . . . weird right now," she said, eyes focused on her pea extraction.

"Everything like . . . Noah?" Lisa guessed. Rose had tried to act like it wasn't a big deal when he started dating Steph that summer, but Lisa had shared a wall with her for too long to be fooled. And in the years before they were sisters, they'd filled countless weekend sleepovers with whispered secrets and giggly games of Truth or Dare. In all that time, Lisa couldn't remember a time when Noah Hanley wasn't one of Rose's biggest Truths. Even if she never told him.

Rose nodded miserably. "Among other things." She cut Lisa a withering look. "Speaking of which, could you not talk to your boyfriend about my personal life?"

"Why? What happened?"

"He gave me a pep talk. About Noah. Which could not have been more awkward if it had come from my actual dad."

Lisa couldn't help but laugh, despite Rose's mortification. "Okay, I'm sorry, but that's hilarious."

"It was *not*," Rose insisted, although a smile tugged at the corners of her mouth.

"I swear I didn't say anything." The last thing Lisa wanted to talk to Shawn about right now was secret crushes. "He must have figured it out on his own."

"Oh *no*," Rose said, dropping her head into her arms on the table. "Is it *that* obvious?"

"Nah," Lisa lied. "But Noah is his best friend, so maybe he's just been paying extra-close attention."

"Maybe," Rose said, sounding unconvinced. She sighed, sticking another bite of casserole in her mouth. A small mountain of peas had accumulated on Lisa's side of the plate. Lisa scooped up a few, trying not to resent Rose for her simple problems and their simple solutions. Not everyone could wear their feelings so plainly on their sleeves.

"Anyway," Rose said, chewing, "it's not just Noah. It's kind of everything right now. I feel like everyone got a manual for what they're supposed to be doing with their lives, and I was, I don't know, absent that day or something."

Lisa shook her head, carefully spearing peas onto her fork in a neat line. "I don't think everyone knows what they're doing," she said softly.

"Could've fooled me," Rose muttered.

Lisa kept her eyes focused on her fork, sure that if she met her sister's gaze, Rose would see all the questions Lisa still couldn't answer. All the parts of herself she didn't dare show, but couldn't bear to hide.

This was the double-edged sword of your mother marrying the father of your best friend. Your best friend became your sister. The window you already had into her soul grew from a single pane into twin houses of crystal-clear glass. Perfect for basking in each other's light.

But impossible when you needed to draw the curtains.

They both looked up at the sound of the front door opening. "Hello? Lees?"

"In here, Char," Lisa called.

Rose raised an eyebrow. "Charlene is here now?"

"Yeah, we weren't actually finished with the bonfire prep," Lisa admitted. "She just dropped me off before running out for some more supplies." It would've made sense to stay at Charlene's house, since that's where the bonfire would be, if Charlene's mother and her never-ending political commentary hadn't been there, too. Charlene's parents were good friends and major donors of Diane's opponent in the upcoming mayoral election, and apparently having Diane's daughter in her home did nothing to dissuade Moira Derrin from enumerating her many complaints about Diane's candidacy.

After an hour, Lisa couldn't take it anymore. She either had to say something or spontaneously combust, neither of which would have worked out in her favor. Charlene's parents already hated that their daughter's best friend was Black, and that her mother was running against their beloved Franklin for mayor; all it would take was one instance of Lisa losing control for them to forbid the two of them from seeing each other entirely.

Lisa and Charlene couldn't risk that. So instead, they'd left.

Charlene walked into the kitchen, her arms loaded with poster board, a brown fast food bag dangling from one hand. "Oh, hi, Rose."

Charlene had actually been Rose's friend first, back in fourth grade. Lisa had stayed home for a week with chicken pox, and when she returned to school, a new girl with blonde pigtails was pushing Rose on the swings. They quickly hit it off and stayed a trio throughout the rest of elementary and middle school.

Since high school, though, their dynamic had shifted. Rose had branched off toward Noah, Lisa had started dating Shawn, and somewhere in the midst of all that, she and Charlene had become . . . something else.

Now Charlene's round cheeks were flushed from the unseasonable heat, setting off her freckles in stark contrast to her fair skin. Blonde curls pulled free of her ponytail to cling to her neck, and she had a smear of blue paint across her forehead where she'd brushed her hair out of her eyes with stained fingers.

She looked beautiful.

Lisa grinned, standing hastily and shoving the mostly empty casserole plate toward Rose. "Hey, would you mind putting that in the dishwasher?" she asked, eyes still on Charlene.

"Oh. I guess. Sure."

"We can talk more later tonight, though?" Lisa said. She took the fast food bag from Charlene, their fingers brushing. A shiver of heat ran up Lisa's arm.

"Want to go work on this up in my room?" she asked. Charlene nodded before the question had finished leaving her lips.

Rose said something else, maybe *yeah* or *okay* or some other single-breath agreement, but Lisa didn't catch what it was, or remember what exactly she had asked.

We'll talk later, Lisa assured herself as she and Charlene hurried up the stairs.

Chapter Four

SHAWN

Shawn waited for Rose to drive away before pulling his house key from his pocket and letting himself inside. Carefully, he untied his sneakers and placed them on the rack by the front door, keeping an eye out for any renegade crumbs of dirt that might try to sneak from his shoes onto the spotless linoleum. His eyes fell on his schoolbooks, the citizenship-award plaque perched neatly on top. For a second, he considered leaving the plaque on the hall table for his father to see when he arrived home, but then picked up the whole stack. Wouldn't want to create clutter.

After dropping the books off in his room, Shawn walked into the kitchen and opened the fridge. He stared inside for a minute, wishing he'd thought to actually go *into* the grocery store when he'd stopped to see Rose and Noah. Breakfast for dinner it was.

Draping his headphones around his neck, Shawn got to work cracking eggs and arranging bacon in a skillet. He sang along to the music trickling out of the tiny speakers, swapping out the lyrics on occasion for whatever similar rhymes popped into his head. He was in a good mood tonight; finally, he had done something that his father might actually be proud of.

He was in the middle of running a block of bright-yellow cheddar over a box grater, repeating an absentminded chorus about "sweet dreams of shredded cheese," when he froze, listening. A familiar mechanical hum rumbled over the music.

The garage door. His dad was home early.

Shawn looked over the messy countertop in dismay, taking in the open egg carton, the half-empty package of bacon, the little flecks of cheese that had escaped the bowl he'd placed under the grater. He'd thought there would be time to clean up.

Stupid, stupid, stupid.

Moving quickly, he put away the eggs and bacon, and was just sweeping the cheese crumbs into his hand when his dad walked in. Shawn straightened, closing his fingers around the detritus in his palm.

His dad frowned, his copper mustache pulling down at the corners. "You planning on keeping that, son?"

"Sorry." Shawn dumped the crumbs down the sink as he washed his hands, deflecting the flow of the water to make sure no bits of food lingered in the gleaming basin.

Shawn cleared his throat as he dried his hands. "Dad, I've got some good news."

"Hrm." His father didn't bother to look at him as he flipped through the mail.

"I won the Buford County Citizenship Award today."

Shawn waited for his father to respond, maybe even congratulate him, but he just kept examining the stack of bills, his expression unchanging. Did he not understand what a big deal this was?

"It's full tuition, for four years," Shawn explained, pressing ahead. He searched his father's face for pride, relief, surprise, *anything* that might indicate even mild interest in his son's accomplishment. His father had never praised him for good grades or championship-worthy athletic seasons—excellence was expected for the son of Gabe Rothman; anything less was to fail—but surely even he could see that *this* went above and beyond mere excellence. "They only award one a year for the whole county, out of hundreds of applicants. It's a really big honor—"

"I know what it is, son."

Shawn swallowed, his throat thick. "So you don't have to worry about money for college. The award will cover all of it."

Finally, his father looked at him, his expression inscrutable. After a long moment, he spoke, his tone icy. "So even after our discussions about what you would do after graduation, you went ahead and applied for this award anyway. Behind my back."

"I wanted it to be a surprise," Shawn said, his heart thunking down into his stomach. "It was a long shot anyway, so I just thought—"

"Did you?" his father interrupted. "Think, I mean?"

"I—I mean, you said you weren't going to pay for college, so I figured—"

"I said you didn't need to *go* to college. Not when you have a perfectly good career waiting for you right here. Or is what I do for a living not good enough for you?"

Shawn took a deep breath, willing himself to remain calm. Getting emotional only ever made his father angrier. He didn't know why he'd allowed himself to hope that the award might make a difference, no matter how impressive it was, or how hard it had been to earn. Gabe Rothman had only ever seen one acceptable path for his son: his own.

It doesn't matter, Shawn told himself. *Who cares if he doesn't approve?*

After all, with the citizenship award, he didn't *need* his dad's blessing. He could go wherever he wanted, far away from here, and there wasn't a damned thing his father could do to stop him.

Still, Shawn couldn't bring himself to let it go. Not yet. "Dad, just because I want to go to college doesn't mean I don't respect what you do. I have a lot of respect for you and your business. I just feel—"

"Listen to you, all *I want* and *I feel*. That's the problem with kids today. You think it's all about your *feelings*. No consideration for anyone but yourself."

"I just think that—"

"You don't *think*. You just do whatever you want to do, and then when it doesn't work out, you'll expect me to come in and fix it all for you. Well, I'm telling you now, son, I won't do it. Once you leave this house, you're on your own. Don't come crawling to me when things don't work out the way you want."

Shawn fought the urge to ball his hands into fists. "But, Dad, I don't—"

His father held up a hand, cutting him off. "Just stop, son. You're only embarrassing yourself. This conversation is over." He closed his eyes for a long moment, exhaling slowly out his nose. On the stove, the bacon was starting to smoke. He nodded to the pan. "You're burning your dinner."

"I made enough for both of us," Shawn said quietly.

"I've lost my appetite."

Shawn stood frozen in the kitchen as his father ascended the stairs. He waited until he heard the bathroom door close and the shower turn on, before driving a fist into his leg, over and over, biting back the urge to yell until the throbbing in his thigh drowned it out. He'd have a bruise later, but it didn't matter. No one would see it.

For a second, he just stood there, relishing the ache in his leg, breathing in the sharp stench of burning grease as smoke stung his eyes.

Ten more months.

Forty-three weeks.

Three-hundred-something days.

He could make it ten more months. Then he could leave.

Taking a deep breath, Shawn turned off the stove, picked up the spitting pan, and threw it in the spotless sink.

Chapter Five

JUSTIN

"Why'd you say you'd go if you didn't want to go?"

"To piss Dave off," I say, dropping my keys on the kitchen counter and opening the fridge, then the pantry. Ugh. How do we never have any food? Grabbing a pad of Post-its off the counter, I start making a list of things we need from the store.

"You know what would piss Dave off even *more*?" Alyssa says as I add milk, bread, peanut butter to my list. "Actually going."

"Yeah, but then *my* night would suck."

Pasta sauce

Vegetables???

Aluminum foil

"You don't know that. It could be fun. Besides, we're seniors. This is the last bonfire we'll ever have."

"You say that like it's a bad thing."

The door to the basement opens and Stan emerges, balancing a stack of dirty dishes in one hand as he leans heavily on the railing with the other. "You're home from school," he announces gruffly, as if I didn't already know.

"No shit," I mutter under my breath. I cross **vegetables???** off the list and replace it with **ramen**.

"Hey, Stan," Alyssa says with a smile, taking the dishes from him and depositing them in the sink.

"Hey there, sweetheart," Stan says, grinning at her like the creeper he is. "Draw anything new today?"

Her eyes light up, and a second later, her sketch pad is in her hand. She flips through it to her assembly sketch of me and holds it out for Stan's evaluation. Alyssa has always thought Stan is charming. It's the one thing she is consistently wrong about.

Stan is kind of hard to explain. He's my grandfather's cousin, or cousin's cousin, or something, and the only member of our family who still talks to us. My grandmother—Mom's mother—was an only child, whose parents died just a couple of years before she did. That left my grandfather's side of the family, who took Mom in and raised her after my grandparents died in the high school fire. But they cut off all contact with her after she got pregnant with me, the result of a one-night stand with some guy she met at a party her sophomore—and final—year of college.

The way she tells it, the pregnancy was just an excuse. They were convinced that if my grandmother had never gotten pregnant with my mom, then their son wouldn't have married her, and he would still be alive. They'd only taken Mom in out of guilt, and jumped at the chance to kick her out.

Anyway, not long after that, Stan showed up, saying he'd heard about what had happened through the family grapevine. While he couldn't mend things with the rest of the family, he offered to help out however he could. He even bought this house for her so we could all stay together, one big happy dysfunctional family.

Mom was so grateful that, when I was born, she named me after him. Justin Stanley Warren.

I know this makes Stan sound like some kind of saint, but he's not. He's grumpy and mean and has probably never had a single moment of fun in his entire existence. He's always there for Mom, making excuses for her every time she gets fired and picking her up at three in the morning when she's too wasted to drive home, but can't be bothered to care about my life, unless it's to tell me what a screwup I am or how I'm being unfair for expecting her to act like an actual adult.

Stan finishes examining Alyssa's drawing—he proclaims it *incredible*, a word that apparently applies only to pictures of me, but not actually *me* me—then shuffles toward me. He looks over my shoulder at my shopping list, his nasty old-man breath brushing my cheek. "Oreos."

I lean away. "Oreos are expensive, Stan." I'm arguing mostly because I'm allergic to agreeing with Stan on anything. Oreos are delicious.

"Here," Stan says, digging a crumpled twenty out of his pocket and handing it over.

"Ew," I say, wrinkling my nose at the softened bill. "Where'd this come from, your mattress?" Stan deals almost entirely in cash. When I asked him why he doesn't just get a credit card—or even a debit card—like a normal person, he gave me a long-winded speech about our society's overreliance on technology, which I tuned out after about fifteen seconds.

He shrugs. "If you don't want it, give it back," he says, holding out his hand.

"Not if you want your Oreos," I say, shoving the bill into my pocket. It may be a gross bill, but money is money. And maybe if I get him his stupid cookies, he'll forget to ask for the change.

"You talk to your mom today?" Stan asks me, getting himself a glass of water from the sink before lowering himself slowly into a chair at the table. He's moving more stiffly than usual. His bad knee must be acting up. Some injury from when he was a teenager that left him with a gnarly scar that looks like a smiley face. Probably means it's going to rain.

I shake my head. "Why? You think she got fired again?"

Stan sighs. "You know you're allowed to text your mother just because she's your mother, right, Justin?"

"I could lick the crust off all the dirty dishes in the sink just because it's food. Doesn't make it appealing."

"Do you have to act like such a brat all the time?"

"Nope, I do it special just for you, Stan."

Alyssa elbows me as she walks by, mouthing *stop it* when I look up from my list to meet her eyes. I roll my eyes, but resist the urge to keep messing with Stan. For now.

He just makes it so *easy*.

She sits across from him at the table and folds her hands. "You need anything else from the store? We're getting ready to run out."

"That's sweet of you, dear, but I think I'm good," Stan says, patting her arm.

Alyssa smiles, placing her hand over his and giving it a brief squeeze. I consider making gagging noises but decide against it, since I don't want to piss off Alyssa. Even if her affection for Stan *is* super gross. "Well, you just let us know if you think of anything, okay?"

"Will do."

For the life of me, I cannot understand why she likes him. He spends about 80 percent of his time in the basement with his weird old-man hobbies that he keeps trying to rope me into, 20 percent of his time parked in a recliner watching *The Young and the Restless*, and zero percent being even slightly normal or cool. Once I asked her what she saw in him, and she said he was "cute," and I had to resist the urge to vomit.

"I'm done," I announce, pocketing the Post-it and picking the keys back up. "You ready?"

Alyssa nods, refilling Stan's glass of water and giving him a little wave before joining me at the door.

Stan and I don't bother saying goodbye to each other. We never do.

Back in my Mustang—purchased off Craigslist last summer for $1,500, which was probably too much considering its mismatched

33

paint job, rattly transmission, and slightly sour smell—I steer toward the Dollar Tree, where I can probably get most of the stuff on my list with my employee discount. We're nearly there when Alyssa gasps, staring at her phone. "Oh my god."

"What happened?"

"They found a *body* in the river."

"Who found a body in what river?"

"Some guy walking his dog out near Wilson Bridge, and the Stone." I glance over and see her switching between various social media apps, where kids from school are already filming videos and snapping selfies from the bridge. From the animated way they're talking to their cameras, I assume there are already a few dozen dead-body theories being crafted into hashtags.

Alyssa's got her phone muted, and I can't make out the auto-generated captions while driving, so I wait for her to fill in the details. "Oh, people are saying it's not actually a body; it's just human remains," she says, clicking to a new video.

"What's the difference?" I find a space near the front of the lot and steer in.

"A body is whole. Remains are, like . . . pieces, I think," Alyssa says.

"Gross."

"But it's not like someone got hacked up," she continues. "It seems like these remains are super old. Maybe even decades old."

"Ah, so no one we know, then." Pity. Could've been Dave. You've got to cross over Wilson Bridge to get to his house.

"Still pretty cool, though," Alyssa says. She looks up at me, mischief in her eyes. "Want to go check it out?"

I point to the store. "I need to get groceries."

"We can come back here after."

"They've probably got the whole area blocked off anyway. We won't even be able to see anything."

"Let's go find out."

Chapter Six

Lisa

"You want to go roller-skating?" Lisa asked, stretching out across her bed to turn down the radio, currently blasting Madonna. She glanced at Charlene, whose nose was adorably wrinkled as she focused on blowing a giant pink bubble with her strawberry Bubble Yum.

The bubble popped, and Charlene shook her head. "I'm kinda tired."

Truthfully, so was Lisa. After Charlene had arrived with more supplies, they'd spent the rest of the afternoon slathering squares of poster board with blue and gold paint and piles of glitter, making signs for the bonfire. She glanced in the mirror over her dresser and lightly brushed her hand over the edges of her neat Afro, dislodging a few stray sparkles that fluttered onto her bedroom carpet.

Still, as tired as she was, it was Friday night, and she longed to go out into the world and do something fun. Something where she could hold Charlene's hand and no one would think it was strange. Tomorrow was about her family and Shawn and keeping up all the appearances she needed to maintain, but tonight, it was just her and Charlene.

"A movie then?" Lisa suggested. "We haven't seen the one about those kids who go underground yet. I've heard it's good." Plus, a darkened theater sounded really appealing at the moment.

Charlene shrugged, her eyes flitting over to the calendar tacked to Lisa's bulletin board. "Sure, whatever."

Lisa sat up, tilting her head. "What's wrong?"

"Nothing." Charlene stretched out her gum, twirling it around a finger before popping it back in her mouth. She wouldn't meet Lisa's eyes.

Lisa peered at the calendar to see what was so distracting to Charlene. "The brunch?" she guessed quietly.

Charlene sighed, pulling a Kleenex from the box on Lisa's nightstand and wrapping her gum in it. She pitched it into the trash can in the corner as she flopped onto her back on the bed. Lisa dropped down beside her, their shoulders bumping against one another.

"It's really not a big deal," Lisa said, trying to convince herself as much as Charlene. Her family was going to brunch in the morning at Emerson's Tearoom as part of a campaign photo op. Shawn was meeting them there. As Lisa's boyfriend, he was already scheduled to be part of it, but the citizenship-award win that afternoon would definitely be a plus. The picture was set to accompany a profile of Lisa's mom in the *Stone Lake Gazette* next week leading up to the debate.

"Lisa," Charlene said softly.

"It's just a stupid brunch," Lisa insisted. Her stomach twisted, belying what she'd just said, but she kept her smile glued on.

"Is it?"

Lisa was quiet. She knew it was more than that. It wasn't just eating pancakes and drinking orange juice while a local photographer snapped photos. It was the public picture they were painting of who their family was: two loving parents, one cherubic baby, two supportive teenage daughters, one award-winning boyfriend.

The perfect family.

"Everyone knows these things don't really mean anything," Lisa said, picking at the purple polish on her nails.

"If it doesn't mean anything, then don't go."

"I have to go."

"Then tell Shawn not to go."

"You know I can't do that."

"Why not?" Charlene propped herself up with her elbow, a challenge in her eyes. "Give me one good reason why not."

"You know why not."

"Do *you*?" Charlene's lower lip trembled, pink rising in her cheeks. Her emerald eyes shimmered.

Lisa reached up to trace a finger along Charlene's jawline. "You know I'd bring you if I could," she said softly.

"Would you?" Charlene's hand closed over hers, and she dropped her head onto Lisa's shoulder, their fingers weaving together. "I just feel so . . . invisible sometimes," she said, her voice small.

"You're not," Lisa insisted. "I see you."

"You just don't want anyone *else* to see me."

Lisa frowned, twirling a tendril of Charlene's golden hair around her finger. "Do you *want* anyone else to see you? With me, I mean?"

Charlene sighed. "No. My parents would flip out."

"Yeah." Lisa still didn't know how her own mother and stepfather would react. Better than Charlene's parents, she thought. Or at least, she hoped. But there was only one way to find out, and she wasn't ready for that yet.

"But you have this whole other life that you want people to see, and I'm not in it," Charlene continued. "I just have to sit around waiting for whenever you can squeeze me in. And it's never the important stuff. I only get the parts that don't matter."

"Are you kidding?" Lisa squeezed Charlene's hand. "You get the parts that matter the *most*."

"You know what I mean. In the paper next week, it's not going to be me sitting next to you. It's going to be him."

"That wasn't *my* idea." The decision to include Shawn in the photo had been all Veronica, Diane's campaign manager. Lisa had never asked for her reasoning, but she suspected Veronica thought Diane would get

37

more votes if their "family" photo included someone who looked like the majority of the people voting.

Lisa hated that she was probably right.

"But you think it's a good idea, don't you?"

Lisa bit her lip.

"It is a good idea," Charlene said quietly, answering her own question. "*He's* a good idea, and I'm a bad idea."

"Char, no." Lisa held her tight, wishing there were something she could say, some magic string of words that could fix this. That could make it easy. But those words didn't exist. "It's just complicated," she said.

"Can't you just break up? I don't think it would be so bad if you weren't together."

"I can't break up with him. Not right before the election."

"Is it *really* such a big deal that you stay with him? Rose is single."

"My mom is a Black woman running for public office against a rich white man. *Everything* is a big deal." Lisa frowned, chewing the inside of her cheek. This was a debate she'd had with herself countless times already. It always ended with the same result. "Rose being single is not the same as me dumping the Buford County Citizenship Award winner. Everyone loves Shawn, especially right now. And if Shawn . . ."

"Loves you," Charlene offered.

"Loves our *family*," Lisa continued, as if that had been what she'd intended to say all along, "it can only make my mom look better. And you know in a race like this, every vote counts. What if people seeing him with our family is the thing that makes the difference between my mom winning and losing?"

Charlene sighed, her fingers tapping out the seconds against Lisa's wrist. Finally, Lisa felt her concede with a tiny shrug. "Yeah. I get it. And I do want your mom to win, if for no other reason than to see the look on *my* mom's face." Charlene lifted their intertwined fingers to her lips to kiss the back of Lisa's hand. "But it still sucks."

"I know," Lisa agreed, trailing the tips of her fingers along Charlene's spine.

Charlene nestled even closer to Lisa's side, her cheek coming to rest just over Lisa's heart as she squeezed her hand. "I'm sorry for being a Jealous Judy."

"A what?"

"Oh, did I not tell you about the new Sunday school curriculum my mom bought?" Lisa could practically feel her roll her eyes. "There are all these picture books, and each one is a cautionary tale about a different character. There's Jealous Judy and Gossiping Gladys and Proud Patsy and—"

"Are they all girls?"

"Yup."

"Wow."

"Are you even surprised?"

"Not really."

Charlene was quiet for a second, then giggled. "Slutty Sally."

"Are you *serious*?"

"No."

Lisa burst out laughing, her shoulders convulsing hard enough to shake the bed. "Kleptomaniac Karen," she managed to gasp. "Murderous Mabel."

"Farting Francine."

"Burping Betsy."

"Cussing Cathy."

"Lesbian Lisa."

That was enough to make Charlene lift her head, looking at Lisa with her mouth open. "You really just used the *L*-word!"

"I really did."

"While talking about my *mother*."

"Oh yuck, don't make it weird. But see, this is why you have nothing to worry about. I could never feel about him the way I feel about you."

"Promise?" Charlene grinned, leaning in for a kiss.

"Promise," Lisa said, and they melted into each other. Charlene tasted like strawberries and summer; her soft curves felt like home. Lisa wished they could stay like this forever, just the two of them in their own little world.

"Char?" Lisa whispered into Charlene's sweet scent. Her heart raced, but she was ready. She knew she was ready. And this felt like the right time. "I have another *L*-word for you."

Charlene pulled back, looking into her eyes. Her face was flushed and hopeful, but a teasing smile still played on her lips. "Lemon? Light bulb? Lettuce?"

Lisa laughed. "Yup. Lettuce. You guessed it." She swallowed, the rush of her own blood filling her ears, flooding her body with heat. She felt like she was teetering on the edge of a cliff, wind tickling the back of her neck, gravity already tugging her shoulders, urging her over the edge. Would she fall, or would she fly?

Her eyes met Charlene's.

"I . . . lettuce you," Lisa said, her voice soft.

Fly, her heart whispered.

Charlene smiled, resting her forehead against Lisa's. Their breath mingled together, their heartbeats a shared song. "I lettuce you, too."

Chapter Seven

JUSTIN

We park on the side of the road, then walk out onto the sidewalks edging the mile-long black ribbon that spans the width of Stone River, dodging ponytailed moms with jogging strollers and bare-chested men sporting athletic shorts and AirPods. By day, Wilson Bridge boasts a steady stream of outdoor fitness enthusiasts, but once the sun sets, it tends to remain empty, save the occasional first-date blowhard trying to convince their companion that it's haunted.

I guess that contingent has a lot more ammo now that a genuine dead body has turned up. Bonus points for it being so old that they can make up any creepy story they want about its origins; anything may as well be true.

We stop about halfway across, massive steel beams rising up on either side of us to crisscross far above our heads, and lean over the railing to look down at the churning water below. It's a long drop, at least fifty feet. On the north riverbank, a couple of police cars and a boxy white van sit parked at crooked angles, their passengers picking along the shoreline like uniformed ants. The van has BUFORD COUNTY CORONER printed on the side.

I'd pictured crews out with shovels, digging up the shoreline, maybe some divers in scuba gear combing the river bottom. What I see is far less exciting, just a few uniformed officers milling about, sipping coffee from disposable cups. There isn't even a body bag.

Even at this distance, I can make out Sheriff Gibson's imposing silhouette striding lazily among the officers. More than once, I've awakened in the middle of the night to find him at our door, holding my mom by the arm to keep her from tipping over.

We aren't the only macabre spectators on the bridge; a few yards to our right, a group of excited twentysomethings with perfect hair wave selfie sticks, stretching for the best angles to capture the entirely unimpressive scene down below. Farther down the sidewalk, a bearded guy in a matching scarf and beanie sets up a tripod.

"Well, this is depressing," Alyssa says, giving voice to my thoughts.

I nod my agreement. "They could at least turn the police lights on. Make it feel a little more *CSI*-y and not . . ."

"Really boring?"

"I was going to go with *pathetic*, but yeah."

A few minutes later, the coroner's van pulls away, and Alyssa sighs. "There go my dreams of anything exciting ever happening in this town. Even our dead bodies are dull."

"Stone Lake: a very dull place to die," I say.

Alyssa laughs. "We should go change the town sign."

"It would be an improvement." The actual sign reads STONE LAKE: A VERY NICE PLACE TO LIVE. It's like our slogan was created by a dim-witted kindergartner.

Since there doesn't seem to be much point in sticking around—especially with the influencer crowd now striking what I believe are supposed to be Sexy Crime Scene Poses on the sidewalk—we finally head back to the Dollar Tree to procure the items on my list, along with Stan's dumb Oreos.

An hour later, Alyssa and I walk back into my house together, plastic bags dangling from our hands. As soon as I open the front door, the sharp smell of cheap whiskey hits me like a fist.

I can't check my phone to see exactly what time it is—my arms are too weighed down with bags—but we weren't gone *that* long. In my experience, when Mom has the house smelling like a distillery before five p.m., it's never a great sign.

Did she call Stan to pick her up, or did the entire bender happen since she's been home? She never calls me, even though she relies on me for pretty much everything else. I guess asking her kid to come scrape her off a bar floor is a line even she won't cross.

I sigh, my breath mingling with air that is at least 50 percent whiskey fumes. I'm never getting out of this godforsaken town. Someone's always got to be nearby to parent my parent, and Stan won't be around forever.

It takes Alyssa's hand on my arm for me to realize that I'm clenching my jaw so hard it hurts. "Maybe there's an explanation," she whispers.

"The explanation is that she's a drunk," I say through gritted teeth, stomping my way into the kitchen, braced for a fight.

But it's not Mom at the kitchen table, up to her eyeballs in whiskey. It's Stan.

"What the hell?" I don't think I've ever seen Stan so much as sip a beer before. I asked him once if he was a recovering alcoholic and that's why he didn't drink. He just told me it was "none of your damn business," which I took as a yes.

But whether or not there was a wagon to fall off, Stan has definitely plummeted headfirst over the edge since we left the house. He looks like he's been bleached, his skin a sickly gray, making his lank hair and ice-blue eyes seem even paler than usual. He looks at me through a watery haze, both hands clutching a glass on the table. Beside him is a mostly empty bottle of Evan Williams.

Not all of it has gone down Stan's throat. A good bit has made it onto the table, the floor, his shirt. That must be why the smell is so strong.

"Where's Mom?" I ask, alarmed. My mind goes to all the worst places. *She had a heart attack. She passed out and hit her head. She flipped out and burned down a Target.*

At least I can rule out decomposing on the riverbank. I'm pretty sure if she'd driven her car off Wilson Bridge, the police would've been at least a *little* more animated while we were there.

Stan shrugs. "Dunno. Work, I think."

"Is she okay?"

"Far as I know."

I let out a sigh of relief. "Then what's going on?" I take the glass from his hand—his fingers are limp, like there are no bones inside anymore, just lumps of wobbly flesh—and place it on the counter as Alyssa goes to the sink and pours Stan a glass of water.

"D'ja see the news?" he slurs. His eyes slide to Alyssa, and he points at her with a crooked finger. "She knows. She read it already."

Alyssa places the water on the table in front of Stan. "What do I know?" she asks, sliding into the chair beside him. Her voice is gentle, far more than mine would be.

"About the body. By the river."

"The remains the police found?" Alyssa asks.

Stan nods, but although we wait for him to elaborate, he doesn't say anything more.

He takes a sip of water, then frowns at it, like he'd forgotten that we took away his whiskey.

"We actually went to the bridge," Alyssa ventures. "But the police were nearly done by then. I'm sure they'll figure out what happened."

Stan snorts. "Fat chance. That lazy-ass sheriff couldn't put together a two-piece puzzle."

"What is your deal, Stan?" I ask. My baseline annoyance with Stan is increasing at an exponential rate. "Why do you care about the stupid body?"

His bloodshot gaze slides to me. "Doesn't matter."

"If you know something, you can tell the police—"

He chuckles, shaking his head, but it's a dark laugh, filled with anger. "You don't get it, kid. It doesn't *matter*. Nothing does. Everything is the way it is, and nothing we do makes any difference."

"Sure it does," Alyssa says, patting his hand reassuringly. "There's always something we can do."

He stares at her, and something in his gaze softens. "I used to think like that, too," he says pleadingly, like he's trying to convince her. "I tried. I really did. But I was too late."

"Of course you did," Alyssa says, her voice soothing, as if Stan's nonsense makes perfect sense to her.

I catch her eye, lowering myself into a chair across from her, and she gives me a small shrug, confirming that she's just playing along. It's hard to follow Stan on a good day, much less now.

He sighs heavily, which leads to a bout of wet coughing. Alyssa pulls her hand back, leaning away as politely as she can to avoid the drops of spittle spraying onto the table. Stan's glassy eyes slide to mine.

"But now I know. None of us can change anything, and the sooner we come to terms with that, the better."

"Sure, Stan," I say, rolling my eyes. I've had enough of this. "C'mon," I say to Alyssa. "Let's go to your house."

Stan turns to me with daggers in his eyes, as if I just suggested burning down our house instead of going to Alyssa's. "For example," he says, raising his voice. He's speaking slowly and deliberately, the way you do when you're trying to prove you're not drunk, even though you know you are. "Your mom was always going to be a drunk. And you were always going to be a stupid, worthless little shit."

"Stan!" Alyssa says, her eyes wide with horror.

I sit frozen, my insides turning to ice. I've always known Stan wasn't my biggest fan, but he's never said anything like that before.

When he looks at Alyssa, his expression becomes almost sad. "You can't fix him, you know," he says quietly. "He's been broken from the beginning."

My fists clench, my nails digging into my palms. Mom is a sloppy, silly drunk, but drunk Stan . . . he's practically a different person.

"Come on," I say to Alyssa. My voice comes out a hoarse scrape. "We're done here."

"I shoulda thrown you in the river the second you were born. Would've been doing you a favor," Stan growls as I push back my chair so hard it nearly topples over. He continues to call after us as I grab Alyssa's hand and drag her from the house. *"I shoulda broken your scrawny neck and thrown you out with the trash. I shoulda—"*

I slam the front door, cutting off his venomous tirade.

I don't remember getting into my car or Alyssa shoving me over so she could get behind the wheel.

When I look down at my hands, they're shaking.

"Has he ever said anything like that before?" Alyssa asks softly as she steers out of my neighborhood.

"Not like that. But he's always hated me."

"He doesn't hate you. He was just drunk."

"Being drunk doesn't change how you feel about someone. It just gives you permission to say it out loud."

She doesn't have a response for that. For a few minutes, we sit in silence as she drives toward her house. Eventually, Alyssa sighs. "It just doesn't make sense."

"What doesn't?"

"Stan. It's obvious he loves your mom. He seems to like me. And we both love you. So what's his problem with you?"

I shrug. I've spent eighteen years grappling with that question. "Maybe he's got a thing for you."

She laughs. "Gross."

"I'm serious. It would make so much sense. I mean, just look at him and my mom. What kind of grown man in his late thirties takes in a pregnant nineteen-year-old he's never met, just because she's his cousin's granddaughter?"

"Someone who cares?"

"Or someone who's a pervert."

"He is *not* a pervert."

"He just admitted he wished he'd committed baby murder. I'm not sure we can rule anything out."

Alyssa shakes her head but doesn't push the issue. "I've never seen him drink before," she says quietly.

"Me neither."

"He must be really upset."

I shrug. I'm not in the mood to make excuses for Stan.

"You think it's because of the remains the police found?"

"I don't know. Maybe."

"Do you think it was someone he knew?"

"Maybe it's someone he killed."

Alyssa glances away from the road, narrowing her eyes at me. "That's not funny."

"I'm not trying to be funny. Once again, I will point out that the man just admitted to considering infanticide. Who's to say he hasn't already killed someone?"

I picture Stan out where the police just were with a shovel, dumping a body by the side of the river. It's not that hard. Maybe that's why he's drinking himself into oblivion right now. He's worried he'll finally be caught.

I imagine myself going down to the sheriff, telling him my suspicion. I picture the cars showing up at our house, Stan leaving in handcuffs. I imagine my mom crying as he's hauled away, the mixed feelings of satisfaction and guilt wrestling inside me as I watch it all unfold.

I can see it all so clearly. Even though I know I won't do it.

Mom will be coming home from work soon, to find Stan drunk in our kitchen. When I think about that scene, it makes me want to sink through the floor of the car to be flattened by my own tires.

I sigh, resting my head against the window as Alyssa pulls into her driveway. "Alyssa?"

"Yeah?"

"Do you think . . . I mean, would your parents mind . . ."

"You want to stay here tonight?"

"Yeah. That okay?"

"Yeah."

Chapter Eight

Karl

Karl stood in the doorway of his parents' room, shifting from foot to foot as his mother methodically opened and slammed drawers, one after another. Each drawer made the same sound.

Shhhh—WHAP.

Karl's older sister, Charlene, was out with her friend Lisa, and his parents were getting ready to head to dinner, which would leave him at home alone. As usual.

Unless his mom couldn't find what she was looking for. Then maybe his parents wouldn't leave after all.

Shhhh—WHAP. Shhhh—WHAP. Shhhh—WHAP.

"Mom?"

"Not now, honey," she muttered, pulling open yet another drawer—*shhhh*—and riffling through it with anxious fingers tipped in sharp red nails. A shiny slip edged with lace spilled over the drawer's edge, onto the floor. She ignored it, shoving the drawer back into the dresser—*WHAP*—and moving on to the next one. The slip tangled under her stockinged feet, and she kicked it aside with an irritated grunt.

"But, Mom, I just wanted—"

She sighed and turned to him, hands moving to her narrow hips, gold bracelets clinking. "*What* is so important, Karl?"

Karl's eyes dropped to the thick cream carpeting. "I just was wondering if it would be okay if I didn't go to the bonfire tomorrow," he muttered.

His mother rolled her eyes, false lashes fluttering against her brightly painted lids like a perturbed butterfly. "That's fine," she said absently, turning her full attention back to the dresser. She opened a drawer, then slammed it with a grunt of disgust. "Ugh, it's not *here*." She glanced over her shoulder and seemed surprised to realize Karl was still there. "Do *you* know where my gold-and-pearl brooch is?"

Karl shrugged. He should've known she wouldn't ask him *why* he didn't want to go. He didn't know why he'd thought she might.

"If you don't find it, will you stay home?" he asked hopefully.

She shook her head, sending her earrings swinging. "Of course not," she said absently, then looked at him and sighed. "Why don't you invite a friend over? You can have a sleepover. Play your video game or something."

"Yeah, maybe," Karl said, his shoulders drooping. *What friend?* he wanted to ask, but he knew she wouldn't be able to answer. The second controller for the brand-new video game system that his parents had given him for his birthday, months ahead of its official release, still sat in its original box, unused. Neither of his parents had noticed.

His mother closed her eyes, crimson-slicked lips moving as she whispered to herself, walking through the last time she could remember wearing the brooch.

Karl backed out of his parents' room and headed downstairs, hands jammed in his pockets. His dad sat on the living room couch in his suit, a *Time* magazine open on his lap. He glanced up as Karl walked past. "Your mom almost ready?"

"She can't find her brooch."

His father groaned, checking his watch before tossing the magazine onto the coffee table. *"Moira, we're going to be late."*

Her frantic voice drifted down from above. "Just another *minute*."

"Oh, for the love of . . ." He stomped toward the stairs. *"Just pick a different one."*

Karl waited for a few seconds, listening to his parents argue above him, before slipping out the front door. Headlights were approaching up their long drive—probably Charlene coming home—so he ducked around the side of the house instead of cutting in front of the garage, disappearing into the thick trees that lined their property.

He pressed into the shadows, keeping his breathing soft as his sister parked her car and climbed out. Karl was one of the smallest kids in his seventh-grade class, including the girls. It made running away hard, but hiding easy. Charlene didn't even glance his way as she walked inside, humming wordlessly along to whatever rock tune leaked from the headphones draped around her neck.

After hearing the front door shut, Karl sank deeper into the woods, navigating more by instinct than by sight. He'd discovered the twisted tree by accident that summer, but in the months since he'd found it, he'd walked the path between his house and the tree more times than he could count, at all times of day and night. By now, he could probably get there even with no light at all.

It was about a ten-minute walk to the tree. He didn't know how far that made it distance-wise; it felt far away from everything, and that's what was important. The moon was full that evening, casting the canvas walls of his fort in a soft glow. Karl swept aside the flap covering the entrance and stepped inside.

It wasn't big, his fort. The twisted tree grew out of the ground like a question mark, its limbs twining out and up over his head. He'd built the fort off it, piece by piece, out of materials he'd found in all sorts of places. A canvas drop cloth from the back of their handyman's pickup truck. A length of clothesline he'd found coiled in the laundry room. A short wooden bookshelf holding empty paint cans in the back of the garage. A kitchen chair from the set his mom had put out in the driveway to donate to the church yard sale.

That one had been particularly thrilling. He'd sat in the kitchen eating a peanut butter and jelly sandwich while his mom paced back and forth, phone pressed to her ear, assuring the volunteer on the other end over and over that yes, she was *sure* she'd set out all eight chairs to be picked up, and no, she didn't have one still in the house, and no, she didn't miscount; *What sort of dining set comes with only seven chairs?* and *What are you, some sort of imbecile?*

Karl sank into the pilfered chair, plucking a flashlight from where it hung off a knot on the side of the tree. He flicked it on just long enough to find the book of matches on the shelf, which he used to light the row of pocket-size candles he'd smuggled, one by one, out of the Food Mart.

He reached into the pocket of his jeans and pulled out his mother's brooch. After turning it over in his hands, running his fingers across the smooth pearls, he placed it on the shelf beside his other treasures—pieces taken from his mother's jewelry box, his sister's nightstand, his father's tray of gleaming cuff links—and watched the flickering candlelight reflect dimly off their shining surfaces.

SATURDAY

Chapter Nine

JUSTIN

"Are you still awake?" Alyssa whispers, hovering between the kitchen and the living room.

I look up over my phone, my feet jammed up against the armrest of the too-short couch. The lock screen tells me it's well after midnight.

"Yeah."

I gave up on sleep a while ago; between the cramped couch and Stan's voice echoing in my head, screaming about how worthless I am, relaxation didn't feel like a thing my body was capable of. So instead I've just been mindlessly scrolling on my phone, hoping I'll eventually pass out from boredom.

Alyssa pads over to the couch in bare feet, clutching two mugs to her chest. I scoot into a sitting position, leaving my legs stretched out under the blankets, and she sits on my feet, handing me one of the mugs. I give it a sniff and raise an eyebrow. "Hot cocoa? What are we, twelve?"

She shrugs. "There's no age limit on deliciousness, Jay."

"Fair enough," I say, raising my mug in a faux toast before taking a sip. It's a slightly awkward drinking situation; she's given me a mug shaped like Appa, the giant white, furry creature from *Avatar: The Last Airbender*. But I manage.

"Why are you still up?" I ask, keeping my voice low. Sitting here in the dark, it feels like quiet is the only option.

She sighs, holding her own mug just under her chin. Hers is printed with a picture of that distracted-guy meme, where the girl with him is "starting the day" and the one walking past is "more coffee." "I just keep thinking about what Stan said this afternoon." She tilts her head to look at me, dark curls tumbling over her shoulders. "Are you really okay?"

"Yeah."

"Justin." She pivots, tucking her feet under the blanket so that they touch mine. Her toes are like ice, but heat radiates up my legs. "You can tell me, you know."

I sigh, buying myself some time with slow sips of hot chocolate. "I guess I just . . . I don't know, I knew he didn't *like* me, but . . ."

"That was really awful, what he said."

"I thought you liked Stan."

"I like you more." She pats my legs through the blanket, giving my ankle a squeeze, and smiles.

I could drown in that smile.

"I'm really glad he didn't do any of those things he said," she says softly. "I'd miss you if you weren't here."

"You wouldn't know me to miss me."

"I think I'd know something was missing anyway. Even if I didn't know it was you. Something wouldn't feel right."

"That's how I feel all the time," I say. "Like I took a wrong turn somewhere, and now everything about me is just . . . off. That thing Stan said about me being broken from the beginning, I think . . . maybe he's right."

I don't normally voice my dark thoughts out loud, but there's something about sitting here with Alyssa in the middle of the night that brings them closer to the surface. Harder to hold in. Plus, between the citizenship-award assembly and the internship applications and Stan's bizarre tirade, today has made it abundantly clear that whatever I'm supposed to be at this point in my life, I'm not it. Like I came from the factory defective."

Alyssa adjusts her position again, pushing my legs to the side and tucking her body into mine to rest her head against my shoulder. My arm goes around her automatically, fitting her into my side like a missing piece. She's always been a cuddler, especially when she's tired. I used to think it meant something, but now I know better—or at least, I try to know better. Her hair tickles my nose, and I smooth it down as best I can with my free hand, resisting my desire to leave my fingers buried in her soft curls.

"I wish you didn't think like that about yourself," she whispers, her voice vibrating softly against my chest.

"I can't help it."

"I don't think you're broken."

"I know." I rest my chin on the top of her head. "What am I going to do when you're gone next year?"

"I won't be *gone* gone. I'll come home on breaks. And we'll still talk all the time."

"Talking isn't . . . this, though."

"Yeah." She sighs, then swivels her head to look up at me. "I'll miss this, too."

I have the overwhelming urge to kiss her. Her dark eyes are infinite, her lips slightly parted, so close I catch a whiff of coconut lip balm mixing with the hot cocoa on her breath. She's right there, just a head tilt away.

Instead, I look up, staring out into the darkness. "That is, until you fall in love with one of your ripped naked models and run away with him," I say, keeping my voice light. "That's all art school is, right? Drawing naked people in soft lighting?"

"Oh, for sure. Hundred percent, that's what it is. And you're right, once I get my freakishly hot naked boyfriend, I probably won't even remember your name," Alyssa says. "But that still leaves at *least* a couple weeks for me to miss you before I completely forget you exist."

I smile, trying to ignore the ache in my chest, trying to pretend there's no truth in our jokes. Maybe it won't be a hot naked model—although now I won't be able to get that image out of my head; thanks, brain—but I've always known she deserves someone better than me. Someone who will do something with his life. Someone who won't drag her down like a heavy chain, sinking us both.

I clear my throat, then tug at the hem of her *Grey's Anatomy* T-shirt. "But I don't think you get to be the judge of who is and is not broken, anyway, given your embarrassingly bad taste in pretty much everything."

She smacks my arm playfully. "Shut up. I like what I like. Don't media-shame me."

"I don't have to shame you; you should already *be* ashamed."

"You are such a butt."

"As long as I'm your favorite butt."

"Nope. That honor goes to Chris Hemsworth."

"Wow, I did not need to know that information."

"Sorry—you sleep at my house, you have to talk about Avenger butts with me. Those are just the rules."

"Fine. Which Avenger do you think has the worst farts?"

"Gross."

"You are the one who demanded we talk about Avenger butts."

"I take it back. You're the worst." She groans but doesn't make any move to extract herself from my side.

Which is fine by me. I would happily stay like this forever.

At some point, we fall asleep, and later, Alyssa drifts back up to her room. Once she's gone, though, I lie awake, missing her heat, her scent, the steady sound of her breathing.

We are just friends, I remind myself over and over again. Best friends. Bamboo-shoots-under-my-fingernails platonic freaking soul-mates, even.

But that is all we are, and all we can ever be.

Chapter Ten

Rose

"Girls, let's go!" Diane's voice rang through the house as Rose and Lisa crowded in front of their shared bathroom mirror, putting the finishing touches on their hair and makeup for the morning's photo shoot.

Or rather, Lisa was putting on finishing touches. Rose kept starting over, each attempt to make herself presentable even more disappointing than the last.

"Just a minute!" Lisa called down the stairs, leaning close to the mirror to dab at her eye shadow with her finger. Rose watched her sister enviously, wishing she were even half as beautiful. No matter what she tried, or how closely she mimicked what Lisa was doing, she always wound up looking like a kid playing dress-up, while Lisa could've stepped straight out of a magazine.

Rose frowned, pulling her ponytail holder free yet again and shaking out her mane of dark hair. She didn't have the stick-straight obsidian hair of her father's side of the family; her mother's Irish genes had thickened and lightened it just enough to turn it a rich, wavy brown. Sometimes, she appreciated that her hair was just a little bit different from all the other girls at school.

But not today.

"Nothing is *working*," Rose whined, sweeping it all onto the top of her head and frowning at the bumps.

"You want me to try?" Lisa asked, fastening her earrings. "I'm pretty much ready."

"Please," Rose said gratefully, shifting to stand in front of her sister and handing over her hairbrush.

After her mother's accident when Rose was five, her father hadn't paid much attention to Rose's hair—or anything else, for that matter—and it had grown long and wild, tumbling down her back in thick tangles. It was Lisa's mother, Diane, who had put a stop to her wild-child phase, inviting her over one day after kindergarten and combing through the nest of knots while Rose and Lisa perched on kitchen chairs, sharing a bowl of potato chips and watching *The Price Is Right* on their grainy kitchen TV.

Lisa's dad had come home from work to find them like that. He'd laughed—he was still vibrant and burly back then, barely resembling the gaunt ghost he'd become three years later, toward the end—and said they looked like a set of mismatched twins.

Lisa had frowned and told him that didn't make any sense. Twins were *supposed* to match; if they didn't, they weren't twins.

He'd just shaken his head and chuckled, letting the subject drop.

Funny how things worked out.

"You remember that game we used to play when we were little?" Rose mused as Lisa tugged at her hair. "'Teenagers'?"

Lisa laughed. "When we thought we'd be married with kids by fifteen?"

"We were eight. We had no concept of anything."

"I remember you were always putting your toys in time-out. Just a creepy row of Barbies and Weebles all facing the wall because 'the children were misbehaving.'"

"I was a weird kid."

"Weird like a child of the corn."

Rose laughed, shaking her head at the memory. "Didn't you decide you were going to marry the mailman or something? I remember you kept saying how you loved a man in uniform."

"No, even worse, it was the *garbage*man." Lisa groaned. "I think I must have heard someone say it on TV once? I don't know."

"Hmm, should we tell Shawn he needs to borrow a pair of his dad's coveralls?" Rose joked.

Lisa's laugh felt like it came a second too late and a smidge too high, like she was forcing it. But when Rose looked at her in the mirror, Lisa grinned back at her, and Rose wondered whether she was simply losing her ability to read her sister's mood. Was all the time they'd been spending apart lately turning them into strangers?

Lisa gave Rose's head a friendly pat. "All done," she proclaimed, stepping back to examine her handiwork. Rose turned her head from side to side, admiring the way Lisa had tamed her stubborn waves by weaving them into braids on the sides, then securing everything in the back with a bright-green clip that matched Rose's dress.

"You're the best," Rose said in relief.

"I know," Lisa said cheerfully.

In the car, their little sister, Emmie, squeezed between Lisa and Rose in the back seat, while Diane and Rose's dad, Jim, sat up front. As Diane drove, Jim twisted around in his seat to smile at the three of them.

"So, girls," he said brightly, "just so you know, Veronica will have already placed our order by the time we arrive. We know that's a little unusual, but she thought it was important to consider the overall look of the table in the photo so that, you know—"

"It's fine, Dad," Rose said, saving him the trouble of having to explain, yet again, how closely their family was being scrutinized for this campaign. Everything they were wearing, down to Lisa's reserved gold hoops and Emmie's pink hair bow, had been approved by Diane's campaign manager, Veronica, earlier in the week, and Rose was sure she'd paid a visit to Shawn's house to sign off on his outfit, too. But it wasn't just that; they'd been reminded a hundred times to be careful about who they spoke to, where they went after school, what they bought at the grocery store, since they never knew when a reporter might be lurking nearby.

Even Lisa's friendship with Charlene had briefly been a point of contention, until Diane insisted that no member of her family was going to be forced to give up friends for this campaign. Eventually, Veronica had relented.

Still, none of it seemed fair. Rose doubted that Franklin Gibson and his family spent a quarter as much energy fretting over their every move as the members of the Lewis-Yin household. But when the *Stone Lake Gazette* once reported that Diane wearing a mismatched pair of macaroni earrings Lisa had made in kindergarten to a school board meeting was "a silent yet pointed indictment of the public school system," which "begs the question whether even Lewis-Yin herself truly believes in her controversial education plan," there was no such thing as too careful.

Rose supposed she should be glad no reporters were skulking around the Food Mart yesterday. She could only imagine how they would've spun their fundraising efforts for Mrs. Hanley. Local Teens Harass Shoppers in Desperate Cash Grab, perhaps, or maybe, Lewis-Yin Family Caught Soliciting Gifts from Local Businesses.

She hadn't known, at the beginning of the campaign, how bizarre this would all feel. Her dad and Diane had called a family meeting before she announced her candidacy, and while Rose and Lisa had been surprised at first, they'd all agreed it was a good idea. Being elected mayor of Stone Lake wasn't exactly becoming president, but Diane had so many ideas about how she might use the role to improve life in their small town that they couldn't help getting excited.

But now that the election was getting close, everything about it felt . . . weird.

It was weird to think of people voting for Diane; it was weird to think of people voting *against* Diane. It was weird to have strangers tell Rose how much they admired her stepmother, and it was weird to overhear people talking about her family like they weren't even human.

Sometimes, Rose silently hoped Diane would lose, just so things could go back to normal. It was hard being someone people recognized and expected things from. Someone that strangers felt entitled to stop on the street and douse in their opinions. Before the campaign, she may have been anonymous, but at least people had left her alone.

Other times—like when she saw the scraps of abandoned police tape waving in the breeze around Mrs. Hanley's blackened garage, or she looked through her AP reading list and realized there wasn't a single author on it who hadn't been dead for decades—she thought that if she had to live through one more second of "normal," she'd lose her mind. On those days, she wanted Diane to win so badly, she could barely breathe.

She didn't know what kind of day today was yet.

Rose shook her head, smoothing her hands over her skirt and taking a deep breath as Diane parked the car. If she kept thinking like this, she was going to give herself an upset stomach before this brunch even started.

"Ready?" her dad said excitedly, practically leaping out of the car. Rose was pretty sure Jim Yin had never expected to be a political spouse when he married first a kindergarten teacher, then a librarian, but sometimes it seemed like he was born to be one. He celebrated every step of Diane's campaign like she had landed on the moon.

Rose hoisted Emmie out of the car and handed her to their dad, then followed her out, fixing what she hoped was a picture-perfect smile onto her face. "Ready."

Chapter Eleven

LISA

Emerson's Tearoom was a small building off the town square with lilac walls and lacy tablecloths. A cardboard sign in the front window read **CLOSED FOR PRIVATE EVENT**. Shawn stood in the middle of the room, looking perfectly at ease in khaki pants and a blue blazer, warm bronze hair gelled meticulously into place. His face lit up when Lisa walked in, and she did her best to return his smile, her chest tight.

When she closed her eyes, she could still feel the velvety softness of Charlene's skin against her fingertips the night before, taste her sweetness on her lips. Could still hear her voice as her breath brushed Lisa's ear. *I lettuce you, too.*

So Lisa kept her eyes wide open as she walked toward Shawn, letting him wrap her in a hug.

Meanwhile, Veronica bustled around the room like a nervous blonde bird, turquoise heels clacking against the tile floor as she adjusted chairs and muttered to the photographer.

"Rose! Lisa!" Veronica called, waving them toward the table, which was already filled with small plates of beautifully presented food. As Veronica rotated a tray of pancakes a fraction of an inch one way, then another, Lisa caught Rose's eye and grimaced, wondering if they'd actually be allowed to eat at this brunch, or whether this was a see-and-smell-only kind of meal.

"Don't touch that," Veronica said, swatting the back of Shawn's hand as he reached for a pile of bacon.

Well, that answered that question.

Shawn raised his eyebrows, sinking back into his seat beside Lisa. "So it's a no-brunch brunch?" he whispered.

Lisa shrugged, folding her hands in her lap. With her eyes, she tracked the photographer, who paced slowly around the room with a bulky black camera hanging from his neck. There were no reporters here today; her mother had given her interview to the paper last week. All they needed was an image to run with the story. The reporter had suggested a family meal at a local restaurant, to show Diane engaging with both her family and the community at the same time.

When her mother and Jim had explained the purpose of the brunch to her and Rose, they'd told them it would be fun, and that they'd barely notice the photographer. Just a normal family outing.

Somehow, that's not what it felt like.

Lisa looked around the elegant dining room, at the photographer adjusting his lights, Diane speaking quietly with Veronica, her father bouncing Emmie on his hip. She thought of all the people who would look at this photo in the paper, read the interview with Diane, and feel like they knew their family. Like they knew *her*.

When the truth was, her own family didn't even know her.

Shawn reached for her hand under the table. She resisted the urge to pull away as he wove their fingers together. "This is more intense than I thought it would be," he whispered.

Lisa nodded. "Have to look perfect for the paper."

He smiled at her, his eyes flicking over the sleeveless lavender blouse that Veronica had helped her pick out. "Well, you nailed that."

Lisa's face tightened as she returned his smile. She fought the desire to cross her arms, cover herself up. *Relax,* she told herself, trying to remember the way she used to feel when he looked at her like that.

Maybe it had never sent butterflies soaring through her stomach, but it had been at least pleasant.

She'd always gotten along well with Shawn, so when he first asked her out at the beginning of junior year, it felt like such a simple thing to say yes. And for a while, it had been nice. He made her laugh and was easy to talk to, and even if she didn't swoon over him the way the other girls at school did, it was impossible not to notice how handsome he was. They had fun together. It should've been easy to get swept away by him.

But although she kept waiting to fall head over heels, her feet remained stubbornly planted on the ground.

Eventually, he'd said the thing she had been dreading for months, and she hadn't been able to say it back, as much as she wished she could. For a moment, she'd been relieved. Now that he knew she didn't feel the way she was supposed to, she was certain he'd cut her loose and find someone who could love him back.

But he hadn't. She'd broken his heart, and still he stayed, leaving her holding all the pieces.

Now that she knew what it was like to say it to someone and mean it, she wished more than ever that she could give those pieces back. But he didn't seem to want them. So she shaved off tiny bits of her heart and offered him those instead—nothing much, just what she could spare. Barely more than crumbs, really.

It wasn't enough, for either of them. But it was all she had to give.

"Did you tell your dad about the award?" she asked.

He nodded stiffly. "Didn't go great," he said under his breath.

"Really? He wasn't even a little bit excited?"

Shawn shook his head, pressing his lips together. "It's my own dumb fault. I should've realized his hang-up about college was never about the money."

"What's it about?"

"Rothman and Son."

"Oh." Lisa sighed, wishing she could take Shawn's father by the shoulders and shake him. He had such an amazing son, but he refused to see it.

This was the part Lisa couldn't explain to Charlene, because she knew she'd never understand. It wasn't just about the campaign. Lisa couldn't break up with Shawn because he didn't have anyone else. Everyone liked him, but barely anyone really knew him. "Shawn, I'm sorry."

He shrugged. "It's not a big deal."

She frowned, knowing how much Shawn had risked—how much they *both* had—to get that award. Nothing was a bigger deal to him than this. "Listen, even if your father—"

But she was cut off when Veronica clapped her hands breathlessly, eager to get the not-brunch underway.

As Jim and Diane took their seats and the photographer started snapping pictures, Shawn's expression changed like a channel, flipping from frustrated to cheerful in the blink of an eye. Sometimes it was unnerving to Lisa, just how good he was at dusting away the parts of himself he didn't want anyone else to see, leaving nothing but a gleaming facade.

Then again, maybe that's what made them perfect for each other. Both of them knew how to put on a show.

Lisa went through all the proper motions as the photographer clicked away, smiling for the camera and holding Shawn's hand between their plates and feeding Emmie bites of muffin. She laughed at Jim's jokes—but not too hard, not opening her mouth too wide or showing too many teeth—kept her shoulders straight, her ankles crossed, her elbows off the table.

When it was over, the photographer claimed he had some great shots, and Lisa was sure he did. The photographs would undoubtedly be beautiful.

They just wouldn't be real.

Chapter Twelve

SHAWN

His father was in the garage when he got home from brunch, his tools and supplies spread out before him on the pristine concrete floor. Saturdays were maintenance days, when Gabe Rothman meticulously inventoried, catalogued, and cleaned all the tools of his trade, down to the smallest scrap of copper wire. Even though Shawn doubted that anything changed significantly enough from week to week to warrant this level of reorganization, his father was insistent that it was necessary.

Shawn hurried up the driveway, hoping to get into the house before his father spotted him.

"In here, son," Gabe called.

Shawn halted just a few feet from the front door. He squeezed his eyes shut for a second, steeling himself, then walked over, loosening his tie and shrugging off his jacket. His father's garage was cleaner than most people's kitchens, and there were plenty of hooks and bars on which a jacket could hang, but everything had its purpose here, none of which was clothing storage. He draped it over his arm instead.

"Where have you been this morning?" Shawn's father asked. He bent over an array of needle-nose pliers, each lined up perfectly parallel to the one beside it, and made marks on a clipboard.

"I was invited to have brunch with Lisa's family," Shawn said, swallowing. "Remember, I told you on Thursday—"

"Don't you take that tone with me, son," Gabe snapped. "I am not your secretary."

"Sorry, sir. I should've reminded you before I left," Shawn said, kicking himself for not saying anything that morning.

His father's eyes flitted briefly to him, then back to his tools. "I have good news," he said. "I wanted to tell you earlier, but of course, you were nowhere to be found."

"I'm sorry," Shawn apologized again. Sometimes, it felt like all he did was apologize.

"Got a call from Mr. Reese over at the bowling alley. He's got some lanes down. Thought you could go with me this afternoon, learn a few things while I get them working again. Bet you've never seen how a pinsetter works. It'll be a real interesting job."

Years of practice had taught Shawn to keep his face neutral, but disappointment coiled in his stomach. Really? His dad's idea of good news was accompanying him on a job to fix a faulty pinsetter at the bowling alley? He wondered if his dad even remembered that Shawn planned to go to the bonfire tonight.

But he didn't dare bring up the bonfire now, after their confrontation last night. He'd just have to hope that they finished up at the bowling alley in time for him to go. "Sounds great, Dad," Shawn said.

His father rocked back on his heels, dabbing his brow with a handkerchief. "This is important real-world experience," he said. "When you're in charge, you'll appreciate that I made it a priority to carve out these opportunities for you."

"In charge of . . . ?"

"Of the business, son!" His dad shook his head, chuckling. "I know your old man's in good shape now, but I won't live forever. One day you'll have to step into my shoes."

"Dad," Shawn said, his stomach sinking. "Don't—don't you remember? I won the citizenship award. So I don't need . . . I mean, I wasn't planning on—"

"I know all about your *award*," Gabe said, spitting out the word like it was a fantasy Shawn should've outgrown years ago, like the tooth fairy. "I'm not an idiot, son."

"I didn't mean—"

"I just assumed that after having the night to think it over, you'd have come to your senses."

Shawn scrambled for something, anything, to say that wouldn't make this worse, but his mind was blank. All he could think was how stupid he'd been to assume that last night would be the end of this, that his father wouldn't seize every opportunity from now until the day he graduated from college—and probably beyond—to remind Shawn that he was making a mistake.

Gabe Rothman didn't lose arguments. Gabe Rothman didn't even come to a draw. Gabe Rothman only won.

"Excuse me if I want to provide my son with a solid foundation in a respectable trade, or offer him a good job right out of high school," his father continued, on a roll now. "If I want to make sure you possess the knowledge and skills that will help you actually make a *living* someday." He shook his head, looking disgusted. "I'd ask how you turned out to be so ungrateful, but I suppose I shouldn't be surprised. You're just like your mother that way."

Shawn took a step back, the knot in his stomach making it hard to breathe. "I'm not trying to be ungrateful, Dad," he said quietly. "I just want something *different*."

His father let out a mirthless laugh. "That's what your mother used to say, before she left. That she needed something different. But I told her she didn't want that. I knew she'd be begging some other poor sap to take her in soon enough, but she'd never have it as good as she did with me."

He began putting tools away, slotting them carefully into neatly labeled drawers and shelves and pegs. "And don't you know," he continued, not looking at Shawn, "I was right. Sure enough, she gets married again, and he knocks her up with another kid, and now she's stuck, just like I told her she would be. He can't buy her the nice house, the pretty clothes that she was used to. He can't take her out to fancy dinners, make her feel special. She had her chance for all that, for someone to take care of her and treat her right, and she blew it. She knows now that she was wrong, and I was right." He wagged a wrench at Shawn, his mouth set in a hard line. "She didn't know what was best for her, and neither do you. Yet here you are, acting just like her."

Shawn swallowed, his heart twisting in his chest. Was his father right? Was he being naive? He desperately wanted to leave Stone Lake, make a life of his own outside his father's heavy shadow, but was he just deluding himself?

It had been years since Shawn had seen his mother. He'd gone to visit her a few times in the years immediately following the divorce, but the visits had gotten fewer and further between after her first child with her new husband was born . . . until eventually they'd stopped altogether.

Lisa said it was probably just too painful for her to be reminded of her life with his dad. That it wasn't anything he'd done wrong. That she probably would have taken him with her, if she could.

Shawn wished he could believe that.

But even if it meant following in his mother's painful footsteps, he couldn't see another way out. Staying here would kill him. Maybe not right away, maybe not in a way anyone else would notice, but eventually, Gabe would drain the life from him, leaving nothing but a shell.

"It's not that I don't appreciate the opportunity," Shawn said, still—foolishly—hoping he might convince his father to see his side. "But with this award, I could—"

"We all *could* do a lot of things, son," his father said. "But most people won't do a fraction of what they *could* do. I'm giving you the opportunity to *do* something, never mind the *could*. And you're throwing it all away for a shot at a maybe." He shook his head, looking disgusted. "*Maybe* this is for the best. *Maybe* I don't want someone so selfish and short-sighted working for me anyway."

"But, Dad—"

"Get out," his father said, waving him out of the garage. "Go do whatever you *want* to do today. I'll go do Mr. Reese's job by myself."

"But—"

"Go. I don't want to look at you anymore," his father said, turning his back on him.

Shawn moved slowly toward the house, his face burning. As he hung his jacket in his closet and listened to the sound of his father's van backing out of the driveway, he realized he was actually *sad* that he wasn't accompanying his father to the bowling-alley job. It was infuriating, but part of him wanted to be there, learning from his dad, making him proud.

Instead, he'd go to the bonfire. Which he'd been looking forward to all week but now felt like nothing more than a pitiful consolation prize.

Chapter Thirteen

VERONICA

"You sure you don't want to walk with us, Veronica?" Jim asked, holding the door of Emerson's Tearoom open for Diane. Rose and Lisa had taken the car home with Emmie, but Diane and Jim had decided to take advantage of the lovely weather and walk.

Veronica smiled. Diane and Jim weren't an obvious couple—Diane was slightly taller, especially in heels with her hair up, and her energy could fill a ballroom, while Jim was slight and unassuming—but they made sense in an unexpected way. Veronica had never met Jim's first wife or Diane's first husband, both of whom had passed away years before, but she loved that they had found each other after.

"Thanks, but I'm good. I've got my car here," Veronica said, waving them off.

Outside, Diane and Jim moved down the sidewalk arm in arm, while Veronica headed in the opposite direction, to the parking lot in the back of the building. As she walked to her car, she admired the posters she'd tacked up on the brick wall facing the lot, with their glossy blue text urging the residents of Stone Lake to **VOTE FOR DIANE LEWIS-YIN FOR MAYOR!**

It still seemed a little unreal that Veronica was managing Diane's campaign. When she and Bill had moved back here after grad school at the University of Pennsylvania, into the house her parents had left her after being killed in a car crash the year before, Diane had been the only one willing to hire her. The pay for an assistant at the public library was abysmal, and the job had little to do with Veronica's degree in marketing, but Veronica didn't mind. She loved going to work every day, not because of the job itself, but because of Diane. They talked about everything, from their families to their career ambitions to their frustrations and fears. Diane admitted that she'd always secretly dreamed of running for office, and Veronica had urged her to do it.

One day, both of their arms loaded with books needing to be reshelved, Diane had asked Veronica if she'd consider running her campaign for mayor. At first, Veronica had thought she was joking. She'd only recently returned to work part-time after delivering Millie, and had little experience in politics.

Experience is all well and good, Diane had said, *but I need someone I trust, and who believes in what I'm trying to do here. Someone who won't quit when things get hard, because they will. Someone smart and hungry, who knows what it's like to get smacked down and then get back on her feet. Someone like you.*

A month later, when Diane had publicly announced her candidacy, Veronica had stood proudly by her side.

Veronica jiggled her key in the lock of her ancient Volvo, eager to get home to Bill and Millie, when she heard a voice calling her name. "Hey, Ronnie! Ronnie, wait up!"

Veronica closed her eyes, lamenting the curse of a small town as Kenny Gibson jogged toward her car, sunlight gleaming off his sheriff's department badge. Charming, handsome, and now a newly minted deputy, Kenny moved through life like an ice cream truck on the hottest day of summer. Stone Lake adored him.

Which was why they weren't the biggest fans of Veronica, the girl who had broken his heart. At least, that was the way he told it.

When she'd moved back to Stone Lake, newly married to Bill and five months into her pregnancy with Millie, people would take one look at the ring on her finger and her swelling belly and their expressions would turn to ice. Come to find out, when she'd broken up with Kenny two years earlier, he'd conveniently forgotten to inform anyone else. Apparently, he'd been walking around the whole time with a ring in his pocket and the delusion that she'd change her mind.

If not for Diane, she wouldn't have even been able to find a job.

"Hey, Ronnie," Kenny said, barely winded as he leaned against the door Veronica had just been trying to open. He blasted her with a dazzling smile that, at one point in her life, would have turned her knees to jelly. Now it just hurt her eyes.

"I told you to stop calling me that, Kenny," Veronica said, crossing her arms.

"Sorry, *Veronica*," he said with a wink. "Old habits just die hard. You know how it is."

"Mm-hmm."

He blocked the door handle with his body, his thumbs hooked in the belt loops of his khaki uniform as his eyes slid over her like oil. "You're looking good."

She stifled a groan. What did she have to do to get him to lose interest? Marrying another man hadn't worked. Neither had running the campaign of his father's opponent in the mayoral race.

Maybe she should stop brushing her teeth. Or stuff her bra with bologna.

Veronica gave him a tight smile. "Thanks, but I really am in a hurry."

"Look," Kenny said, giving no indication of moving, "I just wanted to say that I hope there's no bad blood with us because of all this political stuff." He gestured at Diane's posters, giving her that killer smile again. "You know I don't pay any mind to all that."

"Well, I do," Veronica said, tapping her foot against the pavement. "It is my job, after all."

Kenny laughed, shaking his head. "I remember you telling me once you didn't want a job; you just wanted to cook nice dinners for your husband and raise fat babies."

"I said a lot of things when I was fourteen," Veronica said. "If I recall, that was about the same time you wanted to be a rodeo clown."

"Still do, a little," Kenny said with a grin.

"Aren't you supposed to be working?" Veronica asked, looking pointedly at the badge on his chest and the gun at his hip.

He shrugged. "Technically, sure, but it's perfectly within bounds for a deputy to stop and chat now and again. Preferred, even. Makes the people feel safer, knowing we care."

"I'm not 'the people,' Kenny, and it's hard to feel safe around you knowing how much your dad's team loves to spin anything I say into a headline about how I—I don't know—hate puppies or think all babies are ugly or something."

Kenny narrowed his eyes. "You think I'm just mining for quotes? Ronnie, none of that campaign stuff has anything to do with me."

"Sure, Kenny."

"I swear. Of course I want my dad to win, but you've got to know I would never do anything to hurt you."

She tilted her head, wondering if he even heard himself. "Yeah. I'm sure it's just a coincidence that the papers keep calling me Diane's 'controversial' campaign manager. Or that your dad's ad has our freaking *prom* photo in it while talking about the importance of 'reliability' and 'family values.'"

"None of that was *my* decision!"

"No, it was just your decision to let the whole town think we were engaged after we *broke up*."

"That was just a misunderstanding."

Veronica let out an incredulous laugh, shaking her head. "Okay, fine. You are totally innocent. Can you please let me get to my car now?"

He shook his head but finally stepped aside, pursing his lips like she'd just shoved a lemon in his mouth. As she turned the car on, he rapped on her window with his knuckle, leaning over to peer in at her.

She could tell he was waiting for her to roll down the window, but she just looked at him. "What?"

"I won't tell my dad that I talked to you," he said, his raised voice slightly muffled by the glass.

"I appreciate that."

"See, I'm still a good person."

Veronica fought the urge to roll her eyes. *This is why I couldn't marry you,* she thought. "I know you are," she said, giving him the validation she knew he needed before he'd allow her to leave.

Satisfied, he finally stepped away from her car.

Chapter Fourteen

JUSTIN

My shift the next morning goes horribly. The computers go down at work, which makes the customers grouchy, and then when they come back online, they can't process credit cards, which makes the customers mean. I actually have an old lady tell me I should be ashamed of myself when the machine declines her Visa, because it's supposed to be accepted everywhere.

Okay, first off, lady, your issue should be with Visa's false advertising, not me. Second, it's not like it was my choice for the machines to stop working. But the way she looks at me is like she's caught me with a severed Ethernet cable in one hand and a pair of scissors in the other.

After my shift ends at five, I head back to Alyssa's house, since I can't imagine hungover Stan is much of an improvement on drunk Stan. I'll give him a couple of days to detox, then test the waters again. I texted my mom over lunch to let her know where I'd be, and she's predictably fine with it. As long as I'm not dead, she doesn't care if I'm at home. She probably actually prefers that I'm not.

But all my plans to avoid the people I live with go up in smoke when I pull into Alyssa's driveway to find Stan's car parked outside.

I consider just heading home. If Stan is here, he's not there, and Mission Avoid Stan is still pretty much my top priority. But if I do that, he'll still have to come home eventually—probably sooner rather than later, once he realizes I'm not returning to Alyssa's house. So I'd only be buying myself maybe an hour, max.

While I'm pondering where else I could go that Stan can't find me, my phone buzzes. I glance down to see I've missed a series of texts from Alyssa while I was driving.

Are you on your way back yet?

Stan is here

At my house I mean

He says he's really sorry about yesterday

He seems really messed up

Get here soon please

I grit my teeth, fighting the urge to throw the phone out the window. It's one thing to split when no one knew where I was; it's another to ignore a plea from the one person in the world who actually cares about me.

Heaving a sigh, I pull my key out of the ignition and head inside.

Stan is sitting on the couch in the living room when I walk in, his leg bouncing up and down with enough nervous energy to break concrete. Alyssa perches in an armchair on the other side of the room, back straight. Neither of them is talking. Alyssa's phone is in her hand, her head down as she types furiously. Probably another text for me, wondering where I am.

When he sees me, Stan practically leaps to his feet.

"I didn't mean what I said yesterday," he says, his words tumbling out in a rush. "I had a really bad day and I screwed up. But that wasn't me. You've got to know it wasn't me."

"How'd you even know where I was?" I ask, even though it wouldn't have taken a rocket scientist to figure it out. It's not like I have a ton of friends with couches I could've crashed on.

Stan ignores my question, grabbing my arm. "You have to come home."

I yank my arm out of his grasp so hard he takes a stumbling step forward. "No, I don't."

"Look, I know I said some stuff I shouldn't have, but this is really important."

"*What* is really important?"

Stan's eyes dart to Alyssa. "It's a family thing."

"Like you and I have ever really been family."

His expression darkens, fury flashing behind his eyes. His hand moves so fast I don't have time to react, his grip around my arm so tight it feels like he's trying to break my bones. To my horror, tears spring to my eyes as I try unsuccessfully to wrench my arm away. "You ungrateful little brat. If you had *any* idea what I've done for our family—"

"Hey!" Alyssa jumps in between us, pulling at his hand to aid in my useless struggle. When did Stan get so *strong*? His fingers feel like they've been carved from stone. "Let him go!"

At the sound of Alyssa's voice, his grip loosens just enough for me to pull free of him. I stumble back, making sure to stay out of arm's reach, rubbing the spot on my arm that I'm sure will later turn black with bruises. "What the hell is wrong with you?"

"I just . . ." His eyes dart around the room, as if he's searching for the answer somewhere on Alyssa's ceiling. If I didn't know better, I'd wonder if he's on something.

Then again, after the way he's been acting, maybe I don't know better after all.

He tries to grab me again, but I dodge him this time, his hand closing on empty air.

"Leave me *alone*."

"Stan, maybe you should go," Alyssa says firmly, coming to stand by me.

Stan's restless gaze settles on her, his manic expression softening, just for a second. "He has never deserved you," he murmurs.

"That's it," I say. My skin feels hot, my nerves all crackling like a thousand lit fuses. My arm throbs painfully. I take Alyssa's hand and pull her toward the door. "Come on. Let's go to the bonfire." I glare at Stan. "You'd better be gone by the time we get back."

Before we can get away from him, Stan literally *lunges* at me, throwing his arms around me from behind and hauling me away from the door. "You're not going to that."

"Get *off* me!" I shove him away, blinking in disbelief. "Are you *serious* right now?"

"Listen to me," he says, his hands hovering in the air between us. "Just listen. You can't go to that bonfire tonight. Trust me."

"Why would I trust you after the things you've said to me?"

He shakes his head, his eyes wild. "If you'd just *listen*—"

I've had enough. I push him roughly aside, taking satisfaction in the thick *thud* his shoulder makes as he stumbles into the door of the coat closet. Now I won't be the only one walking away with bruises tonight.

Alyssa lets out a little squeak of shock, but holds tight to my hand as I pull her through the front door and down the steps.

"Justin!" Stan calls after me as we jump into my car and slam the doors. He's limping more than usual, still favoring his bad knee. "Don't go! Come home with me. Please!"

I give him a funny look as I shove the keys in the ignition. Stan never says *please*. At least not to me.

The engine turns over and the Mustang grinds to life. I back down Alyssa's drive and onto the street, Stan still shouting behind me. I can't make out what else he's saying over the roar of the engine, and I don't care. I shove Stan out of my brain as we head toward the bonfire.

Chapter Fifteen

ROSE

Cars were already packed onto the Derrins' expansive lawn by the time Rose emerged from the tree-lined drive. She gritted her teeth, knuckles white on the wheel as she hunted for a space. She'd finally agreed to attend the bonfire with Lisa and Shawn after prolonged begging from Lisa, but when Shawn arrived to pick them up, he'd seemed upset. Feeling like a third wheel, Rose had volunteered to drive herself in order to give them some time alone. Now, hunting for a parking space, she kind of wished she'd just stayed home.

Eventually, Rose created a makeshift spot behind a massive FRANKLIN GIBSON FOR MAYOR sign, trying her best to ignore the way the giant red letters made her stomach clench.

Straightening her skirt and smoothing her hair, Rose moved toward the crowd gathered around the dancing flames in the center of the Derrins' sprawling front yard. The marching band blasted the school fight song into the dimming twilight, the notes mingling with the glowing embers that wound up into the air.

The lawn was filled with students, teachers, and parents. The PTA sold refreshments from behind folding tables lined with posters touting various school activities, while a little farther down, Rose spotted some of the teachers from her school, looking oddly casual in jeans and

T-shirts and sneakers. Veronica was there, too, rocking slowly from side to side, her toddler in her arms, as she laughed at something Rose's history teacher said. In Rose's mind, she associated Veronica with the campaign, and forgot sometimes that she was married to the school guidance counselor.

Rose turned away hurriedly, before Veronica could spot her. Tonight, Rose didn't want to think about the campaign or anything else having to do with her family. She just wanted to have fun.

Once she reached the edges of the teeming masses, though, she stopped, uncertain where to go next. There was Shawn, moving through the crowd with an ease she would never understand, bouncing from one group to another, his smile a glowing constant. If she didn't know better, she'd assume this was his house, his party, instead of a school event where he was just another kid in the crowd.

Speaking of the owner of the house, where was Charlene? Rose didn't see her or Lisa anywhere. She'd hoped to hang out with them, but that wouldn't be an option if she couldn't find them.

Rose made her way to the nearest refreshment table, figuring that getting something to eat would at least give her something to do with her hands. She'd just finished paying for a baggie of chocolate chip cookies when someone poked her in the shoulder.

"Hey, you!" Noah grinned at her as she turned. He was freshly shaved and smelled of warm spice, and she had to resist the urge to lean in and inhale deeply. "When you didn't show up with Lisa and Shawn, I worried you weren't coming."

"Just drove separately," Rose said, unable to hold back her smile.

"I would've given you a ride!"

"It was a last-minute decision." She laughed, her heart giving a little flutter at his obvious disappointment that she hadn't asked. Had he wanted to go to the bonfire together? "Want to go find a place to sit? I think I see a spot over there."

"Oh. Uh, I kind of . . . came here with Steph . . ." His eyes drifted from hers, and Rose belatedly noticed the two cups of pink punch in his hands. He was wearing a black-and-red striped polo shirt she'd never seen before. It must be new.

Of course. Steph. The girlfriend.

Would she ever get used to that?

"Never mind," she said hurriedly, wishing the grass would turn into quicksand and swallow her whole.

"You can come join us if you want," he offered. "Steph went to find a good spot."

"No, that's okay—I was, um . . ." Rose cast around for someone, *anyone*, she could claim was waiting on her, but she knew he'd never buy a lie. He knew her too well.

"Come on; it's totally fine. She won't mind," he said, leading the way.

Not knowing what else to do, she followed him to the faded red blanket that they had once used to construct elaborate forts in his basement, now spread out near the fire. Steph sat in the middle of it with her arms hugging her knees, her eyes searching the crowd. When she spotted them, she waved excitedly.

"Rose, Noah, over here!" Steph called happily, scooting her legs over to make room.

Part of Rose wanted to shove Steph off the blanket, tell her that it was *theirs*, hers and Noah's, and that Steph had no place in their memories.

Instead, she waved back.

Steph Sanchez had been a surprise that summer. They'd met her at a car wash Rose had helped Noah organize for Mrs. Hanley in July, shortly after Steph's family moved to Stone Lake from Philadelphia. She'd brought her mom's car to be washed, but when she asked what they were raising money for, she wound up staying to help out. A week later, she and Noah were dating.

Rose still couldn't believe it had happened that fast. Not when she'd spent months working up the nerve to tell Noah how she felt, only to have the fire ruin all her plans.

What made it worse was that, try as she might, Rose couldn't bring herself to hate Steph. She even thought they might've been friends, if things were different.

Rose tucked her legs underneath her, trying to make herself as small as possible as she perched stiffly at the edge of the blanket. Despite being surrounded by half the school, sitting beside them on their date felt like she was intruding on something private, like she'd stormed into Noah's bedroom without knocking.

The thought conjured an image of Noah and Steph in bed together, so sudden and vivid that Rose found herself squeezing her eyelids shut to try to block it out, and had to make a conscious effort to drag them back open again.

"—*so* sorry about that," Steph was saying. "I definitely want to join you guys next time."

"Next . . . what?" Rose blinked, realizing she'd zoned out of the conversation.

"Earth to Rose." Noah laughed. "Next time we fundraise. If there *is* a next time. We didn't exactly rake in a fortune."

His arm was around Steph's shoulders, his thumb moving slowly up and down against the skin of her neck. Rose folded her hands tightly in her lap to keep them from drifting to her own neck, wondering what his touch must feel like.

She swallowed, forcing a smile to her face. "Next time we'll just have to have Shawn with us from the beginning."

"That guy." Noah shook his head in amazement. "I'd be such a jerk if I were him."

"You would not," Steph said, laughing.

"Sure, I would. Look at those cheekbones. Dude could stab me, and I'd probably thank him."

"Don't sell yourself short." Steph tilted her head to smile up at him, her lips only inches from his. "Your cheekbones aren't so bad."

"You think?" Noah gazed back at Steph, and there wasn't a doubt in Rose's mind that if she weren't sitting there, watching them, he'd have kissed her.

"I just remembered," Rose said, scrambling to her feet. "I agreed to watch Emmie tonight."

"Really?" Noah looked up in surprise.

"Yeah, I've gotta get back home." She didn't meet his eyes. If she did, she knew he'd be able to tell she was lying.

"I'll walk you to your car," Noah offered, disentangling himself from Steph.

"No. You stay."

"You sure?" he said, already in a crouch, ready to spring to his feet.

Rose nodded, her throat thick. "Totally. Talk to you later?"

"Yeah. Okay."

Rose thought she heard a note of disappointment in his voice, but it was probably wishful thinking.

She hurried away as fast as she could without breaking into a run, trying to will away the burning that prickled the backs of her eyes. Why was she doing this to herself? He wasn't *hers*. They were friends; that's all they'd ever been. He didn't owe her anything, even if she'd once thought . . .

She shook her head. She needed to get over this stupid crush on Noah. He clearly didn't feel the same way about her, and if she couldn't figure out a way to be around him and Steph without bursting into tears, she was going to lose him entirely.

So *what* if he liked Steph and not her? He was still one of her best friends, ever since they were in elementary school. Just because he had a girlfriend now didn't change that. And it's not like Steph was terrible or anything. She was actually great. Exactly the type of girl Rose would've picked for Noah, if she were in the business of picking girls for him who were not herself.

When she reached her car, she risked a glance back at them—and wished she hadn't. He hadn't even waited until Rose was gone to kiss her.

Once Rose had seen them, though, she found she couldn't look away. For a few long seconds, she just watched them, imagining it was her lips pressed softly against Noah's, her hair twined through his fingers.

Her chest tightened until she struggled to breathe, her heart thudding painfully against walls that were too thin, too fragile.

Blinking away tears, she climbed into her car and drove away.

Chapter Sixteen

SHAWN

No one seemed to notice his plastic smile as he moved through the throngs of people, slapping shoulders and shaking hands on auto-pilot. Everyone kept congratulating him on the citizenship award—classmates, teachers, parents—and he kept up a steady stream of warm gratitude, despite the cold hollowness inside him. Like the Tin Man in *The Wizard of Oz*.

Thank you so much; it was a real honor.

There were so many good candidates!

I just feel really fortunate to live in such a generous town.

Oh, absolutely, my dad is just thrilled.

He imagined rapping his knuckles against his chest and could almost hear the dull *clang* of echoing metal.

Still, this was part of what had won him the award in the first place, this ability to work a crowd, to turn on charm like a faucet, to make friends with everyone. He scanned the faces at the bonfire, searching for Lisa, whom he'd lost in the crowd shortly after they'd arrived.

In the car on the way over, he'd told her what his dad had said that morning.

"That's ridiculous," Lisa had responded. "First of all, you definitely told him about the brunch. You *told* me that you told him."

"Yeah, but I should've reminded him," Shawn said, still kicking himself that he hadn't.

"Why? You're not his babysitter. He forgot, big deal. Suck it up and move on."

Shawn laughed, trying to picture his father's face if anyone ever told him to "suck it up and move on." Would he shoot fire out of his ears, or simply explode?

"Second of all," Lisa continued, "it's *your* life. Not his. He had a kid, not a clone. He can't expect you to just do everything exactly the way he did."

"He has worked really hard, though," Shawn argued, not entirely sure why he was defending his dad. "He built his business from nothing, and it *is* really generous to offer to share it with a kid just out of high school—"

"You're not just some kid, Shawn. You're his son. He's not being generous; he's being controlling. Has he ever even asked you what *you* want?"

Shawn bit his lip, then shook his head. "But you have to understand," he hurried to say, "he just wants what's best for me. He's worried I might make a mistake. He doesn't want me to wind up like my mom."

Lisa sighed, shaking her head. "Shawn, the only mistake your mom made was when she decided that leaving your dad meant she had to leave you, too."

"No," Shawn insisted, "she didn't know what she wanted, and then she made these huge life decisions without all the information, and—"

"Stop," Lisa said, holding up a hand. "That's your dad's version, but how would he know anything about how she feels now? He hasn't talked to her in years. He's making it up because he's trying to control you the same way he tried to control her."

Shawn frowned, kneading the steering wheel. His father wouldn't do that. Integrity was too important to him. It was even part of his company slogan: *Quality and integrity you can count on.* He wouldn't make up stories.

Would he?

"Look," Lisa had said, shifting in her seat so her whole body faced him, one long leg crossed up in front of her on the bench with her ankle propped on her knee. "Think of what you did to win that award. All that work you put in. All those years of studying and volunteering and training. That wasn't just luck. It was planning and dedication and . . . and *grit*. Are you seriously telling me that after all that, you're still worried you haven't put enough thought into your future?"

A glimmer of a smile tugged at Shawn's mouth. "I guess not."

"Honestly, your dad is in idiot if he thinks that the biggest mistake you could make right now is going to college. And since when do you care what idiots think?"

He chuckled under his breath. "Okay, you've made your point."

"Good," said Lisa as they pulled onto the Derrins' lawn. "Because I can't be seen associating with a guy who caters to idiots." She grinned at him as he parked the car. "You okay?"

He nodded, reaching for her hand. She let him take it, but after a quick squeeze, she pulled away, swinging open her door and hopping out of the truck. He sighed, watching her weave through the cars, toward the fire, before turning and beckoning for him to follow.

She always knew the right thing to say to make him feel better.

Except, of course, for the one thing she'd never said.

Chapter Seventeen

JUSTIN

When we pull up to the Derrin family's bloated estate, festivities are already in full swing. A staccato drumbeat rattles the windows of the Mustang as the marching band blasts the school fight song across a lawn the size of a football field.

Kids, teachers, and parents are everywhere, clustered on the wraparound porch, spilling down the front steps, scattered across the grass, and gathered around the massive bonfire in the middle of the yard. At tables set up around the lawn, PTA moms trade cups of lemonade and brownies wrapped in cellophane for wrinkled dollar bills.

I take a deep breath as Alyssa jumps out of the car. This is so not my scene.

"Come on!" she yells, her voice nearly drowned by the clash of drums and cymbals, already bouncing in place to the beat of the music. I would have done anything to get away from Stan, but I wish I'd suggested we go bowling, or see a movie, or go ice fishing, or *anything* other than this bonfire. These kids aren't my friends, and this isn't my idea of fun. But she wanted to go, and I wanted to leave, so . . . here we are.

I force a smile onto my face and reluctantly follow her into the teeming mass of humanity.

The air is thick with noise—music and voices and car engines and maxed-out phone speakers all competing for precious seconds of attention. I feel instantly overwhelmed, but Alyssa is in her element, dipping in and out of conversations as easily as skimming her fingers across the surface of a fountain.

I trail awkwardly behind her like toilet paper stuck to a shoe, barely able to track what one group is talking about before we've moved on to the next. In a matter of minutes, Alyssa has weighed in on the citizenship-award winner ("I mean, was anyone *really* surprised?"), the city hall internship ("*such* an amazing opportunity"), the human remains in Stone River ("so creepy and cool, right?"), and the latest senior-class relationship drama ("I feel like it's none of our business, honestly"). In every group, Alyssa is quickly absorbed into their midst, the seams between *us* and *them* blending into nothing the instant she appears. Meanwhile, I keep finding myself squeezed out into the periphery like an inflamed zit, blocked by squared shoulders and jutted hips and tossed hair.

After we extract ourselves from a conversation about some social media influencer I've never heard of, Dave stumbles his way through the crowd, stopping directly in front of Alyssa. His eyes rake over her like claws, and I have to smother an overwhelming urge to punch him in the face.

"Yo, you came!" he shouts over the din of the crowd, leering openly at her, like I'm not even there. "You wanna see my room?" His breath reeks of booze.

"No, thanks," Alyssa says, trying to work her way around him, but he blocks her path.

"It's pretty awesome." He grins. "Lotta cool stuff up there. I think you'd like it."

"She said no, Dave," I say, inserting myself between them as I scan the lawn for somewhere we can go that he can't follow us.

Dave frowns at me, as if noticing my presence for the first time. "I told you you weren't invited, *Bore*-en."

"And I told you that's not a thing, you wet toe sock."

His eyes narrow for a second, but then his face relaxes and he smiles, smacking me on the shoulder. "Yeah, guess you're right." He glances around, then reaches into his pocket and pulls out a flask. "Truce?"

I look warily at it, and he rolls his eyes. "What, you think I'm trying to poison you? Look." He unscrews the cap and takes a swig, then holds it out to me again. "See? Totally fine."

I debate for a second, then decide—what the hell. If Stan and Mom can both drink away their problems, I might as well do the same. Maybe some mild intoxication therapy will do me good. I accept the flask from Dave and gulp down a mouthful of whatever's inside, which turns out to be whiskey. My throat ignites as it burns its way down to my stomach. I chase it with another deep swig.

"Justin . . . ," Alyssa mutters under her breath.

"Damn, Warren," Dave says, laughing. "Here, you hang on to that. I've got more where that came from."

"No, he's done," Alyssa says, trying to grab the flask from me. "Come on, Justin, give it back."

I turn away from her, blocking her with one arm. It may be psychosomatic, but already I can feel my nerves uncoiling inside me, soothed by a gentle warmth.

"No worries." Dave grins. "I'll just grab it from you later. Have a great night, kids."

He saunters off toward the house, hands in his pockets, as Alyssa continues to try to grab the flask from me. My head swims with a gentle waviness as I tip more whiskey down my throat. By the feel of it, I've already downed half the contents. "Stop it," I mutter as I bat away Alyssa's insistent hands.

She crosses her arms, glaring at me. "Your mom is an *alcoholic*, Jay. And from the looks of things yesterday, I think Stan might be one, too. How can you *possibly* think getting drunk right now is a good idea? Plus, you got that thing from *Dave*. There's no way he's not up to something."

Now it's my turn to be annoyed. "I'm not a little kid, Alyssa. I don't need you to take care of me."

"*Someone* has to."

I shake my head, turning my back on her. "Just leave me alone, okay?"

"Justin, come on, what are you doing?"

I wave one hand over my head, not bothering to turn back to her as I walk away. "Having fun. That's what you wanted, right?"

Chapter Eighteen

LISA

Lisa spotted Charlene at the edge of the driveway, flattening out one of the colorful signs they'd made the day before that had somehow gotten folded in half. Her heart gave an excited flutter at the sight of Charlene in her pink skirt and bright jacket, her golden hair pinned up on one side of her head and cascading down the other in curls that sparkled in the glow of the fire.

"What happened here?" Lisa asked, crouching down next to her.

"Stupidity," Charlene said with a sigh. She wore a roll of duct tape around one wrist like a bracelet; she tore off a length to attach the sign to a new stake. The old one lay in pieces beside them, half in the ground, half broken off in the grass. "Dumb game that involved half the basketball team and a lot of jumping and, of course, some idiot falling on a sign he could've easily just walked around."

"Wow, sounds like I missed a lot," Lisa said, helping Charlene push the stake back into the earth. They both leaned back to survey their work. The sign was obviously a little worse for wear, but at least it was legible.

"Yeah," Charlene said, brushing a stray curl out of her eyes. "Where were you? I thought you were supposed to get here earlier."

"I did, actually," Lisa said. "But we stayed in the truck for a little bit. Shawn needed to talk."

Something flickered behind Charlene's eyes. "About what?"

Lisa winced internally, knowing Charlene wasn't going to like the answer. "It's . . . private. I'm sorry," she hurried to say. "It's just that it's his business, not mine, you know?"

"But you're the one he talks to about it," Charlene said.

"Yes, but only because he doesn't have anyone else."

"Really?" Charlene raised her eyebrows and stood, taking a few steps into the driveway. She craned her neck, searching the crowd around the fire, until she found what she was looking for and pointed. "*That* guy doesn't have anyone else to talk to?"

Lisa followed Charlene's finger with her eyes. Shawn stood in the middle of a crowd of their classmates, laughing with his head thrown back as admirers pressed ever closer to him, like moths to a flame. "That's different," Lisa said quietly.

"How?"

"They don't know him like I do," she tried to explain. "He needs me."

Charlene nodded slowly, biting her lip, and Lisa realized what she must be thinking. "Not like you, though," she rushed to say. "And, of course, after the election—"

"Will things really change after the election, Lisa?" Charlene asked. "If he *needs* you now, won't he need you then, too?"

"I-I don't—That's not—" Lisa stammered, trying to come up with the right thing to say. In her head, the election was such a clear gateway. She'd step through, and everything would be different on the other side. But when she tried to explain why she felt that way, the words danced just out of her reach, fizzling to dust the instant she touched them.

Charlene took a deep breath, her shoulders trembling slightly. She hugged her arms to her chest, her green eyes watery. "Be honest. Do you love him? Is that why you won't break up with him?"

Lisa opened and closed her mouth, unable to form the words she knew Charlene wanted to hear. The truth was, she *did* love him. Not in the way he loved her, but she cared about him. She was one of few people who knew him for who he truly was, who kept the secrets no one else knew. She couldn't abandon him, not now. Not when he had trusted her with so much.

Would it help for her to admit that out loud, or just make everything worse? She couldn't decide.

The silence between them stretched out excruciatingly.

Charlene closed her eyes for a few seconds, then opened them, giving Lisa a tight smile. "That wasn't fair. I shouldn't have asked that. I'm sorry."

She chewed her lip, and Lisa could tell there was more she wasn't saying. She had hoped that after last night, after what they'd said to each other, everything was okay now. That Charlene wouldn't feel threatened by Shawn, that Lisa wouldn't feel torn between them, and that things could just go on as they had been. Better, even, because she'd *said* it. Out loud. The *L*-word. Or, not *the* *L*-word, but they both knew what it meant.

She'd never been able to say it to Shawn. Not any version of the *L*-word. Shouldn't that count for something? Didn't Charlene know what a big deal that was?

Lisa waited for Charlene to say what they both knew she was thinking, while desperately hoping she wouldn't.

"The thing is," Charlene said slowly, "I know it's hard for you. But it's hard for me, too. I thought I would be able to handle it, but . . . I don't know if I can anymore."

She shifted so her back was to the fire, blocking Lisa's view of Shawn, and his of her. Charlene took Lisa's hand in hers, winding their fingers together. "I don't want to lose you," she said, looking down at their hands. "But I also know I can't keep doing . . . whatever this is."

She waved her free hand at the air between them, indicating that by *this*, she meant the messy, undefined *something* that bound them together. "I think I just need some space."

Lisa's heart raced. She clutched Charlene's hand, as if she were a kite Lisa could keep from slipping away just by gripping tighter. "For how long?"

Charlene sighed and looked up at the night sky, blinking rapidly. "I don't know. I need to figure out some stuff on my own, I think. I've been trying to be strong, because I thought you *needed* me to be strong, but the truth is, I don't think I am. And I can't keep pretending that this is all fine with me when it's not."

"But—" Lisa's heart beat frantically, threatening to shatter, and break her chest, all at once. "But you're saying that if I *do* break up with him—"

"Not *if* anything, Lees. This isn't an ultimatum. You do what you need to do, and I'll do what I need to do, and we'll see where that takes us."

"But last night . . . we said—Char, I—"

"Lettuce you," Charlene whispered with tears in her eyes, dropping Lisa's hand.

Lisa felt her body turning to stone. She stood rooted in place, staring at Charlene. Had that really just happened?

Footsteps approached, and Shawn appeared over Charlene's shoulder, a wide smile lighting up his face. "There you are!" he exclaimed. "I've been looking everywhere for you." He reached for Lisa's hand, but she moved away, crossing her arms. The thought of him touching her now, while her heart was breaking, was more than she could bear.

"Well, you found us," she said, trying to remember what smiling felt like. She hoped she had come close.

"Hey, Charlene," Shawn said, turning his sparkling grin toward her.

"Hey." Charlene's eyes were on the ground, the house, the sky, anywhere but on Lisa or Shawn.

"You want to go sit with Noah and Steph?" Shawn asked, turning back to Lisa. "They've got a blanket near the fire."

"Um," Lisa said, looking uneasily from Shawn to Charlene. She needed him to leave, needed to be alone with Charlene, needed to fix this. "It's just, Charlene and I were kind of in the middle of—"

99

"It's fine," Charlene said. "I was just leaving."

"Oh," Lisa said, her stomach aching like it was slowly filling with cement. "Are you sure you didn't want to . . ."

She trailed off as Charlene walked away, not even waiting until Lisa had finished her sentence. Her whole body felt like it had turned to glass. One tap, and she would shatter.

Shawn looked from Charlene to Lisa, his forehead crinkled. "Everything okay?"

"Yeah. Fine," Lisa said. Her voice sounded like it was coming from far away. Roaring filled her ears.

Shawn cleared his throat, then reached for Lisa's hand. "Anyway, let's go—"

Lisa tugged her fingers free, stepping away from him. "Actually, Shawn, I'm sorry." Her voice trembled, and it took everything she had to keep it from breaking. "I just remembered I need to—Can I find you later?"

"Oh, sure. I'll just—"

"Thanks."

She walked, then ran, around the back of the house, away from Shawn, away from the revelry around the fire, away from Charlene and her sparkling eyes and her trembling mouth and her aching whispers. And when she was away from it all, where no one could see, she finally let herself cry.

Chapter Nineteen

JUSTIN

Half an hour into the bonfire, mild intoxication therapy has turned into moderate intoxication therapy. Dave's flask is now empty, the remainder of its contents dumped into the red Solo cup of lemonade in my hand, which is also mostly empty. I'm pleasantly buzzed, and don't care about my mom or Stan or Alyssa or any of it, which is exactly what I was going for.

The sun has long since finished setting, the dim orange glow of the fire the only real light, the dancing flames sending up sparks that twirl through the black sky and disappear above the treetops. I sit in a lawn chair by the fire near a group of kids I share a couple of classes with, nodding here and there but paying little attention to the conversation, which has circled back to the body in the river. A passionate debate has arisen between Team Accidental Drowning and Team Unidentified Zodiac Killer Victim, neither of which appears to have anything supporting their positions outside of whatever is in their Solo cups (which I'm beginning to suspect is similar to what's in *my* Solo cup).

Personally, I'm rooting for Team Zodiac Killer. At least that would be interesting.

On the other side of the fire, Alyssa sits on the edge of a wide blue cooler, sharing a ziplock bag of PTA cookies with Danny, a guy I work with who I don't think has shown up to a school function since we were sophomores. Up until junior year, Danny presented as female, but as soon as he came out, some kids made it their mission to make school impossible for him, and he eventually withdrew to take online courses instead. Now he's laughing, and Alyssa is smiling, and I am the worst because the sight of her enjoying herself so much with someone who is not me makes me want to vomit.

I know I should be glad that he's here. Danny is a good guy, and he deserves to have some fun with what's left of high school. If I were a good person, I'd be happy he felt comfortable enough to show up, and that Alyssa was the person who made him feel welcome.

But alas, I'm just my usual petty self, and every time Alyssa's arm brushes against his, I find myself wishing he would get hit with a sudden wave of explosive diarrhea.

I've been trying not to watch them, but occasionally I'll hear her laugh and I'll glance over to see her face lit up by firelight, dark curls bouncing as she talks animatedly, waving her hands to illustrate whatever point she's making.

All that pleading with me to come to this thing, and she doesn't even care that we haven't hung out since we got here.

Suddenly, I don't want to be here anymore. I mean, I never wanted to be at this stupid fire in the first place, but now I specifically don't want to be *here*, sitting with people I don't even like, watching Alyssa hang out with another guy.

I stand, not really sure where I'm going until gravity does its thing and I realize I have to pee. Throwing back the final remnants of my drink and tossing my cup in the general vicinity of the nearest trash can, I make my way toward the colossal house to locate a bathroom.

The inside of the Derrins' house looks like the "after" tour in one of those HGTV makeover shows my mom is always watching (which has always felt a little masochistic to me, considering our house is about the size of my gym locker, and only half as nice). Derrin Family Jams moved the actual jam-making business out of their kitchen and into a factory thirty miles up the road decades ago, but the money has always stayed right here.

Chalkboard signs covered with artistically scrawled script point the way to the various bathrooms like they're announcing the specials at a coffee shop. I follow the directions to **Downstairs Bathroom, North** like it's a normal thing to have so many bathrooms in your house that you need a freaking compass.

There's a short line, so while I wait, I study the family portraits lining the walls in their dark wood frames. The first one is Dave and his siblings with their parents: a short, unsmiling man with wiry hair and hard features, and a thin, Stepford-looking woman in heels and pearls. In the next one, I recognize his dad again but this time as a kid, probably around eleven or twelve, with a pretty older sister and parents who look at least marginally happier than the one he'll grow up to become.

More portraits continue on down the hall in matching frames, each a generation older than the last, until the final black-and-white image captures a brood of smiling Derrin children, each holding a jar of homemade jam. They sit in front of the much more normal-size farmhouse that used to sit in this spot, before it was replaced by this sparkling modern monstrosity with its cardinal-direction bathrooms.

When I'm done, my hands smelling of organic lavender soap that probably cost more than my shoes, I start to make my way out of the house—but I'm stopped on the porch.

"This is him?" asks a stern-looking man I recognize from the picture in the hall as Dave's father. He's frowning at me but talking to Dave, who looks *way* too happy for my liking.

Along with Dave and his dad, the sheriff is also here, thick arms folded just above the spot where the buttons of his uniform fight valiantly to hold back the swelling tide of his growing beer gut. I don't know what's going on, but I'm 100 percent certain it is not good for me.

Dave nods, and before I can ask what on earth they're talking about, his dad is in my face, grabbing my arm. "You've been going through my liquor cabinet, son?"

"Huh?"

"Don't lie to me, kid; I can smell it on your breath."

My thoughts are sluggish from the whiskey, but even with my brain functioning on power-saver mode, a few things are crystal clear.

Son of a bitch. I narrow my eyes at Dave, who hovers behind the adults, a Joker grin stretched across his face. "I didn't do anything," I say through gritted teeth.

"Check his pockets," Dave suggests, nearly jumping up and down in excitement. "I think I saw him take one of your flasks."

I'm going to kill him. Not in a metaphorical way. I'm going to literally put my hands around his neck and wring the life out of him.

"Let's see what's in those pockets, son," the sheriff says, puffing himself up like a blowfish. Sheriff Gibson has always struck me as one of those guys who peaked in high school and has been chasing the glory days of his youth ever since.

I weigh my options and decide there's no use in stalling. They'll find it sooner or later. Sighing, I pull the flask out of my pocket and hand it to the sheriff, who in turn hands it to Mr. Derrin.

"I didn't take it," I can't help myself from saying.

The sheriff chuckles, shaking his head. "This is Lissa Warren's boy," he says under his breath to Mr. Derrin, like I'm not even here. "Like mother, like son, I guess."

"I know the kind," Mr. Derrin mutters as he sniffs at the flask and wrinkles his nose, as though I've somehow contaminated it. I fight an urge to grab it out of his hands, tear through the yard, and hurl it into the fire. He finds me and my "kind" offensive? How about we let the fire burn every trace of me off his precious flask? See how he likes it then.

Mr. Derrin turns to me. "I'm going to need to ask you to leave, son."

"But—"

He frowns, holding up a hand. "I don't want to hear it. I'm cutting you a break here. I could have Sheriff Gibson take you down to the station."

"But I didn't do anything!"

Mr. Derrin narrows his eyes at me. "Everyone's done something," he says ominously. "You'd do well not to fight me on this. I could make your life very difficult."

I look from him to the sheriff, my mouth agape. Is he seriously threatening to have me *arrested* over this stupid flask? "Fine," I say through gritted teeth. "I'll go."

"Want me to get you a Lyft?" Dave asks, his eyes filled with fake concern. His shoulders shake in barely contained laughter.

"No, thanks, I'm here with someone," I say pointedly. "I'll go home with *her*."

The satisfaction I feel at watching Dave's smug smile crack is almost, *almost* enough to make this whole thing worth it.

I hurry away from the house, my ears ringing with Sheriff Gibson's warning that if I'm not gone in five minutes, he'll have to "take measures," whatever that means. Alyssa is probably still over by the fire. We can go back to her house, watch Netflix, warm up a frozen pizza, and pretend today never happened.

But my steps slow as I get closer. Alyssa and Danny are still sitting side by side on the cooler, but they've been joined by Brian Bruhe and Kennedy Ramberstein and Mikayla Jenkins and a few other kids I can't recognize from this distance. They're clustered in a loose knot, some sitting in folding camping chairs, others on the ground, talking and laughing and having fun.

Danny, who'd been so nervous to come to this thing, seems like he's having a good time, leaning into the conversation, his elbows braced on his knees, his smile relaxed. And Alyssa is beaming, talking a mile a minute as the others hang on her every word. This is the experience she wanted tonight, one where she could laugh and unwind from the stress I continually dump in her lap.

I can't ask her to leave.

Alyssa glances up and squints in my general direction, but I turn away, shoving my hands in my pockets as I head toward my car. I've nearly convinced myself she didn't see me, when I hear footsteps on the grass behind me.

"Justin?"

For a second, I seriously consider breaking into a sprint. My car is only one row over. I could probably be in it and halfway out of the parking lot before she has time to process just how much of an asshole I am.

"Are you *leaving*? Without me?"

"You looked like you were having fun," I mutter, not wanting to turn around. "I'm sure Danny can give you a ride."

"That's not the point."

"I was gonna text you."

"Are you serious? You can't just ditch me and then think—come *on*, Justin, will you please look at me?" She grabs my arm, spinning me to face her, and frowns as, despite my best efforts, I sway slightly. "You can't drive like this. You're drunk."

"Therapeutically intoxicated."

"That's not a thing."

"It is and I'm it."

"Give me your keys."

"No."

"Give them to me *now*." She holds out her hand.

"*No.* You're the one who wanted to come to this stupid bonfire, 'Loossa." *Loossa?* Damn, I'm drunker than I thought. Short sentences it is. I examine each word carefully in my head before I let it escape my mouth. "Go. Have fun. I'll be fine."

"I'm not going to let you do this."

"Not your choice."

"I'm calling Stan," she says, pulling out her phone.

Before she can unlock her screen, I grab the phone out of her hand and hurl it into the darkness as hard as I can. Our gym teacher spent freshman year trying to convince me to join the baseball team, saying I had a pretty good arm on me, but eventually gave up when he realized I had no interest in team sports—or any other sports, for that matter.

Now my untapped throwing talent rises to the occasion. The phone arcs high into the night sky, spinning over the last row of cars, and disappears.

"Are you *serious*?" Alyssa shrieks. She may as well shoot laser beams out of her eyes. I swear I smell something burning. "I cannot *believe* you did that," she says through gritted teeth.

"Guess you're gonna have to go look for it," I say with a shrug.

She hesitates for a second, then goes stomping off after the phone. "Don't you dare leave," she calls over her shoulder, but I'm already unlocking the Mustang and slipping behind the wheel.

"Justin!" she yells, her voice swallowed by the growl of the engine as I turn my key in the ignition.

I pause for a moment and look up at her, running back toward me in the glow of the headlights, her phone forgotten. I roll forward, wheels bumping through the grass, as she bangs on my window. "Stop the car, Justin," she yells, her voice muffled by the glass as she jogs to keep up. "Come on. At least let me drive."

"Leave me alone, Alyssa," I call to her. "I'm not your problem, okay? Go do what you want."

She yells something else, but I don't want to hear it. I crank the wheel and hit the gas, shooting out onto the driveway and leaving her behind.

Stan was right. I should never have come here.

Chapter Twenty

JUSTIN

I glance at my phone as the Mustang traces the winding road south, toward Wilson Bridge.

Come back. Don't be stupid.

Too late, Alyssa. Crossed that line a while ago.

It's started to rain, and the windshield begins to fog up. The defroster tries to turn on, but the fan is sluggish and barely any air drips from the vents. I lean forward to wipe away a circle of condensation with my hand, improving the nighttime visibility about as much as swapping out a blindfold for sunglasses.

My phone buzzes again. Please? We need to talk.

I sigh, wringing my hands around the steering wheel. I can't believe I just *left* her there. It seemed like the right thing to do at the time—noble, even—but now it feels like yet another bad decision shoveled onto the steaming dung heap that is my life.

On the off chance I haven't already screwed things up between us permanently, I should probably go back. Eventually, if I keep pulling crap like this, she's going to decide I'm not worth the effort, and I'll have lost the one thing in my life that's actually decent.

I should apologize. As much as my life sucks, I can't even imagine how much worse it would be without her.

I fumble at my phone, figuring I'll call and tell her I'm on my way back, but the liquor has made me clumsy, and I drop the phone into the floorboards. Awesome.

I look down and spot the phone by my foot, and think of a story I heard once about a guy who had something roll under his brake pedal, making it impossible for him to stop the car. It crashed, he died, and it was all very tragic.

No thanks.

I'm on Wilson Bridge now, crossing high over Stone River, the only car traveling in either direction. I make sure the headlights are lined up straight, then bend down to grope for the phone. It takes longer than I expect to find it, but finally, my fingers close around it, and I straighten.

There's something in the road.

At first, I think it's a deer, but then I realize it's a person—standing right in the path of my car, washed white by my headlights.

I don't even have time to wonder what sort of idiot goes walking in the rain, on a bridge, in dark clothing, at night, before I slam on my brakes, my heart leaping into my throat. The car skids, spinning like a coin, the wheels slipping over the rain-slicked pavement.

I can't remember what I'm supposed to do. Blood pounds in my ears, my chest clenching like a fist.

What am I supposed to do? Turn into the skid?

I yank the wheel, but nothing happens. The car is out of control. I have no idea which way I'm pointing, what's happening, until the car slams to a stop with a sound like a thunderclap.

My shoulder and head smash into the door.

Lights explode behind my eyelids as pain blossoms between my ears. I feel like I just got run through a blender.

But the car has stopped moving, and I'm alive.

Relief washes through me. For the first time since I hit the brakes, I venture a breath, taking inventory of my body. Nothing hurts when I breathe in, which is a good sign, I think. My head aches, and I probably have a concussion, but nothing feels broken. All my limbs are present and accounted for. I don't even think I'm bleeding.

Slowly, my eyes adjust to the view through my windshield. I blink through a whiskey-fogged haze, my brain sloshing around in my head like half-melted ice. For a minute, I'm disoriented. It's just . . . *sky*.

The car groans forward, pitching me over the steering wheel. Twinkling lights flicker below me, and for one wild second, I'm convinced the world has turned upside down, and I'm looking down on outer space. Then my brain reorients itself, and I realize it's not the stars I'm seeing, but moonlight glistening off black, rippling water.

Suddenly, I know exactly where I am.

My car is hanging off the bridge, teetering over the river.

Oh God oh God oh God. I don't know if I'm praying or cursing. Maybe both. My hands feel fused to the wheel.

I try to breathe, but my whole body is frozen. Do I open the door? Climb into the back seat? Stay still?

My phone buzzes—it somehow wound up on the dashboard, right in front of my face—and, ridiculously, I look at it.

Are you ok? I'm worried about you.

I laugh. *Me too,* I want to respond. I think I might be in shock.

Maybe it's my laughter; maybe it's gas shifting in the tank; maybe it's the wind. I wish I knew what it was, but I never will.

The car dips lower, and suddenly it doesn't matter if I stay still or move or scream or hold my breath.

I try to resist, but gravity grabs hold of me, pulling me forward as I feel the back wheels lift off the pavement. I brace my arms against the steering wheel, pressing my back against the seat, but it's no use.

The car tips like a teapot, threatening to pour me out.
Then—
It falls.
In slow motion, then all at once.
The last thing I see is the reflection of my headlights in the water.

Chapter Twenty-One

ROSE

Rose kneaded her hands on the steering wheel as she drove home, her headlights the only illumination on the winding road leading to Wilson Bridge. She sighed, biting her lip. No matter how many logical arguments she ran through her head, the ache in her chest remained. She wondered if it would ever fully go away.

The road spilled out of the trees, giving way to the airy openness of the bridge. Tomorrow, she decided. After church, she'd find Noah and apologize for acting so weird tonight. She didn't think she could explain to him what the problem *really* was—that would just make things worse—but it wouldn't be lying to talk about how she was stressed out about the campaign and the pressure their family was under and how weird everything felt right now. Maybe then, they could—

There was a body in the road.

Not at the edges of her headlights, in the distance.

Right in front of her. Like it had appeared out of nowhere.

Rose slammed on her brakes, jerking the wheel to one side. The tires shrieked in protest, skidding across the pavement, and for a moment, she feared she'd lost control. A horrific image flashed through her mind of her car flying off the bridge, plummeting to the river below.

The front of her car bucked angrily as the tire hit the sidewalk, sending her lurching over the wheel as the car squealed to an abrupt stop.

She sat frozen, eyes squeezed shut, fingers clenched on the wheel. Breaths came rapidly, her heartbeat racing as she realized the car was no longer moving. She pried her eyes open to survey the damage, and realized that, miraculously, she hadn't even hit anything, other than the sidewalk. The steel railing of the bridge sliced the beams of her headlights into glowing ribbons a few feet in front of her car.

Hands shaking, she shifted into reverse, the front tire slowly dropping back onto the road. Rose put the car in park and opened her door.

"Hello? Are you okay?" she called, her legs still feeling a little wobbly as she stepped into the road. Her headlights were pointed away, out over the water, but she could still make the person out in the hazy glow of the bridge lights. A boy, lying on his side, limbs askew, like a dropped doll. Her breath caught in her throat as she approached, forcing herself closer even as her feet itched to run away. She didn't *think* she'd hit him, but she really wished he'd move so she could be sure. "Hey!"

She was standing over him now, close enough to be certain that she didn't recognize him from school, although there was something vaguely familiar about him. From here, she could see that he was, in fact, breathing. And there didn't appear to be any blood. He was fair-skinned, with shaggy hair dyed a weird shade of red-orange, although it appeared blond at the roots. He seemed to be made up entirely of angles, with bony limbs and sharp, pointed features.

Tentatively, she nudged him with her toe. "Hello?"

To her relief, he groaned, rolling onto his back and rubbing his eyes. He mumbled something that sounded a little like *Lisa*.

"You know Lisa? I'm Rose, her sister," she said, tapping her chest.

"Huh?" He blinked at her, frowning. Slowly, he pushed himself to a sitting position, wincing as he did. "Alyssa doesn't have a sister."

"Oh, I thought you said—never mind. Are you okay?"

"I'm . . . not sure." After a couple of false starts, he managed to get his feet under him. He looked around, bewildered, hands linked behind his head. "Where's my car?"

Rose shrugged helplessly. "I was just driving home from the bonfire and saw you on the bridge."

"What time is it?"

"A little after eight."

He seemed disoriented, looking up at the sky, then down at the pavement, before walking a little unevenly to the railing and peering down into the river. "What the hell?" he muttered.

Rose couldn't agree more. "What's the matter?"

Instead of answering, he squinted at her again. "Can I use your phone? I think mine was in my car . . . Are you *sure* you haven't seen my car?"

He didn't look like he'd been hit by a car, but she was starting to think he had a concussion. "Do you want me to take you to the hospital or something?"

"No, I just need to figure out what happened to my freaking car." His head swiveled in all directions, as if a car might magically appear if he caught it at the right angle, then groaned, pressing the heels of his hands to his eyes. "I'm never drinking again," he said under his breath, although Rose didn't think he was talking to her.

"Well," she said hesitantly, "where was the last place you saw it?"

He laughed, shaking his head. Despite the strangeness of the situation, Rose couldn't help but notice that he had a nice smile. "I could've sworn I drove it into the river, but"—he spread his hands wide, gesturing to the empty road—"clearly *that* didn't happen, so I sincerely hope it's still at the bonfire."

"You were at the bonfire? Do you go to Stone Lake High?" She'd never seen him before, which may have seemed normal at a bigger school but was strange at Stone Lake.

He gave her an odd look, like *she* was the one acting bizarre here. "You mean Warren High?"

"I think I know the name of my own school." She was beginning to think this guy was on something. How could you tell the difference between a concussion and someone who was just high? She didn't have much experience with either.

"Clearly not, since there *is* no Stone Lake High."

"What are you talking about?"

"What are you talking about? It's been Warren High for decades now. Ever since the fire."

"The bonfire?"

"No, the one that killed . . ." He trailed off, tilting his head to squint at her like she had sprouted a third eye. "You seriously don't know this? It's, like, common knowledge."

"I literally have no idea what you're talking about."

"Half the school burned down in 1985. Killed two people. They renamed the school."

Rose shook her head, utterly lost. "There hasn't been any fire at the school this year."

"Who said anything about this year?"

Maybe he was high *and* had a concussion.

"*You* did. Just now." Her brows knit together. "1985."

Chapter Twenty-Two

JUSTIN

"What?"

"What?"

For a minute, we just stare at each other. I cannot figure out this girl's deal. I don't recognize her from school, making me wonder what she's doing out here. She's Asian, with dark hair that falls past her shoulders and a heart-shaped mouth that is currently pinched in confusion. At first, I thought she'd genuinely stopped to help me, but now I'm thinking she must be pulling some sort of weird prank, although I have no idea why some girl I've never met would try to mess with me.

Also, where the hell is my car? Did I seriously hallucinate the entire accident? I clearly hallucinated the rain, considering the pavement is bone-dry. And if I imagined it, how on earth did I *get* here? Did I walk?

Memories flash through my mind. Mom stumbling around our house after a drunken night out, insisting that the stories Stan or the police or the neighbors were telling weren't true, that she didn't do what they said she did, that she couldn't have been where they said she was.

Oh god, am I turning into her?

But . . . every time Mom has ever lost her grip on reality, it has been accompanied by vomiting, headaches, a general inability to move or speak or do anything resembling healthy human behavior. If I was so drunk that I hallucinated everything since I left the bonfire, why do I feel fine?

"Look," I say, needing this night to be over, "can you please just let me use your phone? I've had a really sucky weekend and I just—"

"I'll take you to the hospital, but I'm not taking you to my house."

"Who said anything about your house?"

She doesn't *look* like she's messing with me. Her eyes are narrowed, her body tense, like she's waiting for me to attack her. "You asked to use my phone."

"Not your *house* phone."

"Well, I don't have a *car* phone!"

I pinch the bridge of my nose, the last drops of my patience draining away. "How about you just take me back to Dave's, and I'll see if my car's still there or get a ride with one of my friends?"

"Who's Dave?"

"Dave Derrin. The bonfire's at his house?" Who *is* this girl? How does she not know whose house she was just at?

She shakes her head. "The bonfire is at *Charlene* Derrin's house."

"Fine, whatever. I don't know his sister's name."

"Charlene's brother is named Karl. And her dad is Jack."

This whole conversation is so deeply weird that I almost feel stupid trying to make sense of it. Especially when my brain sluggishly circles back around to the bizarre thing she said a minute ago, and I realize that *I* am not the problem here. Or at least, not the only problem. At least I know what year it is, unlike this strange girl, who has apparently suffered some sort of break from reality.

"Can I just ask . . . What do you think the date is?" I feel a little dumb that it's taken me this long to realize that this girl may be more than a few bricks shy of a load.

"September twenty-eighth."

That's not right—it's the thirtieth—but that's not really what I'm getting at. "What, uh, year?"

She gives me a funny look but answers, "1985. What year do *you* think it is?"

Okay, seriously, what the hell? I feel like I'm trapped in an episode of *The Twilight Zone*. "You're off by a few decades," I say, reaching into my back pocket to pull out my wallet. I hold up my driver's license, tapping the date with my index finger. "See?"

I glance at her car, a boxy, old-model sedan, and wonder what she's doing out here. She said she was at the bonfire, but if she's living in some kind of delusion, I probably shouldn't trust her to know where she came from. Did she steal this car? Maybe I should be the one taking *her* to the hospital.

"Listen," I say, trying to make my voice as nonthreatening as possible, "I think you're confused. Where do you live? Let me drive you home." I don't really want to devote any more of my evening to this girl, but I feel bad just leaving her here. If she at least knows her address, I can pass her off to her parents or someone else who—and I cannot stress this enough—isn't me.

She's shaking her head, frowning as she examines my license, and digs her own out of her purse. "*I'm* not the one who's confused, and you are *definitely* not driving my car." She fans a handful of multicolored cards under my nose. It takes me a second to figure out what I'm looking at as I try to parse the typewritten text on each card, but after a moment, I realize she's showing me a driver's license, library card, and student ID.

The license lists her birthday as August 12, 1968; the library card says it was issued in 1982; and the ID is for the 1985–1986 school year. They're all issued to a Rose Yin. No photos, though. Is she walking around with her grandmother's expired documents in her wallet or something?

"Who's Rose Yin?" I ask, still keeping my voice as nonthreatening as I can.

"*I'm* Rose Yin," she huffs. "Obviously."

I shake my head, holding my hands up in defeat. "You know what? Never mind. I give up. You win. It's 1985. Have a nice life."

I turn away from her and begin walking along the sidewalk, toward the south side of the bridge. It's a two-mile walk to my house, but I don't think I have it in me to go back to Dave's tonight, not after getting thrown out and hallucinating a car accident and having to deal with this weird girl and her *Back to the Future* schtick.

"Hey, where are you going?"

"Away," I call over my shoulder.

Behind me, I hear her car door slam and the engine rumble to life. I wait for her to zip past me, but to my dismay, she pulls up alongside me and rolls down her window, her car idling loudly. "What year do *you* think it is?"

I ignore her, staring straight ahead. I don't have a lot of patience on a good day, but tonight I feel like I'm working from a significant deficit.

"Where'd you get that weird shiny driver's license?"

"DMV, same as anyone else."

"Come on, where?"

"Why do you think it's 1985?"

"Because it is. Do you think you're from the *future*?"

I sigh. "No, I think I'm from right now."

"Which is . . . ?"

I roll my eyes. "2023."

Her forehead wrinkles as her car continues to creep along the bridge next to me. I walk a little faster, knowing I won't be able to outpace a car but just wanting this bizarre night to be over as soon as possible.

"How'd you get in the middle of the—"

Before she can finish her question, she's interrupted by flashing red lights flickering on behind us.

My heart thunks into my shoes. Did the police find my car? Is it somewhere stupid, like the middle of the woods or half-submerged at the riverbank, or parked in the Derrins' living room? All this hellish weekend needs is for me to get arrested for something I don't even remember, giving Stan yet another reason to wish he'd drowned me as a baby.

"Shoot," Rose mutters, glancing in her rearview mirror before throwing her car into park and grabbing her purse off the passenger seat.

I consider making a break for it, but quickly decide that running from the cops isn't the wisest move in any decade. I dig out my wallet again and attempt to sneakily sniff my breath, hoping that the smell of whiskey has faded.

The door to the police car opens, and an officer walks over to Rose's window. She smiles nervously when she sees him. "Sorry," she calls through the open window. "I know I wasn't going the speed limit."

"Everything okay, miss?" His voice sounds vaguely familiar.

"Yeah, sorry," Rose says again. "I was just heading home."

"This guy bothering you?"

Not really sure how *I* could be the one bothering *her* when she was the one choosing to drive next to me at three miles per hour, but okay.

Rose shakes her head. "We were just talking."

"Not a great place to talk. You're lucky you didn't get hit. License and registration?"

She hands it over, and I wait for him to point out that it's out of date by a few decades, but he just scans it quickly, looking bored, and then turns to me. "Yours too, son."

Seriously, has *everyone* lost their minds tonight? In what universe is her archaic driver's license an acceptable form of identification? I'm so busy gaping at him that I forget to do what he asked, until he clears his throat. "*Now*, kid."

Come to think of it, this guy looks kind of familiar, too, although I can't place him. Maybe he brought Mom home one night after one of her benders or something.

"What'd I do? I was just walking."

"Don't make me ask again."

I hand over my ID, but he barely glances at it before he narrows his eyes and hands it back. "Very funny. C'mon, kid, show me your real ID."

"This *is* a Real ID." I tap the gold star on it.

"I'm not playing here."

"Neither am I. Just *look*—"

I stop as my eyes flick down at the name on his badge, then back to his face. *Gibson.*

That's why he looks familiar. He reminds me of the sheriff, although this guy's no more than twenty-five, and without the sheriff's beer gut and receding hairline. But his voice, eyes, and towering height are all the same. His badge says DEPUTY, and I wonder exactly what flavor of nepotism we're serving up here.

"Are you related to Sheriff Gibson? Is he like . . . your dad or something?"

"*I'm* Deputy Gibson. The sheriff's Montague."

"But is there, like, another Gibson? Do you have an uncle or something in the police department?"

"I'm the only Gibson at the Stone Lake Police Department," he says, one hand going to the handcuffs at his waist. One finger taps against them threateningly. "Now if I have to ask you one more time for that ID—"

"Can you just—" I interrupt, holding my hands up for him to wait. My jumbled thoughts tumble over one another like dice. What the hell is going on here? "Sorry, I know this is weird, but can you just tell me . . ."

My pulse races. I can't believe I'm about to ask this.

I swallow, feeling like I'm losing my mind. "What year is it?"

Chapter Twenty-Three

Rose

Deputy Gibson frowned, his hands tightening on the handcuffs at his waist. "Okay, kid, I think you'd better come with me," he said, reaching for one of the strange boy's outstretched wrists.

All the blood rapidly drained out of the boy's face as the officer twisted his arm behind his back.

"Wait," he said, his breaths coming faster now. "Wait, you don't understand!"

Rose watched, her own heart rate increasing as the boy's wide eyes met hers, filled with fear and confusion and desperation. She could tell he wasn't lying—or didn't think he was—but it was more than that. Her mind was seized by a prickling thought that kept nagging at her, despite being completely impossible: *he's telling the truth.*

Nothing he said made sense. Some of it was verifiably false. And yet, a part of her believed him. Maybe even the biggest part.

Something in Rose's heart twisted, then gave.

"Officer, wait!"

She jumped out of her car before fully considering what she was doing. Gibson pivoted toward her, one hand still holding the boy's wrist behind his back, the other grasping a dangling pair of handcuffs. "Miss, I'm going to need you to stay back."

"He's my cousin!"

Gibson frowned as the boy stared at her, mouth agape. "Your . . . cousin?" His eyes slid suspiciously from her to the boy, and back, one eyebrow raising at the obvious lack of physical resemblance between them.

"On my mom's side," she said, thinking quickly. "He's visiting from, uh, Hawthorne. We were just heading back from the bonfire, but he, um, had to get out of the car for a minute to, uh . . ."

Crap. Why would he have to get out of the car? Her mind was totally blank.

"I felt dizzy," the boy supplied, his voice shaking.

Gibson raised an eyebrow, his gaze shifting to the dazed-looking boy. "Dizzy?"

Rose nodded, her throat thick, heart hammering. What was she thinking? She was *lying* to a *police officer*, all to help a complete stranger who thought he was from the future. If anyone found out about this, she'd be grounded for the rest of her life, and Diane's campaign would be ruined. And that was a best-case scenario, assuming this guy didn't kill her and dump her in the river.

But she couldn't just sit there and watch him get arrested. Not when there was a small but insistent part of her that was—inexplicably—sure he was telling the truth.

Deputy Gibson chewed on his lower lip, narrowing his eyes. "Yin," he repeated to himself. He peered into her face. "You're the stepdaughter, aren't you? Of the woman running for mayor?"

Rose noticed the disdain in his voice, confirming her suspicion that he was likely related to Franklin Gibson, Diane's opponent. "Yes, sir."

He snorted, shaking his head and muttering under his breath. Rose couldn't make it all out, but she definitely caught the words *these people*.

Her face grew warm, but she hoped the officer couldn't tell in the flashing red lights of his patrol car. In the six years since her dad had married Diane, she'd still never gotten used to the comments. For a while after the wedding, kids would make buzzing noises whenever she or Lisa passed them in the halls. Eventually, she learned it was because their family was half-Black, half-Asian—black and yellow, like a bumblebee.

The buzzing had stopped after a few months, but there were still times when Rose was caught off-guard by a dirty look, a mumbled comment, a mean-spirited laugh. Things that she and her family had never done anything to deserve, except exist.

Which was why they had to be perfect. All the time. No exceptions.

If Diane and her father knew what she was doing right now, they would *kill* her.

Deputy Gibson sighed and checked his watch, then finally dropped the boy's arm. "Okay, Miss Yin, if you want to take responsibility for him, be my guest. But he's gotta get in the car, and you've gotta drive the speed limit. I don't want to see either of you out here again. Understand?"

Rose nodded around the lump in her throat. She just wanted to be back at home, where she could shower this whole night off her.

Gibson strolled back to his car, then paused with his hand on the door. "1985," he called.

"What?"

"Kid asked the year. It's 1985," Gibson said with a grin, his shoulders shaking with barely suppressed laughter as he climbed into the patrol car.

Rose looked at the boy, whose face was as white as a sheet and oddly waxy in the moonlight. He looked like he might throw up, but she very much hoped he didn't, since she now had no choice but to give him a ride. "Get in the car," she hissed through clenched teeth as she climbed back into the driver's seat.

He nodded, drifting to the other side of the car like a zombie and flopping into his seat without a word. Rose started the engine, glanced in her rearview mirror—the lights were no longer flashing, but Deputy Gibson was still sitting there, watching—and eased her foot onto the accelerator. Once she started moving, so did the police car behind her, matching her pace across the bridge. She fervently hoped that he wasn't planning to follow her home.

The boy whispered something she couldn't quite make out.

"What?"

He cleared his throat. "Is it really 1985?" His voice sounded dull, like it was covered in dust.

Rose nodded. For some reason, she wasn't nervous anymore. Sometime during their encounter with Deputy Gibson, her apprehension had disappeared, replaced by curiosity. "What's your name?"

"Justin. Justin Warren."

Rose thought for a second. "You said the school is named Warren. In . . . where you're from."

He let out a humorless laugh. "Yeah. After my grandparents. They died there. Or I guess . . . they *will* die there."

Rose didn't say anything, but her stomach clenched as her mind made the obvious connections. Veronica, Diane's campaign manager, was married to Bill Warren, the school guidance counselor. They had a baby—a little girl. Veronica brought her to their house sometimes for campaign meetings. She and Emmie would play together. Rose and Lisa would take turns holding her.

Was Justin really talking about *those* Warrens? Were Bill and Veronica in danger?

And why on earth did she actually believe any of this? Was she losing her mind?

Justin pinched the bridge of his nose. "I think I'm losing my mind."

Rose's stomach flipped a second time at the sound of the words she'd just been thinking. Again, she was struck by the sense that they were somehow uniquely aligned with one another. Like the moon passing over the sun. "I don't think you're losing your mind," she said.

"You're just saying that because you're trapped in a car with me."

"No, I'm not. I mean, I *am* trapped in a car with you, but that's not why."

"Why, then?"

She tilted her head, her hands tight on the steering wheel. "I honestly don't know. It's just a feeling, I guess."

"A feeling. Sure. Why not." He sighed, dropping his head back to thump rhythmically against the back of his seat.

"How'd you get in the middle of the road?"

He shrugged, not pausing his thumping.

"I can't help you if you won't talk to me."

He turned to face her. "You can't help me anyway."

"How can you be sure?"

"Because you're not real."

"Yes I am."

"That's just what a not-real person would say."

"Why don't you think I'm real?"

He twisted around in his seat, pointing back behind them. "Because the last thing I remember that made sense was driving my car off Wilson Bridge. So, as best I can figure, I'm either in a coma, and you're a product of my subconscious, or I'm dead, and you're . . . I don't know. An afterlife fairy or something."

"An afterlife *fairy?*"

He spread his hands. "Or an imaginary being of your choosing, I don't care."

"There's a third possibility, you know."

"Oh yeah?"

"You're really here."

"Here . . . in 1985."

"Yep."

He rolled his eyes. "I don't think so."

She sighed, repressing an urge to roll her own in return. She wasn't scared of him anymore, but apparently frustration was a whole other matter. "You know, you are awfully chill for someone who thinks they're dead."

"I mean, if I'm dead, there's not much I can do about it, is there?"

"Even so, you'd think you'd be a little more, I don't know, freaked out?"

126

He shrugged. "Maybe I'm in shock."

"Can dead people go into shock?"

Another shrug. "Apparently so."

The police car was no longer behind her, so Rose decided to pull into the parking lot of the Food Mart to talk, since she'd realized after she told him to get in the car that she had no idea where to take him, and she didn't want him to know where she lived until she felt confident he wasn't going to murder her whole family in their sleep. She didn't *think* he was dangerous, but that wasn't the sort of thing she wanted to risk being wrong about. At least the parking lot was public and well lit, making murder less likely, if not impossible.

But first things first. If he really was from the future—an idea so incredibly bizarre, she couldn't believe she was even considering it— they needed to figure out what had happened.

"Why'd you drive off the bridge?"

He threw her another sideways look. "I didn't do it on purpose, if that's what you're thinking."

"I wasn't—"

"Someone ran in front of my car, and I swerved to keep from hitting him. Or her, I guess. I didn't get a good look since it was raining."

"But it's not raining," Rose interjected, only to immediately regret it when Justin tossed her a withering look. "It's not raining *here*," she amended.

"No kidding," he grumbled. "Anyway, my car spun out, and then . . ." He flicked his fingers in front of his face, puffing out his cheeks in a pantomimed explosion.

"Okay. So your car went off the bridge, and then what? Do you remember hitting the water?"

"I remember *seeing* the water." He squinted, as if trying to examine his memory more closely, then shook his head. "No, that's it. I remember the car tipping forward, and seeing the water, and feeling my stomach drop, and thinking I was going to die, and then . . . I woke up on the bridge."

"Hmm." That must have been when it happened—when he some-how fell out of his time, and into hers. But of course, she still had no idea how or why, or why she was able to think about any of this as though it made even the slightest bit of sense.

"See?" he said, pointing at her face, which was scrunched up in thought. "I told you, you can't help me. Even if I actually . . . *time traveled*"—he snorted, as if he couldn't believe he'd just uttered those words—"it's not like you can get me back. Unless you want to drive off the bridge again."

"Not particularly," she said, her brain churning. People didn't just *time travel*. As far as she knew, this had never happened to anyone else in the history of humanity. She supposed it could've happened to someone at some point and she just didn't know about it, but at the very least, it couldn't be a very common occurrence.

There had to be a reason he was here.

Unless I'm losing my mind.

"We need to figure out why you're here," she said a little too loudly, shoving the persistent thought away. "Maybe it's fate or something."

"Fate?"

"You know, like you're here to fix something that went wrong. Put the universe back on track or something."

"Like, what, prevent the JFK assassination? I read that book; it doesn't work."

"What? That was back in the sixties."

"Yeah, I know. I was just trying to—never mind, that's not important."

"Anyway, I meant something more related to you. Something per-sonal that happens this year?"

"You mean like my grandparents dying in a fire?"

"Oh, right. Yes, like that." A chill went down her spine as she thought of the fire that had already occurred that summer. "Do they know what caused it?"

"I mean, they know *how* it was started. But they still don't know who it was."

"But you're saying it was a person? Like, the fire was set intentionally?"

"Seems likely."

Rose's mind spun. Mrs. Hanley's fire had been intentional, too. The police weren't doing much to figure out who had set it, but they knew it wasn't accidental. No one had been hurt that time, but if Justin was right, then whoever set the next one would be guilty of murder.

This had to be it. The reason he was here. They'd find the arsonist, stop them from setting the fire, save his grandparents, and—hopefully—send Justin back to where he'd come from.

Gooseflesh rose on her arms. Was this why she couldn't stop thinking of Mrs. Hanley's fire? Because it was the key to saving two more people? Noah kept telling her to let it go, but she never could. Maybe some part of her had known that it would be important. That *she* would be important.

After all, was it a coincidence that *she* was the one who was here right when Justin showed up, even though nearly everyone else in town had crossed this bridge at some point this evening? Or had their paths crossed because they were meant to?

"When does it happen?" she asked, practically breathless as she realized the implications of what Justin was saying. "The fire at the school."

He kicked at the floorboards. "October fifth."

Rose's stomach did a nervous little flutter. That gave them one week.

One week to change the future.

Interlude

After, and Before

For a long time, he disappeared.

Not literally, much as he'd hoped he might. And not to himself, although he wished he could.

He climbed on a bus as the smell of smoke still lingered in his nostrils, not caring about the destination, and rode until his money ran out, in a place where nothing and no one was familiar. He gave himself a new name, and every person he met got a new story, each one more sensational than the last, until he got tired of keeping up with all the versions of himself.

After that, he stuck to one story, one that was easy for him to remember and easy for everyone else to forget.

For a while he thought someone might come looking for him. He slept fitfully, his eyes never fully closed, twitching awake at the slightest noise. He envisioned federal agents kicking down his door, armed with questions, suspicions, accusations.

But they never came.

Over time, his memories began to fade, their sharp edges dulled like something out of a dream. He didn't even know why he was running anymore. What sort of life he was trying to protect? Wouldn't it be better, he sometimes thought, to have it all be over?

He thought about ending it. He spent days, weeks, planning what he'd do, what it would feel like, how he'd be sure to do it right. He thought through every last detail. Assembled everything he'd need. Spent hours staring at the instruments of finality, spread across his bed like he was packing for a trip.

But he couldn't do it. Didn't *want* to do it.

He'd never wanted to die. Just didn't want to be *here*, in this world that was not his world, answering to a name that was not his name, living a life that was not his life.

But he didn't have a choice. Not really.

He spent months working up the courage to do what he knew he had to do. He never wanted to go back there, where the ashes of his failure still hung heavy in the air. But there was nowhere else to go.

By the time he returned, it had been years. No one knew him, although he knew everyone. He walked the familiar streets as a stranger, time dragging on like claws in his skin.

And he waited.

SUNDAY

Chapter Twenty-Four

JUSTIN

I've been here for less than a day, and I'm already over 1985.

I slept in Rose's car last night, tossing fitfully in the back seat, jerking awake at every sound, expecting to open my eyes to a hospital, or a riverbed, or the afterlife, or anything that made more sense than this, but I remained stubbornly here, two decades before I was born. Rose sneaked me food this morning—a foil-wrapped Pop-Tart and a box of Hi-C—and told me that as soon as she and her family arrived back home from church in the afternoon, we'd "figure things out." As if fixing my accidental time-travel problem is something that can be accomplished in a single Sunday afternoon.

That left me with a few more hours to kill, during which I stupidly walked to my house, just because I had to see for myself. Long before I got there, though, daylight revealed all the things I'd missed in my panicked state the night before. Wooded areas where neighborhoods should be. Storefronts that looked nothing like I remembered them, on the rare occasions when they were at least the same business, which, most often, they weren't. Houses that were different colors, or missing additions, or had totally different landscaping from what I was used to seeing every day.

By the time I got to my house, it was barely even a shock to find the driveway covered in chalked hopscotch grids, and the lawn littered with brightly colored plastic toys. Of course it was wrong. Everything here was wrong.

I ran back to Rose's house, tears stinging my eyes. I'm not normally a crier, but it turns out that even when home kind of sucks, it's still a gut punch to realize it's actually *gone*. Or rather, that it's still there, somewhere, but you may never be able to see it again.

Fortunately, I had composed myself by the time Rose got home and finished lunch with her family. They had pot roast; I had a gas station burger whose best feature was that it cost only fifty cents. Good thing I never returned Stan's Oreo money to him—twenty bucks goes a long way in 1985.

Afterward, the first words out of Rose's mouth were "let's get to work." I could absolutely not have dealt with that level of group-project-leader intensity if I had still been crying.

The first item of "work" on Rose's list turned out to be finding me a place to stay, which I assumed would be a massive headache but wound up being no big deal. She arranged for me to crash with an elderly woman named Mrs. Hanley, who was the grandmother of one of Rose's friends. She told Mrs. Hanley I was her pen pal visiting from out of town, and just like that, I had a room to myself, a key to the back door, and a thick-cut turkey sandwich, due to Mrs. Hanley's assessment that I was "too skinny."

Once I was settled in Mrs. Hanley's guest bedroom—didn't take long, given my complete lack of possessions—Rose revealed her ulterior motive for my lodging situation. The detached garage behind Mrs. Hanley's house was blackened, blocked off with the tattered remnants of yellow police tape. The fire had occurred a few months earlier, but already the police had lost interest in their investigation, leaving the garage as a charred monument to indifference. Rose was adamant that the odds of there being *two* arsonists in a small town like Stone Lake were slim. She reasoned that it couldn't hurt for me to live at the scene of the first crime, where I might stumble upon a clue that could help me solve the second.

Hence, Rose's presence across a plastic patio table from me on Mrs. Hanley's back deck, with a yellow legal pad and a pencil, the charred garage looming over her shoulder. "So," she says, pencil poised to take notes, "tell me everything you know about the school fire."

"Uh, should we really be talking out in the open like this?" Mrs. Hanley is in the living room with the television on, but the kitchen window is open. Plus, neighbors could walk by and overhear what is bound to be an absolutely unhinged conversation.

But Rose waves her hand. "It's fine. She's getting a little hard of hearing, and we can see if anyone is coming," she says, gesturing to the empty backyards on either side of us.

"Okay," I say, still feeling pretty dumb. On the other hand, I guess there's nowhere we could have this conversation where it'd feel normal.

I take a deep breath and begin telling her what I know.

Unfortunately, it isn't much.

Here's the thing about my grandparents, and I don't want to sound like some sort of monster, but the fact is I never really . . . cared how they died. I mean, obviously I knew the same broad strokes that everyone did, but to me, they were strangers. Strangers whose dramatic deaths led to getting a high school named after them, sure, but if anything, that made me even less interested to dig into the details of their lives. To be honest, until I was sitting here across from Rose and her #2 pencil, I'd never really considered them as *people* at all. They've always just been specters, determinedly haunting me no matter how much I wished they—and my entire messed-up family tree—would just go away.

Still, I do know *some* stuff, beyond just the normal things everyone in town knows, and it's not because I'm interested, or because I'm related to them.

It's because Stan. Is. Obsessed.

Look, I get that I'm not exactly fair to Stan or whatever—*I* don't really think that's true, but Alyssa does, and she's right about most things—but I do not think I'm being even the slightest bit uncharitable when I say that it is freaking *weird* to have a full-fledged murder board in the basement, complete with red yarn and newspaper clippings and stalker-y black-and-white photographs that Stan probably took while disguised as a tree. Right?

Stan's tried a bunch of times to pull me into his bizarre *CSI* delusion, insisting that it's "important" that I be a part of it, but I've mostly managed to avoid getting sucked into the crazy with him. Still, when a murder board takes up half the room in which you do laundry, and you live with an obsessive true crime junkie, you tend to pick up a few things.

So here's what I know: The fire started in the guidance office on Saturday, October 5, around 6:30 p.m. It was pretty amateurish; whoever did it just doused the carpet in high-proof liquor, then lit it with a cigarette. It was mostly concentrated in one corner of the room and could probably have even been contained by the fire department if they'd gotten there in time. But most of the town was off at some political thing—

"The debate?" Rose interrupts.

"The what?"

"The mayoral debate at the community center next Saturday night between my stepmom, Diane, and Franklin Gibson. Diane and Veronica have been preparing for it for weeks." Rose wrinkles her nose. "What would Veronica have been doing at the high school at six thirty when the debate is supposed to start at seven?"

I shrug. "Maybe they saw the smoke on their way over and stopped to help?"

"The high school isn't on the way to the community center from their house. They would've been driving in the complete wrong direction." Rose pulls her dark ponytail over her shoulder and begins absently twirling a few strands around her finger. My chest tightens with a sudden pang. Alyssa plays with her hair when she's thinking, too.

I wonder what she's doing today. Is she still mad at me? Has she noticed I'm gone yet? Is she worried?

I clear my throat in an effort to banish the complicated emotions now clogging it up, and Rose looks at me in alarm. "Are you okay?"

"Yeah," I say, trying for a smile. "Just thinking about home."

Something about the word—*home*—snags like a thorn. All I've wanted for as long as I can remember was a life other than the one I had. But since I knew it wasn't possible, I never allowed myself to hope.

Then somehow, I got my wish. And now all I want is to go back.

How messed up is that?

Rose's expression softens. "I'm sorry. This must be really hard."

"Honestly," I say, shaking my head a little, "I still don't think I've wrapped my brain around it enough for it to be hard."

"We'll get you back," Rose says confidently, leaning across the table to give my shoulder a reassuring—if slightly awkward—pat. "I promise."

"Thanks," I say, wishing I shared her certainty. About anything.

I shift in my chair, tapping a finger on her legal pad, needing to give my thoughts another track to tear down instead of the dangerous one they're on. "Anyway, I don't know *why* they were there, but for some reason they were, and they went inside."

"What about Millie?"

Millie. So that's what Mom's parents called her. Not Lissa, short for Millicent, which she goes by now. Millie. I wonder if she knows that used to be her name.

"They left her in the car."

"Veronica wouldn't do that."

I shrug, not knowing what else to say. This is one of the facts of the case I'm clearest on. Mom was found in the back seat of their still-running car in the middle of the parking lot while her parents burned to death inside. It's not a detail you can really forget.

"All I know is what happened," I say. "The police think the arsonist attacked Bill—coroner's report said he suffered a head injury before he

139

died—and then Veronica died trying to get him out. But I don't know anything about why they were there or what made them do any of the things they did."

Rose lets out a frustrated sigh but lowers her head to make more notes on her pad, chewing on her lower lip as she scratches away with her pencil. "Fine. So that's what happened. Did the police ever figure out who did it?"

I sigh. "Depends on what you believe."

Shortly after the fire, the sheriff's department arrested a guy named Michael McMillain, a janitor at the school who, it turned out, had previously served two years in prison for marijuana possession and lied about it on his job application. He'd been fired the day before, which seemed like a decent enough motivation. McMillain's lawyer argued that his conviction as a teenager was irrelevant, but it didn't do him any good. Between his lack of an alibi—he claimed he was home alone during the time of the fire—and the town's ravenous need to convict *someone*, he never stood a chance. He spent the next thirty-two years in prison.

Stan went to visit him a few times, and even tried to get me to go with him a couple of times after McMillain was released. I always refused. Didn't see the point.

The thing is, Stan was convinced that McMillain was innocent. He wouldn't even put his photo up on the murder board. Thirty-eight years later, Stan still hasn't been able to come up with a convincing theory of who may have set the fire, but he continues to stubbornly maintain that it wasn't Michael McMillain.

Rose taps her pencil against her lips after I tell her all this, thinking. "So what about Mrs. Hanley's fire? Did the police think he set that one, too?"

I shrug. "I don't think so. I only ever remember Stan talking about the school fire in connection with McMillain's case. I don't think I ever heard him talk about another fire at all."

"So he didn't think the two were connected?"

"Not as far as I know."

Rose grumbles something unintelligible under her breath as she makes more notes, her brow furrowed. Now it's my turn to ask, "What's wrong?"

She sighs. "The police think Mrs. Hanley started the fire herself."

"Seriously? Why?"

"To get the insurance money. They figured her husband had recently died, she was living on a fixed income, so she decided she may as well burn down a garage full of old stuff she didn't use in exchange for a little more cash. But they don't *know* Mrs. Hanley. All her old photographs of her husband and kids were in there. All their old art projects and report cards and Christmas ornaments. There's no way she would have destroyed all that on purpose."

I press my lips together, considering. I haven't known Rose for long, but I can already tell she has a lot more faith in humanity than I do. "I don't know," I say slowly, thinking back to my tenth birthday, when a neighbor gave me their used Xbox and a bunch of games. I had it a week before Mom sold it for booze money. "Money can be a pretty powerful motivator."

"She didn't even *get* any money, though. The insurance company won't pay since they think she did it herself."

"Well, yeah, but she wouldn't have known that at the time. She could have thought—"

"She didn't set the fire, Justin!"

"How can you be sure?"

"Because I was *there*." She sighs, looking over at the charred garage, her eyes full of regret. "I was there that day," she says wistfully, "and I couldn't do anything to help."

Interlude

Rose, Three Months Earlier

"This *sucks*," Noah said, tossing another rust-stained rag onto the rapidly growing pile. He pulled the back of his arm across his dripping brow, leaving a smear of grime on his sweaty skin.

Rose continued scrubbing away at the leg of a chair, hair escaping from her purple scrunchie in damp tendrils that clung to her face like creeping vines. "It's not so bad," she said, panting slightly. Her skin felt hot, like she was burning up from the inside.

"We've been working at this for hours, and we've barely made a dent," Noah said, plucking a new rag out of the laundry basket between them and tipping the tin of WD-40 onto it. They were using ripped-up, old T-shirts that had been culled from the donation bin at church for being too tattered to give away. There was always a pile of such things after every clothing drive, with well-meaning but oblivious people hauling in plastic bags of their trash because "someone might want it."

Noah stood and stretched, joints cracking after spending so long crouching down to chisel rust from the seemingly infinite ridges and crevices of the floral-patterned set. The day was unusually hot, even for July, with temperatures swelling into triple digits. They'd plugged in two box fans to create a breeze, but all that did was push the thick air around, caking their sweaty skin with thirty years' worth of accumulated crud.

"Let's take a break," Noah said. "Go get some of Gran's lemonade and sit inside by the air conditioner for a while. Then we can come back out here and finish up."

Rose dropped her hands to her sides and stretched her neck, rolling her head back, then side to side, releasing a couple of alarmingly loud *pops*. "Sounds good to me."

As Noah tossed his rag onto a chair, her heart gave a little flutter. Would this be a good time to talk? She'd been putting it off all summer, but Lisa was right. She needed to just tell him how she felt and get it over with.

Especially since she was beginning to think that maybe, just *maybe* . . . he might like her, too. The thought filled her with butter-flies so big she thought she might actually take flight.

Before they left the garage, Rose suggested dousing a few of the dirty rags with more WD-40 and placing them over the worst of the rust spots, in hopes that the chemicals would do more work for them while they were inside. When they'd finished, the furniture looked like it had been partially mummified, albeit poorly.

As soon as they stepped into the fresh air, Noah sucked in a deep breath, blowing it out theatrically. "Wow. I didn't realize how fumey it was in there until we came out here."

"Same," Rose said. She glanced at him, and the corners of her mouth twitched, fighting a smile. "I also didn't realize how *gross* you were in there." Gray dust streaked his brown skin and clumped on his clothing, and his glasses were so speckled with grit she was surprised he could see.

"You're one to talk," he said, making a show of plucking a cobweb from her hair.

"Ew," she squealed, wrinkling her nose. She jogged to the side of the garage and unwound a few coils of the garden hose from its hook, spraying down her arms and legs, then splashing more water onto her face with her hands.

Noah joined her, and she hosed him off as well. As he dried his glasses on his shirt, giving her a glimpse of his smooth, flat stomach, Rose tore her eyes away before he could notice she was staring.

Then a devious, delicious idea sprang into her head, and she pointed the hose at him again.

He looked up, his eyes widening. "Don't you dare," he said, taking a step back.

She matched him step for step, still brandishing the hose. "Or else what?"

"Or else I'll . . . uh . . . I'll—" But he didn't get a chance to figure out what he'd do before she sprayed him square in the center of his chest, instantly drenching his shirt and shorts. They clung to him like a second skin, and Rose couldn't help herself. She burst out laughing.

He stared at her with his mouth hanging open, his dripping arms held wide by his sides. "I can't believe you did that."

"I did you a favor." She giggled, feeling almost giddy in the summer heat. "You stink."

"Oh, do I?" He pulled his soaked shirt up over his head, then twirled it quickly between his hands, rolling it up into a tight rope.

Her gaze caught on the sight of his bare chest, but she didn't have time to gape; she skittered to the side, her hands held out in front of her like she was guarding him in basketball. She knew turnabout was fair play, but somehow getting smacked with a wet T-shirt did *not* feel like it was on the same level as getting doused with the hose.

Noah leaned in, holding the two ends of his rolled shirt taut, his right hand extended toward her. He grinned, then gave her a wink that set the butterflies in her stomach wildly flapping.

"Don't even—" Rose yelped as he flicked the wet shirt toward her, not hard enough to sting, just enough to splatter water across her stomach.

"Now who stinks?" he asked, getting ready to strike again.

"I don't have any spare clothes here!" she shrieked as she darted toward the house, skipping slightly in her efforts to keep out of his reach.

"Should have thought of that before you started this!" he bellowed, chasing after her, continuing to splatter her with water from his dripping shirt until she reached the back door and yanked it open.

After scrambling inside, she closed it in his face and held it shut, grinning at him through the screen.

He smiled back, spreading his hands. Their faces were inches apart, separated by the thin screen. Rose leaned toward him, closing the gap.

"Don't worry," Noah said breathlessly. "I'm not gonna keep chasing you in my gran's house."

Another flutter of the butterflies. "Leave that out there," Rose said, gesturing with her chin.

"My shirt?" Noah raised an eyebrow, dropping the wet shirt on the steps, where it landed with a splat. "I didn't realize you wanted my shirt off so bad."

"Oh. I didn't mean—never mind." Rose's cheeks went hot. She stepped back from the door. Could he tell how she'd been feeling? Had she been embarrassing herself all this time?

"Rose, I was just kidding," Noah said, opening the door and stepping into the kitchen. He left his shirt on the step. Moisture glistened on his bare skin. "I'm sorry if I made it weird."

"No—you're—*it's* fine," Rose said, turning abruptly toward the refrigerator and trying to get her rapid breathing in order. "So, lemonade?" she said, her voice a little too bright.

"Let me go grab a new shirt and I'll be right back. We've got a date with the air conditioner."

Rose tried not to read anything into the word *date*, but she couldn't help it; her stomach did a happy little cartwheel.

The window air conditioner was in the living room, but Rose sank into a chair at the table while Noah changed, sipping her glass of lemonade. Her heart pounded as she thought about what she'd say when he came back.

Noah, we've been friends for a long time.

Noah, is it just me, or have things felt a little different between us lately?

Noah, you know me better than anyone in the world.

Before she could come up with the perfect opening, Noah returned and plopped down across from her, picking up the glass of lemonade she'd poured for him and draining half of it in one gulp. When he put it down, he opened his mouth to speak, but she beat him to it.

"Noah," she said, "we need to—"

A crash sounded from outside. Rose sat up a little straighter in her chair, looking toward the window. "Did you hear that?"

"Mm-hmm." He was already moving toward the back door. He swung it open, scanning the yard. "I don't see anything," he said.

Then they smelled the smoke.

MONDAY

Chapter Twenty-Five

ROSE

"He's your what now?"

"My pen pal," Rose repeated, taking a bite of her turkey and cheese sandwich.

"Since when do you have a pen pal?" Lisa asked. Her own sandwich sat on the cafeteria tray in front of her, still tightly bound in its plastic-wrap cocoon, untouched.

They were gathered around their usual lunch table, but the seating was a little off today. Shawn and Lisa still sat together, but Charlene had moved to the other side of the table for some reason. Since Steph and Noah also were seated together beside Charlene, Rose wound up in the seat next to Lisa, who had been acting weirdly moody all weekend.

"We've been writing each other for a while," Rose said. They'd come up with the story together at Mrs. Hanley's house the day before. Rose knew she'd need an excuse for spending all her time with a boy no one in town had ever heard of, especially the week before the debate. And it's not like anyone had taken much interest in her life lately. It seemed plausible that she could have a pen pal no one knew about.

Sure enough, when she'd told her parents last night, neither had batted an eye. "That's nice, dear," her father had said, while Diane merely smiled, distracted by her phone call with Veronica.

"But I've literally *never* seen you writing letters," Lisa protested. "Or getting any letters, for that matter."

"I guess you just didn't notice," Rose said, feeling slightly guilty at the hurt expression that flickered across Lisa's face. But this was how it had to be; the truth just wasn't an option.

"I think it's great," Shawn said with one of his easy smiles, wolfing down half his sandwich in one bite. "Pen pals are fun. I had one for a while in middle school."

"Wasn't that the girl who made you the bracelet out of her own hair?" Noah asked.

"I'm sorry, she *what*?" Steph said as the rest of them dissolved into laughter.

"She was nice!" Shawn gasped through his laughter. "Just . . . a little weird, I guess."

"But that's the thing with pen pals, right?" Noah said. He took off his glasses and wiped them on his shirt, giving Rose a sideways glance as he did. "They can seem nice and normal and then, boom, envelope of human hair."

"Justin isn't like that," Rose insisted. At least, she *hoped* not. She tried not to imagine what Noah would say if he found out that Justin claimed to be a time traveler from the future or, even worse, that she *believed* him.

"How do you know, though? It's weird that he just showed up unannounced, right?" Noah said around bites of pepperoni pizza. "Shouldn't he have at least checked with you first that this was a good time? I mean, he can't even stay with you this week."

"I told you, it was just a spur-of-the-moment thing," Rose said. "I'd always told him he should come visit, and the opportunity came up all of a sudden, so he just got on a bus."

Noah rolled his eyes and shoved another bite of pizza in his mouth, chomping unnecessarily aggressively.

He was acting weirdly annoyed, and Rose suspected she knew why. She'd known that asking her parents if a teenage boy they'd never met could stay with them, especially the week before the debate, would be a nonstarter, so she'd asked the one person she knew would never turn away a surprise houseguest: Noah's grandmother.

As long as Rose had known her, Mrs. Hanley had always had a heart for strays, whether of the animal or human varieties. Every time Noah and Rose went over there, her home contained a rotating selection of dogs, cats, and people who needed a temporary place to stay. Since Noah's grandfather had passed, she hadn't taken in as many animals, but Rose knew she wouldn't say no to a person.

Plus, she had an ulterior motive. If Justin stayed with Mrs. Hanley, he'd have a front-row seat to her garage, which they needed to investigate if they were going to figure out who had started the fire.

Not that she could tell her friends about that part of Justin's "visit." Part of her still felt crazy that *she* believed it. As far as they knew, he was just her pen pal, who had spontaneously traveled to see her from out of town.

At the end of the period, after dumping her tray, Rose automatically turned to head to her next class. A moment later, she heard someone calling her name. "Rose, hey, wait up!"

She turned to see Noah jogging up to join her and gave him an odd look. "What are you doing?"

"I'm walking to English," he said, falling into step beside her.

"I mean, why aren't you walking Steph to class first?" Even though Rose and Noah had AP English together, he'd been in the habit, since the beginning of the year, of detouring by the chorus room to drop Steph off. A tiny flutter of hope that maybe something had happened between the two of them, something that might lead to a breakup, sparked in Rose's chest, but she quickly tamped it down. They'd been acting perfectly fine at lunch. Whatever had prompted the split from Noah's routine, it wasn't that.

Noah shrugged. "Just thought I'd walk with you today. That's okay, right?"

Rose nodded, her eyes narrowing. *Something* was going on. "What's up, Noah?"

"You're asking me?" he said with raised eyebrows. "What's going on with *you*?"

Now it was her turn to shrug. "Nothing." She hoped he didn't notice the slight quickening of her pulse. Of course he'd take an interest in her life *now*, when she couldn't tell him the truth.

He stopped walking, forcing the sea of students to split and go around them, like a stream flowing around a rock. A few gave them dirty looks as they went by, and Rose heard at least a couple of racial slurs tossed anonymously into the air. They both tensed but otherwise ignored them, the result of years of practice.

Noah grabbed her wrist, spinning her to face him, his touch sending a light shiver rippling through her skin. "It's not nothing, Rosie," he said, keeping his voice low, his eyes searching hers. "You're acting . . . different."

She pulled her wrist away, moving down the hall again. "Am I? Or have you just not been paying attention?"

"Look, I know we haven't been hanging out as much as we used to," he said, falling back into step beside her, "but seriously, I'm worried about you. A secret pen pal none of us have ever heard of? That's not you, Rose."

"Maybe it is now."

"Are . . . are you okay?" he asked, leaning closer to her and dropping his voice to a whisper. "Is something wrong? You can tell me, you know."

Rose swallowed, but it did nothing to clear the lump that had risen in her throat. She wished, more than anything, that she could tell him. But she couldn't, because it wasn't her who had changed; it was *them*. Her and Noah, together. She wasn't his priority anymore, and she couldn't lean on him like she had. That just seemed like a good way to fall.

"I'm fine, Noah," she said with a forced smile as they reached the door to their classroom. "Everything's fine. I really didn't mean to keep it a secret. Everyone's just had so much going on that I guess it didn't come up."

"But—"

"Class is about to start," she said, turning away from him to head to her desk. She dug her copy of *I Know Why the Caged Bird Sings* out of her backpack and buried her nose in the pages, pretending she couldn't feel his eyes still on her, couldn't feel his questions burning into her skin. At the end of class, she was out the door before the bell finished ringing.

Chapter Twenty-Six

KARL

He wished his mom would stop wrapping his sandwiches in aluminum foil.

Karl perched on the back of the toilet, his backpack laid as flat as he could make it across his knees as a makeshift table, and hurried to unwrap his bologna-and-cheese before anyone else came into the bathroom. The foil scraped and squeaked, like some sort of nightmare bird squawking his presence to whomever might be within hearing distance.

He'd just gotten one triangle of his sandwich loose when the door to the bathroom slammed open and a pair of boys spilled inside, laughing and talking loudly. Karl ate as quietly as he could, surrounded by the sounds of urine hitting porcelain and water swirling down the drain.

A faucet turned on, and a familiar voice shouted, "Yo, careful!"

"Sorry," another boy said, and Karl heard the water stop. "Did I mess you up? Did any of it wash off?"

"No, I think it's okay," Robbie Reynolds said.

Careful not to make any noise, Karl leaned forward, peering through the gap at the edge of the stall door.

Robbie had his sleeve pushed up to his elbow and was resting his wrist on the edge of one of the white sinks, a blue BIC pen clutched in his other hand. A wrinkled piece of paper was propped up by the faucets, and Robbie was in the process of carefully transferring whatever was written on it to his forearm.

The other kid—Steve Burks, Karl saw now; his sneaker print from last week was still etched in purple on Karl's thigh—dried his hands on a paper towel while peering over Robbie's shoulder. "You sure about these?"

Robbie nodded. "They better be right, for what I paid for them."

"Because you know your mom said if you flunk another test, we can't do sleepovers anymore."

"Dude, chill out," Robbie said, capping his pen and tugging his sleeve back into place. He ripped the sheet of answers into tiny strips and then—to Karl's horror—turned toward the row of stalls.

Karl pressed himself against the cinder-block wall, hugging his backpack to his chest and holding his breath as Robbie's footsteps approached.

"It's gonna be fine," Robbie was saying. "I just gotta—"

He quieted as his hand slapped against Karl's unyielding door. "Yo, who's in there?" he called, a hint of nervousness creeping into his voice.

Karl didn't say anything. He realized he was clutching his sandwich so hard that bits of bologna and cheese had turned to paste between his fingers. He stared at Robbie's shoes on the other side of the door, willing them to just give up, walk away, leave him alone.

Robbie's face appeared at the bottom of the stall door, a wide grin stretching from ear to ear as he met Karl's terrified gaze. "Derrin, my man, have you been eavesdropping on us?"

Karl shook his head, his throat dry. *Please leave, please leave, please—*

"I think you're lying, Derrin. I think you *were* listening."

"I wasn't," Karl whispered, frozen in place. His hands had gone numb. "I promise."

"Why don't you open the door and come on out here so we can talk? This is making my neck hurt," Robbie said, that same rictus grin still plastered across his face.

"No thanks," Karl rasped. "I think I'll just stay in—*aughhh!*"

He screeched as Steve appeared beside him from the adjacent stall, sliding under the divider and popping to his feet in one smooth motion. "Hey, Derrin," Steve said jovially, throwing an arm around his neck and dragging him off the back of the toilet as he used his other hand to unlock the stall. Karl's backpack fell to the bathroom floor, his lunch scattered across the tiles as he struggled to get away, but it was no use. Steve's arm might as well have been made of cement.

After dropping his handful of shredded test answers into the toilet, Robbie turned to face Karl, arms folded across his chest. "What are we going to do with you, Derrin?"

"I won't tell anyone," Karl gasped, moisture gathering at the corners of his eyes. "I swear."

"I want to believe you, Derrin, I really do," Robbie said, dropping a meaty hand onto Karl's shoulder and squeezing, his thumb digging painfully into the soft spot just under Karl's collarbone, making him wince. "But I think I'm gonna need some convincing."

Robbie's eyes fell to the smushed bologna-and-cheese sandwich on the ground, still tangled up in aluminum foil. He picked it up, looking pensively from the sandwich to Karl. "Aw, man, you didn't get a chance to finish your lunch, Derrin! You must be hungry."

"No. No thanks. I'm good." Karl's heart hammered so hard, it was a wonder Steve was able to hold his arm in place.

"Come to think of it, you look thirsty, too."

Robbie stepped into the nearest stall and bent down, dunking the corner of the sandwich into the toilet bowl. It came up dripping, the white bread falling apart in soggy chunks.

He held the toilet-soaked sandwich out to Karl, fake concern making his eyes wide. "Here you go, Derrin. Take a bite."

Karl wriggled and kicked, pushing against Steve's arm around his throat, but Steve only tightened his grip.

"C'mon, open up. Yummm," Robbie said, circling the sandwich in front of Karl's face like he was trying to feed a baby. *"My bologna has a first name, it's O-S-C-A-R,"* he sang in a high-pitched voice, the sopping sandwich hovering closer and closer to Karl's mouth until it brushed his lips.

The bread was cold and wet, and while it didn't *smell* like anything but bologna, Karl couldn't stop himself from thinking about all the other things that had been in that toilet bowl. His stomach gurgled queasily. He pressed his lips together, straining away from Robbie as much as he could—but thanks to Steve's chest against his back, that was barely at all.

"My bologna has a second name, it's M-A-Y-E-R."

Without warning, Robbie drew back his fist and punched Karl in the stomach. Karl's knees buckled as he clutched at his middle, coughing and gasping for breath.

As soon as his mouth opened to gulp air, Robbie shoved the sandwich inside. Slimy, wet bread filled Karl's mouth, all the way to the back of his throat. He gagged and tried to spit it out, but Robbie clamped a hand over his mouth. "Swallow! Swallow!" he commanded, laughing so hard tears spilled from his eyes.

Karl didn't have a choice. Chewing as quickly as he could and fighting the urge to vomit, he choked down the sandwich. It took him a few attempts to get it all down, interspersed with fits of retching. Snot streamed from his nose and his eyes burned with the effort, but finally, finally, the sandwich was gone.

Steve released him, and Robbie dropped his hand from his mouth and frowned at the flecks of wet bread and meat smeared on his palm. "Gross, Derrin," he said, wiping his hand down the front of Karl's shirt.

Karl kept his gaze fixed on a spot on the wall, avoiding their eyes. He hoped that Robbie didn't realize there was still another half of his sandwich on the floor. He willed himself not to look at it.

Robbie's smile fell from his face, his eyes cold. "Just remember, you tell *anyone* what you overheard in here, and next time, you'll be eating something else out of the toilet. Got it?"

Karl nodded wordlessly, not trusting himself to speak without throwing up.

Satisfied, Robbie and Steve left the bathroom, cackling and slapping each other on the back. With shaking hands, Karl gathered up the ruined remnants of his lunch and tossed it all into the garbage can.

He dared to look at his reflection over the sink. Bits of food flecked his chin and the front of his shirt. His neck was a little red where Steve had held him in place, but it was fading fast enough that he'd be fine by the time he went to class.

The bell rang while Karl was still attempting to clean himself up with warm water and paper towels. He picked up his backpack and gingerly threaded his arms through the straps, wincing slightly at how the motion aggravated the bruises on his neck. After taking a last look in the mirror, Karl took a deep breath and pushed his way into the hall.

The door bumped something solid, and for a horrible second, Karl thought it was Robbie and Steve, lurking outside the bathroom waiting for him to come out. Adrenaline flooded his system and his legs tensed, ready to sprint down the hall, before he realized it wasn't a student he'd hit; it was an adult.

The guidance counselor, Mr. Warren, jumped out of the way of the swinging door. "Sorry, didn't see you there, kiddo," he said.

Karl shrugged, working to keep his breathing even so Mr. Warren wouldn't ask questions. He ducked his head, hunching his shoulders to hide the redness on his neck. The last thing he needed was Robbie thinking Karl had ratted him out. He tried to squeeze around Mr. Warren to get to class, but the guidance counselor stood blocking his path, his head tilted. "Everything okay, Karl?"

"I'm fine," he muttered.

Mr. Warren considered him for a moment, frowning slightly. "Want to go talk about it in my office? I'll write you a pass for class," he said, putting a hand on Karl's shoulder.

"I said I'm *fine*," Karl snarled. Wrenching free of Mr. Warren, he spun around and fled down the hall.

Chapter Twenty-Seven

BILL

"You coming in, or you just going to lurk there like a gargoyle?" Bill asked, a cigarette dangling from his lips, not looking up from the papers on his desk.

Pat Shaw filled the doorway of his office like an eclipse, blocking out the light from the hall. Pat was tall enough that his wavy hair brushed the top of the frame and broad enough that he could've served as a decent door himself.

The history teacher came in and folded himself awkwardly into one of the rounded armchairs opposite Bill, which were an adequate size for the students but seemed like doll furniture compared to Pat. "Gargoyle? Really?" He had a low voice, like distant thunder.

Bill gave a one-shoulder shrug, his pencil still scratching across the file in front of him. "I mean, they lurk, right? Basically all they do."

"They more perch, I think. Like birds. Not really lurkers."

"Okay, then, what's something that lurks?"

Pat cocked his head, his bushy mustache twitching in thought. "A vampire maybe? Or . . . perhaps a mummy? Although I'm not sure if it's considered lurking if it's still in a sarcophagus."

"How about a yeti?"

Pat nodded slowly. "Yeah, I could be a yeti."

"You pretty much *are* a yeti."

He laughed, running a hand over his dark beard, which he kept neatly trimmed to an inch below his jawline. "You're just jealous that you can't look this—"

"Sasquatch-adjacent?"

"Rugged and handsome, but sure."

Bill closed the file, giving up on the idea of getting any more work done that afternoon. Pat was a great history teacher, but outside the classroom, he could often be worse than the students. "What can I do for you, Pat? Or did you just come in here to distract me from working?" He opened his top desk drawer and pulled out an ashtray, setting it on the desk and extinguishing his cigarette.

"That last part is just a bonus," Pat rumbled, digging a small gift box out of his pocket and sliding it across the desk. "I finished it."

"Really? Already?" Bill opened the box excitedly and carefully lifted out a thin gold chain. From it dangled an intricately carved wooden pendant, fashioned into a delicate Möbius twist from a single piece of wood. Into the wood, Pat had carved *love you forever* over and over in wide script, so that the words seemed to flow back into themselves, like the wood itself.

Bill had asked Pat a couple of months earlier if he would make a custom necklace for his and Veronica's two-year anniversary next month. Pat's hobby was woodworking, and although he'd never made anything quite like Bill's request before, he'd been up to the challenge. But even though Bill had known Pat was good, the necklace exceeded his expectations.

"Pat, this is amazing," Bill said.

Pat shrugged. "I think it's a little thick at the bottom," he said. "And the spacing between the words on one side isn't quite even."

Bill shook his head. "It's perfect. She's going to love it."

"Let me know if she doesn't," Pat said. "I can try again."

"That definitely won't be necessary," Bill said, closing the box and tucking it away in his top desk drawer. "I can't believe you finished it so early, too."

"Yeah, well, you know how I work in my garage when I'm feeling stressed?"

"Uh-oh," Bill said, leaning back in his chair. "What's up?"

Pat tossed a folder onto Bill's desk. "I need your advice."

Bill flipped open the folder. "What am I looking at?"

"That," Pat said with a sigh, "is last year's ninth-grade World War II unit test."

"Okay . . ."

Pat leaned forward and slid the top paper to the side. Underneath was a similar-looking test, this one filled in in neat pencil. Most of the answers were marked out with red Xs. Pat tapped the sheet with a meaty forefinger. "And that is *this* year's ninth-grade World War II unit test. Notice anything interesting?"

Bill glanced at the name at the top of the test. "Andrew Reese needs to study more?"

"Look again."

Bill read through Andrew's answers, and quickly realized that many of them made no sense. For example, he'd written that the war had begun with the invasion of "the Battle of Britain," and that one of the leading generals in the Spanish Civil War was "Communism." It didn't take long to figure out what had happened. "He answered the questions from last year's test on this year's test?"

Pat nodded. "You know how I was reading that book by William Shirer this summer?"

"The one with . . . the cover?" Pat never went anywhere without a book, but his attempts to hide the cover of that particular book had been a source of constant amusement for Bill that summer. Pat had taken to carrying it around in a padded leather Bible case in order to mask the large offensive symbol on the front. Bill had made a habit of teasing him about it any time he saw him paging through it at the community pool, asking him how he was enjoying the "Good Book."

"Well, it was fascinating, so naturally, I wanted to incorporate some of it into the unit. I've been using the same tests for the past few years, but I decided to rewrite it this year so I could reflect a little bit of the new material. Same format, same number of questions, but I changed up the order, rephrased some stuff, introduced a couple new things. Nothing major. Should've been about the same difficulty level as the last one." He sighed, shaking his head. "And then *this* happened."

It was easy enough to fill in the blanks. "So Andy got a copy of last year's test, memorized the answers, and just filled them all in without actually reading the questions," Bill surmised.

"Oh, it's worse than that. If it was just one kid cheating, I mean, it sucks, but I've dealt with that before. But this . . ." Pat readjusted his position in his too-small chair, leaning forward to rest his elbows on his knees, fingers laced together. He glanced at the door to Bill's office before lowering his voice. "Bill, I don't think it's just Andy. I went through all my other classes, and I don't know for sure, but I just . . . have my suspicions that something is going on. That's what I needed your advice about."

"Do you have proof?"

Pat shook his head. "Andy is the only one so far that I can prove. I have a few others I suspect. But if I'm right, I doubt it's contained to just my class. It may be all over the school."

Bill blew out a long breath, then reached into his bottom desk drawer and pulled out a bottle of Bacardi 151. Spinning around in his chair, he grabbed two Styrofoam cups that were stacked next to the coffeepot behind him, then turned back to face Pat. Wordlessly, he poured an inch of rum into each of the cups and handed one to Pat.

Pat took a sip, closing his eyes for a moment to savor. "You know it's a big deal if you're breaking out the good stuff."

"I just . . ." Bill shook his head. "If word gets out that we've got a school-wide cheating scandal, that's going to be another blow to Diane's campaign."

Pat wrinkled his forehead. "How's that?"

"You know Gibson has been attacking her education plan every chance he gets," Bill said. "He'll say it's ridiculous to invest more money into public education and increase teacher pay when this is what's already happening in our schools. Then he'll say the only way to curb cheating in high school is to agree to *his* proposal to increase the police budget, so that kids will have more incentive to follow the rules."

"That's ridiculous. If anything, schools need *more* support to—"

"It won't matter. Parents will want someone to blame, and Gibson won't have any trouble making this Diane's fault. Especially since her campaign manager is married to me, and this is happening where I work. I know how men like him think, Pat. If Diane pushes back, he'll say she's just trying to protect Veronica's husband. If she doesn't, he'll say it's because she knows he's right." Bill sighed. "Any chance we'll be able to keep a lid on this, at least for a little while?"

Pat frowned. "You know I don't like to embarrass the kids when stuff like this happens. I've never seen that help. But I can't see any way to look into this without word getting around about what's going on."

Bill took another sip of his drink. It burned its way pleasantly down his throat, easing the tension in his belly. "Well, let's start with Andy. Maybe we can get to the bottom of it before the rumor mill starts churning. At least get a better idea what we're dealing with."

"Tomorrow? I'll bring him in here?"

"Yeah, that works." Although the school had an official zero-tolerance policy when it came to cheating, the reality was that teachers each dealt with cheating in their own way. Lots of them liked to loop in the guidance counselor when having these conversations, so that Bill could play the good cop. Especially for teachers like Pat, who tended to intimidate the students simply by existing, it was helpful to have someone else there.

Pat drained his cup and tossed it into the plastic trash can by Bill's desk. "Thanks, buddy," he said, bracing his hands on his knees and rising. "I appreciate it."

"Any time," Bill said automatically.

Pat barked out one of his wolf laughs. "I hope not."

Bill grinned. "Fair."

"Veronica doing good? And the baby?"

"Yep. Millie's walking now, saying a bunch of words. And Veronica is gearing up for Diane's big debate this weekend."

Pat's mustache twitched, indicating a slight smile underneath the pile of coarse hair. "I hope she mops the floor with that soggy skid mark."

"Oh, she will. Veronica's actually been working with Diane on toning down her vocabulary just a little bit, so she doesn't come across as *too* much smarter than him."

Pat snorted. "Anyone who watches them for more than two seconds will tell she's smarter than him. I mean, she's a librarian and he's a used-car salesman."

"Yeah, but if the gap seems too wide, she comes across as snobby. It's a delicate balancing act."

"Politics, man. What a shit show."

"You're telling me."

Chapter Twenty-Eight

JUSTIN

Since I'm already staying at Mrs. Hanley's house, I'm the one tasked with investigating her fire while Rose works on McMillain over at the high school. I spend most of Monday combing through the police report on the fire, along with every inch of the garage, while she's in school.

I don't know what I'm hoping to find, but the answer so far is . . . nothing. I'm no detective, but from where I sit, odds are not looking great for me getting back home.

If there even is a way back home.

I'm sitting on the couch in Mrs. Hanley's living room, hunched over the coffee table as I pore over the file yet again next to a growing pile of Twinkie wrappers, when she sits next to me and plops down a plate holding a sandwich. Thick-cut roast chicken is piled high between slices of wheat bread. My mouth instantly starts watering.

"Twinkies aren't food," she proclaims. "I keep those in the pantry for my grandkids, but a growing boy like you needs more than just sugar."

"I don't think I'm growing much more," I say, and receive a knuckle in my ribs in response. "Ow!"

"There's more than one direction to grow in," she says. "You need some meat on your bones."

Obediently, I take a bite of the sandwich, closing my eyes in momentary bliss as Mrs. Hanley leans forward to examine the contents of the coffee table. She taps the thin stack of papers with a pointed red nail. "I can find you something better to read if you want. I think my grandson left some books here with some space monsters on the covers. Probably find more truth in those than in here."

I look up in surprise at the old woman. "So what's in here isn't accurate?"

She shrugs, leaning back and folding her hands in her lap over her flowered dress. "I'm sure they *think* it's accurate. As much as they think about it at all."

I look back at the file in confusion, flipping through the pages. I'm not an expert on police files by any stretch, but nothing jumps out at me as obviously wrong.

Mrs. Hanley chuckles, patting my hand. "It's not anything that's *there*, sugar."

"Are you saying there's something missing?" I ask, trying to understand. "Like evidence of an intruder?"

"Oh, honey, I don't know what's missing, and they don't care," she says, shaking her head. "Door was unlocked, lighter belonged to me. My grandson was home. Case closed. They acted like they were doing us a favor by not charging him with arson."

"But even if it *was* your grandson—which I'm not saying it was," I amend hurriedly at the look on Mrs. Hanley's face, "shouldn't the insurance company still pay, since he doesn't live here?"

She gives a humorless chuckle. "They figure that I *asked* him to start the fire while I was out. Or that's their excuse anyway."

"You think there's another reason they're not paying?"

"Yup. They're a buncha thieves," Mrs. Hanley says matter-of-factly. "Well, that's what they are," she insists when she notices my eyebrows go up. "First, they don't want us to own our own homes at all, but then when we go and do it anyway, they say, 'Well, you have to buy this insurance, too,' so then we do *that*, but then when it's time for that insurance to pay, they won't. It's a racket."

I look over my notes and the police file again, chewing the inside of my lip. "Can you think of anyone who might have a motive to hurt you? Or would want to destroy your stuff?"

Mrs. Hanley spreads her hands helplessly. "I just don't know, sugar. I've lived in this house for thirty years now, and there have always been people who didn't like that. I've known my share of unkindness over the years. But as far as a name, or a reason? Could be anyone, for any reason they like, or no reason at all." She looks lovingly at the framed family portrait hanging on the wall, her smile a little sad. "I just know it wasn't my Noah. That's what I know."

I don't know what it's like to have grandparents, but I think it would be nice to have a grandmother like Mrs. Hanley.

I hope I can help her.

Chapter Twenty-Nine

ROSE

"Do you believe in fate?" Justin asked, staring up at the ceiling of Mrs. Hanley's guest bedroom, one arm tucked behind his head.

Rose looked up in surprise from where she sat cross-legged at the foot of the bed. She'd come straight to Mrs. Hanley's after her first attempt to talk to Michael McMillain after school—not particularly encouraging, but she still had the rest of the week—and she and Justin had gone up to his room to compare notes. Although Justin's "notes" turned out to just be a rant about how insurance systems were a scam, which was hardly helpful.

"I think kind of," Rose said, putting down her pencil. She'd been writing up a to-do list for them to follow for the rest of the week, although it had far more blanks on it than she'd like. "Like I feel like there's meaning in everything, but not everything *has* to happen the way it does. Does that make sense?"

"I think so," Justin said. "So kind of like 'everything happens for a reason'?"

"No," Rose said, shaking her head adamantly. "I *hate* that."

"Really?" Justin sat up, tilting his head so his shaggy hair fell across his eyes. "Isn't that why you're so sure that we have to stop this fire?"

"Not exactly." Rose frowned, trying to figure out how to put her thoughts into words. "So my mom died when I was little," she said. "Car accident."

"Oh wow," Justin said. "I didn't know. I'm sorry."

She waved away his condolences, not wanting to linger in those memories. "Anyway, after that, I spent a lot of time at my best friend Lisa's house. And Lisa's mom wound up doing a lot of 'mom' things for me, like taking me bathing suit shopping and teaching me to braid my hair. And then a few years later, Lisa's dad died of cancer. And then a couple years after that, my dad and Lisa's mom got married."

Justin's eyes had widened as she explained how her family had come to look the way it did, but he didn't interrupt or make a stupid comment about how lucky they were, or how everything worked out in the end, or any of the other asinine things people sometimes said without thinking.

He just listened, his blue eyes holding steady on hers, waiting for her to finish.

"So," she said, blowing out a shaky breath. Talking about this was harder than she'd expected. She hadn't picked at this old wound for a while and was surprised to find it was still a little sore. Maybe it always would be. "I can believe that there was meaning in all of that, but I can't believe that the *reason* my mom died was for my dad to marry Diane. Like, I don't think fate causes things to happen, but once they do happen, they have significance. Does that make sense?"

He nodded slowly, running a hand through his hair. "That's pretty intense."

"I've thought about it a lot."

"I can tell. So where does my whole . . . situation place on the meaning-reason spectrum?"

She sighed. The truth was, she hadn't completely figured that out yet. Time travel hadn't factored into her existential calculus until a couple of days ago. "I think there's definitely meaning in it," she started slowly. "And the rules of cause and effect mean that there has to be *some* sort of reason why it happened."

"And you think that's to save my grandparents."

"Yeah."

"So not everything happens for a reason . . . except for me being here, right now, with you, which definitely *did* happen for a reason."

Rose shrugged, spreading her hands. "Maybe? It feels like time travel is an exception to a lot of things. So maybe it makes sense that there would be a reason for this, even if there doesn't have to be one for everything else."

"Huh. Interesting," Justin said. He was quiet for a moment, his forehead crinkled. "But what about—"

"Ooh, I love this song," Rose interrupted, leaning over him to turn up the radio volume. She bobbed her head to the energetic beat as the British singer promised his love that she was never second best. Must be nice, Rose thought, to know you were someone's first choice.

Justin listened for a second; then his eyes widened in recognition. "Oh, I've heard this one," he exclaimed, sounding surprised. "They did a COVID cover of it. I watched it on YouTube during lockdown."

"They did a . . . what?" Rose said. Most of the words that had just come out of his mouth sounded like total gibberish.

"Um, you know what?" he said, his forehead creasing slightly. "Let's just say the band re-recorded it a couple years ago—in my time—and I watched a video of it."

"Which one of those words meant that?"

"All of them. Sort of."

Rose shook her head, wondering if she'd ever get used to all the ways his world was different from hers. "You know, it's been forever since I've heard this song," she said thoughtfully. The last time had probably been when she and Lisa were on their *Valley Girl* kick last year and nearly wore out the library's VHS copy of the film. "They played it a lot on the radio when it first came out, but that was a couple years ago. Maybe it's a sign."

Justin raised an eyebrow. "A sign of what?"

"That we're going to succeed. I mean, a song about two people taking on the world together and changing the future? That's gotta mean something, right?"

"Okay, first of all, I didn't think you believed in signs. Whatever happened to 'not everything happens for a reason'?"

"Well, yeah, not *everything*. But a song on the radio is just one tiny thing. It could be a little nod that we're on the right track."

"You are seriously moving the goalposts, but fine. Second of all, that is *not* what this song is about."

Rose listened for a few more seconds as the singer repeated the chorus. "Yes, it is. He's talking about things getting better when he's with her. And how the world stops when they're together."

"No, he's talking about how the world is about to actually *stop*. It's about a nuclear apocalypse. Like, the chorus is about them physically fusing together."

"With love."

"Nope. With radiation."

"*No*. No way." Rose ran back through the lyrics in her head as the song faded to an end, wishing she had it on cassette so she could rewind it. It was a love song. Wasn't it? That was definitely how it had been used in *Valley Girl*.

"I'm telling you, I looked it up when they did the cover, and that's totally what it's about," Justin insisted.

"There's a *book* about this song?"

"No, it's just on the internet. I told you about—"

"Oh right, I remember." He'd described the "internet" as an infinite library that everyone had access to through their computers, a concept she still couldn't quite wrap her brain around. "So they *die*?"

"I mean, maybe not *during* the song, but death is definitely imminent."

"But . . . but he says things are changing! And that the future—"

"It's supposed to be ironic. They're totally dead. He literally says they melt."

Rose dropped her head into her hands. "You just ruined this song for me."

"It's not *my* fault some British dude decided to write a super-peppy song about having sex during a nuclear blast. That's for him and his therapist to work out."

She groaned, then cut her eyes to the radio, which had moved on to the next song. "What about this one? You going to tell me it's really about running someone over with your car or something?"

Justin shrugged, reaching over to turn down the volume. "I mean, I think it's just about the power of love, but if you want to get all morbid about it—"

She smacked him with a pillow, sending him tumbling off the bed, even though she definitely hadn't hit him hard enough for that.

He didn't bother climbing back up, just propped his arms on the edge of the mattress and rested his chin on his hand. "So my point is, if that song was a sign, it probably means we're doomed."

"Or maybe it's just a sign that it's good we found each other," Rose said. "Those people seemed pretty happy not to be alone, even if the world was about to end."

"Well, yeah, I mean, if you're gonna die, that's probably the way to go."

"Not just *that*," Rose said, fighting the blush she could feel rising in her cheeks. "But even if it *is* about dying—"

"It is."

"—isn't it also about the importance of having someone with you when things feel impossible? That maybe sometimes, even if you can't change anything, it's good to be with someone who makes you believe that you can?"

"So now you're saying it's a sign that we're delusional and this whole plan is a waste?"

"Are you *trying* to be irritating?"

"Just comes naturally."

Rose gave a frustrated sigh, although the corners of her mouth kept insisting on tugging upward. As irritating as he could be, there was something energizing about him. Like she had to remain alert in case he changed direction without warning. Most of the time, it was kind of fun. "I'm saying that maybe it's good to have someone in your corner who can push you to keep hoping when it would be easier to give up."

Justin thought for a second, then nodded slowly. "Yeah, I can get behind that. You can be my motivational apocalypse buddy."

"Maybe without the apocalypse part."

"We'll see."

She tapped her eraser against the legal pad. "So let's make a plan and hopefully we can avoid that?"

"Sure thing," he said, hauling himself back up onto the bed. "But first, subject change. Tell me something about your mom."

That was *not* what she was expecting. "Why do you want to know about my mom?"

"Because it feels like she's a big part of why you're helping me, and why we're even making this whole stop-the-fire plan." He shrugged. "Plus, it just seems like you think about her a lot. So I thought you might want to talk about her."

"Um," she said, flustered. "I mean, I was only five when she died . . ."

"But you still have some memories of her, right? Or stories your dad told you?" He scratched the side of his head, giving her a crooked smile. "Sorry, am I being too much? Alyssa says I can be a lot."

"Is Alyssa your sister?"

"My friend," he said, his cheeks turning slightly pink, making her wonder if this Alyssa was his "friend" in the same way that Noah was hers. "I, uh, don't have much of a filter. I just say whatever stuff comes into my brain. ADHD thing."

"What's ADHD?"

"Attention deficit hyperactivity disorder. Do you not know what that is here?"

She shook her head. "I know what ADD is."

"Oh, weird. Okay, well, yeah, it's basically the same thing. It's what doctors call an executive function disorder. So it's like the ringleader in my brain is asleep most of the time, so whatever monkeys or clowns or contortionists feel like performing, they just run onstage and shove out whoever's already there, since there's no one to keep everything in order. Or sometimes they perform at the same time. Or maybe they merge into a single act. Just a free-for-all circus." His arms waved around his head, pantomiming the internal chaos. "No one driving the ship, icebergs everywhere. Fun times."

Rose laughed. "So your brain is an out-of-control three-ring circus . . . on the *Titanic*?"

"I'm honestly not entirely sure where I was going with the circus metaphor *or* the ship metaphor. Both just seemed to work at the time." He shrugged. "Welcome to my brain."

"It seems fun."

"Tell that to my teachers." He straightened abruptly. "But *you* were going to tell me something about your mom."

"Was I? I don't remember agreeing to that." Rose couldn't keep the smile from her face, though. As bizarre as their situation was, it was easy to talk to Justin. She didn't second-guess everything that came out of her mouth with him. Maybe because he didn't even first-guess what came out of his.

"Come on. I may never see my mom again either, but all my memories of her kind of suck. Give me a good one instead."

"Okay, just a minute." Rose closed her eyes, conjuring a memory. Most of her impressions of her mother were hazy wisps, barely more than a splash of color here, a whiff of scent there. But she had a couple that were solid enough to grab on to, worn soft from years of frequent handling.

"She used to put me on her lap when she played the piano," she said, the memory spooling out against the backs of her eyelids. "I would put my hands on hers, and close my eyes and let her move my arms up and down the keyboard, and I'd listen to the music and pretend that I *was* her. That I was the one playing, in the future, all grown up."

She opened her eyes to find Justin staring intently at her, a smile playing on his lips. Had he moved closer, or had she just gotten so caught up in the memory that she'd forgotten where she was? Slight warmth seeped up the sides of her neck, into her cheeks.

"Do you still play?" he asked.

She shook her head sadly. "I never learned. She had planned to teach me herself. After she died, Dad offered to find me a teacher, but I didn't want to learn anymore. Dad sold the piano a couple years later."

"Do you wish he hadn't?"

She let out a surprised little laugh. She'd never known someone who asked questions the way he did, like they barely had a chance to skip off the surface of his brain before tumbling from his mouth. "Sometimes," she admitted.

He nodded thoughtfully. "Yeah, I think I would, too."

"Do *you* believe in fate?" Rose asked, turning his original question back on him.

Justin flopped onto his back, setting the mattress bouncing slightly. Rose's pencil rolled off her legal pad, onto the comforter. Justin picked it up, twirling it around his fingers. "I don't know," he said, staring at the slowly rotating pencil. "If you asked me a couple days ago, I would've said no. Now . . . I'm undecided."

"Really?" Rose was surprised. She would've thought that time travel was a pretty compelling argument for believing that there were larger forces at work in the universe.

He looked at her, pointing with the pencil. "I mean, I take it you believe in God, right?"

She nodded. Her parents had attended church only sporadically before her mom died, and then her dad stopped going completely afterward. But later, Rose started attending Sunday school with Lisa, and eventually, when her father and Diane got together, he accompanied them to church, too. Yet faith in God wasn't something she remembered deciding to have; faith simply felt like something that had always been inside her. She knew some people found it hard to believe in something they couldn't see or prove, but for Rose, it was impossible not to.

"So, naturally, it makes sense to you that all of this would be part of some bigger *thing*, right, because you already believed there *was* a bigger thing," Justin reasoned.

Rose considered, tapping her fingers on her notepad. "Yeah, I guess so."

"Whereas for me," Justin continued, "I believed everything was random and pointless, and then this time-travel thing happened, and I can't decide if that's just the *most* random and pointless thing imaginable, or a sign that things actually *aren't* random and pointless. Like, the evidence fits in both columns, you know?"

Rose reached over and grabbed her pencil from him, holding up the pad. "So then why are you going along with this whole fire theory anyway, if it's all random and pointless?"

He shrugged. "Better than the alternative." He grinned at her when she raised an eyebrow. "Throwing myself off a bridge," he clarified.

"No, we wouldn't want that," Rose agreed.

"We?"

Rose gave him an incredulous look. "Are you seriously surprised that I don't want you to throw yourself off a bridge?"

He dropped his eyes to the comforter, fiddling with a loose thread. "I'm just . . . not really used to people caring what happens to me," he said quietly.

Rose's heart sagged. Was he really that lonely, back in his time? "Well, I care," she said, a little too brightly. She cleared her throat. "I'm in your corner, remember?"

"Right." He gave her a small smile. "You and me versus the end of the world."

"Exactly." She nudged his leg with her foot. "C'mon. Get up, and let's figure out what we're doing tomorrow so you don't melt."

"Whatever you say, apocalypse buddy."

TUESDAY

Chapter Thirty

VERONICA

"Ugh, no, thank you," Veronica said, waving away the plate of slightly runny scrambled eggs her husband was trying to place in front of her. Her stomach turned at their glossy yellow sheen, the way they wobbled on the plate.

Bill frowned, examining the eggs. "Not a fan of eggs à la Bill anymore?" he said, exhaling a cloud of smoke. "And here I thought I'd perfected my method."

"It's not that. It's—can you put that thing out?" She didn't normally mind Bill's smoking habit, but this morning it was giving her a headache. She picked up the folded newspaper as he snubbed the cigarette out in the ashtray on the kitchen table. "Thanks," she said. "I just feel . . . ugh." She scanned the front page yet again, hoping that maybe this time, it wouldn't make her want to throw up.

Nope, still terrible.

Bill tilted his head sideways so he could read the headline that accompanied the photo of Diane and her family at brunch. "Yikes. I thought it was supposed to be a friendly profile of Diane?"

"It *was*. They totally screwed us." Veronica flipped the paper over so she couldn't look at it anymore. Lewis-Yin's Lavish Lifestyle: Living Large as Polling Plummets. The article was ridiculous, using barely any of the thoughtful quotes Diane had provided, and contorting the facts to make it seem as though she had given up on the idea of winning after the latest polls and was squandering her remaining campaign money on extravagant outings for her family.

"Emerson *donated* the use of the Tearoom for the photo shoot!" Veronica lamented, dropping her head into her arms. "And the polling numbers aren't even down that much! A lousy *point*. Although it's probably more after this. I swear, I could strangle Franklin Gibson with my bare hands."

Bill gave her a sympathetic smile, scraping the eggs onto his own plate before dropping into the chair next to her and rubbing her back. "I'm really sorry, honey." Beside him, Millie babbled in her high chair, happily rubbing eggs into her hair. "Millie, baby, we eat with our *mouths*, not our hair," he said, tapping the messy plastic tray with his finger.

"Ha!" Millie exclaimed, offering her daddy a gummy grin.

Veronica smiled in spite of herself. "I think she's trying to say *hair*."

"Are you saying *hair*, Millie? Have you learned another new word? Are you a precious little genius? I think you are, yes I do," Bill said in baby-speak, making his voice high and cartoonish.

"Ha, Daddy!" Millie squealed again, picking up another handful of eggs and smashing them into her ear.

Veronica watched Bill as he tried to convince Millie to eat her food instead of accessorize with it, exaggerating his own motions as he shoveled bites of his breakfast into his mouth. "See how Daddy eats with his mouth? See how my teeth go *chomp chomp chomp*? Can you go *chomp chomp*, Millie?"

"Bill?"

"Hmm?" he said absently, still focused on their daughter. "I'm going to have to give you another bath before school, aren't I?" he muttered despairingly as Millie smeared eggs into her lap.

"Am I insane, to think we can still win?"

He shook his head. "You're absolutely not insane. We've known since the beginning that coverage from the *Gazette* wasn't going to be fair, considering how much money Gibson funnels into that business. I mean, I don't think anyone was prepared for just how bad it would get, but we were never expecting them to be in our corner. Yet Diane's numbers have been pretty good, all things considered."

"He's got more money, though. And it's getting worse."

"I know, but I just don't think—" Bill distracted himself by looking at Millie, then groaned. "Baby girl, did you really just stuff eggs in your diaper?"

"Poop!" Millie hollered in glee.

"You just don't think . . . ?" Veronica prompted.

Bill pivoted in his seat to face her, taking her hand on the table. "In a small town like Stone Lake, with a candidate like Diane, I just don't think we can know which way it's going to go, even with all his money and influence. She may inspire people to vote who don't typically care about local elections."

"On both sides," Veronica pointed out. "You know how awful people can be."

"Maybe they'll surprise you. When they hear what Diane has to say, how can they *not* root for her?"

She loved her husband more than anything, but some days, she just wanted to take him by the shoulders and shake him. His relentless optimism was one of the things that made him so good at his job— teenagers needed someone to believe in them, and Bill wore his belief like a finely tailored suit—but sometimes it was maddening that they saw the world so differently.

It wasn't entirely his fault. Good grades, good looks, and a wealthy family had ensured that every door in Bill's life had swung wide open for him—until he met Veronica, the poor girl with no parents, no money, and an overeager uterus.

The Warrens were sure that Veronica had gotten pregnant on purpose, in order to trap Bill into marriage. They hadn't even bothered to come to the wedding. They told Bill it was because their family had been hit with a bout of flu, but Veronica knew better.

Not that she was surprised. She knew their type, and they would never approve of hers. Veronica always had to shoulder her way through every door herself, throwing her full weight against it until it began to budge, an inch at a time.

Which was why she couldn't take anything for granted, especially with the election only a few weeks away.

"The debate is in *five days*, Bill. This profile was supposed to give us a bump going into it. Now . . . I just don't know what we're going to do. Which is a problem, since it's my job to know what to do."

Bill put an arm around her, rubbing gentle circles into her back. "Is there anything *I* can do?"

She gave him a weak smile, then gestured at Millie, who by this point seemed more egg than baby. "De-egg our child? I'll figure out this other stuff. I just needed to freak out about it for a little bit."

"I'm always here for freak-outs," Bill said, planting a kiss on the top of her head before turning to the baby and wrinkling his nose. "Good grief, child; it's a good thing you're cute."

Veronica took a deep breath as Bill scooped Millie out of her chair and swept her into the bathroom. Her stomach still churned uncomfortably, and the sight of smashed egg all over Millie's high chair was doing nothing to help. She dropped her eyes back to the paper, focusing on her breathing as she spun through ideas for the day.

In. Maybe Bill was right, and more people could see through the blatant misinformation in the paper than she thought.

Out. But she had to prepare for the worst. The gap between Gibson and Diane hadn't been much, but was probably wider now. Would the debate be enough to make up the difference?

In. They'd just have to prepare more. And get the word out. Make sure people showed up. People who may be receptive to what Diane had to say. People who . . . who . . .

Out. Really needed to throw up.

She barely made it to the sink before retching up her morning coffee. As she leaned over the breakfast dishes, rinsing her mouth with handfuls of running water, her thoughts were interrupted by a knock on the front door. Veronica closed her eyes briefly, steeling herself for yet another unexpected problem. People didn't knock on doors unannounced at six thirty in the morning just to say hello.

The second she opened the front door, her day got worse.

"What are you doing here?" she hissed under her breath at Kenny Gibson, standing in full uniform on her front porch. She hurriedly shut the door behind her, hoping Bill hadn't heard it open over the sound of the bathtub faucet and Millie's squeals.

"Hey, Ronnie," he said. His lake-blue eyes scanned her approvingly. "How's the family?"

She crossed her arms over her chest. "What do you want, Kenny? Cornering me in parking lots is one thing, but this is my *home*."

He ran a hand through his straw-colored hair. "I need to talk to you about the campaign."

"I thought you said the campaign had nothing to do with you."

"It doesn't. I mean *your* campaign."

She raised an eyebrow.

"Look, I made a traffic stop the other night. Car driving real slow across Wilson Bridge, and some kid walking next to it, right in the middle of the road. Really weird kid. Never seen him before. Didn't seem to know what year it was. I was going to bring him in, but then the other kid, the one driving the car, she vouched for him. Said he was her cousin visiting from out of town, and that he'd gotten light-headed. So I let them both go with a warning."

He took a step closer to her, bending down so he could lower his voice. "Ronnie, it was one of Diane's kids. Rose. I don't know who the boy is, but I don't think he's her cousin. And I don't think her parents know he even exists."

Veronica closed her eyes for a moment, collecting her thoughts. This was the last thing she needed. One of Diane's kids sneaking out with some mystery boy, lying to her parents right before the debate. If the press got wind of this, they'd have a field day. "Why are you telling me this? What's in it for you?"

Kenny sighed again, looking at her with a slightly sad expression. "Ronnie, I know you've made me into some sort of villain in your head, but I don't want all your hard work to go to waste because of some stupid kids." He stepped closer, his eyes soft. "I still care about you, you know."

She leaned away from him. "Does your dad know?"

He shook his head, giving her a fraction more space. "I haven't told him, and I didn't log the stop on Saturday either, although maybe I should have. That's why I came here before my shift today. I thought you'd want to deal with it privately." He hooked his thumbs in his pockets, giving her a small smile. "I'm trying to do the right thing here, Ronnie. I didn't have to tell you, but I actually am a decent person, believe it or not."

There it was. The fishing for credit. He just couldn't resist.

"Thanks for telling me," she said, her mind already whirling through ways to approach this new development.

"You're welcome." He seemed a little disappointed, probably because she hadn't dropped what she was doing to throw him a parade. But she just did not have the energy to stroke his ego right now.

"Well, if there's nothing else . . . ?" She raised an eyebrow, one hand on the front door handle, eager to get back inside so she could figure out her next step.

"Nope, nothing else," Kenny said, slipping on his sunglasses. "But I'll tell you what—if I find out anything else on this kid, I'll let you know."

"Great," Veronica said.

He smiled. "Kinda nice, isn't it? You and me, working together on something again? Like it used to be."

Veronica opened the front door. "Thanks for your help," she said, her voice measured. "But it's not like it used to be. And it never will be." With that, she shut the door, locking him out.

Chapter Thirty-One

LISA

"Mama? Can we talk?"

Lisa tied her fingers into knots in her lap, her bottom lip caught between her teeth. She stared into the dregs of milk at the bottom of her cereal bowl, heart hammering.

"Hmm? Sure, baby, what is it?" Her mother's eyes didn't lift from the newspaper she had spread across the table beside her mug of coffee. She was still in her bathrobe, her face bare of makeup. One finger absently twirled the end of the silk scarf wrapped snugly around her hair.

Lisa fidgeted in her seat, searching for just the right opening words. If she was going to make things right with Charlene, she had to tell someone the truth. And her mother would love her no matter what, right? Even if it might make the campaign harder?

Of course I will, she could almost hear her mother say.

She took a deep breath. "Mama, I—"

"Morning, ladies," Jim said, shuffling into the kitchen with a pajama-clad Emmie on his hip. She was the only one who looked truly awake, kicking her chubby legs gleefully as her daddy attempted to stuff her into her high chair. "Ba ba ba!" she chanted urgently, pointing at Lisa's empty bowl.

"I hear you, Emmie-girl. I'm getting there," Jim said patiently, clipping on the plastic tray. As far as Lisa could tell, none of Emmie's noises actually meant anything yet—right now, *ba* seemed to mean *breakfast*, but later it could just as easily mean *diaper* or *milk* or *car*—but her mom and Jim always talked to her as if they knew exactly what she was trying to say.

He picked up the Cheerios box and shook it. "Gotta get to the store soon," he muttered to no one in particular, shaking a smattering of o's onto Emmie's tray before glancing at the table. "Is Rose still in bed?" he asked, sounding surprised.

Lisa swallowed thickly, her face hot. She picked up her bowl and empty glass and walked them to the sink. "I'll go check."

"Hang on, baby," her mom said, catching her arm as she passed by the table. "What did you want to talk about?"

Diane tore her eyes from the paper, from a story that Lisa now saw contained the brunch photo they'd taken on Saturday. The headline read, Lewis-Yin's Lavish Lifestyle: Living Large as Polling Plummets.

Lisa's heart sank. "I thought it was going to be a good article," she said softly.

"We all did, sweetheart," Jim said, patting her shoulder as he passed behind her on his way to his seat. "This is just how it goes, sometimes."

Lisa looked from her mother to Jim, wondering how they were both so calm. If it were her, she'd be furious. She *was* furious. "Is there something we can do? Tell people that they're lying?"

"How?" Diane said. "Make a statement to the paper?"

Lisa shook her head, sinking back down into her seat, rage boiling inside her. It wasn't right that the newspaper, whose owners played golf with Franklin Gibson every weekend, could just print complete lies about her mother—about their family—and they had no choice but to sit there and take it. "It shouldn't be like this," she muttered, glaring at the paper.

Her mom looked tired, more tired than she'd seemed in years, but she still managed a smile. She leaned forward, taking Lisa's face between her hands. "This is just the road, baby. We knew when we started that it would be bumpy."

"It's not bumpy for *him*," Lisa grumbled.

"Maybe not," her mom said, "but if we can just stay on it through to the end, maybe we can smooth out some of these bumps for the people walking after us." She smiled at Emmie in her high chair, shoving handfuls of Cheerios into her mouth with her stubby fingers. When she noticed her mom looking at her, Emmie grinned, her brown button nose crinkling, bits of saliva-soaked cereal flecking her lips.

"It's not fair," Lisa said quietly, leaning over to wipe Emmie's mouth with a napkin. Emmie twisted her face, arching away from the napkin and swatting at her sister's hand. Lisa looked at Emmie's wispy, dark curls, at the slight crescent shape of her eyes, and a simultaneous wave of envy and fierce protectiveness washed over her. Emmie didn't know yet how hard it was to be different, and Lisa wished she could keep her from ever finding out.

"It's not," her mom agreed. "It's not fair at all."

Lisa had always appreciated this about her mom, how she didn't try to sugarcoat bad things in pretty words. A scraped knee got a matter-of-fact *That looks like it really hurts*, while a mean taunt on the playground received a sympathetic *Sometimes people are just cruel. There's no excuse for it, and it's never okay.*

And when her dad had died and Lisa had sobbed herself to sleep every night for two months, her mom had simply sat on the side of her bed and stroked her back, saying, *This is a big sadness, baby girl. It's all right to feel it.*

Lisa pulled in a long breath. This was the thing Charlene didn't get. She knew the world was hard and rarely fair, but there were layers of complexity that she just didn't understand, and probably never would. It wasn't her fault; their roads were just different.

Her mom cleared her throat, folding her hands. "Now, honey, what was it you wanted to talk to me about?"

"Nothing," Lisa said quickly. She couldn't talk to her mom about her and Charlene now. Not when there was so much other stuff going on.

Her mom pursed her lips, giving her a practiced *I-don't-believe-that-for-a-second* look.

Jim paused with his spoon midway to his mouth, catching his wife's eye. They had a quick conversation using only their eyes—a language Lisa had never learned to speak, despite her efforts—then he cleared his throat. "Well, I'm going to go finish taking care of all this," he said, straightening to gesture at his white undershirt and the couple of flecks of red-spotted toilet paper dotting his chin, as if he'd never intended to sit and eat breakfast in the first place.

After Jim had hurried out of the room, her mom raised her eyebrows at Lisa. "C'mon, baby girl, you and I both know you didn't ask to talk about *nothing*."

"Well," Lisa amended, casting around for an effective distraction. "I was just going to ask if you needed me this weekend. To help prepare for the debate."

It worked. Her mom's eyes instantly became clouded, and Lisa knew she was running through her long list of things to do. "Oh, honey, that's so sweet, but don't you worry about that. Actually, other than the setup Saturday morning, it's probably for the best if you and Rosie lay a little bit low for the rest of the week. The press . . ." She sighed, her gaze dropping back to the paper as she trailed off.

Lisa pasted a smile on her face, determined not to make the road her mom was walking any bumpier than it had to be. "Absolutely."

"And you know, I know you love to hang out with Charlene, and of course we love her, too, but in light of the article and considering how close her family is with the Gibsons, we were wondering if maybe you might take some . . . space. From each other."

Unexpected tears sprang to Lisa's eyes at the sound of Charlene's words echoed in her mother's voice. Abruptly, she stood to retrieve her glass from the sink, pretending she'd suddenly decided on a refill. She blinked rapidly as she rinsed out the glass and filled it with water, trying to banish the tears from her eyes.

"Not for long," Diane hurried to say, likely mistaking Lisa's heart-break for annoyance. "Maybe just until after the debate? Then we'll see where we are."

Char doesn't want to see me anyway, Lisa reminded herself. It should be easy enough to say yes. To give her mom what she needed. To give Charlene what she wanted. Really, nothing was even changing. Nothing was being taken away that she hadn't already lost.

Then why did it feel like she was being torn in two?

Lisa took a deep breath. Her tears seemed mostly under control now, even as her heart felt like it was being slowly crushed. She turned to face her mother, her smile frozen in place. "Sure thing. No problem at all."

She excused herself and walked back upstairs to brush her teeth, wondering just how many pieces of herself she'd have to give up by the time this was all over, and if she'd even recognize herself anymore by then.

Chapter Thirty-Two

BILL

The door clicked shut behind Andy, who walked out of Bill's office stiffly, his hall pass to in-school suspension crumpled in his hand. Once Andy was safely on the other side of the door, Pat walked over to the window, running his hand slowly over his beard, and blew out a long breath. "Well, shit."

He cracked the window open and pulled a cigarette out of his shirt pocket. "Want one?" he said, holding the box out to Bill.

"It's nine a.m., Pat. Class is in session."

"I opened the window."

As Pat lit his cigarette and inhaled deeply, Bill eyed the desk drawer that held the Bacardi. If only it weren't nine o'clock in the morning during a school day, he'd be pouring himself a drink. He leaned back in his chair, pressing the heels of his hands to his eyes until he saw spots, trying to think through what to do next.

It hadn't taken long for Andy to crack. As soon as Pat had shown him the tests, the truth had come pouring out. Andy wasn't a bad kid, but he'd quickly become overwhelmed by the increase in the amount of work for high school as opposed to middle school. Someone had told him about a way to buy tests, so he'd scraped together the money to purchase three. He wrote down all the answers on a piece of paper he hid in his shirtsleeve, and until this morning, he thought he'd gotten away with it. Two of the other tests he'd already gotten back with A-plus results. His face when he saw his failing history grade had made Bill wonder if he was going to burst into tears.

Andy didn't know who he'd bought the test from. He knew who'd told him about the system, but that person had never purchased a test; they just knew how it worked. Apparently, it was a pretty widely known secret among the students at the school: Put an envelope in locker 247 containing the money, your locker number, and which classes and tests you need. The next day, either the test appears in your locker or your money is returned to you.

"Do we tell the faculty?" Pat asked, blowing a stream of smoke out the open window. "Sounds like it's practically every class."

Bill shook his head. "Until we know who it is, we need to keep this between us. We don't want to risk them finding out we know. We'll tell the rest of the faculty once we have a name." And maybe, if he was lucky, they could get this wrapped up before the mayoral debate this weekend. More support for public schools was one of Diane's biggest campaign platforms. If news of a school-wide cheating scandal came out right before the debate, Bill just knew Gibson's people would have a field day with it, adding to Veronica's already overflowing plate of stress.

"Andy could tell someone. Warn them we're looking."

"He's not going to. Did you see that kid's face? He won't be going anywhere near that locker for a while. And he definitely isn't going to want word to get around that he's the one who told the teachers about it."

"So what do we do then?"

Bill sighed. "I think we need to set up a sting."

Chapter Thirty-Three

ROSE

Rose tapped her pencil against her desk. She'd finished her homework in the first ten minutes of study hall, leaving her with nothing to do for the next half hour. At the front of the classroom, Mr. Shaw hunched over his desk, a red pen in his hand and a stack of papers in front of him.

When Rose had first walked into the classroom at the beginning of the period, Mr. Warren had been there, talking quietly with Mr. Shaw. The guidance counselor's brow had been furrowed, like their conversation was a matter of life and death. If only he knew what he should *really* be worried about.

It felt a little ridiculous to be sitting in study hall right now knowing that unless she and Justin solved a mystery that hadn't even happened yet, Mr. Warren would be dead by the end of the week.

Rose was jolted out of her fog by a note sliding onto her desk. *You okay?*

She turned to see Lisa peering at her concernedly over her calculus textbook and gave a small smile. *Just a lot on my mind,* she jotted underneath Lisa's handwriting before passing the note back.

Lisa's eyes darted to the door; then she looked at Rose with raised eyebrows, her question clear. *Want to get out of here?*

Rose nodded, and Lisa's hand shot up. "Mr. Shaw, may Rose and I please go to the library?"

He grunted his assent, and a minute later, they were both out the door, each clutching a bright-pink hall pass.

"What's going on with you?" Lisa whispered once they were in the hallway.

Rose sighed. As much as she yearned to talk about it, there was nothing she could safely say without sounding insane. "Nothing," she said.

"Uh-uh," Lisa said, shaking her head, sending her painted green earrings swinging. "Something is up. You have some guy show up out of the blue, that no one has ever heard of, who you've apparently been writing letters to for long enough that he decided to come visit you?"

"He just had some free time, that's all."

"Why would you keep a pen pal a secret?" Lisa pressed. "Why haven't I ever seen any of his letters? Have you been hiding them? It's just the two of us now. You can tell me if something's going on. I promise I won't tell anyone else."

"Nothing's going on," Rose insisted. "Maybe you just didn't notice. You've been really busy lately."

Lisa paused in the door of the library, frowning slightly. "You still could've told me."

Rose shrugged. "I just didn't think it was that big a deal." She knew it was a little mean to imply that it was Lisa's fault she didn't know about Justin, when the reality was that neither had Rose until a few days ago. But she couldn't help it. Sure, Lisa couldn't have known about Justin, but there were plenty of *other* things she'd missed.

After showing their passes to the librarian, they picked a table in the back corner of the library, dropping their stacks of books onto it between them. Lisa leaned forward, folding her hands on the table. "So tell me about him. How did you guys become pen pals? What did you talk about in your letters?"

Rose bit her lip. She really didn't want to dig deeper into her lie. She knew the truth wasn't an option, but the idea of concocting a whole complex history that didn't exist created an uncomfortable pit in her stomach. Was there anything she could be honest about?

"We talk about fate," she said finally, hoping Lisa wouldn't press her on the question of how they'd met. "You know, like whether there is a purpose for everything."

"Oh." Lisa blinked, tilting her head in thought. After a moment, she said, "I believe in fate."

"You do?" That was surprising. Of course, Lisa attended church along with the rest of their family, but she'd never given Rose the impression that she bought into any of it.

"I mean, I want to, anyway," Lisa said. "It would be nice to believe there's a reason why things are the way they are. That it's not all just pointless and cruel."

Rose smiled. "You sound like him."

"Yeah? Maybe we should hang out sometime."

"No," Rose said quickly. She winced at Lisa's hurt expression. "I mean, you're just always so busy," she amended. "And he's not going to be here that long." *I hope,* she added to herself.

Part of her wanted to introduce Justin to her friends. He seemed so lonely, and she didn't think he had many friends at home. Maybe he'd fit in better here than he did in his time.

But that would create a whole pile of problems on top of the ones they already had. Justin barely knew anything about the time he was living in and was constantly mentioning things that didn't even exist yet. The more people he interacted with, the more likely someone was to notice something about him that didn't add up.

Plus, there was a little part of her that selfishly wanted to keep him for herself. Right now, she was the most important person in his world. She'd never been that before, to anyone, and she wanted to hold on to it as long as possible.

"I'm actually . . . not that busy right now," Lisa said, studying her hands.

Rose raised an eyebrow. "Lisa, you practically live at Charlene's."

"No, I don't," Lisa said. "If you'd been around this week, maybe you'd have noticed."

"If *I'd* been around?" That was rich. "*You're* the one who's never around."

"You don't know what you're talking about," Lisa snapped. Her lower lip trembled slightly and her hands balled into tight fists on the table, causing Rose to wonder if something could be wrong.

"Lisa," Rose ventured, "is everything okay?"

Lisa was quiet for a long moment, then pushed her chair back, standing abruptly. "You know, I actually just remembered," she said, a little too loudly, "I have a question for Mrs. Thompson, so I should probably get to Calc a few minutes early." She scooped her books into her arms. "I'll see you later."

"Oh," Rose said, deflating. Had Lisa even heard her question? "What do you need to ask her about?"

"Um, you know, the current lesson," Lisa said hurriedly, pushing in her chair. "I don't really get it."

"Really?" Rose was surprised to hear Lisa was struggling with math, since that was one of her best subjects. "What part? I could—"

"Oh, you know," Lisa said, waving the question away without answering. "See you later!"

"Wait—" Rose started to say, but realized it was no use. Lisa was already gone.

Chapter Thirty-Four

VERONICA

"Diane." Veronica hurried over to the front desk of the library, taking advantage of the brief lull between patrons. She'd been waiting for an opportunity to talk to Diane all morning, but between books needing to be shelved and people asking to use the copier and a slight cataloging disaster in the microfiche section, her first chance didn't arrive until after lunch.

Before running Diane's campaign, Veronica had never considered how difficult it was to run for public office while also holding down a full-time job. No wonder most people didn't want to do it. Must be nice to be rich like Franklin Gibson, who was able to devote himself to his campaign full time while his employees ran his car dealership. "I need to talk to you for a minute."

"I know, I know," Diane said, slipping her reading glasses off her nose as Veronica approached. "I talked to Lloyd again and he swears those buttons will be ready by Saturday afternoon, which I realize is cutting it close, but I think—"

"It's not about the buttons," Veronica said hurriedly, although that *did* check one more thing off her list. She made a mental note to call Lloyd at the printshop later to confirm. "It's kind of delicate."

"Oh?" Diane arched an eyebrow.

"It's actually about Rose." Nervously, Veronica twisted her wedding ring around her finger. She didn't like getting involved in family matters, but she had to say something. "I have some concerns."

Diane straightened from the desk, folding her arms. "What sorts of concerns?"

Already, this didn't feel like it was going great. Veronica knew how she'd react if someone came up to her with unsolicited advice about Millie. "It's just this new boy."

"The pen pal."

"Yes, except . . . Diane, I'm not sure he is who he says he is."

"What do you mean? Who else would he be?"

Veronica took a step closer, lowering her voice. She knew it was silly to assume anyone was listening to them in the library, but after the story in the paper that morning, she wouldn't put anything past Gibson's goons. "On Saturday, Rose told Kenny Gibson he was her cousin."

Diane shook her head, confused. "Cousin? No, he's not her cousin."

"That's not all. Kenny said that when he ran into the two of them on Saturday night, Justin kept asking him what year it was. He's worried he may not be, you know . . . all there," Veronica said, tapping the tip of her finger to her temple.

"What?" Diane waved a hand dismissively, shaking her head. "Honey, don't you see what this is? That boy would do just about anything to get you to pay attention to him, and even more to make you feel like you owe him something." She pursed her lips disapprovingly. "You'd think that ring on your finger would keep him away, but men like that feel entitled to everything, and everyone."

"Diane, I know exactly who and what Kenny is," Veronica said softly. "I've known him my whole life. You know better than anyone that his act doesn't work on me anymore. But I don't think he's lying about this."

Diane frowned. "So you're telling me that the pen pal isn't a pen pal?"

"I don't know. Maybe he *is* really her pen pal, and he's lying about something else."

"But in that case, why would he claim to be her cousin? And why would Rose go along with it?" Diane wagged her head slowly from side to side. "This isn't like her, Veronica. I can count on one hand the number of times that girl has ever lied to me or Jim."

"Maybe it's the boy," Veronica suggested. "Maybe he's manipulating her."

"Manipulating her to do *what*, though? What would he want with Rose?"

Veronica spread her hands helplessly. She had no idea.

Diane picked a date stamp up off the counter, examined it, then set it back down. "All right. I'll talk to her." She sighed. "She's not going to like it."

"It's for her own good."

Diane chuckled humorlessly. "Would you have believed that when you were her age?"

Veronica smiled ruefully. As a matter of fact, her parents *had* tried to warn her off Kenny Gibson. It was probably part of why she'd dated him for so long.

"I'll try to look into it more, too," Veronica said. "Maybe it was just a misunderstanding."

"Maybe." Diane sounded unconvinced. She closed her eyes, rubbing her temples. "First Lisa, now Rose. I am not winning any popularity contests in my house this week."

"You're a good mom," Veronica tried to reassure her. "You're just trying to do what's best for your kids."

"I doubt they'll see it that way."

"Hey." Veronica laid a hand on Diane's arm and gave it a squeeze. "When Millie's a teenager, I'll be happy if I'm half the mom you are."

"Oh, honey, you'll be great," Diane said, patting her hand. "Anyone can tell you love that sweet baby more than breathing. Hold on to that, and you'll figure out the rest."

"I hope so," Veronica said. "Sometimes it all seems so overwhelming."

"It doesn't get any less overwhelming when they get older," Diane said. "Just in a different way. And you just learn to take what they give you as it comes and love them through it all no matter what. There's no secret. Just love." She smiled, then tucked a strand of Veronica's hair behind her ear. "Enjoy these years. One day she'll be a teenager, and you'll be the mama having to sit your child down for the hard talks."

Veronica shook her head, trying and failing to imagine Millie as anything other than a round little dumpling in bloomers and puffed sleeves. "I can't even picture her that big."

Diane laughed. "I couldn't either, when I was in your shoes," she said. "But believe it or not, the years go fast. And the future will be here before you know it."

Chapter Thirty-Five

JUSTIN

For a brief, shining few hours, Rose had me believing that we really could change the past, save my grandparents, and get me back to my time. She was so certain that I'd come here for a reason that I bought into it, even though I don't really believe in that sort of stuff. Listening to her talk, I honestly thought we could rewrite history and fix my life.

Then I started trying to find answers, and reality came crashing down.

I lay in bed on Tuesday morning staring at the ceiling, knowing I should get up but unable to will my body to move. Yesterday I walked around the burned-out husk of the garage for hours and found nothing that could possibly be a clue, although I'm not sure I'd recognize one even if I did see it. I read through the police file over and over, until the words started blurring and my brain refused to let me focus anymore, but there was nothing useful in it.

Rose didn't get anywhere with McMillain either. She told me she tried to talk to him after school, but he didn't want to talk to her while he was working. So she waited in the library until he was ready to leave for the day, and it turned out he didn't want to talk to her then either. She's going to try again today, but I somehow doubt he's going to suddenly decide to spill his guts to her.

Which leaves me without a lot of other options. My column in Rose's to-do list is pitifully short. I could get up and pick through the garage again, but I can't see how that could help. I could ask Mrs. Hanley more questions, but I can't think of anything I haven't asked already.

I could go to Wilson Bridge and hurl myself off, in the hopes that whatever invisible rip in space-time got me here works both ways. But I'm not quite desperate enough to try that yet.

There's one other thing I can do. I really don't want to, and it probably won't get me anywhere. But considering I have no ideas other than jumping off a bridge or staying in bed all day and resigning myself to 1985, this is all I've got.

I haul myself out of bed and shower, pulling on the same black jeans I've been wearing since Saturday and one of Noah's old shirts from the dresser in Mrs. Hanley's guest room. The selection isn't great, and I wind up in a loose-fitting purple button-down that—even though Noah is about my size—feels about eight sizes too big. But it was either that or a Hawaiian shirt, and I just couldn't bring myself to go there yet. I don't know how long I'd have to live in the '80s to brainwash myself into thinking Hawaiian shirts look good, but I know it's longer than a few days.

Mrs. Hanley told me she'd be out for most of the day today attending her ladies' Bible study and then going to lunch with a friend, which means I have the house to myself. I cut myself a slice of the homemade pound cake in the fridge, pull a chair up next to the wall-mounted phone, and get to work.

Wishing for Google for the thousandth time since I wound up stuck in 1985, I start with the heavy yellow phone book Mrs. Hanley keeps in one of her kitchen drawers. Stan was probably around my age in 1985, maybe a little older, so I'm not sure if he'd have been living on his own or with his parents. I'm actually not even sure if he was living in Stone Lake at all. I know he lived here for a while when he was young, before spending most of his young adulthood bouncing around from state to state, but if he ever told me how old he was when he lived here, or when he left, I must not have been paying attention.

It takes me an embarrassingly long time to figure out how to dial Mrs. Hanley's phone, which has a spinning dial with little holes over each number. First, I try pushing the numbers, but nothing happens. Then, after a few minutes, I realize I'm supposed to spin them, but when I pick up the handset to initiate the call after entering the number, all I hear is an interminable dial tone. There's no "Send" or "Call" or "Dial" button anywhere. Eventually, I figure out that I have to pick up the handset *before* dialing and am finally rewarded by the sound of ringing on the other end.

I find myself simultaneously wishing Rose had been here to explain to me how to use the phone, and glad she wasn't here to witness just how bad I am at existing in this stupid decade.

Once I get the hang of dialing, I spin the same story over and over: I'm a friend of Stan's who moved away a while ago and is trying to get back in touch. I will say this for the people of 1985: they're way more generous with personal details than the people of the future. A couple of times, I think I've found him—they have a cousin with that name, or know someone in the next county over—only to get my hopes dashed when they tell me he's in his fifties, or married with kids, or dead.

I'm not sure what I hope finding Stan will accomplish. Obviously, the fire hasn't even happened yet, and his obsessive quest hasn't begun, so it's not like he can tell me anything about it. And even if I were somehow able to call up future Stan and have him consult his murder board for me, he still couldn't tell me for sure what to do since he's never managed to solve the case. I only know that he says he knew my grandparents, and that he really cared about what happened to them.

I guess I figure that if I can talk to him, something might jump out at me. Maybe a word that seems meaningful, or a clue he doesn't realize he has. Or maybe, once I see him, the sight of his face might jostle free one of my own memories that I'd previously forgotten.

It's the longest of long shots, but it's something to do, and at the moment, I'll take what I can get.

And—I can barely admit this, even to myself—it might be nice to see a familiar face. Even if it's Stan's.

But by the time I've gone through every possible number in the phone book that could be him, it's early afternoon, and I have nothing to show for my half day of work. I truly am the world's shittiest detective.

There are other things I could do today. I could take yet another tour through the garage and the police file. I could go to the bridge. I could seek out my grandparents, see if I can determine what leads them to the school instead of the debate on Saturday night, or talk to McMillain myself.

Instead, I wind up on Mrs. Hanley's couch.

It's not that I don't want to make the most of the day, or that I don't care about getting home. It's that I want those things *so badly* that I feel paralyzed.

I know it doesn't make sense. It's just the way I've always been. Alyssa used to get on my case about procrastinating on stuff, but the truth is, I don't think that what I do counts as procrastination. Procrastinating is telling yourself, *I'll do it later.* What *I* do is tell myself, *I'll do it now*, and then I just . . . don't.

When I'm on my medication, it's better, but still hard. When I'm off it . . . well. You may as well ask me to run a triathlon as do my homework. Beginning either seems equally daunting.

Mrs. Hanley comes home from her lunch to find me still sprawled on the couch, paging through the old issues of *Better Homes and Gardens* on her coffee table while a grainy soap opera plays on the tiny living room TV.

Listen, when you're staying with an old lady in 1985 who doesn't even have cable, entertainment options are limited.

She starts shaking her head as soon as she sees me, making disapproving "mm-*mm*" noises through pursed lips. She switches off the

TV—I consider protesting, since I was actually kind of invested in seeing what happened when the guy found out his wife was being impersonated by her evil twin sister—and plucks the magazine out of my hands. "Have you been inside all day?"

I nod, and she actually smacks the side of my head like I'm a faulty microwave. It doesn't hurt, just surprises me. "Hey!"

"Get outside. It's a beautiful day, and if you're going to stay under my roof, you're not going to waste all your time in front of the TV."

"But—"

"*Out.*"

She points toward the front door, her expression leaving no room for argument. So I do the only thing I can—I leave.

Chapter Thirty-Six

KARL

His breath coming in ragged gasps, Karl pushed down hard on the pedals of his bike as he rounded the corner, legs pumping furiously. He risked a glance over his shoulder—and let out a dismayed cry. Robbie Reynolds and his crew—Steve Burks and Kevin Thomas, flanking Robbie on their bikes—were still right behind him, just a dozen or so yards back.

"Get back here, Derrin!" Robbie shouted, rapidly shrinking the short distance between them.

"Leave me *alone*!" Karl shouted, fear spiking his voice up several octaves.

Harsh laughter carried over the roar of the wind in his ears. Karl's legs burned, and his back and shoulders ached from where the straps of his backpack pulled and bounced.

Where was he even *going*? He didn't have a plan. His idea had been to ride toward the center of town, hoping that the people milling about the sidewalks would discourage Robbie and his gang. It hadn't worked—Robbie was closer than ever, and now Karl was too tired to outpace them all the way back to his house, which involved riding across Wilson Bridge and through the woods.

If he tried, they'd be sure to catch him, and he knew all too well what would happen then, in the woods, with no one to hear his cries for help.

His parents didn't believe that Robbie was dangerous, but they also didn't believe that Robbie had held him underwater at the pool that summer until black spots bloomed in his vision, or that he'd been the one to push Karl down the steps at school last May, sending him tumbling across the floor and giving him bruises so deep they turned black.

Karl was flushed with a sudden, burning rage. It should be *Robbie* crying and cowering and wetting his bed from the terror of his nightmares. It should be *Robbie* feeling this overwhelming fear, this utter helplessness.

It was *Robbie* who deserved to suffer. Not Karl.

So why was it Karl?

And why didn't anyone care?

Stinging sweat dripped into Karl's eyes, and he blinked hard, shaking his head to clear his vision, his anger and the strength that had accompanied it vanishing as quickly as they had come, replaced by cold fear. Maybe he should've just let them catch him after school, when there were still teachers around who probably wouldn't have let it go too far. He'd have some bruises, maybe a black eye, but that would've been the worst of it, and then Robbie and the others would've left him alone, at least for a while.

But he'd been too scared to stand his ground. As soon as Robbie started moving toward him through the middle school courtyard, he'd taken off running, jumping on his bike and pedaling as fast as he could, his heart in his throat.

That just made Robbie mad. Before, Karl had been an amusement. Now, he was prey.

Something bumped against his back tire and Karl nearly lost control of the bike, wobbling wildly for a few terrifying seconds before regaining his balance. He didn't have to look back to see what it was;

he could hear the heavy panting of the boy behind him, so close he imagined he could feel Robbie's breath on the back of his neck.

Making a last-second decision, Karl leaned hard to the left, dropping his foot and letting it skim the ground as he cut into the alley that ran between the post office and the barbershop. The alley was narrow, and Robbie's group wasn't expecting the turn; maybe Karl could increase his lead enough to lose them on the other side.

He pedaled faster, not noticing the stick until it was too late.

It caught in Karl's front tire, spinning around and biting into the skin of his ankle before becoming entangled in the chain. A cry of dismay escaped Karl's lips as he went shooting up and over his handlebars, momentarily weightless. Instinctively, he thrust his hands out in front of him, a futile attempt to catch himself before crashing hard into the pavement.

There was no pain in the impact, just shock, as his palm struck the ground, hard, followed an instant later by his shoulder. He rolled, dizzy, the world blurring and spinning around him, until he came to a crumpled stop.

For a second, he was disoriented, unable to draw breath or understand what had happened. Then every sensation hit at once, sharp and burning. His knees, back, shoulders, hands, arms—everything hurt, like the skin had been sanded off and rubbed with salt, tanning him like leather.

And his wrist. He gasped at the sudden agony. Something was *very* wrong with his wrist, which ached with such a strong, piercing pain that he was afraid to look at it.

Gradually, over the throbbing in his ears, Karl heard the sounds of bikes scraping to a stop and hitting the ground. He felt like he'd been lying here for ages, but only moments had passed, and Robbie's gang had finally caught up with him.

Move! Run! his brain screamed, and Karl tried, he really did, but his limbs had taken on a mind of their own, refusing to cooperate. His knees curled into his stomach, and he clutched his hurt wrist to his chest, tucking his head down and squeezing his eyes shut, bracing for the inevitable beating.

To his horror, a pathetic whimper squeaked out of him, and the other boys laughed. "Are you *crying*?" he heard Robbie exclaim gleefully.

Karl didn't answer, knowing he couldn't speak without sobbing. *Just let it be quick,* he prayed silently. Let them do whatever they were going to do, get bored, and go home.

He waited for the first blow, knowing Robbie would go for a sensitive spot. Would it be his face? Groin? Stomach?

Probably groin, Karl decided. That wouldn't leave any marks that his parents or teachers would see. Plus, Robbie would think it was funny.

Karl pressed his knees together, rolling away from Robbie and the others, trying not to give them a clear target.

The first kick hit him in the middle of the back, sending fireworks of pain exploding all along his body and radiating down his limbs.

It hurt—it hurt *so much,* but Karl knew this was just the beginning.

His body couldn't take it, seizing control away from him in its efforts to protect itself. Even though he knew it wasn't safe, even though he *knew* they wouldn't let him leave until they were finished, he tried to roll to his hands and knees so he could crawl away.

The next kick landed on his stomach, knocking the air out of his lungs and collapsing his legs from under him, leaving him coughing and gagging, struggling for air.

He couldn't take any more of this. He'd do anything to make it stop. How could he make it stop?

"Hey!" someone shouted, and at first Karl thought it was Robbie, trying to get a reaction out of him.

If he answered, would that make Robbie hurt him less? Or more?

"Hey, assholes, leave that kid alone!"

Wait. That wasn't Robbie's voice, or any of his gang's. This boy sounded older, his voice deeper.

And he was telling them to stop.

Chapter Thirty-Seven

Justin

The way I see it, I have a few options.

I can go to Wilson Bridge. But considering the only thing I can think to do there is jump off, no thanks.

I can continue looking for Stan. Go to the addresses of the people I couldn't reach this morning and see if I have more luck in person. But that would require me to go back into Mrs. Hanley's house and explain to her why I'm ripping a page out of her phone book, and that sounds only slightly more appealing than jumping off a bridge.

I can go to my grandparents' house. I'm not sure what this will accomplish, but considering the entire focus of my week—and maybe my life—is to save them, it probably can't hurt to talk to them face to face.

But for reasons I can't fully explain to myself, I really, *really* don't want to do that. Just the thought of actually looking them in the eyes makes me feel sick to my stomach. And since I know *they* didn't set the fire, I don't have a hard time convincing myself that there's no need for us to meet. Rose and I can do this whole investigation without me, Bill, and Veronica ever having to breathe the same air.

That leaves going to the high school and seeing if I can catch Rose after classes dismiss. As the only sort-of friend I have in this miserable town, that is the least horrible option, so I start in that direction.

Fortunately, the roads in Stone Lake haven't changed much in nearly four decades, so navigating my way to the school is easy. If I were driving, I'd take the four-lane road that circles around the outside of town, since cutting through the tiny downtown area of Stone Lake is a traffic nightmare. But since I'm walking, I pick the shorter route.

Anyway, that's how I find myself walking by the post office right as some kid is getting beaten up in the alley outside.

The kid is tiny, probably only about eight or nine years old, while the kids gleefully kicking him look like teenagers. Baby teenagers, sure, but still twice the size of the poor kid on the ground. Plus, there are three of them and only one of him. Sick little freaks.

Without thinking, I run at them, waving my arms. "Hey, assholes, leave that kid alone!"

Normally, I can't say I'm the type to rush into a fight to defend a stranger, but these kids are puny and their victim looks like he should still be riding a bike with training wheels, so it's kind of a no-brainer.

As I continue yelling threats and insults and whatever else comes to mind, the boys scatter, picking bikes up off the ground and pedaling away, throwing a few insults over their shoulders as they go. I can't tell if they're intended for me or for the kid on the ground, covered in dirt and blood.

Once it's just me and the kid alone in the alley, I realize I have no idea what to do next. The boy is sobbing, one arm still covering his head, the other held tight to his chest. It feels weirdly invasive to be here, like I'm trespassing on something private, but leaving seems worse.

A bike lies abandoned a little way down the alley, a thick branch caught in the spokes of one tire. More for something to do than anything else, I walk over to it and assess the damage. It seems to still be in decent shape—a lot better than its owner, anyway. I toss the stick aside and wheel the bike over to the kid, who's still turtled up on the ground.

"Is this your bike?"

He doesn't answer, and after spending an awkward few seconds just standing there, I lean the bike against a brick wall and kneel down beside him. "You okay, dude?"

In response, he emits a kind of sad little whine, like a dog who's been locked in a hot car. His hair is the same color as the dirt that streaks his face and clothes, and the holes in the knees of his jeans and the elbow of his shirt all reveal ragged scrapes leaking fresh blood. Up close, I realize he may be older than I previously thought.

"They're gone, if that's what you're worried about. It's just you and me. And I'm not gonna hurt you."

At that, he finally opens his eyes, his lashes wet with tears. Slowly, he pushes himself upright, still cradling one arm to his chest, and I see that his wrist is red and beginning to swell. He sniffs, wiping his nose on the cuff of his shirt, leaving a smear of red across his face. I don't even think he realizes he's bleeding.

He blinks up at me, looking bewildered, but flinches away when I reach out my hand to help him up. "I'm fine," he mutters, not meeting my eyes.

"Okay." He's clearly not fine, but I get wanting to pretend he is. "What's your name?"

"Karl."

"I'm Justin. Can I help you get home? Where do you live?"

He looks me up and down. "I don't know you," he announces, saying it like an accusation.

"I'm from out of town," I say, giving him the same lie we've been giving everyone else. "I'm visiting a friend."

"What friend?"

"Rose Yin."

I can tell her name means something to him, as his shoulders relax just a little. "I know her."

Hoping that means he might trust me, I try again. "What's your phone number? I can call your parents." I gesture toward the pay phone in front of the post office. It's been an adjustment, not having a phone in my pocket all the time, but I think I've got a couple of quarters.

"Don't call them!" he yells, his voice suddenly panicked. Then he adds, almost in a whisper, "They can't know."

"Okay." I rack my brain, trying to think of what to do. I'm the last one to force him to go to his parents if he doesn't want to—experience tells me that involving parents can often create more problems than solutions—but I can't just leave this kid here with a mangled bike and a possibly broken wrist.

"You want to come with me?" I suggest, pointing back in the direction I just came from. "I'm staying just a few blocks from here. We can probably find some ice for that wrist."

To my relief, Karl nods. I help him to his feet, then go retrieve his bike. He's in no condition to push it, so I do.

"What grade are you in?" I say as we walk. I don't actually care, but I know if I were him, the last thing I'd want to talk about is what just happened, or the boys who were chasing him. And small talk feels less awkward than walking in silence.

"Seventh."

"At, uh, Stone Lake Middle?" I almost called it Warren Middle; the middle and high schools share a campus, so when the name of one changed, so did the other.

He nods. "I hate it there."

"It gets better," I say automatically, parroting the same words that I've heard repeated over and over by well-meaning adults and overly earnest social media campaigns—only to realize after I've said it that I'm in a unique position to know it's all a lie. The future isn't better than this. The future is a mess.

Not for the first time, I ask myself why I'm so eager to get back there. Is there anything good waiting for me in 2023? Or am I running toward my own destruction, simply because it's familiar?

I don't have an answer, and the lack of knowing scares me. But what can I do? The future may suck, but I know I don't belong here. Maybe I don't belong anywhere.

"Are you in high school?" he asks.

"Technically."

"What's that mean?"

"It means I'm enrolled, but I'm not currently attending."

"Why not?"

"Because no one's making me."

He laughs at that. "I wish no one would make *me*," he says wistfully.

"Careful what you wish for," I say, smiling humorlessly to myself. "School doesn't seem so bad compared to some of the alternatives."

He wrinkles his nose. "*I* can't think of anything worse than school."

"Sure you can. I mean, wouldn't you rather be in school than . . ." I think for a minute. Probably not a great idea to finish that sentence with *stuck in the wrong time period*. "Inspecting manure?"

"What's manure?"

"Animal poop."

Karl laughs. "That's not a job."

"It totally is. Some people get out of bed every morning to go inspect poop." Thanks, YouTube, for that horrifying nugget of knowledge.

"*Why?*"

"Some people use it for, like, gardening and stuff."

Karl's eyes get wide. "So when everything smells bad after the gardeners come, that's because they used *poop?*"

I shrug. "Maybe."

"Gross." Karl laughs, looking delighted.

We spend the next few minutes coming up with more jobs worse than school: sewer cleaner, maggot farmer, and the person who cleans vomit off roller coasters all make the cut, until it seems like Karl has mostly put the incident in the alley behind him. He becomes more animated as we walk, moving on to talk about his favorite comic book (*Spider-Man*) and movie (*E.T.*). I get the impression that this is a kid

213

without many—or possibly *any*—friends, and that he doesn't get the opportunity to talk about the stuff he likes with an actual human being very often. I don't weigh in much, but just nodding along and adding the occasional *oh wow* seems to be enough for him.

He's so absorbed in what he's talking about that he doesn't even seem to be aware of his surroundings until I turn his bike into Mrs. Hanley's driveway. He freezes on the sidewalk, his eyes suddenly wide as his gaze jumps between the house and the burned garage, the police tape lightly flapping in the breeze.

"Come on," I say, nodding toward the house. "This is where I'm staying."

"I—I just remembered I have to go help my mom with something," Karl stammers, edging backward on the sidewalk. His round face is pale.

"Hey, it's fine," I say, trying to sound more reassuring than annoyed. "Let's just get some ice for your wrist."

"That's okay," he says, already turning away from me. "It actually doesn't hurt that bad."

He's clearly lying; his wrist is obviously swollen and turning an ugly shade of purple. He'll be lucky if he hasn't broken it.

"But—"

"Thanks for your help!" he calls as he runs away, his voice already fading into the sound of his sneakers smacking the sidewalk.

I'm so surprised by Karl's abrupt departure that it takes me a second to realize I've still got his bike. I call after him, but either he doesn't hear me or he just doesn't care, as he sprints back up the street, running like he's being pursued by something horrible only he can see.

Chapter Thirty-Eight

ROSE

"But . . . I don't understand," Rose said, her head swiveling between her father and Diane as they sat across the table from her, wearing matching unyielding expressions. "He didn't do anything wrong."

"He lied to the police, honey," Diane said, her eyes skirting briefly to her husband before jumping back to Rose.

"You can see why we're concerned," her father added.

"That was just a misunderstanding," Rose said.

"How did Deputy Gibson misunderstand?" Diane asked. "Did he or did he not say he was your cousin?"

"*I* said that, not him," Rose said. "And just because that officer was being really mean. I thought if I said we were related, he'd be more likely to leave us alone."

"Then show us the letters," her father said.

Rose stared at him blankly.

"The letters he wrote to you," her father clarified. "You told Deputy Gibson he was your cousin because you were scared, but he's really your pen pal, right? Which means you have letters from him. Go get them and show them to us."

"They're—they're private," Rose stammered, her heart racing.

Her father frowned. "I thought I raised you better than to lie to us."

"I'm not—"

He held up a hand, cutting her off. "Do not make this worse, Rose."

"We just want the truth," Diane added.

Rose's mind spun frantically. She couldn't think of anything to say. She couldn't tell them the truth, but she couldn't lie either.

"He didn't have anywhere else to go," she said finally. "I wanted to help him. Isn't that why you're running for mayor? To help people?"

"That's different."

"No, it isn't. You told us that you saw a need and wanted to do something about it," Rose argued. "Well, so did I. I met someone who needed help, and I helped him. He didn't hurt anyone. He didn't break any laws. He just needed help."

"If he needs help, there are ways we can help him," Diane said. "There are programs—"

"He doesn't need a *program*."

"Or there is a wonderful homeless ministry down at—"

"He's not homeless either. You don't understand!"

"We're trying to understand, Rose, but you still haven't given us any—"

"If you would just believe me that I know what I'm doing—"

"*Rose,*" her father cut in sharply, "stop interrupting your mother."

"She is *not* my mother."

She regretted the words as soon as they came out of her mouth. For six years, Diane had packed her lunches, kissed her scrapes, attended her parent-teacher conferences. She'd held her hair back when she had the flu and wiped her tears when she had nightmares. No, she wasn't her mom. But she was the closest thing she had.

Still, she couldn't bring herself to take it back. Not when Diane and her father were about to ruin everything.

Her father looked as though he'd been slapped. Diane swallowed, patting his hand, her head bobbing in a slow, rhythmic nod. "You're right," she said eventually, still patting Rose's dad's hand as if it were the only way she could make her mouth form words. "I told you I would never try to replace your mother, Rose, and I still mean that. But I do love you like you're my own, even if that's not how you think of me."

"*My* mom would trust me."

"*Rose!*"

Her father was suddenly on his feet, his fingers spread on the table as if to anchor himself in place. Rose glared back, knowing she'd gone too far but refusing to be the one to back down first.

Diane rose slowly, holding up a hand to her husband, keeping control of the conversation. "Perhaps that's true," she said in a low voice, her dark eyes locked on Rose's, unblinking. "But here are the facts. We did not know that this boy existed until this week. So either you just met him, or you've known him for a while and have been keeping him secret. Either way, you have shown a serious lack of judgment. Since he's been in town, you have *both* lied to the police. Deputy Gibson has not made that information public yet, but he *could*. And after this morning's story, we can only guess what the press would do with it. But even if the press were not a concern, your safety is, and the fact remains that we do not know the first thing about this boy. So no, your actions have not engendered a lot of *trust*." She spit out the word *trust* like it was rancid. "You are not to see that boy again. Is that clear?"

Her voice had lost its conciliatory tone and was now as sharp as broken glass. Still, Rose couldn't help but throw herself against its edges. "You can't do that. Without me, he won't have *anyone*."

Diane shook her head, pursing her lips. "Baby girl, he's going to have to sort that out for himself, because you are *done* with that boy. And if you have an ounce of sense left in that head of yours, you will not say another word right now unless it's *yes, ma'am*. You hear me?"

Rose's fists clenched in her lap, but she nodded, knowing the battle was lost. "Yes, ma'am."

"Good girl," Diane said, straightening up and placing a hand on her husband's back. "C'mon, let's go put Emmie to bed."

Jim's gaze lingered on Rose, but she looked away, quietly seething. He didn't understand. Neither of them did.

God didn't send people back in time for no reason. Or even for small reasons. At least, she didn't think that was how God worked. Which meant that her parents had just thrown a giant wrench into a cosmic plan.

Assuming, of course, it was God. And not just some random freak accident, like Justin thought.

She tried to push the thought away, but it refused to leave, clawing back into her mind like a stubborn cat. Where *was* God in all this? He flings a boy back decades in time to change the universe and then what? Can't stop his only ally from getting grounded? What sort of all-powerful, all-knowing Creator was he, if he could be tripped up by a couple of paranoid parents?

Rose sighed, digging her nails into her palms as she searched for a solution. They'd said she couldn't see Justin, but they hadn't said anything about who *else* she could talk to. She could still look into McMillain, and talk to Noah and Mrs. Hanley. Maybe she would go visit Mrs. Hanley with Noah, and Justin would just happen to be there . . .

She never lied to her parents. She wasn't a kid who sneaked out or made up stories. She always colored within the lines.

But at least two lives depended on her now. So maybe it was time to get a little messy.

WEDNESDAY

Chapter Thirty-Nine

ROSE

As had become her routine, Rose watched the buses pull out of the lot from her table in the school library, her chin propped in her hand as she gazed out the window. In front of her was her calculus textbook, open to the page of problems her teacher had assigned for homework that evening, although the notebook paper in front of her remained blank. Rose sighed, chewing the side of her pencil absently as she stared at the yellow parade carrying her classmates to their homes, then shifted in her seat to bend over her paper.

School ended each day at two forty-five, and it typically took the buses around ten minutes to clear the lot, which left her with another hour to kill before Mr. McMillain wrapped up his shift. Rose had learned better than to try to talk to him before he was finished. When she'd tried, she had managed to squeeze only a collective dozen words from him, and half of them were, "Kid, can't you see I'm working?"

She worked through a few problems, the sound of graphite scratching onto paper mixing with the low whispers of the study group meeting at a neighboring table and the soft clacking of Mrs. Fein, the school librarian, sorting through book returns at her desk.

Every few minutes, Rose's eyes would flit to the clock over the library entrance, willing the long hand to complete another slow revolution. The librarian smiled as she caught Rose's wandering gaze. Rose had always liked Mrs. Fein, but she'd been even warmer toward Rose and Lisa this semester than before. Rose suspected it was due to Diane's campaign; librarians, she'd found, tended to have one another's backs.

She frowned a little thinking about the campaign, and how she was no longer allowed to see Justin because of it. The truth was, Diane and her dad were so busy lately, they probably wouldn't even *notice* if she followed their stupid rule. They just trusted that she'd obey them because she always did. She couldn't remember ever disregarding a rule they'd given her, much less a punishment.

But there was a first time for everything.

Finally, Rose heard what she'd been waiting for: the low rumble of the janitorial cart being pushed past the library entrance. Rose shoved her textbook and half-finished homework back into her bag, then hurried out into the hallway, giving Mrs. Fein a little wave as she passed her desk.

Just as she'd hoped, Mr. McMillain was in the midst of pushing the cart back into the supply closet, his keys jangling from his hip. She stood behind him, waiting for him to finish locking the door. His shoulders rose and fell in a sigh, before he spoke without turning around.

"Back again, Walters?"

He'd started calling her Walters after the female *20/20* cohost, thanks to her incessant questioning during the first day she'd stayed after school. That time, she'd pretended that she'd left something behind in a locked classroom. The second, she'd claimed to be waiting for a ride after missing her bus. But he'd quickly seen through both ruses, and she eventually admitted that things were awkward at home and she was avoiding her family.

She was surprised to find that it felt like the truth.

"Just finishing up my homework." Rose tipped a shoulder to show him her backpack, as if the presence of her schoolbooks proved the validity of her claim. "I was on my way out."

"Sure you were," Mr. McMillain said, shaking his head slightly as he began to walk toward the exit. He was young, probably in his midtwenties, with dark-brown skin, close-cropped black hair, and a narrow whisper of a mustache over his top lip.

Rose hurried to keep up with his long strides. He was tall and thin, with a slightly stretched appearance, as if his skin had come a size too small for his skeleton but was trying its best to fit anyway.

"So halfway to the weekend, yay!" Rose waved her arms in a weak display of enthusiasm, cringing inwardly at her own awkwardness.

Mr. McMillain gave her an odd look but didn't break his stride. "Yup. Love those Wednesdays."

Rose cleared her throat. "So do you have any big plans this weekend?"

He stopped walking and frowned, narrowing his eyes. "What's your deal, Walters?"

"What?"

"Why do you care what I'm doing this weekend?"

"Just making conversation," she said, her cheeks growing hot. It's not like she could just come out and ask him if he planned on burning down the school.

"Why? Why do you keep showing up here?"

"I told you, things at home are—"

"Naw, I don't buy that." He took a wary step away from her. "You've got friends, Walters; I've seen y'all during the day. If you don't want to go home, you could hang out with one of them. Yet here you are, again. What do you want?"

"I, uh," Rose stammered, searching for something she could say that would defuse his suspicion while leaving the door open for her to continue to ask questions. It turned out that trying to casually suss out the weekend routine and possible arsonous tendencies of a total stranger—and an adult, at that—was no easy task. Yet if she was going to figure out if McMillain had anything to do with the school fire, that was exactly what she had to do. "Do you know Mrs. Hanley?" she blurted out.

He raised an eyebrow. "Who?"

"Her grandkids go to school here. Her garage burned down over the summer?"

"Oh yeah, I think I heard something about that."

"It happened in July. July 11."

"Okay . . ." McMillain gave her an odd look, like she'd suddenly started reciting Shakespeare out of the blue.

"Do you, um, remember what you were doing on July 11?"

Something flickered behind McMillain's eyes, his expression going from bemused to guarded. "Look," he said, keeping his head down as he began to walk toward the exit again, moving faster now. "I don't know what your deal is, but I don't need your kind of trouble. I've got enough of my own. Go find someone else to interrogate."

"Wait!" Rose hurried to keep up with him, following him out of the school into the bright afternoon sunlight. She could feel her window closing with every step. Asking about Mrs. Hanley's fire had been a mistake. She needed to switch tactics, or she was going to lose him entirely. "I'm sorry," she said, her mind racing. "I'm just—uh—I'm just trying to help out my mom."

He paused, frowning. "You're what?"

"My stepmom, actually, Diane Lewis-Yin? She's running for mayor."

"Yeah, I've seen her signs." McMillain still looked suspicious, but at least he wasn't running away from her anymore. "She's the Black lady, right?"

"Yes! And, um, well, there's this debate she's participating in this weekend, and we're trying to get more supporters to attend so—"

"How do you know I'm a supporter?"

"Uh . . ." Rose's cheeks grow hot. "I-I don't," she said, stumbling over her words. "I just . . . hoped . . ."

He gave a small chuckle but didn't seem amused. "Chill out, Walters. Truth is, I don't know much about her, but I guess I probably like her more than that other guy. Doesn't matter, though; I'm not voting."

He started walking toward the parking lot again, the conversation apparently over in his eyes, but Rose hurried after him, determined to keep him talking. "Why not?"

He didn't bother to look at her. "Gotta work."

"But we have the day off school."

"*You* have the day off," he said with a shrug.

"Oh." It had never occurred to her to think about what the custodial staff did when school wasn't in session. "There are other ways to vote, though. There's absentee voting, or—"

"Not really interested in that, Walters."

"Well, maybe if you come to the debate, you'll change your mind."

"Unlikely."

"Why?"

He cut her a nervous glance. "I really don't think that's any of your business." They had reached his car by then. He paused after he unlocked the door, his keys dangling from his hand. "Look, Walters, you're a nice kid, and maybe you really are just trying to help your mama, but I think you need to find something else to do with yourself after school from now on."

"But—"

"See you around, Walters," he said, keeping his eyes down as he got into his car and slammed the door.

Rose stood outside the driver's side window, desperately searching for something to say that might salvage the situation, but her mind remained stubbornly blank. She continued to stand frozen in place as he peeled out of the parking lot, leaving her clouded in the lingering smell of exhaust and failure.

She bit her lip, trying to think if she had learned anything useful at all in her half week of sleuthing. From what she could tell, he took his job seriously and did it well, so she had no idea what was going to lead to him getting fired in a couple days. She hadn't seen anything particularly suspicious in the janitor's closet, but it wasn't like he was going to keep evidence of his darkest impulses at school, so that didn't mean much. And perhaps the most important piece of the puzzle—his alibi for the weekend, or lack thereof—was still a frustrating question mark.

He didn't *seem* like the type of person to burn down a school. But then again, it wasn't like she knew a lot of other arsonists to compare him to. And she had no idea how he might react to getting fired. If she was honest, even after days of waiting after school and trying to get him to talk to her, she still didn't really know Michael McMillain at all.

She didn't think he'd do it. But she couldn't be sure he wouldn't. Which meant she basically knew nothing.

Chapter Forty

JUSTIN

After my weird run-in with Karl yesterday, I don't have much of a desire to go to the school. But my other options haven't gotten more appealing since yesterday either. Since Mrs. Hanley doesn't want me loafing around all day, I walked out to Wilson Bridge this morning. But once again, I couldn't think of anything to really *do* other than jump off, and I'm still not there yet.

Instead, I pace slowly up and down the sidewalk that lines the bridge, staring out over the gently rippling water. I can't fully explain the pull the bridge has for me. Anytime I try to think about what I should be doing here in 1985, it's the first image that pops into my head. Even though it has nothing to do with the fire, it still feels important somehow. Maybe because it's the place I would've died, if I hadn't come here instead. For others, it's just a bridge, but for me, it's a place of death and life and mystery.

I don't think it can answer any of the questions I have about why I'm here, or how to get back. It's just the only place I feel calm. Like myself. Probably because this was the last place I was ever really *me*, before I was here, in a place where I was never even supposed to exist.

I probably could've stayed there, listening to the sounds of the river all day. But in the early afternoon, the sky begins to rumble menacingly, so I head back to Mrs. Hanley's house, grab an umbrella, and decide to walk over to Rose's house to wait for her to come home from school.

Her family seemed to buy her weak story about me being her pen pal, so they won't be completely confused if I show up on her doorstep, but that still doesn't mean I want to invite myself into her living room to hang out with her parents for an hour until she gets home. So I walk slowly around her block, hunched under my umbrella as the rain first peppers, then pummels the thin fabric, counting down the minutes until she'll be home.

I miss Netflix. And texting.

Not really social media, though. It's funny, how quickly my anxious brain has adapted to the relative quiet of 1985. To not knowing everything that's happening, everywhere, all the time. If not for the whole being-stuck-in-the-wrong-decade thing, I think I'd actually find it kind of soothing.

On my fourth orbit around the block, I slow as a car pulls into the driveway. A young woman gets out, wearing a deep-purple skirt suit with wide padded shoulders, her blonde hair curled into a fluffy cloud around her face. I stop and stare as she opens the back door of the car, umbrella outstretched in her free hand, and pulls out a chubby baby.

"Mom?" I hear myself say under my breath, even though it can't be her. The woman looks so much like her, though, that for a moment, my lungs forget how to move air in and out of my body. They just hold it, frozen along with the rest of me, at the sight of this woman who has Lissa Warren etched in every curve and angle of her face.

She notices me standing on the sidewalk staring, and tilts her head curiously, hiking the baby up in her arms. "Hello?"

"Hi," I say, waving sheepishly.

"Can I help you?" Her voice is friendly, but her smile is reserved. Probably wondering if I'm some sort of pervert.

"No, that's okay. I'm just waiting for my friend to get home from school."

"Who's your friend?"

I clear my throat. "Uh, Rose Yin?"

Something odd flickers behind her eyes. "Oh, you must be the pen pal. Justin, right?"

"She told you?"

"Mm-hmm," she says, adjusting the baby again to unlock the front door. "Please, come inside."

"That's okay," I say, pointing up at my umbrella. "I'm fine out here."

"Don't be ridiculous. It's pouring."

Reluctantly, I follow her inside, feeling incredibly out of place. Rose's house is warm and soft, with rich wood furniture and framed family photos on every surface. I follow the woman, who has to be Veronica, Rose's stepmother's campaign manager, and also my grandmother, into the wood-paneled living room. I sit on a plump sofa covered in a blue floral pattern and accept a can of Tab from Veronica, who plops her daughter—my mom—down on the brown shag carpet in front of me.

"No one is home yet, but Diane should be here any minute," Veronica says, hanging her coat on a rack by the front door. "She had an errand to run after work, but it shouldn't take long. So it's just us until she gets here. Oh, I'm so sorry, I forgot to introduce myself. Veronica Warren," she says, sticking her hand out to shake. "And this is Millie." She indicates the baby, who is toddling precariously around the room, arms outstretched to touch everything in her path.

Millie. That's right. I'd forgotten that her name would be different here, even though Rose already told me. I wonder if Mom's grandparents changed the nickname on purpose when they took her in, or if they simply never knew what her own parents called her.

"Nice to meet you." My hands feel numb, and I don't think it's from the cold can of soda.

"So," Veronica says, sitting across from me in a plaid armchair and folding her hands on her crossed knees. "Tell me about yourself." She stares at me intently with blue eyes just a shade darker than my mom's.

"Um," I say, feeling like I'm being interrogated. My hands are clammy; I wipe them on my jeans. "Well, I'm Justin. I'm eighteen."

"Have you graduated yet?"

"No."

"Then why aren't you in school?"

Wow. I am *not* prepared for this. "I'm homeschooled," I blurt out in a moment of brilliance. "So my breaks are . . . different."

"Hmm," Veronica says, and I can practically *see* her make a mental note. "And you decided to use your break from school to come visit Rose."

"Yeah."

"Why?"

A tiny laugh escapes involuntarily. Is my entire family allergic to subtlety? I always figured that Mom was a drunk, and I had my neurodivergent brain, and Stan was, well, *Stan*, but Veronica is not any of those things—I think—yet here she is blasting away with her shotgun full of questions. Maybe it's genetic. "I just . . . wanted to see her," I say.

"But you knew we all had the debate this weekend, correct?"

I nod, swallowing. My mind was not meant to race this fast. It already has a cramp. "I didn't think it would be a problem."

"But—"

Just then, the front door swings open. Literally anyone could walk in and I'd be happy to see them. Dave. Stan. The cast of *Jersey Shore*. Anyone who can provide a temporary reprieve from this barrage of questions from this woman who looks and sounds like my mom but is *not* my mom and is sending me into full-on existential-crisis mode.

But then I see who it is, and suddenly, it's worse.

"Look who it is, sweetheart!" Veronica coos to the baby, who lets out a squeal of joy. "It's your daddy!"

"Sorry I'm late, hon," the rain-splattered man says breathlessly. "I'll get her out of your hair in just a sec." His hair is shorter than mine, his shoulders a little broader, his nose a little wider, but this is undoubtedly him. Bill. My grandfather. He's not a mirror image of me, but more like

230

what a sketch artist would draw if someone described me. Same sharp chin, same pale eyes, same weirdly small ears.

For a second, I forget to breathe. Can they see it? How can they not?

But apparently they don't, because Bill looks at me like a stranger, sticking out his hand. "Oh, hello, I don't think we've met. I'm Bill Warren. I'm the counselor over at the school."

"Justin," I croak, my mouth dry as I shake his hand. I take a swig of Tab and immediately choke, and for a few seconds, the only sound in the room is my gross hacking.

"What brings you here this afternoon, Justin?" Bill asks as Veronica continues to size me up.

"Justin is Rose's friend," she supplies, watching me through slightly narrowed eyes.

"Oh, wonderful," Bill says, completely unfazed. Is he used to his wife being this intense all the time, or is he just oblivious? He tilts his head at me. "Do you go to the high school? I try to make it a point to meet with every student, but I'm so sorry, I don't think I've seen you before."

"Homeschooled," I manage to rasp out.

"Ah." His expression clears, and he turns to Millie, who is concentrating fiercely on the zipper of her diaper bag, her little brow furrowed as she tries to pinch the tab between her stubby fingers. "Well, Millie girl, what do you say we get out of Mommy's hair so she can work, hmm?"

Millie shakes her head, sending her wispy curls bouncing, but Bill scoops her up anyway, causing her to emit a howl of protest. "I'll see you at home," Bill says, planting a quick kiss on Veronica's lips before hefting the diaper bag onto his shoulder and turning to me. The only indication that he's aware of his daughter's screeching is his slightly raised voice when he says, "Lovely to meet you, Justin."

Watching the three of them together—a *family*—I feel like my veins have been filled with battery acid. The way Bill and Veronica look at each other, look at Millie . . . no one has ever looked at me like that. Not even my mom.

Maybe she never learned how. She never knew her parents, never heard her father call her *Millie girl* or her mother call her *sweetheart*. Before they could teach her how to love the way they did, they were burned alive, their flesh melting off their bones and fusing with the cheap school carpet.

I didn't want to meet these people. I was okay with this ludicrous mission to save my grandparents being something theoretical, which could work or not work, when the only one who would bear any of the consequences either way would be me.

Now, faced with two living, breathing people—one of whom looks just like my mom, while the other looks like me—it's like my entire reality shatters again. I was never convinced that preventing this fire was my ticket back home anyway, but now, failing at this task won't simply mean that dead people will stay dead.

It will mean this woman right here, who just invited me in from the rain and served me a Tab and shook my hand, will die. And her husband, who makes it a point to know the face of every kid in his school, will die beside her. And their baby, who reached out with a chubby hand to steady herself on my knee as she passed by on her way to the diaper bag, will be an orphan.

And instead of a thing that just *is*, like it's been my whole life, it will be my fault.

Chapter Forty-One

Rose

Voices floated out of the living room when she opened the front door. Rose peered around the entryway to find Justin sitting stiffly on the couch beside Veronica, looking a bit dazed. The blood drained from Rose's face as she looked from Justin to her mother.

"Oh. Hello." The last thing Rose had expected after her blowout with her parents the day before was to find Justin in her house after school.

"Oh, hi, honey!" Diane said, rising from the blue velour armchair in the corner, her voice alarmingly chipper. "How was your day?"

"Fine . . . What's going on?"

"Oh, that's on me," Veronica said with a too-broad smile. "I saw your friend outside, and I invited him in until you got home. He's just been keeping us company while we work."

Justin caught Rose's eye and shrugged, his expression a little lost, like he had no idea how he'd wound up in this situation.

Diane pulled Rose in for a hug, leaning close to her ear. "So I suppose you didn't get an opportunity to tell him about our little talk last night?" Diane whispered. All the cheeriness had vanished from her voice.

Rose shook her head. "I didn't know he'd come over here, I promise," she replied, her heart racing. It was one thing to defy her parents' orders; it was another thing to do it right in front of them.

"You'll tell him *now*," Diane ordered.

"In front of everyone?"

"You can go outside, but only for a few minutes. Then I expect to see you back in here. *Alone.*" Her tone left no room for negotiation.

Rose nodded, swallowing thickly, then pulled out of the hug and gave Diane a tight smile. "Let's, uh, go outside," she said to Justin, who practically jumped from the couch.

"Don't go far," Diane said, a warning in her voice.

"We won't."

As soon as he was within reach, Rose all but dragged Justin through the front door after her. The rain had slowed to a lazy drizzle, light enough to walk without an umbrella. Rose would rather get a little damp than risk Diane and Veronica overhearing them.

"Didn't expect to see you in my living room," Rose said by way of apology as they headed down the sidewalk, elbows bumping as they shared the narrow strip of cement.

"Yeah, I noticed," Justin said. "Your face was like you found Freddy Krueger sitting on your couch."

"Sorry," she said, driving her elbow into his side on purpose this time. "I thought you might, I don't know, say something."

"What, 'Greetings, Mrs. Future Mayor? I am a future boy from the future, here to convince your daughter to help me save the future'? Yes, because that's a thing I'm just *dying* to share with people."

"I didn't mean you'd say it like *that*," Rose laughed.

"Trust me, I'm not planning to say it like *anything*."

Rose paused, playing his words back over again in her head. "Future mayor? So does that mean she wins?"

He was quiet for a few seconds. "I thought you didn't want to know anything about the future."

That wasn't entirely true. That had been his proposed rule, which he'd justified by giving her a long speech about maintaining the Space Pie Conundrum or something like that. Or maybe it was Pi Conundrum? That would probably make more sense, although she had still never heard of whatever equation he was referring to. She'd just agreed to it because he'd been so adamant.

Still, now she second-guessed herself, questioning whether she really wanted to know. If Justin said Diane lost, what could she do with that information? Agonize over whether to say anything to her family for a few more days? But if the answer was that she won, would it really gain her anything? Or would she spend the next few days second-guessing every little thing she did, wondering if she might be throwing the entire Space Pi Conundrum off its axis?

"No," she said finally, deflating a little. "I don't want to know."

He blew out a long breath. "Okay, good. I mean, that's probably safest, you know? Wouldn't want to upset the space-time continuum."

Space-time continuum. That was it.

"But seriously, why were you at my house? I thought I was supposed to meet you at Mrs. Hanley's in half an hour." She'd planned on telling Diane she was going to study with Noah.

"She got tired of me hanging around the house, so I decided to come kill time over here. I was just going to walk around the block, but then my gran—*Veronica* saw me and made me come inside."

"Sorry about that," Rose said. "I, um, well, there's a . . . thing I should probably tell you."

"Okay . . ."

"I've kind of been . . . forbidden from spending time with you."

His eyebrows shot up. "How'd you manage that?"

"That police officer that stopped us the first night? I guess he told Veronica that I told him you were my cousin."

"Wait. Are we not cousins?"

Rose moved to elbow him again, but he skipped out of reach. "So now Diane's pissed at me for lying to the police, and I'm grounded from seeing you."

"Well, bang-up job you're doing being grounded."

"She told me I could see you just long enough to tell you I can't see you."

He snorted. "Can Diane be my mom, too? I like her style."

A smile tugged at Rose's mouth. "Cousins isn't enough for you? Now you want to be siblings?"

"I'd be a great brother."

"Would you?"

"Yup. I'd forge your dad's signature on progress reports and intimidate your boyfriends."

"Ha. What boyfriends?" Rose said dryly.

Justin caught her eye, raising an eyebrow. "Really? No one?"

She shook her head. "Nope. No one's ever been interested."

"I highly doubt *that's* true," he said. He glanced at her, then quickly looked away, smiling slightly as he kicked a stray pebble down the sidewalk.

Heat rushed to Rose's face, and she dropped her gaze, too, hoping he didn't notice the sudden redness in her cheeks. What had he meant by *that*? She played it over and over in her brain, committing everything about it to memory.

But this wasn't why he was here, and they didn't have much more time before she'd have to go inside. She cleared her throat, pivoting back to their investigation. "Anyway, I don't know how much I'll be able to help you now, with my parents on my case."

Justin sighed, his breath clouding in the humid fall air. "Well, then I'm screwed," he said flatly.

"Don't say that."

"Rose, this plan was a long shot to begin with. But without your help? It's impossible."

"No, it isn't."

"I have *zero* leads, Rose. Zero. Other than this McMillain guy—"

"I don't think it's McMillain."

He gave a humorless chuckle. "Great. You and Stan, both."

"But I'm also not sure it's *not* McMillain."

"What is that supposed to mean?"

"It's just a feeling. Like there's something we're missing, something that has nothing to do with him. Not that we can know for sure based on feelings. But . . . I don't know. I just don't think he'd do this."

Justin snorted. "You're not superstitious, but you are a little stitious."

"I'm . . . what? That's not a word."

"I know; that's the joke."

"What joke?"

"It's an *Office* reference."

"What office? What are you talking about?"

At that, he stopped walking, doubling over with laughter.

"What is so *funny?*"

"It's nothing," he said, his shoulders still shaking. "It's just . . . this is so messed up. You know? Like, we're trying to solve a crime based mostly on *feelings*, because all the actual *clues* are in the future. So this is already pretty much impossible, right? But now I'm even more screwed, because the only friend I have here got grounded. *Grounded.* From solving a murder. That hasn't happened. But we know it's *going* to happen, because I'm from the *future.* All the shows and movies and songs I know, all the technology I'm used to—none of it exists yet. You are old enough to be my *grandmother.* Isn't that just . . . just piss-your-pants hilarious?"

He let out another peal of high-pitched laughter. Rose looked around, alarmed. What would any of her neighbors think if they looked out their windows to see her consoling some sort of hysterical boy on the sidewalk? Or worse, what would *Diane* think? "Justin," she whispered, shaking his arm slightly. *"Justin."*

"What?"

"Get a grip."

"That's what she said." Justin dissolved into another fit of giggles.

Rose looped her arm through his and half coaxed, half dragged him down the sidewalk until finally he stopped howling with laughter and straightened up to walk like a normal person. Rose kept her arm linked through his, just in case.

"What's going on?" she hissed at him under her breath. She was starting to get worried.

"It's just . . . I met Veronica and Bill today," he said, a touch of awe in his voice. "And Millie. The baby. They call her Millie."

"Yeah," Rose said softly. "I know."

"And you know how, what we're doing, it was all kind of theoretical before? 'Maybe I'm here for this reason, and here's how we test it.' Like a scientific experiment, right?"

She nodded.

"But it's *not* an experiment, because if I know something bad is coming and don't stop it, it's kind of my fault. Not stopping it is, in a way, like making it happen."

"I don't think I'd go that fa—"

"If I don't save them, they're going to die. And that baby is going to lose her parents." His voice cracked as he ran his hands through his hair, causing it to stick out in all directions. "She's going to grow up to have no one and nothing, except me, and I'm going to *leave* her when I'm fucking *eighteen*, which will be *my* fault, because *I couldn't save her parents*. Do you have any idea how messed up that is?"

He laughed again, but less wildly this time, his head dropping back to look up at the gray sky. She was worried he might tumble into fits of hysteria again, but instead his laughter trailed into silence. "What if we can't do it?"

She shrugged. "We have to."

"Just because we want something doesn't mean we can make it happen. Trust me, if that were a thing, I'd know." He cut his eyes toward her, then down to the ground, running a hand through his hair.

"But this isn't like winning the lottery or wishing someone would like you. Something in the universe rearranged the very fabric of its

238

being in order for you to be right here, right now. It has to work, because the entire cosmos tied itself into a knot to make it happen."

"Or maybe it just tripped and fell, and I am just like . . . a cosmic penny that accidentally rolled into the sewer."

"Well, if that's the case, then nothing we do matters anyway, so we may as well act as if it *does* matter, right?" She barely understood what she'd just said, but he seemed to follow along.

"Okay, fine," he agreed, "but we could still get it wrong. If, by your logic, the cosmos is *really* invested in making sure this goes right, then that has to mean there's some chance of getting it wrong. Otherwise the stakes would be nonexistent, in which case, why put in all that effort?"

"I'm not trying to talk hypothetical logic problems here," she said, coming to a stop and turning to face him with her hands on her hips. "It has to work, because . . . it *has* to. Okay?"

She couldn't figure out how to put it into better words, but she knew at her core that the answer was vital to who she was, what she believed. After all, if there was no greater meaning to someone traveling through *time*, then how was she supposed to believe that there was any sort of meaning to the rest of it? To her mom, to Lisa's dad, to Mrs. Hanley's fire. To herself.

Maybe this was what that feeling had been, the night she first met Justin on the bridge. Maybe what she'd thought was certainty was really just a deep longing to matter.

"I'm not talking hypotheticals either," he said, looking at her with a gaze like icy flames. "I just realized a few minutes ago that in a couple days, I'm either going to succeed or I'm going to murder two people. There's no other option." He hung his head. "And I still have no idea how to succeed."

Moving almost by instinct, she reached out and grabbed his hand. "We're going to figure it out," she said. "I promise."

He didn't pull away, but instead tightened his fingers around hers. They were thin and lightly calloused in her hand, his skin warm. She resisted the urge to trace her thumb over his knuckles, debating whether it was less awkward to drop his hand or keep holding it. Unbidden, her brain replayed his words from a few minutes ago, when she said no one was interested in being her boyfriend.

I highly doubt that's *true.*

"I haven't made any progress either," he said, not meeting her eyes. It took her a second to remember what they were talking about: their investigation, right.

Not where *her* brain was, still dwelling on her hypothetical boyfriends.

"I couldn't find Stan," Justin said. "I couldn't find any clues at the bridge. Mrs. Hanley doesn't know anything." He shrugged, his hand slipping out of hers in the process. The motion was almost casual enough for her to convince herself that maybe he hadn't even noticed the hand-holding, which must have felt electric only to her. "Oh, but I did accidentally take some kid's bike?"

"You did what?"

"It's a long story," he said. "I don't know his last name, but his first name's Karl, he's in seventh grade, he has an older sister—oh, I think she knows you—"

"I know who it is." Rose sighed. How on earth had Justin ended up with Karl Derrin's bike?

"Great, then you can help me get it back to him. I mean, what else am I doing with a kid-size bike?"

"I'm sure you could get creative."

He looked at her with a raised eyebrow. "How creative do you mean?"

She nudged him playfully, her cheeks growing hot. "I was thinking like a science experiment, you pervert."

"*I'm* the pervert? You're the one talking about all the dirty bike stuff."

She laughed, dropping her head so that her hair covered her rapidly warming cheeks. She knew if she looked in a mirror, they'd be glowing red. When she glanced up at him, he was grinning at her, his smile stretching across his typically dour face like the sun breaking through the clouds.

Something did a little flip in her stomach, but she ignored it. If everything went right, he'd be here only a few more days. And then she'd never see him again.

She cleared her throat, forcing her mind to stay focused. "I'll ask Noah to return it. He's got a bike rack on his mom's car already. I can ask him whenever he gets home."

"Great. So I'll see you back at Mrs. Hanley's?"

Rose nodded. "Now you'd better leave before Diane chases you off with a broom."

"She didn't strike me as the chase-you-with-a-broom type."

"She's the do-what-I-say-or-else type."

"I've always kind of liked that type," he said with a wink. "Come to think of it, you kind of *resemble* that type . . ."

"Go," she laughed, shoving his arm.

He gave her a salute, then obediently turned and ambled down the sidewalk, back toward Mrs. Hanley's house. "Never mind, nothing bossy about you at *all*," he called over his shoulder, tossing her one last grin.

She smiled as she watched him go, pretending there wasn't a part of her that wished he could stay.

Chapter Forty-Two

LISA

"Now isn't a good time," Mrs. Derrin said coolly when she answered the door. "You should have called first."

"I'm sorry," Lisa said. Charlene's mother had opened the door only a crack, and was filling the space with her body, barring Lisa's view inside. "But since I'm here, can I just talk to Charlene for a minute? I won't take up much of her time, I promise."

Mrs. Derrin sighed, her long artificial eyelashes fluttering theatrically as she rolled her eyes. "All right. Wait here." She shut the door in Lisa's face, leaving her standing on the wraparound porch.

Lisa took a deep breath, trying to calm the frustration that surged inside her every time she had to interact with Charlene's parents. They had never been the biggest fans of Charlene and Lisa's friendship, and their frostiness had seemed to double when Lisa's mom announced her campaign for mayor. Although they'd never come out and said it, Lisa got the impression that they were offended at the very idea of a Black woman running for office. They seemed to think Gibson deserved to be mayor simply because he wanted it.

That was one of the many reasons why she and Charlene preferred to hang out at Lisa's house. Or at least they had, until everything changed on Saturday. Since then, Charlene hadn't exactly been ignoring her—she still sat with their group at lunch—but there was a distance between them now that hadn't been there before. She definitely wasn't coming over to Lisa's house anymore.

Which was why Lisa was now standing at the door of the Derrins' enormous mansion, being treated like a servant trying to crash the ball.

The front door opened again, and Charlene came out, still in the aqua blazer that she'd worn to school. "I'll just be a few minutes, Mom," she said to her mother, who hovered behind her in the doorway, her bright-red lips puckered like she'd licked a lemon.

Mrs. Derrin exhaled a disapproving puff of air through her nose, but turned and went back inside, shutting the door behind her just a smidge too hard.

Charlene's eyes briefly met Lisa's, then slid off, down to the white-washed boards of the porch. With one hand, she absently fiddled with the thin gold chain around her neck, which held the locket Lisa had given her for her birthday that summer. At least she hadn't taken it off. "Why are you here?" she asked quietly.

Lisa forced a smile, trying not to let the ache in her heart bleed through. "I have something for you."

At that, Charlene's eyes bounced up to her face, her expression wary. "Lisa, I told you, I don't think—"

"Just look at it, okay?" Lisa's heart pounded. Her idea had seemed so romantic when it first occurred to her, but now she wondered if it was just stupid.

She gestured to the white wicker patio set beside the front door, where a perfectly round head of iceberg lettuce sat in the center of the table.

Charlene blinked at it for a second, her mouth twitching. Did she love it? Hate it?

Oh no. Did she not even *get* it?

"It's lettuce," Lisa said, feeling ridiculous. This was such a bad idea.

"I can see that."

Lisa cleared her throat. Bad idea or not, she was in it now. No choice but to keep moving forward. "Can we talk? Just for a minute?"

Charlene nodded, and they sat across from each other at the table, the lettuce between them. Lisa imagined she could see a face in the leaves, taunting her. "Um, so I've been thinking a lot about what you said on Saturday," she started. She risked reaching across the table and lightly touching the back of Charlene's hand with her fingers. Charlene stiffened, but didn't pull away. "And I miss you, Char," Lisa said.

Charlene nodded, her chin trembling slightly. "Me too," she whispered. She didn't look at Lisa, but stared intently at the head of lettuce, as if it might hold the answers they were both looking for.

"I want to fix us."

"I do, too. It's just—" Charlene sighed, pulling her hands away and dropping them into her lap. "Everything I said on Saturday is still true. I know you're not ready to tell everyone yet, and that's fine. I'm not either. You know how my parents would be."

"Mine too," Lisa agreed. "My mom actually told me yesterday that she doesn't want me to be seen in public with you anymore until after the election."

Charlene nodded. "Mine said the same thing."

"Yesterday?"

"No, a while ago."

"Oh." That was good, right? That Charlene had kept hanging out with her even after her parents had told her not to? Then again, maybe it wasn't, since Charlene hadn't bothered to tell her.

Still, Lisa opted for the optimistic interpretation. "Well, thanks for not ditching me."

Charlene looked at her hands uncomfortably, giving a little shrug. Here, there weren't any of the distractions of school that could help them fake normalcy. Lisa hadn't been prepared for just how awkward it would be. And that damned lettuce kept making faces at her.

Why had she led with the lettuce?

"But I can't be with you while you're with someone else," Charlene continued. "Even if it's not real for you, it's real for him. It's too much for me, Lees."

"I know." Lisa took a deep breath, her heart racing. "That's what I came to talk to you about. I've been thinking about it a lot, and I think . . . I think I'm ready to tell him."

Charlene's eyes widened. "Really?"

Lisa swallowed, nodding. "Yeah. I don't know if I'm ready for anyone else to know. But I think he'd keep it a secret if I asked him. And you're right. It's not fair to keep letting him wait for me when I know I'm not going to feel what he wants me to feel."

Charlene bit her lip, her hand going to her necklace. "Are you going to tell him about me?"

"That's why I came over here today. I wanted to ask what you wanted me to do. I can just tell him about me, if you'd be more comfortable with that."

Lisa watched her closely, trying to tell what she was thinking. She knew—or at least thought she knew—that she could trust Shawn not to tell anyone, but just because *she* believed that didn't mean Charlene would. Would Lisa be telling Shawn the story of an *I*, or the story of a *we*?

Whatever Charlene decided, Lisa hoped desperately that they were still a *we*.

Charlene kept her eyes downcast, focused on a spot on the table as she pulled the locket back and forth on its chain. Lisa wanted to move around to the other side of the table, slide her chair alongside Charlene's so she could put her arms around her, but she held herself back. Charlene had been the one to put up the boundary between them; only she could take it down.

"Okay," Charlene said at last. "You can tell him about me. About us."

Lisa couldn't keep the grin from her face. "Really?"

Charlene nodded. "And then I guess we'll go from there." She met Lisa's eyes, a smile creeping back onto her own face, and placed one of her hands on the table, palm up. Lisa reached across and took it in both of hers, squeezing tight.

She'd missed being able to touch her. Her heart attempted to fly out of her chest.

"I like the lettuce," Charlene said, rubbing her thumb over Lisa's fingers.

Lisa laughed. "I'm so sorry. I thought it would be romantic."

"It *is* romantic," Charlene said, picking it up with her free hand and admiring it. "I hereby name it Casanova."

Lisa snorted. "You're giving it a *name?*"

"Seems like it should have one, if it's going to be our mascot."

"It's going to be a stinky mascot in a couple weeks."

"Well, there's no rule that a mascot can't also be a salad." Charlene grinned, and even though it had been only a few days since they'd broken up, Lisa drank in her smile like water in a desert.

"When will you talk to him?" Charlene asked.

Lisa cleared her throat, her stomach suddenly tight. She'd been so excited about making things right with Charlene that for a second, she'd forgotten all about her conversation with Shawn. "Tomorrow, I think," she said. "I feel like I need to tell him in person."

"That makes sense. Call me after?"

"You bet." The relief Lisa felt to know that Charlene would be waiting for her on the other side was almost enough to drown out her dread.

Chapter Forty-Three

SHAWN

"I just don't understand girls."

Shawn whipped the stone out of his hand and watched it skip along the surface of the river before disappearing into the gurgling current. He'd originally thought it might be nice to have a picnic by the river with Lisa after school today, but when she was busy—again—he'd asked Noah. They'd skipped the picnic, though, opting to skip stones instead.

Shawn dropped his gaze to the bank and began searching for another one, nudging the rocks with the toe of his shoe.

"We were great all last year. And then summer arrives, and suddenly she'll barely even let me touch her. She spends all her time with Charlene now. I hardly even see her outside of school." He found another rock, tossed it. Two skips. "I get that they're best friends, but I'm her boyfriend. Shouldn't that mean she wants to spend time with *me*?"

"I don't know, man," Noah said. He sat on the bank, making some sort of rock sculpture, his sweatshirt balled underneath him as a cushion. "Maybe she's just not feeling it anymore."

"I should never have told her I loved her. I think that's what screwed it all up."

"*Do* you love her?"

Shawn sighed, flinging another rock into the water as he thought about Noah's question. Only one skip that time.

That conversation, when he told her he loved her, had been his big mistake. He *knew* she wouldn't say it back, but he'd foolishly said it anyway, hoping maybe she'd prove him wrong. Of course she hadn't. She'd been pulling away for months by then, always wanting to go out to big, crowded places rather than be alone with him.

But at the end of the school year, after finals, he'd thought they were better. For a while, it even felt like they were a team again. Like he might actually be the most important person in her world, the way she was in his. So he said it.

Stupid, stupid, stupid.

Even now, though, he couldn't help it. Even if she'd never love him, she was the only girl he'd ever brought home who had seen his life as it was, seen *him* for who he was. Not the carefully shellacked vision his father tried to drag into reality, but reality as it actually was.

"Yeah," Shawn admitted. "I think I do."

"Well, then, it was good that you told her. Even if she doesn't feel the same way."

Shawn looked sideways at Noah. "You're one to talk."

Noah furrowed his brow, making his glasses slip a little down his nose. He pushed them back up with one finger. "What do you mean? Steph and I have only been together for a couple months. It's way too early to—"

"Not Steph." Shawn raised his eyebrows meaningfully at Noah's confused expression. "You can't pretend you don't know who I'm talking about."

"I really don't."

"Rose, dude. The girl you've been in love with since we were twelve."

Noah blinked at him, looking slightly stunned, then shook his head. "No way. She's my best friend, that's all."

"I think the only two people who believe that are you and her."

Noah returned his attention to his rock creation, creating a lopsided tower. "Anyway," he said, not meeting Shawn's eyes, "I think you just need to talk to Lisa. Ask her what's up."

"But what if she really isn't into me anymore? What if she wants to break up?"

"Then you'll know." Noah frowned as he misplaced a rock and half the tower collapsed with a clatter. He examined it for a second, then kicked out his foot to knock the rest of it down. "I mean, it would suck, but do you really want to keep dating a girl who isn't into you? Like, who is that good for?"

"Yeah. I know." Shawn found a perfectly flat, smooth stone, and slung it into the river. Four skips. His best yet. "I just . . . no one knows me like that, you know?"

"Dude, I do *not* need to know about how well Lisa 'knows' you," Noah said, waving his hands like he was wafting away a bad odor.

"Not like that." Shawn laughed, although his voice came out a little strained. The truth was, Lisa didn't know him at *all* in the way Noah was implying. They'd had plenty of opportunities, but he could tell she wasn't super into it, so they'd never gone very far. Eventually, he'd stopped trying. "I mean I've told her stuff no one else knows. About me. About my life. I've always been able to talk to her in a way I haven't been able to talk to anyone else. If we broke up . . ."

Noah came to stand beside him, scooping up a rock on his way and flinging it out across the water. Five skips. Damn. "You want to talk to me about it?"

Shawn quirked one side of his mouth. "You asking to be my girlfriend?"

Noah shoved his shoulder, sending Shawn hopping a few steps down the bank. "Seriously, dude, if there's something on your mind, we can talk about it. She's not your shrink; she's your girlfriend. You can't keep dating her just so you can use her for free therapy."

"You're not my shrink either."

"No, but I *am* your friend. And I'm volunteering."

249

Shawn was quiet for a minute. "I don't know, dude. I'm kind of messed up." He looked at Noah, wondering how much he could say. The only reason Lisa knew about his dad was because she'd witnessed some of it firsthand. But Gabe Rothman was great at charming people. It was why people were happy to invite him into their homes to install their lights and rewire their televisions. They didn't know who he was, beneath the surface.

Maybe that's why his mom had gone to a new town, leaving Shawn and his father and their whole life behind. Maybe no one here would have understood why she'd leave someone like Gabe. Maybe leaving them both was the only way she wouldn't feel crazy.

There were some days when Shawn thought he understood what it must have been like for her. When there was nothing he wouldn't do to get away.

Noah shrugged. "Everyone's kind of messed up. But that's what friends are for, right? To be there through the mess? Honestly, if you want to talk, we can talk."

Shawn sighed. He spotted another good skipping stone on the bank, flat and smooth. He picked it up, hefting its weight in his hand. "Not yet," he decided. "But thanks. Seriously."

"Well, the offer stands."

"Same for you." Shawn turned the rock over and over in his hands. It really was perfect.

He tossed it out into the water and turned away before he could see it start to skip, walking up the bank toward Noah's mom's car. "C'mon. Let's go home."

Chapter Forty-Four

JUSTIN

A couple of hours after I leave Rose's house and she obediently returns to her "grounding," Noah's car pulls into Mrs. Hanley's driveway, with Rose in the passenger seat. It's still weird to me how people will just disappear for hours in 1985, and you'll have no idea what they're doing until they resurface. Rose told me she'd talk to Noah when he got home, and now here they are. No text to say they're on their way, no social media check-in with their location. Just there, then nothing, then here.

When they arrive, driving a station wagon with a bike rack strapped to the back as promised, Noah seems less than thrilled to see me standing in the driveway. He climbs out of the driver's side and looks at me. "So I hear you stole Karl Derrin's bike."

Rose rolls her eyes, but I can't help but notice how she seems happier in his presence. More relaxed. Like the sun coming out from behind a cloud. My stomach does a strange little flip. "Not exactly," I say. "You okay taking it back?"

"Of course."

As Noah loads the bike up onto the rack, he grins at Rose and says in a weirdly high-pitched voice, "I don't *wanna* go that fast!"

Rose dissolves into giggles, then pitches her voice up several octaves, too. "Like a *snake?*"

I look from one to the other, totally lost as Rose doubles over in laughter, and Noah's shoulders shake as he secures the bike to the rack with bright-orange straps. Briefly, he wraps the end of a strap around his own waist and makes a comically horrified expression, stretching his eyes and mouth wide, making them both laugh even harder.

Rose catches me staring at them in confusion, and manages to gasp out, "Noah's sister, when his mom first got this rack—"

"She was eight," Noah jumps in, lifting his glasses to wipe away tears.

"She asked what it was for, and Noah told her—"

"I said it was for bikes."

"But she thought that meant while people were *riding* the bikes—"

"And that one person got tied to the rack, and then the rest would get tied on behind them—"

"And they'd all get pulled by the car like a train. She called it a bike snake."

"And she got *so scared* that we were going to make her ride the bike snake—"

"Which you *totally* let her believe—"

"I mean, *I* was not going to be the one to kill the dream of the bike snake!"

By now they are laughing so hard it's all I can do to follow their tag-team story. I wonder if they realize that they talk like two people sharing one voice. Like when one of them breathes in, it's the other who breathes out.

Is she different, with him? Brighter, sharper, more vibrant?

Or is this who she is all the time when she's not with me? Is relying on her to help me fix all my absurd problems . . . dimming her somehow?

I'm still stuck in my own head, wondering if I somehow make the people around me worse, when I hear Rose say something about me riding with the two of them, which I find moderately alarming, considering I am nowhere near fluent in this language of shared inside jokes that they speak.

Noah looks at me, his keys dangling from one finger as the laughter fades from his eyes. He's still smiling, but the truth couldn't be plainer if it were tattooed across his face: I'm a third wheel, and he planned for only two. "Actually," he says, "since you know the way there, Rose, why don't you two just go and I'll head home? My mom won't mind if you drive her car."

"Are you sure?" Rose asks, and there it is. The dimming.

"Yeah. I told Steph I'd call her when I was done over here anyway," Noah says, hands in his pockets. He doesn't meet her eyes.

"Oh," Rose says, her expression flickering for just a second before she gives him a tight smile. "Sure, yeah, of course."

She's quiet during the drive over. I feel like there's obviously something going on with her and Noah, but I don't know the right way to ask about it, or if it's even any of my business. So I don't say anything either.

When we pull into the Derrins' driveway, I get the weirdest sense of déjà vu. The house looks largely the same as it did when I was here last weekend, thirty-eight years in the future. The landscaping is different, of course, and I think some of the trim may be a different color, but otherwise it looks just like it did the last time I watched it shrink in my rearview mirror as I drove away with Alyssa screaming at me to stop.

A few seconds after Rose parks in the wide driveway, the front door opens and a girl emerges from the house. She's pretty and petite, about our age, with a round face that looks like it should be selling bubble gum, and green eyes frosted in a shocking smear of bright-blue eye shadow. Her peach-colored shirt is about eight sizes too big, with the face of some dude who looks like he just escaped from *Jumanji* printed across the chest and something unintelligible scrawled in purple script down the sleeve, and her blonde hair is tightly curled into a frizzy halo that makes her look like she shoved her finger in an electric socket.

I have been stuck in 1985 for more than four days now, but I don't feel any closer to understanding any of its bizarre fashion choices.

"Hey," she says, looking at both of us and trying to hide her confusion at my presence. Her eyes settle on Rose. "I'm sorry, did we have plans or something?"

"No, Justin just noticed that Karl left his bike by the school, so we came here to drop it off," Rose says. She gestures toward me as I lift the bike off the rack. "Charlene, this is my friend Justin. My pen pal that I told you about. Justin, this is Charlene, Karl's sister."

Charlene sticks out her hand to shake, which seems a little formal, but I go with it. I expect her hand to be soft, given the swankiness of her house and the gentleness of her features, but her fingers are calloused and her grip is firm. Looking at her up close, it finally comes to me where I've seen her before: the family portrait, when I went inside to use the bathroom during the bonfire. She was in the one with Dave's grandparents. Which would make her Dave's aunt.

Poor girl.

"Is Lisa here?" Rose asks as I wheel the bike over to the garage and lean it against the outside of the house.

Charlene shakes her head. "No. Not today."

"Oh. Okay," Rose says. She's smiling, but something about it feels odd. Like she's posing.

I want to jump back in the car, away from this decidedly weird vibe. This whole thing is uncomfortable, but since this is my first time meeting Charlene, I'm not sure if I'm the one causing it, or if this is always the dynamic between the two of them.

Rose and Charlene make stilted small talk for another minute or two before Charlene puts us all out of our misery by saying she has to get back to her homework. We say an awkward goodbye and get back in the car, while Charlene returns to the house.

My seat belt somehow gets all twisted, and as I turn in my seat to untangle it, a slight motion at the top of the driveway catches my eye. It's Karl, his wrist now bandaged, half-hidden in the bushes at the edge of the woods. He startles when he notices me, his eyes going wide. For a second, we just stare at each other, while Rose starts the car. Then he turns and disappears into the trees like he was never there.

Chapter Forty-Five

ROSE

"I've met him before."

"Who?" Rose said, looking over her shoulder as she backed up, turning around in the Derrins' skating rink–size front drive.

"Karl. In my time."

Rose blinked at Justin, his words taking a second to fully register. Was he willing to talk about the future now? Despite the risk to the space-time continuum?

Since he was the one bringing it up, she had to admit, she was curious. "Oh yeah?" she said, approaching this new subject carefully, like a deer she hoped to touch before it bounded back into the trees.

He nodded, his eyes far off. "I didn't recognize him at first, but after seeing his house again . . ." He laughed, a little incredulously. "He kicked me out of that house, the night of the bonfire. That's actually why I was on the bridge that night. If not for Karl, I wouldn't be here."

"Why'd he kick you out?"

"Because his son hates me."

"Karl has a son?"

Justin nodded. "He's the worst." He shook his head, seeming dazed as Rose steered away from the house and down the winding drive. "It's so weird, you know? You have this idea about why things are the way they are, but you never really *think* about it. Like, I go to school every day in a building named after my dead grandparents, and I know they died in a fire at the school, but I never actually thought about them as, like, *people* people, with personalities and responsibilities and, I don't know, smells and stuff."

Rose raised an eyebrow as she turned onto Wilson Bridge. "Smells?"

Justin shrugged, fidgeting a bit in his seat. "You know, like how some people have certain smells—you can't necessarily describe them, but as soon as you smell their scent, you know exactly who it is? Like Mrs. Hanley. Or like you, even."

"I *smell?*"

"It's a good smell. Like something sweet but also . . ." He trailed off, his cheeks turning slightly pink as he ran a hand over the back of his neck. "Nope, I just said that I can't describe it and I'm sticking to that. Just trust me, it's a good smell."

Rose wished more than anything that she could bend her head down and check to see if she smelled just then, and if it actually *was* a good smell or if he was just being polite, but there was no way to do that inconspicuously.

But if she was being honest, she knew exactly what he was talking about. Noah had a warm, slightly spicy scent to him, subtle but always present. She'd recognize it anywhere.

Justin's scent was cooler, crisper. Different, but still pleasant. She fought a sudden strong urge to lean toward him and inhale deeply, but even though he was the one who had brought up smells in the first place, that seemed a little too strange.

"I never really thought about it before, how people smell," Justin mused. He tilted his head sideways, considering. "Honestly, this whole time smells different."

"How can *time* smell different?"

"It just does. I can't explain it. Different chemicals in the air, I guess. Also, you guys smoke a *lot.*"

"I don't smoke!"

"I didn't mean you *personally*."

"So, wait, people don't smoke in the future?"

"No, they do, but you can't smoke in public anymore. Although some places will still let you vape."

"Vape?"

He shook his head. "Never mind. It's dumb."

They sat in silence for a minute, Rose kneading her hands on the steering wheel, her mind brimming with questions. This was the most he'd talked about the future since they'd met, and as much as she didn't want to overwhelm him, she was hungry for more answers. She cleared her throat. "What else is different? You don't have to tell me any of the big stuff, like who's president or anything—"

Justin snorted. "Depends on who you ask."

"Huh?"

"Trust me, you really don't want to know."

Well, now she kind of *did* want to know, but she'd said she wasn't asking, so she didn't push the subject. "Tell me something little. Something that won't matter if I know it in advance."

He ran a hand through his hair, staring out the window. "Pluto isn't a planet anymore."

"*What?* What happened to Pluto?"

He shrugged. "Nothing. Just got . . . demoted or something."

"Demoted to what?"

Another shrug. "No idea."

"Wow." She caught herself looking up at the sky, like she might be able to spot Pluto in the distance.

"Friendship is different, in the future," he said softly, pulling her attention away from the clouds.

Rose wrinkled her brows, confused. "How can *friendship* be different?"

"It's hard to explain. It's like . . . in the future, we're all constantly in touch with each other through our phones and social media and stuff"—he'd explained to her that first night, when he kept asking to use her phone, what *smartphones* were, which, no matter how hard she tried to wrap her brain around them, still sounded like something out of science fiction—"but no one is ever really fully . . . *there*. Present. In the moment. We're all always multitasking, and no one ever really gives anyone else their full attention. Not like people do here."

Rose laughed humorlessly, thinking of Lisa, Noah—even her dad and Diane. "People don't really do that here either."

"Sure they do." He looked at her, his blue eyes piercing. "You do. You've given me your full attention since the minute I got here." He held her gaze a second longer, then looked away, flushing slightly as he ran a hand through his hair.

Her mouth went dry, heat trickling down the back of her neck. She cleared her throat a few times, unable to dislodge the lump that had suddenly appeared. "I just wish I was actually helping," she said softly.

He sighed, dropping his head back against the headrest. "At least you're trying," he said, glancing at her sideways. "That's more than I can say for most of the people in my life. If I even have a life anymore."

"Not that it's doing any good. The fire is this weekend, and we're no closer to answers than we were on Saturday."

"Yeah." Justin pressed the heels of his hands into his eyes and groaned. "Maybe it's time we just admit it's hopeless and give up."

Rose shook her head, even though she knew he couldn't see her with his hands still over his eyes. "Don't say that." She was quiet for a minute, debating with herself, then decided it couldn't hurt to tell him. "You remember the night we met?"

Justin nodded. "Wow, that was only a few days ago, wasn't it? Feels like longer."

"Did you ever wonder why I lied for you? And why I believed you so fast?"

"I just figured you were nuts."

Rose smiled nervously, wondering if she was about to confirm that theory. "Something inside me just *knew*, right away, that you were telling the truth. Even if it didn't make any sense, or even seem possible. I couldn't explain it, but I knew I was supposed to help you."

"So what you're saying is you *were* nuts."

"It was like the way you know to hold your breath when you go underwater," Rose said. "No one has to explain it to you. You just *know*. And that feeling hasn't gone away. I still think you're here for a reason. We just . . . haven't found it yet."

"We're kind of running out of time to find it."

"We'll know it when we see it." She didn't know how she was still so sure. She just was.

They rode in silence the rest of the way back. At some point, Justin dropped his hands, but his eyes stayed closed. Rose wondered if he'd fallen asleep.

She pulled into Mrs. Hanley's driveway and turned off the engine, her lips pursed in thought. Yellow police tape still crisscrossed the burned-out husk of the garage, which gaped in front of them like a yawning black mouth. "Let's go check for clues again."

Justin finally opened his eyes. His leg jiggled up and down, causing the whole front seat to vibrate. "Rose, we've been over every inch of that place. We've read the police file and talked to Noah and Mrs. Hanley. And you were *there*, and didn't even notice anything. We're not going to find anything. This is impossible. It was stupid to think we could change anything."

"No, it's not. There *has* to be something we missed."

"Why?" He looked at her with narrowed eyes, his voice edged in anger.

"Because people don't just fall back through time, Justin," she said, repeating the same argument she kept having with herself, over and over. "There's got to be a reason for it, and if you're here for a reason, then finding that reason can't be impossible."

"Why, though? Why does there *have* to be a reason? Why could it not just be, I don't know, like a random fold in space-time or something?"

"Because that's not real! That's science fiction!"

"*Time travel* is science fiction! It's not supposed to be real either!" He balled his hands in his hair, pulling at the ends, making it stick out wildly in all directions. "Maybe I was right that very first night, and I'm dead or in a coma. That's the most real explanation of any of them."

"Stop saying that. You're not dead."

"Why not? I drove off a bridge. I *should* be dead. And this is my own personal hell."

A knife twisted deep inside Rose's chest, but she gave him a small shrug, trying to hide how much it hurt. "If you're dead, then I'm not real, and I *am* real."

"How do you know? Maybe my subconscious made you up."

"Don't be ridiculous."

"Says the girl helping a time traveler solve murders that haven't happened yet." He sighed, staring toward the garage. "You think I *like* the possibility that I'm dead? That I get some sort of kick out of the idea that I will never get back to my life? That I might never see Aly—the people I care about ever again?" He crossed his arms tightly over his chest, his eyes darting uneasily to Rose, then back out the window.

"That's why it's important to focus on what you can do right now. So you don't get stuck thinking about stuff like that."

"But I might already *be* stuck. That's my point. I may not be able to do anything at all, and pretending that I can—believing that there's some sort of higher purpose to all this—*that's* the sort of thinking that will really mess me up. Maybe all this time we've been spending trying to fix things, I should've been working on accepting things the way they are instead."

Rose shook her head, a sense of defiant urgency building inside her. "No, don't you see? If you give up now, they'll die—"

"They're already dead, Rose! They've been dead my whole life." Justin's irritation seemed to be rising to meet her own, his voice growing harsher with each retort.

"They're not dead *now*. Weren't you telling me like two hours ago that not saving them is the same as killing them yourself? How can you suddenly just be okay with letting the fire happen when—"

"I'm not *suddenly* anything. I'm just saying maybe we've been wrong all along, and none of this has anything to do with me. Maybe our biggest mistake was thinking we have any control over any of it."

"Unless—"

"No, not 'unless' anything. If I'm dead—"

"You're not dead!"

"—or dying or whatever, then all of this—you, the time travel, everything—is just some sort of construct that my brain created for some reason, maybe to help me accept the inevitable or maybe just randomly based on miscellaneous pieces of my subconscious."

"I am *not* a piece of your subconscious."

"Maybe *you* are the unhealthy part, keeping me in denial instead of accepting the reality that things are the way they are, and nothing I do is going to change that."

Rose shook her head, her face feeling hot. "So according to your theory, everything—the whole world—is all about you. *Your* life. *Your* friends. *Your* family."

"Not the actual world, but *this* world? Yeah, pretty much." He scrubbed a hand over his face, shaking his head. A muscle in his jaw twitched, like he was clenching his teeth.

Rage blurred Rose's vision, buzzing along her skin. "Well, I hate to burst your bubble, but I had a whole life here before you showed up, Justin, and it had *nothing* to do with you. I have friends, family, people I care about, and who care about me."

Justin made an exaggerated show of looking around. "Really? From where I sit, it seems like they don't care *that* much. You say Noah is your best friend, but he bailed on you today, and hasn't even been around the rest of the week. That Charlene girl barely said two words to you. You don't know where your sister *is* most of the time. And you tell me your parents grounded you, yet here you are. Honestly, it seems to me like you only exist to help me, except not really since we're not actually *doing* anything. You're barely even a *person* without me."

Hot tears pricked the backs of Rose's eyes. She blinked rapidly, refusing to let him see her cry. "Get out," she hissed through clenched teeth.

He hesitated a moment, seeming like he wanted to say something else, but then he just shrugged. "Fine."

He unfolded himself from the passenger seat, slamming the door so hard the whole car shook. Rose kept waiting for him to turn around, to take back what he'd said, but he disappeared into the house without glancing back.

Chapter Forty-Six

Rose

"Honey, Noah's here to see you," her father's voice called through her bedroom door. "Can I tell him he can come up?"

Rose lifted her head from the tear-flecked purple flowers of her bedspread and wiped her eyes. Of course Noah would pick *now* to come over. She glanced at herself in her dresser mirror, and the face looking back at her wasn't pretty. Puffy eyes; drippy, red-tipped nose; tangles of hair stuck to the sides of her face in a crusty glue of snot and tears. She sniffed, her voice coming out thick when she said, "Tell him I'm not here."

"He's in the kitchen."

Rose drew in a deep breath, blinking a few times as if that would magically deflate her swollen eyes. "All right," she said, defeated. "Give me a couple minutes, and then he can come up."

"Oh, also, I noticed earlier that the car is making a weird noise."

"Weirder than usual?" That car always sounded like it was on the verge of an asthma attack.

"Yeah. Going to get it checked out next week. Until then, just short distances, okay?"

"Fine," she agreed numbly. Not like she had any real reason to drive anywhere anyway. As Justin had so kindly pointed out, no one wanted to be around her.

After a trip to the bathroom to scrub the grossness off her face and drag a brush through her hair—still not good, but better, she decided—she returned to her room to find Noah standing in the middle of the floor, twisting his fingers around a stubby pencil.

She pointed to the pencil. "Here to take notes?"

He gave her a little half smile. "I was doing homework when I saw you drive up. Guess I just forgot to put it down. Um, do you have my mom's car keys?"

Of course. He was here for the keys. In her fog, she'd forgotten to return them. She picked them up from her nightstand, dropped them in his hand. "Sorry. Thanks for letting us borrow the car. See you later."

"I don't need to go right away."

"You don't have to stay. I know you've got better things to do."

"No, I don't." His face turned serious, and he straightened his shoulders. "Look, I know we haven't been exactly . . . *us* lately. But you know if something's wrong, you can talk to me."

Rose sighed, unable to meet his eyes. "It's really not a big deal."

"Is it that guy? Justin? Do I need to go beat him up?" Noah pounded his fist into his open palm, his eyes narrowed and his lower lip caught between his teeth in an exaggerated tough-guy expression.

Rose burst out laughing. "Like you'd ever hit anyone."

He shrugged, dropping the act with a grin. "Naw, I guess not. But I could deliver a strongly worded complaint."

"That's more like it."

The phone on her nightstand rang, but Rose ignored it. A second later, her dad's voice called from downstairs, "Rose! Phone!"

"Who is it?"

"Justin."

She hesitated for a second. "I'm not allowed to talk to him, remember?"

"Oh, right! I'll tell him," her dad said, oblivious.

Noah had been watching her closely, and now he took a step closer to her, causing her breath to catch in her chest. "Did he do something?

265

You can tell me if he did. I'm just . . . worried about you, Rosie." He got quiet toward the end, his eyes fixed on hers.

At that moment, Rose wanted to tell him everything. Not just about Justin and their fight and the impossible task they'd set for themselves, but about Lisa hiding something from her, about her conflicted thoughts about the campaign, about her jealousy toward Steph and her guilt about being jealous. She wanted to tell him that she wasn't just crying because it had hurt when Justin said that none of the people she cared about truly cared about her; she was crying because she was pretty sure he was right.

But she and Noah weren't like that anymore. He'd chosen Steph over her. Coming over tonight didn't mean he cared about her *specifically*, any more than Justin scooping Karl out of the street indicated any sort of strong emotional bond between the two of them. All it meant was that he was a decent person.

And that she was pathetic.

"I'm fine." She sniffed and crossed her arms, taking a step away from him. "You don't have to worry about me, Noah. You can go home."

"Why would you—did I do something wrong, Rose?"

She almost laughed. *You picked another girl.*

Instead of giving voice to that thought, she shrugged. "No. We're good."

"We don't *feel* good."

Another shrug.

Noah sighed. "Is this really how it's gonna be now, Rosie?" he said softly. He extended his hands toward her, palms up, pleading. "I miss you. I miss *us*."

Rose looked at him, studying his face intently. Did he mean it? She heard Justin's voice in her head. *Seems like they don't care that much.* Which voice could she believe? "I miss us, too," she said quietly.

"So talk to me. Tell me what's going on." Somehow, he'd gotten close enough that when he spoke, she could feel his breath brush her cheek. His eyes locked on hers, deep pools of dark brown. It was all she could do to keep from sinking.

"I just . . . don't know what to do," she said, her chest tight. Her voice sounded small, swallowed up by the heaviness of the air between them.

Noah's hands came up to grip her arms, his lips curled into a little smile. "Then explain the problem to me, and we'll figure it out together."

His hands were warm and sure against her skin, and she thought his eyes flicked down to her lips, just once, so quickly he may have simply blinked. She breathed in his scent, spicy and safe and familiar, wishing she could stay here in this moment forever. Just the two of them in the quiet, sharing the same space, breathing the same air. No Justin, no Steph, no families or friends or impossible problems to solve. Just her and her Noah.

But he's not mine.

She blinked, cold reality breaking over her like a wave. She could keep him here, unload all her doubts and uncertainties onto him as she had so many times before, knowing she could trust him to hold them gently. He would have the right words, the right reactions. He would know just what to say. He always did.

But he couldn't give her what she wanted. She knew it wasn't his fault, or something to be mad about. She knew he cared about her. But until she learned to be okay with what they were, it wasn't fair to either of them for her to lean on him the way she used to. Not when all she could think about were all the things they weren't.

Maybe, someday, they'd be an *us* again. But today, she wasn't ready.

She stepped back, away from his touch, and swallowed thickly. "I can't. I think this is something I just need to figure out on my own."

His face fell, his expression defeated. "So . . . you want me to go?" He didn't echo her steps this time, apparently unaffected by the gravity that tried to tug her toward him like insistent hands. The few feet between them may as well have been a chasm.

Rose bobbed her head up and down, and he moved toward the door, shoulders slightly slumped. Protests bubbled up inside her—*no, stay, talk to me, ask me what's going on, I'll tell you if you ask again*—but she clenched her jaw tight, trapping them behind her teeth.

Justin may think she was the voice of denial, but he was wrong. This was her accepting things as they were. Noah hadn't chosen her; he'd picked Steph. That was the reality they lived in. Time to actually live in it.

So she stayed silent as Noah turned his back on her and walked away.

Chapter Forty-Seven

JUSTIN

At dinner, Mrs. Hanley piles juicy slices of fried ham and creamy mashed potatoes onto my plate, ignoring my repeated insistences that I can't eat that much.

"You're too skinny," she proclaims for the hundredth time, adding a generous helping of greens beside my ham, and finishing off the plate with a thick slice of crispy cornbread. "Didn't your mama feed you back home?"

"My mom didn't really cook," I say, picking up my fork.

"Hmph," Mrs. Hanley grunts. She smacks the back of my hand with a serving spoon, leaving a splatter of potatoes on my skin. "Boy, put that fork down. You know we say grace in this house."

"Sorry." I start to lift my hand to my mouth to lick off the potatoes, but at a look from Mrs. Hanley, I wipe it on my napkin instead, then accept Mrs. Hanley's open hand. Her wrinkled fingers feel soft and fragile, but her grip is strong as iron.

When Rose first suggested that I stay with Noah's grandmother, I've got to admit, I wasn't thrilled about it. I'm not great at estimating the ages of the elderly—*old is old*, has always been the extent of my understanding—but by my best guess, Mrs. Hanley is in her seventies, and has been living on her own since her husband died earlier this year.

While I appreciated the free room and board, the geriatric roommate was decidedly less appealing.

But honestly, it turns out that Mrs. Hanley kind of rocks. She's funny and smart, and she's lived an incredible life, traveling on buses while her kids were in school to listen to speakers like Martin Luther King Jr. and Malcolm X, and writing letters and joining protests for issues like voting rights and the desegregation of schools.

She mentioned being in jail once, and when I expressed my surprise that she'd ever been arrested, she just gave me a sad smile and said, *Son, jail is just part of growing up for some of us.* But she didn't say any more after that, and as curious as I was, I haven't gotten up the courage to ask. I don't know if that makes me kind, or a coward.

It's simultaneously inspiring and depressing, hearing about Mrs. Hanley's experiences and knowing how much energy she's spent working for change. Alyssa is always attending these protests and rallies for gun control, racial justice, health care, climate change, you name it—I've even participated in a few walkouts at school myself, although I think most of us were just using it as an excuse to get out of class—but I've never really paid much attention to all that. I always figured that whatever happened, my life would probably stay pretty much the same. Alyssa says I'm missing the point, that it's not about me, but I just figured that she and I were wired differently. That she was built to care too much, and I wasn't, and that was fine.

Listening to Mrs. Hanley talk about the things she's lived through, though, I feel like I'm starting to get it. She thinks that Rose's stepmother's campaign for mayor is a sign of better things to come, but decades from now, people like her will still be protesting, getting arrested, getting killed—while fighting for many of the exact same causes. Too little has changed, probably because too many people like me are content to just sit on our asses and assume that everything will sort itself out. And if it doesn't, that's no big deal either, because we'll be fine either way.

If I ever make it back, I owe Alyssa an apology for being a lazy, privileged asshole.

Mrs. Hanley finishes saying grace, releases my hand, and I dig into my meal, trying not to think about all the ways the future is going to do its best to screw over this kind, determined woman. Every bite is amazing, and before I know it, I've polished off my whole plate and am going back for seconds. Mrs. Hanley chuckles to herself. "See, I told you it wasn't too much."

"Yeah, yeah." I grin, helping myself to another piece of cornbread.

"So," Mrs. Hanley says, her tone suddenly serious as she folds her hands in front of her plate, "tell me why you stomped in here tonight looking like someone just drowned your puppy."

My appetite shrinks to a pinpoint, but I stick a bite of ham in my mouth anyway, chewing slowly while I try to come up with an answer that isn't a lie. I've been lying to pretty much everyone except Rose since the moment I got here, but I try to lie to Mrs. Hanley as little as possible.

When I swallow, she's still patiently staring at me, and I haven't come up with anything good, so I opt for vague. "Rose and I had a fight."

"Ah." She leans back in her chair, moving her folded hands to her lap. "About what?"

I might have said that no one here cares about her and that she's barely even a person. "We just disagreed about this . . . project we're working on, and things got a little heated."

"Mm-hmm." She twists her mouth, making it clear that she knows there's more to the truth than that. "And what is this *project*, exactly? Does it have anything to do with why you suddenly showed up to visit your *pen pal* in Stone Lake without even letting her know you were coming?"

"I-I don't . . . ," I sputter, scrambling to come up with an answer that makes sense. Mrs. Hanley has never even hinted that she didn't buy my story, and every explanation I can think up to account for the holes in my tale would involve *massive* lies. I can't risk it; big lies mean more to keep track of, which means more opportunities to slip up.

271

But that leaves me with only one option, which might be even worse.

I flip a mental coin. And then decide—screw it.

"We're trying to figure out who burned down your garage, because we think that whoever it is will do it again, and that people will get hurt next time."

Mrs. Hanley raises an eyebrow. "And why do you think that?"

"Call it a premonition."

She purses her lips, considering me thoughtfully. I assume she's not buying it, but instead of calling me out, she asks, "So what was the disagreement?"

I sigh. What's that expression? In for a penny, in for a pound? "We've got a suspect, but neither of us know if he's the right suspect, and we don't know how to even begin figuring that out. We'd look for someone else, but we have no other leads. The police said it's a dead end, and you've already told us everything you remember from that day. We've got nothing to go on."

Mrs. Hanley pulls in a long breath and blows it out slowly. "Tell me about this premonition you say you received. How do you know it was real?"

That's one line I can't cross. She'll think I'm crazy and may not want a crazy person living in her house. I can't risk her throwing me out. "I just . . . know. I can't explain it."

"And this premonition is why you came to Stone Lake?"

"Rose thinks so."

"What do *you* think?"

I spread my hands, knowing I'm treading dangerously close to the edge, but unable to stop myself now. "I don't know. I was home, and then the next thing I knew, I was just . . . here. I didn't plan it. It just sort of happened. And then once I was here, I couldn't go back. Not until I figure this out." I shrug helplessly. "Except I'm failing miserably at that. And now Rose probably won't even talk to me anymore."

"Let her be the one to decide that." Mrs. Hanley rises from her chair, crossing to the counter. She opens a drawer. "In the meantime, I may be able to help you."

I blink, confused. "Really? How?"

"I didn't tell the police everything about that day. The day of the fire."

"You . . . what? Why?" My mind is spinning. Never in my wildest dreams did I imagine that Mrs. Hanley would've lied to the police.

"I had my reasons," she says, rummaging through the drawer. "But if the good Lord has called you to find the person who set that fire, who am I to stand in his way?"

I squirm uncomfortably in my chair. "I wouldn't say it's a calling, exactly—"

"In my experience, premonitions don't just happen. They are *given*." She finds whatever she's looking for, held tight in her hand, and walks back to me. She picks up my hand, pressing a small, uneven object into my palm. "I found this the day of the fire. I have an idea of what it might mean, but I'll let you draw your own conclusions."

I swallow, staring at my hand, my throat tight. "Mrs. Hanley, I appreciate this a lot, like, a *whole* lot, but . . . I feel like I should tell you, I'm not sure I even believe in God."

"That's all right, sugar," she says, patting me gently on the cheek. "Maybe he believes in you."

THURSDAY

Chapter Forty-Eight

Justin

I pace back and forth in front of Rose's house, waiting impatiently for her to get home from school. I tried calling her last night, after what Mrs. Hanley told me, but her dad wouldn't let me speak to her.

I shouldn't have been surprised. But I *have* to talk to her, which is why I'm waiting outside her house. I was prepared to wait for her outside the school, but her house was dark when I walked by, and I'm gambling on Rose beating her parents home. It'll be easier to corner her here than at school. She may hate me now, but it'll be much harder for her to avoid me if I'm standing right in front of her.

At least, I hope so.

When she finally arrives home, she's not alone. Noah glares at me from behind the wheel of his mom's car as he turns onto their street, Rose seated beside him. She won't meet my eyes as Noah parks in his driveway and I run around to the passenger side.

"Leave me alone, Justin," Rose mutters, trying to get past me as she climbs out of the car.

I block her, shuffling from side to side, arms out like we're on opposing basketball teams. "I need to talk to you."

"I don't *want* to talk to you. And you're not even supposed to be here."

"I know. I was a jerk yesterday, and I'm sorry," I say hurriedly. "But if you would just listen for a second—"

"What are you doing here?" Noah asks from the other side of the car, his expression dark.

"I have to talk to Rose."

"She doesn't want to talk to you."

I frown, wondering what this guy's deal is. I know he's got a girlfriend, although she's currently nowhere to be seen, and every time I see him around Rose, it's like he's confused about which girl he's actually dating.

"Not that it's any of your business," I say, "but this is important."

Noah crosses his arms, and I swear to God, he's *got* to be flexing, because his muscles strain against his shirtsleeves like they're trying to escape. Dude is trying to intimidate me, and it's pissing me off—and not just because my scrawny arms look like twigs, whether or not I'm flexing.

"Fine," he says, nodding slightly, like a bouncer granting me admission to a club. "Say whatever you gotta say."

I roll my eyes. "I'm not saying it in front of *you*."

He shrugs. "Suit yourself, but I'm not leaving." As he's been speaking, he's gradually been moving around the car closer to Rose, like he's caught in her gravity.

I try to catch Rose's eye, which is a feat considering she's trying her best not to look at me. "The thing is, it's kind of . . . private. It's about that *thing*," I say, raising my eyebrows in an attempt to convey that by *thing*, I actually mean *time travel*. "I found something. It might be exactly what we were looking for."

That grabs her attention. She finally looks at me, and I can see her curiosity warring with her desire to stay mad at me.

Curiosity wins. She touches Noah's arm lightly. "It's okay, Noah," she says. "You can go in."

He gapes incredulously at her. "But last night—"

"It's *fine*," she insists, "but thank you." She gives him a shy smile, leaving me wondering what the hell happened last night.

I tell myself that the tightness that twists through my chest is irritation, not jealousy.

Shaking his head, Noah steps around me toward his house, making a point to smack his shoulder into mine as he passes.

Once he's gone, I follow Rose to her house. The second the front door closes behind us, she turns to glare at me. "Well?"

I reach into my pocket, pulling out the object Mrs. Hanley gave me last night. It's a small Han Solo action figure, dirt caked into its tiny indentations, like it has been stomped into the ground.

Rose accepts it, turning it over in her hand, looking confused. "I don't get it."

"Mrs. Hanley found this on her lawn the night of the fire," I say, keeping my voice low since I don't know if anyone else is home. "She didn't tell the police about it because—"

"Because she didn't want to get a kid in trouble," she says, realization dawning in her eyes.

I nod, trying to hold in my excitement. "If we can figure out whose it is, even if he didn't have anything to do with the fire—"

"What makes you so sure it's a *he*?"

I frown at the toy in her hand. "I mean, I just assumed—"

"Girls can like *Star Wars*, too."

"I know that," I say, fighting the exasperation that tries to creep into my voice. "I just meant that it seemed most *likely* that it's a boy."

Rose shrugs. "I just think it doesn't do us any good to jump to conclusions."

"Fine," I say, rolling my eyes. "But anyway, even if he—*or she*—didn't have anything to do with the fire, maybe they saw something we can use."

Rose's head bobs slowly in agreement. "We can start with the kids who live on that street."

"Do you think it could really be a kid who sets the school fire?" I ask. I've been trying to wrap my mind around that idea since last night, that a kid might be the one responsible for murdering two people.

Rose looks at the figurine in her hand. "I don't know," she says, "but we've got two days to figure it out."

Chapter Forty-Nine

ROSE

The last door swung closed with a definitive *click*.

Sighing, Rose crossed the final name off her list, the thick black ink slashing away a bit more of her hope that Justin's discovery of the action figure actually meant something.

They'd spent the whole afternoon knocking on doors, working off a neighborhood directory that Mrs. Hanley kept in a kitchen drawer. Any house with kids went on their list, which turned out to be a *lot* of houses. They'd had to split up in order to get to them all, but their methods were the same.

Claiming they were working on a school project, they started out by asking whether anyone in the house liked *Star Wars*, and then whether they had any *Star Wars* action figures. After that, Rose had caught a few breaks, learning that a birthday party accounted for a bunch of the *Star Wars*–loving kids' whereabouts. There had also been a Girl Scouts meeting that day, along with a soccer game, which knocked another big chunk of names off her list.

Of the remaining kids, though, none of the alibis stuck out as being particularly suspect.

And the payoff for all her labor was . . . nothing. Even if they were right and the owner of the action figure had been there the day of the fire, there was no way to figure out who it was, unless Justin had had better luck than she did—which she doubted, since if he'd uncovered a lead, she assumed he would've found her and told her. Otherwise, with no additional ideas about where to look for the kid, they'd never identify them in time.

Shielding her eyes with one hand, Rose squinted toward the setting sun. Another day, nearly gone. When Justin had first shown up in her life, a week had seemed like plenty of time to change something. Now time was almost up, and they were no closer to solving the mystery of what was going to happen to Bill and Veronica Warren than they had been at the beginning.

I could quit, she thought. *Walk away and never look back.* She hadn't asked for any of this, and Justin certainly didn't *deserve* her help. He'd apologized for the way he treated her the day before only because he needed something from her. And while at first she'd been convinced that her path had intersected with Justin's for a reason—that they were somehow destined to solve this problem together, saving lives and changing the future for the better—now she wondered if she'd just been fooling herself this whole time.

Maybe Justin was right. Maybe they couldn't actually change anything. Maybe this whole thing had been a waste of time.

Or maybe he was wrong about everything, including—especially—the time travel. Maybe there wasn't going to be a fire at all. Maybe he was just delusional.

Her mind kept churning over maybes as she walked slowly back to Mrs. Hanley's house, where they'd agreed to meet after they'd finished up their lists. If Justin was wrong about everything, then there was no point to any of this. She could just walk away, and it wouldn't matter.

She tried to make herself believe it. A big part of her wanted him to be wrong, so that this could all be over. He could disappear, and she'd never have to think about him again.

The problem was, she *didn't* think he was wrong. Despite everything, she was sure that if they didn't succeed in their mission, in two days, two innocent people would die. If anything, that feeling had only grown stronger since he'd first told her his unbelievable story.

Once she was standing in Mrs. Hanley's driveway, she decided to walk around the garage yet again, as if *this* time, she'd suddenly spot something she'd missed the first dozen times she'd done this.

She was crouching behind the garage, examining a smear of soot underneath the windowsill, when she heard the back door of the house creak open, then smack shut. Rose turned to see Mrs. Hanley picking her way through the grass in her house slippers, a tall glass filled nearly to the brim clutched in one hand.

"How's the investigation going?" she said as she got closer, holding out the glass.

Rose accepted it, took a sip. Homemade lemonade, perfectly sweet and tangy. She closed her eyes a moment to savor. "Not great," she admitted. "Everywhere we look seems to be a dead end."

Mrs. Hanley sighed, her eyes roving over the ruined garage. Rose wondered whether she was seeing past the smoke-darkened walls to the years of memories packed lovingly inside, now little more than piles of ash.

If Justin was right—if they couldn't solve this—she'd never even know why.

"Well, in any case, I appreciate you kids for trying." Mrs. Hanley smiled sadly, patting Rose on the cheek. "I've always thought my grandson was particularly skilled at picking his friends."

"Oh," Rose said, her ears heating with embarrassment, "Mrs. Hanley, I'm not actually doing this because of Noah—"

"No matter," Mrs. Hanley said, waving away her explanation. "Doesn't change the fact that you're trying to help out an old lady, even though I'm sure you have better things to do."

Justin came around the side of the house, looking glum. Rose's heart sank, knowing what he was going to say, but needing to confirm it anyway. "No luck?"

He shook his head, kicking at a clump of weeds. Rose searched for something to say, some right next step they could take, but her mind was blank. The action figure had seemed so significant. Like a sign that they were on the right track, that they *could* make a difference. She didn't know what to do with the possibility that it meant . . . nothing.

Plus, there was a part of her that kind of *wanted* him to feel lost and hopeless. Served him right after how he'd acted yesterday.

Although, somehow, that didn't make her feel any better.

The sound of tires crunching on gravel pulled her attention, and she peered toward the front of the house to see the neighbor's car pulling into the driveway. She looked at Justin. "Did you do that house yet?"

"Nope. No one was home."

Hope surged in Rose's chest. "Mrs. Hanley, your neighbors have kids, right?"

The old woman nodded, a slight frown deepening the wrinkles in her face. "One. Nasty little boy."

Rose's jaw dropped slightly. She couldn't remember ever hearing Mrs. Hanley speak so harshly about someone before, much less a child. "Nasty?"

"You remember Tiddlywinks?"

Rose nodded, confused about what Tiddlywinks had to do with Mrs. Hanley's neighbors.

"Tiddlywinks?" Justin whispered under his breath.

"Foster cat," Rose explained. A couple of years before her husband died, Mrs. Hanley had taken in the extremely pregnant stray and, not long after, her two tiny kittens. Rose and Noah had named Tiddlywinks together, along with the kittens, Parcheesi and Boggle. After Tiddlywinks ran away, Rose sometimes stopped by to help give the kittens their bottles, even when Noah was busy.

"We told you kids she ran away, but that wasn't true. We just didn't want to upset you," Mrs. Hanley said, her typically warm eyes narrow.

Rose clapped a hand over her mouth, her eyes widening in dawning horror. "Oh no—what happened?"

Mrs. Hanley frowned, pursing her lips. "His parents found her inside a camping cooler in their garage. He'd piled paint cans on top so she couldn't get out. Poor thing suffocated to death."

Rose's stomach clenched queasily, and a glance at Justin told her he was having a similar reaction. She met his eyes, and he raised an eyebrow. She assumed they were both having the same thought: if the kid was capable of killing a cat, he was probably more than capable of burning down a garage. Living next door would have given him ample opportunity.

And if he'd killed a cat *and* burned down the garage, who was to say he wouldn't burn down the school?

Together, they headed over to the neighboring house, where a tired-looking blonde woman balanced paper grocery bags in her arms as she kicked her car door shut with a maroon high heel. "Robbie," she called to a bored-looking preteen standing in the driveway, bouncing a grotesque rubber ball that looked like a human head. "Can you get the mail?"

He rolled his eyes but caught the ball. "Fine," he grumbled, dragging himself toward the end of the driveway.

"Oh damn," Justin whispered as they approached. "I know that kid."

Rose gave him an incredulous look. *"How?"*

"I mean, I don't *know* know him, but I've seen him before. That's one of the kids that was beating up Karl outside the post office."

Rose added *violent bullying* to her quickly growing mental list of evidence suggesting the Tiddlywinks-murdering Robbie would turn out to be their arsonist. She pasted a smile on her face, forcing herself not to stare daggers at the kid. "Excuse me," she called to his mom. "Do you have a minute to answer a couple questions? It's for a school project."

"Here, let me help you with those," Justin offered, stepping forward to relieve her of the grocery bags. She readily accepted his assistance, tucking a permed curl behind her ear as she thanked him. Rose found herself hit by a sudden wave of frustration at the memory of Noah getting met with hostility for trying to take a similar action, just a few days earlier.

Rose launched into the same rehearsed speech she'd given so many times that afternoon, but when she asked about *Star Wars* action figures, Robbie—who had moved most of the way toward the front door of the house with the mail—spun toward them. "I *did* have an awesome set of action figures," he said, interrupting his mother's polite answer, "until some asshole *stole* some of them."

His mom shook his head, her gaze lifting to the sky for a second as if searching for strength from above. "Honey, we've been over this. You probably just left them at—"

"I *told* you, I didn't *bring* them to the fucking birthday party," Robbie screeched.

"Robbie!" his mother hissed, casting Rose and Justin an apologetic look. "He lost some of his favorites over the summer," she offered by way of explanation, "and he thinks—"

"I don't *think*; I *know*," Robbie interjected again. "Someone was in my room and took them, and now they're probably gone forever because you wouldn't take it seriously—"

"Sweetheart, I wasn't going to call the police about your toys—"

"They're not *toys*; it was a collectible Han Solo and Boba Fett!"

"—when they had a much bigger problem to deal with next door."

"Let the fire department deal with her stupid fire; I was fucking *robbed.*"

"Now, honey, you seem like you're getting a little upset," his mother said. "How about you go inside and cool down, and I'll finish up out here?"

Robbie rolled his eyes, then stomped into the house, slamming the front door behind him. Rose watched incredulously, trying to imagine what her parents would do if she ever talked like that to either of them. The crater left by the force of their rage would be visible from the moon. But Robbie didn't strike her as a kid who'd ever been held accountable for much of anything.

"I'm so sorry," his mother said to Rose, her expression sheepish. "There was a fire at the neighbor's house the day his toys went missing, but of course, you know how kids are. Everything is an emergency!" She threw up her hands with a *what-can-you-do* gesture.

"Well, we'll let you go," Rose said, her heart pounding with what they'd just learned. "Thanks for your time."

Justin walked her groceries inside, then joined Rose in the driveway. They rushed back to Mrs. Hanley's, keeping silent until they were sure they were out of earshot of Robbie and his mother.

Back by the garage, Justin turned to Rose, his eyes wide. "Holy shit."

She nodded breathlessly. "He said it was a Han Solo, right?"

"Yeah. And on the day of the fire."

"But why would he make such a big deal about them being stolen if he set the fire? Wouldn't that just draw more attention to him?"

"Who knows how that little psychopath thinks?" A grin spread across his face, and without warning, he threw his arms around her and scooped her up. She let out an involuntary squeal as he spun her in a circle before setting her back on her feet. His blue eyes sparkled as they locked on hers. "Rose, we *solved* it!"

Rose ran a hand through her hair, feeling her face flush. She knew she was supposed to be mad at him, but she couldn't help the giddy flutters in her stomach. Still, they needed to focus on what they'd just learned. She cleared her throat. "Okay, so assuming it's him, what do we do next? Is there a way to prove he did it? Can we give the action figure to the police?"

Justin shook his head. "Mrs. Hanley won't go for it. And even if she did, Robbie will just keep claiming it was stolen. No way would they hold him through Saturday night."

"Right." Rose chewed on the inside of her cheek, thinking. "Okay, how about this? We know he's been bullying Karl. What if we turned him in to the school? They could contact his parents and maybe—"

Justin laughed. "You saw his mom, right? That kid wouldn't get grounded if he murdered Karl on his front lawn."

"Well, then what's *your* bright idea?"

Justin shrugged. "I don't know. He's a kid, right? Maybe we just, like . . . tie him up until Saturday night?"

"Justin, that is kidnapping."

"We'd let him go eventually."

"No."

He sighed. "Well, we know where he lives. And we know when the fire starts. Maybe we just . . . keep an eye on him on Saturday? We can meet here in the morning and just watch the house until he leaves, and stop him if he tries to go to the school."

"And if we're wrong and he *doesn't* go to the school?"

"Then we can head to the school before the fire starts and wait for someone to show up. But I mean, really—this kid kills a cat, he's basically a playground terrorist, and he just so happens to be missing the exact action figure that was found at the scene of the fire, which he lost on the *day* of the fire? Come on. Tell me that's a coincidence."

Justin seemed convinced, and Rose had to admit that Robbie was by far the most compelling suspect they'd come across yet. And even if they were wrong, Justin was right; if they waited at the school on Saturday, they were bound to see the arsonist, whoever they were.

She *knew* there had to be some sort of purpose in all this. She should never have doubted.

She allowed herself to return Justin's grin. "Okay. It's a plan."

Chapter Fifty

LISA

Lisa gazed at her reflection in the mirror over her dresser, heart hammering so loudly, she wondered if anyone else could hear it. She looked calm, but inside, her stomach was tying itself into a complex series of knots. She took a deep, shaky breath, smoothing a hand down the front of her dress.

Her mom was out doing more debate prep with Veronica. Jim was picking up Emmie from day care. It was just her and Rose in the house. And soon, Shawn.

Any moment. Any moment now.

According to her clock, it was only three minutes later when the doorbell rang, although it felt like hours. She closed her eyes, willing her pulse to stop racing, as she heard the door open, and Shawn's and Rose's voices floated up from downstairs.

Was she really about to do this?

Walking heavily, she waved Shawn up the stairs, her smile too tight, her movements too stiff.

Shawn smiled nervously, but didn't say anything as he joined her in her room. She guessed he wasn't sure what to say. It had been so long since she'd invited him over that he probably thought that she either wanted to finally talk about trying to fix their relationship or break up. Neither of which would be an easy conversation.

Of course, either of those would've been a breeze compared to what she *actually* needed to say to him.

Shawn stood in the center of the room, his hands in the pockets of his jeans, his eyes scanning the posters and photos on her walls. She tried to remember how long it had been since he'd last been in here and was surprised to realize she had no idea.

Reminding herself to breathe, Lisa gestured for Shawn to sit down. He walked to the bed and perched himself stiffly on the edge, looking up at her like he expected her to sit beside him.

But she couldn't sit. Her skin was buzzing with energy, ready for her to just get on the other side of this, whatever that looked like.

"I wanted to talk to you about something," Lisa started, pacing in front of him, her fingers working nervously over one another in an erratic dance. Her voice came out as a rasp, and she cleared her throat and started again. "You remember the end of last year, when I was always suggesting we go out and do stuff, like go roller-skating or to the mall or—"

"I remember," he said, giving her a bemused smile. "Kind of hard to forget that time, you know?"

"Yeah," she said, a nervous laugh leaking out. "Well, that's actually kind of related to what I wanted to talk to you about today. I know you've noticed that I haven't been—I mean, that I sometimes—"

"You've been avoiding me," Shawn said. It wasn't an accusation, just a statement of the obvious.

Lisa nodded, swallowing hard. "I have. And I'm really sorry. That wasn't fair, and you didn't deserve that."

Shawn's shoulders rose and fell, but he didn't say anything. His stormy eyes bored intently into her, like he was trying to see her thoughts, examine them so they made sense. She hoped that by the time she was done, they would.

"It wasn't anything you did," Lisa pressed on. "It was me. I had to . . . figure some stuff out. On my own. Or, well, not on my own." She took another deep breath and blew it out. Hot tears pricked at the backs of her eyes, and she blinked, trying to hold them in. This was harder than she'd thought. "Charlene was . . . helping me."

Shawn's attentive expression hadn't changed, but his body seemed like it was slowly turning into stone. As Lisa spoke, all his softness seemed to melt away, leaving only hard edges.

"The thing is, Charlene and I . . . we've been . . . together. For a few months now." A tear leaked from the corner of her eye; hurriedly, she wiped it away. "I need you to know I didn't plan it. It just . . . when I was with her, I felt . . . I *feel* . . ."

She squeezed her eyes shut, frustrated that her words were coming out all jumbled. This wasn't how she wanted this to go. She'd written a whole eloquent speech in her head, but when she opened her mouth to talk, the words seemed to dissolve from her brain. "I just . . . like her," she whispered. "I didn't know how that was supposed to feel before."

She opened her eyes and looked at Shawn, whose own eyes were now bright. "I'm sorry," she said, her voice coming out as barely more than a breath. "I didn't mean to hurt you."

He studied his hands for a minute, picking at his nails. "So, last year, when you always wanted to go out . . . you just didn't want to be alone with me."

"It wasn't—it was never about *you*," Lisa said. "I was freaked out that I didn't feel the way I was supposed to feel. I didn't want to—I didn't want *you* to think we might—it just all felt easier in public places, for a while," she tried to explain. "I don't think I even realized what was happening, at the time."

Shawn nodded, chuckling slightly as he shook his head. "Well, that explains a lot," he muttered. Lisa couldn't tell whether he was amused or upset.

He rose to his feet and hesitantly took a step toward her, then another. She couldn't read his expression. A muscle in his jaw twitched, his mouth pressed into a thin line. He sucked in a long breath through his nose, his eyes never leaving her.

Then he smiled, his eyes softening to a watery gray.

"I thought you hated me." His voice was a little shaky, but she could hear the relief in it.

She shook her head. "I could never hate you," she said, and suddenly she couldn't hold the tears back anymore. They streamed down her cheeks, dripping from her chin onto the carpet as her shoulders shook in giant, heaving sobs. "You're not mad?" she managed to gasp.

Shawn let out a small laugh. "I know this is going to sound weird, but I honestly feel better now. I was convinced that you couldn't stand me."

She wrapped her arms around him, finally allowing herself to hug him in a way that hadn't felt comfortable in months, since she always worried that he might interpret it as something more. After a second, his arms came around her, too, holding her tight. "That will never be true," she said into his shoulder, her voice coming out slightly muffled. "I love you. You're one of my favorite people."

This time, Shawn's laugh was bigger. "*Now* you say it."

Lisa laughed, too, and it felt so good, to finally have named the wall that she'd put up between them, and in the naming of it, to have knocked it down. "I always wanted to, you know. Just not in the way I knew you'd hear it."

Shawn sighed. "Maybe don't tell me that right now."

"Sorry."

They were both quiet for a long time, until it was suddenly strange that they were still touching, and they pulled apart. The air between them seemed somehow lighter. Easier to breathe.

"Have you told Rose?" Shawn asked.

Lisa shook her head.

He grimaced. "You know it's going to kill her that you told me first."

"Things have just been so weird between us lately."

"Weirder than *this*?" He gestured between the two of them.

She shrugged. "At least I knew *why* things were weird with us. With Rose, I'm not even sure what's going on. It's like she's got this whole different life all of a sudden that I'm not a part of, and I don't know how or why that happened."

Shawn raised his eyebrows. "Gee, I wonder what that must feel like."

She gave him a pointed look.

"Sorry," Shawn said hurriedly, his face flushing a bit. "I meant maybe she's got something going on that has nothing to do with you, but she just doesn't want to tell you. Like you did."

"Maybe," Lisa agreed. She bit her lip, staring at the photos of her and Rose stuck in the frame of her dresser mirror. "I'm just not sure what to do about it."

"You can talk to her," Shawn said with a shrug. "That's what I wish we'd done a long time ago."

"Yeah." Lisa took a deep breath and blew it out slowly. She knew he was right. She and Rose were long overdue for a talk. She just needed to find the right time to do it.

Chapter Fifty-One

BILL

After three days of uneventfully watching locker 247, Bill was beginning to wonder whether the mysterious test vendor was onto them. He and Pat had looked up the locker in the office, hoping their job would be easy, but it wasn't assigned to anyone. Yet there was a combination padlock on it like many of the students used, keeping them from being able to open it.

So they followed the system. They put twenty-five dollars in an envelope, along with one of Pat's classes and another unassigned locker number, and slipped it into locker 247. The locker they picked for their fictitious cheating student was clearly visible from Bill's office.

He stayed every day after school until the building was empty, pretending to work late, and came in first thing in the morning in order to keep watch. They'd put the envelope in 247 on Tuesday, so if Andy was right, there should've been something in the receiving locker by Wednesday. But no one ever approached the locker, and when Bill checked, it was still empty.

He wondered whether maybe he'd put the envelope in 247 too late for a one-day turnaround, and the delivery would happen on Thursday instead. But by the end of the day Thursday, the locker was still empty.

Bill sat at his desk, flipping mindlessly through a *Time* magazine he'd gotten from the teachers' lounge. It was an August issue, with a cover story warning about AIDS: The Growing Threat. He'd finished that article and moved on to one about year-round schooling—interesting, although he didn't think it would fly in Buford County—when he heard footsteps coming down the hall, along with the sound of someone humming.

Bill kept the magazine open and leaned his head on his hand, keeping his chin pointed down like he was still reading, while his eyes watched the hall.

The hummer came into view, and Bill recognized the janitor, Michael McMillain, who must have finished up his shift for the day. He was bouncing as he walked toward the school entrance, moving to a beat only he could hear. A Walkman was clipped to his belt, and headphones covered his ears. He twirled his keys around one finger as he hummed along to the music coming out of his headphones, punctuated by a few muttered lyrics every now and then. Bill thought it might be Stevie Wonder, but he couldn't be sure.

He sighed and stood, ready to call it quits for the day. If there was still nothing tomorrow, he and Pat might need to come up with a new plan.

He stopped midstep, stunned at what he'd just seen.

As Michael passed by the locker Bill had staked out, still grooving to the song, he'd spun around and, in one fluid motion, pulled something from his back pocket and slipped it through the vent on the front of the locker. It happened so quickly Bill would've missed it if he hadn't spent three days watching for it.

Michael looked up and spotted Bill standing in the doorway of his office. He grinned, lifting one side of his headphones so that Bill could hear the music leaking out. "Hey, Mr. Warren, how's that baby doing?"

Bill forced a smile. "She's great. How have you been, Michael?"

"Can't complain, can't complain. Just dancin' with my friend Stevie here." He reached down and dialed the volume up, so Bill could hear

Stevie Wonder's tinny voice scatting while backup singers repeated, *"Part-time lover."* Michael spun around again, swinging his arms and singing along with Stevie, *"Doot-doo-doo-doot-doot-da-da-da-da."*

Michael laughed, putting his headphones back on, and gave Bill a little wave. "You have a great night, Mr. Warren."

"You too, Michael."

After Michael pushed through the front doors of the school and the hall was quiet, Bill took a deep breath and reluctantly approached the locker. He dialed in the combination he'd picked—Millie's birthday—opened the locker, and gazed sadly at the envelope lying there.

He knew what he'd find, but he still picked it up and looked inside. Sure enough, there was a folded copy of the test they'd requested. Bill unfolded it, and to his surprise, a five-dollar bill fell out, along with a small handwritten note. *Sorry it was late. Gave you a discount.*

Bill sighed and shook his head, tucking the money and the test back in the envelope and closing the locker, then headed back into his office to call Pat.

FRIDAY

Chapter Fifty-Two

SHAWN

Shawn didn't mind getting up early on Fridays for his shift in the attendance office. It gave him an excuse to eat breakfast in peace, free of his dad's scathing looks and biting criticism, and to get out of the house before Gabe Rothman emerged from his room.

The streets of Stone Lake were quiet as he drove through town to school. There were a few people out on the sidewalks, sipping from Styrofoam cups of coffee or walking dogs, but overall, the town was still mostly asleep as R.E.M.'s *Murmur* album spilled from his truck's tape deck.

The truck wasn't much to look at, an old Chevy with a rusting paint job and fraying seats, but at least it gave him freedom. He'd purchased it with the money he had earned two summers ago working at the Dairy Queen, and he'd signed up for Auto Shop class so he'd know how to keep it running. After graduation, it would carry him out of this dead-end town once and for all.

He once had hoped Lisa would come with him. But now that dream was gone. All that remained was the promise of a fresh start somewhere else. The citizenship award would let him go anywhere he wanted. Right now, the only criteria he cared about was that it was somewhere far away.

He sang along under his breath to "Perfect Circle" as he pulled into the school parking lot. There were only a few other vehicles here so far, mostly teachers' cars filling up the spaces closest to the school. Shawn grabbed his backpack from the passenger seat and walked inside, letting himself into the front office, where the only other person was the school secretary, Mrs. Swenson. She greeted Shawn when he walked in, then returned her attention to the crossword puzzle on her desk.

Shawn picked up the stack of yesterday's mail from the basket at the front of the office, and took it around to the teacher mailboxes, which were housed in the side hallway that connected the main office to the guidance office and conference rooms. As he sorted the mail into individual cubbies, Mr. Warren's muffled voice drifted through his closed door. Shawn assumed he must be on the phone and didn't pay much attention, focusing on the mail in his hands, until he heard a second man speak. Unlike Mr. Warren's even tone, this person sounded deeply upset.

"Mr. Warren, Dr. Birch, please, my mama's not well. I just needed a little extra money so I can help my sister take care of her. Nurses are expensive. Please, sir, I'm sorry. I know I shouldn't have done it. I just needed the money for my mama. I won't do it again. You're good men. I know you are. Please."

"I'm sorry about your mother, Mr. McMillain," said a new voice, which Shawn recognized as Principal Birch's. "But we just can't allow you to stay after—"

"I'm a good worker. I work hard." McMillain started speaking rapidly. "I don't take time off. Not even sick time. I need this job. I swear, I'll never do it again. I promise on my life."

"Michael," Mr. Warren said, his voice low so that Shawn had to strain to hear, "I wish we could give you another chance. But selling tests to students . . . you know we can't just let that go."

Shawn's jaw dropped. So the secret test supplier behind locker 247 was the janitor? He had always assumed it was a student. But he guessed it made sense. The janitor would have access to all the classrooms after the teachers were gone and would be able to pick up and drop off things in lockers when no one was looking.

"Mr. McMillain"—Principal Birch spoke up again, his voice noticeably cooler than Mr. Warren's—"it has also come to our attention that you lied on your application to work here. You were previously incarcerated, yes?"

There was a heavy silence. Shawn realized he'd taken several steps closer to the door, the mail forgotten. "Sir, I can explain that," McMillain said, his voice trembling. "It's just so hard to find a job . . ."

"Even if facilitating cheating wasn't already a serious offense, we cannot have a convicted felon working around students."

"But, sir—"

"This conversation is over. I expect you to collect your personal belongings and turn in your keys before the students begin arriving. Understood?"

McMillain must have acknowledged Principal Birch somehow, because a second later the door swung open and the principal emerged. Shawn shoved a handful of mail blindly into the nearest mailbox, hoping that it didn't look like he'd been eavesdropping.

Dr. Birch hadn't bothered to shut the door behind him, so it stood partially open, allowing the sound of McMillain's quiet sobs to drift out. Shawn stood just out of sight of the men still in the office, slowly placing letters in random mailboxes—he'd have to redo all this later—straining his ears to listen.

"Michael," Mr. Warren said softly, "I'm sorry. I know you're not a bad person. But we just don't have any other choice."

"I understand, sir." McMillain sniffed, his voice thick. "Mr. Warren, I need you to know about that application, and my jail time . . . I was just a kid. It wasn't even my pot, but someone said it was and I-I panicked and tried to run and—"

"It's okay, Michael," Mr. Warren said. "You don't have to explain."

"I just don't want you to think I'm the kind of person who would, you know . . ." McMillain's voice was jagged, snagging on the words. "I

301

just want you to know, even though I did what I did with the tests, I'm not that guy. I swear I'm not."

The office was quiet for a minute, save for the sound of McMillain's ragged breathing, but Shawn didn't dare peek inside. His head spun as he tried to process what he'd heard.

After a couple of minutes, someone let out a shaky sigh. "You know anywhere that's looking to hire an ex-con who just got fired from the only real job he's ever had?"

"Actually, I think I might," Mr. Warren said slowly.

"Really?" McMillain sounded like Mr. Warren had just told him he had a pet unicorn.

"But I need something from you first. Did you keep any records of who bought tests from you? It seems like we have a lot of students who have been cheating, and we need to address that. Anything you give us could help."

"I-I don't have names. But I have a list of the locker numbers and dates, and which tests they requested. Lots of repeat customers. Keeping track was . . . helpful."

Mr. Warren chuckled. "Michael, you could've made a decent businessman."

"Not a lot of businesses looking to hire men like me."

"I suppose that's true," Mr. Warren said with a sigh. "Well, I'll tell you what. Can you get me that list before you go? Do you have it here at school?"

"No, sir. It's at home."

"In that case, why don't you go home and get that list, then bring it back to the office and drop it off with Shelly. I'll tell her to be on the lookout for it, and to bring it straight to me when she gets it. If you can get it to me before the end of the day, I'll see what I can do about finding you a new job. And even if that doesn't work out, I'll write you up a good reference."

"Thank you! Thank you, sir. I really do appreciate it. You won't regret it, I promise."

Shawn heard the scraping of chairs and took a few steps away from the door, making a show of focusing intently on the mailboxes as McMillain rushed from the office, barely glancing at Shawn as he hurried by.

Mr. Warren appeared in the doorway, then noticed Shawn. "Good morning, Mr. Rothman." He smiled warmly, but his eyes were exhausted. "Didn't realize you were out here."

"Just delivering the mail," Shawn said, his throat dry. He held up the handful of papers he hadn't yet placed in mailboxes, hoping Mr. Warren couldn't tell that his heart was pounding. He didn't think he'd necessarily get in trouble for eavesdropping, but it wouldn't look good either.

"Anything for me?"

Shawn stared at the wall of envelopes, flyers, and slips of paper that he'd made a complete mess of. "Um, not quite done yet. I'll bring it in to you in a few minutes."

"Thanks, Shawn. You're a good kid. Come see me next week; we can talk about your college applications. Lots of possibilities with that citizenship award."

"Yeah." Shawn swallowed, then forced one of his practiced, perfect smiles. "Sounds great."

Chapter Fifty-Three

JUSTIN

I spend the day at the bridge.

That wasn't my plan when I woke up this morning—or, more accurately, when I finally gave up on sleep and rolled out of bed, after spending the night tossing and turning, churning my sheets into a rumpled, sweaty nest. It was one thing to decide to stop our investigation into the fire once we realized Mrs. Hanley was basically living next door to a pint-size supervillain. It was another to just sit around waiting for Saturday to arrive, the day when I'll either prevent two deaths and go home, or fail and remain stuck here—or, worst of all, *succeed* and remain stuck here, proving that there's no reason for any of this, and that it was always just a totally random twist of reality.

I considered spending the day on Mrs. Hanley's sofa watching soap operas (a new obsession, and a secret I am determined to take to my grave), but after an hour of my eyes constantly being pulled from the TV to the window facing the Reynolds's house, I realized that was a surefire way to make the day take a hundred years.

Half an hour later, I found myself back at Wilson Bridge, staring out over the water. I still can't shake the feeling that there's something special about this place. Is it just because it's the last place I was before driving into the river? Or is there more to it than that?

This is the one piece that doesn't seem to sync with the Robbie theory. All week Rose and I have been so focused on *when* I went back in time; we've never stopped to wonder about the *where*. I think part of me hoped that if I came back here, the missing piece would click into place.

But it's just a bridge. Just a river. Nothing special about it.

The river seems angry today, churning and spitting far below my feet. It's like it knows what's going to happen. It's like it shares my anxiety about stopping it.

Hours slip past, and I don't leave. Sometimes I stand; sometimes I pace; sometimes I sit on the sidewalk with my back to the metal barrier that lines the edges of the bridge. Once, I climb up and over it, bits of orange rust flaking off onto my jeans and staining my hands, and look down at the water far below. The water that should've killed me but never got the chance.

I'm not going to jump. I still can't help but wonder what would happen if I tried—the universe snatched me from the grip of gravity once before, flinging me into a totally different time rather than letting me fall—but not enough to actually *do* it. Even though I'm not entirely convinced I'm still alive, I haven't yet made my peace with death.

Besides, we have a suspect. We have a plan. It's going to work. It has to work.

I tell myself this all day, over and over, trying to force my insides to stop tumbling like the water below. Yesterday, for a brief moment when Rose and I returned to Mrs. Hanley's, I felt calm, certain we were on the right path. But the more distance I gain from that moment, the more doubts pick at me, whispering that we might be wrong, we might be missing something, we might fail.

I stare out over the water, a sparkling cerulean ribbon, and wish that, just once, I knew what it was like to feel the certainty that seems to fit itself to Rose like a well-worn jacket. I wish I knew what it was like to have faith in something, anything, other than the universal inevitability of disappointment.

The temperature drops in the afternoon, the sun disappearing behind a wall of thick, rolling clouds. I remember Stan telling me that it was raining the night of the fire. This must be the pregame.

I slowly start to walk back to Mrs. Hanley's house, flipping up the collar of my borrowed jean jacket to block the wind's harsh bite and jamming my hands deep into my pockets to keep my fingers from going numb. The week started out warm, but the weather caught up with the calendar over the last couple of days, and now autumn has arrived in full force.

I should be hungry; I haven't eaten a thing since breakfast this morning, two fried eggs and buttered toast, which I didn't even finish—but I'm not. My stomach feels like it's been filled with cement, which is slowly curing into a hard, heavy lump.

I try not to think about tomorrow, but my mind keeps coming back to it. Is there more I can do, besides stalking Robbie Reynolds? Could I somehow stop Bill and Veronica from—

I freeze midstep, listening intently. I could've sworn I just heard—

There it is again. Clearer this time.

A scream.

Chapter Fifty-Four

KARL

His fort was supposed to be his safe place. His fortress of solitude. The lone place where he was the one with the power, the one in control.

And then Robbie found it.

"Leave me *alone*," Karl screamed, tearing through the trees without paying attention to where he was going.

Karl hadn't seen them until it was too late. He'd been too excited about digging into the newest issue of *Peter Parker, The Spectacular Spider-Man*, which he'd picked up at the comics shop right after school, along with an older *Incredible Hulk* that he'd slipped into his backpack while the shop owner was looking for the *Spider-Man* book. He had planned to spend a blissful afternoon reading in his fort and tuning out the world.

Except no sooner had he entered his fort and pulled the comics out of his backpack than there were Robbie and his goons. Karl had no idea how long they'd been following him. He was sure he would've noticed them crossing the bridge behind him, so maybe they'd already been in the woods when they spotted him.

Not that it mattered. Robbie wasted no time in sweeping the treasures Karl had collected off the shelves onto the ground and ripping down the canvas he'd rigged to provide shelter. At first, Karl tried to stop him, but then he realized that as soon as they got bored with destroying his stuff, the only thing left to destroy would be him.

That's when he ran.

Steve was blocking the path back to his house, so Karl ran in the opposite direction, toward the river. Branches scratched at his face as he crashed through the woods, sneakers crunching on a thick carpet of fallen leaves. Spiderwebs clung to his face and arms where he'd smashed through an invisible barrier, and he tried his best to wipe the sticky silk from his mouth and eyes as he ran.

Sheer surprise gave him a few seconds' head start, but soon Robbie and the others were chasing him, screaming taunts and insults. Karl didn't listen or look back, watching only the ground in front of him, knowing that if he tripped, he'd never get away.

Soon, the shimmering blue of the river appeared through the trees. How far was he from the bridge? He'd never make it all the way across, but maybe if he could get there without Robbie and the others seeing him, he could hide underneath.

As he burst out of the woods onto the rocky bank of the Stone River, the bridge loomed high up to his left. Karl scrambled toward it, thinking he'd take refuge behind one of the thick concrete supports.

He was more than halfway there when the toe of his sneaker caught on a piece of driftwood, and he went sprawling onto the ground. He managed to avoid hitting his sprained wrist this time, but his chin bounced off the stones, and when Karl touched it with his hand, it came away bloody.

"Grab him!" he heard Robbie yell from behind him, and an instant later, two sets of hands wrapped around his arms, hauling him to his feet.

"Stop it! Stop it!" Karl kicked helplessly as Steve and Kevin dragged him toward the water. His heart was hammering so hard his whole body shook.

"Stop whining, Derrin," Robbie said, supervising with a smirk. He plucked a strand of spiderweb from Karl's shirt and twisted his mouth in disgust. "We're just gonna give you a bath. You're gross."

With that, Steve and Kevin threw him down on his back at the river's edge, pushing his shoulders below the surface of the icy water. Karl screamed, but all that escaped his mouth was a stream of bubbles.

After a few seconds, they pulled him back up. He spit out a mouthful of river water, sputtering and coughing, his lungs burning. "Please stop," he begged, tears streaming from his eyes. "Please."

This time, when they pushed him under, he didn't scream. He tried to hold his breath, squeezing his eyes shut, but his body still needed to cough. He fought it as best he could, but then the urge was too strong, and he gave in. Water forced its way into his lungs like greedy fingers, choking him.

They brought him back up, but he couldn't even find the air to plead. He coughed and hacked, straining for oxygen, his gut churning with a bellyful of water.

He didn't know how much more of this he could take. Was this it? Was Robbie actually going to kill him this time?

Suddenly, his right arm was free. Beside him, Kevin took a few stumbling steps down the bank, clutching at his arm. "Hey!" Kevin yelled toward the bridge.

This time, Karl saw the rock strike Steve in the shoulder, and Karl's other arm was released. He scrambled through the shallow water on all fours, until he was back on the bank. His stomach heaved, and he vomited up a sour stream of river water onto the rocks.

Robbie's gang was distracted now, scooping up rocks of their own. "Get him!" Robbie yelled as the trio hurled rocks toward the base of the bridge.

Karl blinked his water-reddened eyes, trying to focus on his rescuer. "Gonna have to do better than that, you pathetic little freaks," the guy yelled, ducking one of Robbie's rocks and then flinging back one of his own, which caught Robbie in the calf.

It was Justin, the same guy who had saved him on Wednesday. He scooped up rocks from the bank and hurled them at Karl's attackers, sending them dodging and scrambling back, away from where Karl knelt by the water. Most of the rocks they sent flying his way missed, but Justin stumbled and fell as one smacked into his leg, sending him to his knees on the rocky ground.

"Shit!" he growled, trying to stand and then falling again as his leg seemed to buckle beneath him. For a second, he stayed there, braced on all fours, panting as his eyes met Karl's. His face was pale, his blue eyes wide, and suddenly Karl realized—he was scared, too.

Karl's stomach dropped. Was this it? Had Robbie and his goons won? Already, they were moving toward Justin; any second, they'd be on him. Karl's eyes darted around, searching for a way out.

But then Justin rose up on his knees and chucked another stone with all his might, gritting his teeth.

This one whizzed right by Robbie's ear, causing him to stumble to a stop midstride. "You're dead!" he yelled at Justin, who already had another rock in his hand, ready to go.

Karl held his breath, wondering whether he meant that literally. And after they finished with Justin, of course Karl would be next. Sweat clung to the thin hair around Justin's face, and his fingertips were white against the stone in his hand.

But instead of charging, Robbie led his crew away down the bank, limping slightly from where Justin had hit him in the leg. Karl could hardly believe his good luck.

Once they were gone, Justin let out a breath, allowing the rock to slip from his fingers. Slowly, he pushed himself to his feet, his legs trembling slightly under his weight. He limped over to Karl and squatted down gingerly, blood seeping through a rip in the knee of his jeans where he'd hit the rocks. "You again, huh?"

"Thank you," Karl managed to gasp, shivering, his voice coming out raw.

Justin sighed, taking in Karl's soaked clothing and bleeding chin. He reached out a hand, helping him up. "Okay, buddy. Let's get you home."

Chapter Fifty-Five

JUSTIN

I don't know what it is about this kid that makes me keep abandoning all sense to try to rescue him. He's not exactly the endearing type, and he grows up to sire *Dave*, of all people. Maybe Rose is rubbing off on me; I feel like I wouldn't keep showing up in the same places where those little asswipes are trying to murder him if there weren't a reason for it.

Or maybe this is just the universe's idea of a sick joke, to make me the one responsible for saving Dave's dad over and over.

Plus, I just missed an opportune chance to bean Prime Arson Suspect Robbie Reynolds in the head with a rock. Sending the kid to the hospital would definitely make my life a lot easier tomorrow.

But I couldn't bring myself to do it. Robbie may be fine with casually brutalizing a twelve-year-old to the point of death, but I'm not. Even if I do feel like the kid is probably going to grow up to be a serial killer.

Yes, there is definitely ample evidence to suggest the universe enjoys screwing with me.

My knee throbs as I walk Karl home, my ripped jeans growing increasingly wet with blood. I doubt I'm going to need stitches or anything, but I don't relish the thought of looking at my mangled knee.

The stone that hit me didn't hurt all that much, but it made my leg go dead for a second so it suddenly couldn't support my weight. The rocks that broke my fall were large and jagged and cut right through my jeans, ripping into my skin like claws. I haven't examined it yet, but from the blood I can feel trickling down my leg, I imagine it looks pretty gnarly.

Fortunately, Karl's house isn't far from the bridge. I don't think I can walk much farther than that.

"So what's up with those kids?" I ask as we limp along, side by side. "Did you do something to piss them off?"

Karl shrugs, his teeth chattering slightly. "They just hate me. I don't know why."

"Kids suck," I say. I have nothing else helpful to offer.

"The biggest one, that's Robbie," Karl says. "He's the leader."

I don't let on that I'm already well acquainted with Robbie. "He seems like a real treat."

That gets a little laugh out of Karl, but the smile quickly falls from his face. "He hates me the most," he says softly.

"How long has this been going on?"

"Since the beginning of middle school."

"Do your parents know? Or any other adults?" I don't have a lot of faith in most adults to have any idea how to deal with bullying this severe—in my experience, they tend to just make things worse—but I'm not sure what else to suggest.

Karl shakes his head. "Mr. Warren, he's the guidance counselor at my school . . ."

My stomach tightens at the mention of my grandfather. Who will probably die tomorrow, if I can't stop it.

"He asked me about it a couple times. But I told him that nothing bad was happening. I think it would just make Robbie madder, if he thought I told."

"Yeah, I get that." His instincts about Robbie are definitely right, but I don't tell Karl what I know about Mrs. Hanley's cat. It would only make the kid more terrified.

Man, my knee is *killing* me. When we get to Karl's house, I think I'm going to need to call Rose and ask her to come pick me up. I can't imagine walking the few miles back to Mrs. Hanley's house. "Have you ever tried to get them back? Learn some self-defense?"

"I can't fight them." He's probably right. All the self-defense classes in the world likely wouldn't make up for the fact that he's half their size and there's three of them.

He goes quiet for a few minutes, and I'm kind of grateful for the silence. It's taking everything in me not to just sit down on the ground and scream in pain. I think it's more than just the scraped-up skin. It feels like there is something seriously *wrong*. Like that rock knocked my kneecap out of place or something. My teeth are clenched, and I can feel sweat beading along my forehead.

"I tried to get back at Robbie once," Karl says suddenly. "But . . . it was a bad idea."

He has a strained expression on his face, like the words are spilling out despite his efforts to hold them in.

"What did you do?"

Tears start leaking from his eyes. "I didn't mean to." He looks up at me, his face crumpled and red. "If I tell you, will you promise not to tell?"

I'm starting to get alarmed, wondering if Karl murdered this kid's dog or something. But I've probably just got animal murder on the brain because of Mrs. Hanley's cat; surely there are not *two* adolescent pet killers in this town. I nod my agreement.

"It's really bad."

"I'm not going to tell. I swear."

He takes a few deep breaths, then says in a shaky voice, "A few months ago, over the summer, I-I broke into Robbie's house. Sometimes I like to . . . take things. That's what I wanted to do. I wanted to take something from Robbie that he would really miss. And then I'd know I could hurt him, too, even if he didn't know it was me. I didn't think anyone was home. I crawled in through the dog door."

313

Something inside me starts to twist. *No.*

"I went up to Robbie's room. I was looking around for something that I could take, something that would mean a lot to him. But then I heard his mom come home, so I grabbed a couple of action figures—he had them set up really cool on his shelf, so I figured they were important—and I ran out the back door. But I was scared she'd come out and find me, so I ran into the neighbor's garage."

I can feel my eyes widening as Karl talks. The action figures, the garage, the way he tore away from Mrs. Hanley's like a bat out of hell when he realized where he was. My vision temporarily blurs; I wonder if I'm about to pass out.

"I didn't mean to do it," he whispers, his voice shaking. "I swear I didn't mean to."

"Karl," I say slowly, feeling like I'm going to throw up. "Are you telling me that *you* started the fire at Mrs. Hanley's?"

He nods miserably. "I didn't mean to," he says again.

"What *happened?*"

The picture he paints is one of just absolutely horrible luck. Karl went into the garage through the back while Noah and Rose were out front goofing around with the hose. He decided to hide between a workbench loaded with tools and a pile of boxes that they had pushed off to the side to make room for the lawn furniture.

After a few minutes, when no one came after him, he started poking around the stuff on the bench, mostly out of boredom. He found a lighter and started messing with it, but accidentally burned his fingers and dropped it. It landed on the pile of WD-40-soaked rags Noah and Rose had been using to clean off the furniture, which immediately ignited.

Karl panicked. He ran out the back door and sprinted away as fast as he could. It was only when his sister later picked him up outside the library that he realized he'd dropped one of the action figures somewhere during his mad flight.

"I'm really sorry," Karl sobs as his house comes into view. "I never meant to do anything bad to that old lady."

I know I should say something, comfort him or offer some words of wisdom, but I can't make my mouth form words. My stomach feels like someone has poured concrete into it.

Mrs. Hanley's fire was an accident. Not Robbie Reynolds acting out of some sadistic desire to watch the world burn. Not Robbie Reynolds at all.

Karl.

By accident.

A total random fluke.

Started by a scared kid who didn't know how to hold a lighter.

It has absolutely nothing to do with the fire tomorrow.

Which means Rose and I have wasted our entire week, and our plan tomorrow is useless.

When we reach Karl's front door, I ask if he would mind if I used the phone. None of the rest of his family is there, thankfully, so I don't need to attempt to make small talk. I dial Rose's number and Lisa picks up. She says Rose isn't there, but she should be back soon. I tell her that I've messed up my knee and need a ride home from the Derrins' house.

"The Derrins'?" Lisa sounds startled. "What are you doing there?"

"It's a long story," I say, squeezing my eyes shut and pressing my fingers to the bridge of my nose. I can feel a massive headache coming on. "Can you just please ask her if she can come pick me up?"

"Okay," she says, her voice sounding a little chilly. "But it may be a while."

"That's fine."

After getting off the phone with Lisa, I ask Karl if he has a first aid kit. He hands me a box of Band-Aids and a tube of Neosporin and points me toward a bathroom—*Downstairs bathroom, North*, I think, wishing I could engage in some moderate intoxication therapy right about now—where I shut myself in and focus on the only thing left within my control.

I wince as I peel off my jeans, the fibers around the tear pulling painfully where dried blood has adhered them to the cuts. Gingerly, I dab at the mess of blood and dirt and gravel around my knee until I can see the injury clearly.

I blink at it for a few seconds, uncomprehending.

I've seen this injury before.

Only the last time I saw it, it wasn't swollen and bleeding. It was old, healed, and scarred. It looked like a smiley face, which I always thought was ironic, given that its owner was one of the most miserable people I'd ever met.

No no no NO NO NO NO NO

It can't be. It *can't* be.

I spin around and vomit into the toilet, the truth ripping me apart, leaving me scattered in a million bloody pieces.

Stan.

I have the same injury as Stan.

I.

Am.

Stan.

Chapter Fifty-Six

Lisa

Lisa sat on the couch, flipping idly through the channels on the TV. Nothing good was on in the afternoon, so she finally settled on MTV, although she wasn't paying much attention to the groups singing on the screen.

Her eyes kept going to the digital clock on the VCR. School had ended more than an hour ago. Where was Rose? She knew she wasn't with Justin; he'd called a few minutes before to ask Rose to pick him up from the Derrins' house. Lisa couldn't believe he'd been stupid enough to call, considering how much trouble Rose would be in if one of their parents picked up. And what on earth was he doing at the Derrins' anyway? Lisa was dying to know, but she didn't really know Justin well enough to press for details. She'd get them from Charlene later.

Since her conversation with Shawn the day before, Lisa felt like a fire had been lit under her. All day at school, she'd felt like she was floating, and had even dared to hold Charlene's hand under the table at lunch. She knew Shawn had noticed—he still sat next to her, after all, since they'd agreed to not officially "break up" until after the election—but when she caught his eye, he just gave her a small smile, then turned to say something to Noah.

Lisa had been so worried about telling Shawn, but it turned out . . . he was fine. Next to him, Rose should be easy.

If only she would get here.

Finally, Lisa heard the front door open. She sprang up, switching off the TV, and ran to meet her. "Where have you been?" she asked, eager for Rose to finish taking off her shoes so that they could talk.

Rose frowned. "Just out walking. And thinking." She sounded exhausted.

"Well, I'm glad you're here," Lisa said. "I wanted to talk to you about—"

"Wait," Rose interrupted, pointing to the hastily jotted note Lisa had left by the phone. "Justin called? What did he want? I can't *believe* you wrote it down. You know Dad and Diane will kill me if they know I'm still talking to him."

"*He* was the one who was dumb enough to call. What was I supposed to do?"

"I don't know—remember it?"

"I didn't want to forget to tell you!"

"Well, then tell me."

"He needs a ride home from the Derrins'."

"What is he doing at the Derrins'?"

Lisa flung her arms wide in exasperation. "He wouldn't tell me. He just said he did something to his knee and asked you to pick him up, and that's all I know. But, Rose, I *really* want to—"

"That doesn't make any sense," Rose muttered to herself, stepping back into her shoes. "I need to get over there."

"Wait," Lisa said, her heart falling. "Can't you just wait a few minutes?"

"I don't have time," Rose said, shaking her head. "Dad?" she yelled. "Can I borrow the car?"

"It's still making a weird noise!" Jim's voice drifted down from upstairs.

"I won't go far!"

"Okay, just make sure you take some quarters!"

"Rose, please, it won't take long."

"We can talk later," Rose said as she scooped the car keys and a few quarters from the dish on the hall table. She sighed, her hand on the doorknob. "I'm sorry if I was snippy just now. It's not your fault. It's just been a really tough week."

"For me too," Lisa said quietly.

Chapter Fifty-Seven

JUSTIN

I don't know how long I sit in the bathroom in my underwear, my ripped jeans crumpled up on the floor, a wad of bloody toilet paper floating in the toilet with the remainder of my breakfast.

My whole life, the person I've hated more than anyone in the world has been *me*. *I'm* the one who made my life a living hell. *I'm* the one who told me he should've drowned me in the river as soon as I was born.

Stan's murder wall was *my* murder wall.

Stan's obsession was *my* obsession.

I riffle through my memories like I'm paging through a book, searching for clues. Stan's hair has long gone silver, and he is stooped and shriveled more from unhappiness than age, but I mentally straighten his hunched shoulders, recolor his limp hair, smooth the wrinkles on his tired face. Now that I know, I can see it. Can see *me*. I've been there all along.

I wonder how I missed it, but then again, of *course* I missed it. No rational person ever stops to wonder whether maybe they're being raised by a grouchy, several-decades-older version of themselves.

All those years, Stan kept trying to drag me down to the basement to drill the particulars of his obsession into my head, because he was trying to change things. Give me the knowledge he never had. Enable me to see the things that he never did.

I never listened. Never cared. Never carved out a single minute of my day to accept what I now realize was the only help he knew how to give me: information he thought might help me get back. And I ignored him.

No wonder he hated me.

I think back to the night I came here, the night I drove off the bridge. I remember Stan trying to tackle me to keep me from going to that party. I remember blocking his number so he'd stop calling me.

He knew I was about to come here.

Because when he was my age, *he* came here.

And he never got back.

I don't move until Karl knocks on the door, telling me Rose is here to pick me up. I slap a few Band-Aids on my knee, trying hard not to look at it as I do. After pulling on my jeans, I limp to where Rose waits by the front door, past a still-sniffling Karl. He hovers by me like he's expecting me to say something, but I can't think of anything to say to him. I feel numb as I drift out the door. Part of me registers that my knee is still jacked up, but I barely feel the pain.

Rose says something to me as I get into the car, and I grunt in response, not paying attention. I stare out the window as we pull out of the Derrins' driveway, taking in the world I am doomed to be stuck in for the rest of my life.

As we drive across Wilson Bridge, I wonder what would happen if I flung open my door, jumped out of the car, and took the leap I've spent all week avoiding.

Would I die, and stop this hellish cycle from repeating?

Would I live, and find myself back in 2023?

Would I just be wet and cold and still stuck in 1985?

In my mind's eye, I see myself reaching for the door handle, rolling across the pavement, flinging myself off the bridge.

But I don't. I just sit there, frozen and useless.

As always.

Rose likes to talk about fate, about purpose, but I know now: I have no fate. I have no purpose.

I don't matter.

I have never mattered.

I never will matter.

And there's nothing I can do about it. It was stupid to believe there was.

I fist my fingers into my hair and twist, hard enough that I hear strands ripping free of my scalp. I want to tear my stupid, useless body apart. Shred it to pieces and let it scatter in the wind. Tears burn my eyes as I let out a scream.

"Justin!"

Rose pulls onto the shoulder of the road and stops the car, then grabs my wrist. I realize I've been punching the dashboard. My knuckles are red and raw. "What's going on?" Her eyes dart between me and the road, one hand on the wheel, one still clamped on my wrist.

It all comes pouring out. Seeing Karl on the riverbank. Throwing rocks at the kids. Falling and mangling my knee. Karl admitting he started the fire at Mrs. Hanley's. Realizing that Stan and I have the same scar.

Rose shakes her head, her forehead crinkling a little as she presses the tips of her fingers to her lips. "So . . . Stan is *you*?"

I nod, feeling a fissure begin to spread through my insides, wondering how long I can hold it together before I shatter. "I'm never getting back," I say, my voice cracking. "We never had a chance of solving this case. Stan's spent his whole life trying to do it, and he's never gotten anywhere." I force myself to say it. "*I* never get anywhere."

That does it.

The dam inside me bursts, and all the fear and confusion and hopelessness come pouring out in giant, hiccuping laugh-sobs. I try to hold it in, but that just makes it worse.

"I . . . *hated* . . . him," I gasp through spasms of violent laughter, tears streaming down my face. "My whole life, I've thought he was the biggest asshole on the planet. And he's *me*."

I get out of the car and hobble into the middle of the road, throwing my arms wide to the sky.

"What are you doing?" Rose calls, but I shake my head, spinning in a circle.

"Doesn't matter."

"Get back here before you get hit by a car."

I stop spinning and face down the road, keeping my arms raised. *"Hit me!"* I scream to no one, and to everything. "I fucking *dare* you!"

"Justin!"

"What?" I turn to face her. "Don't you get it? Nothing *matters*," I shout. "Not me, not you, not this ridiculous quest we've been on all week. It's all meaningless bullshit! Everything is pointless!"

"Stop it!" she yells at me. "Seriously, Justin, get out of the road. Then we can talk about this."

"Or what, I could die?" Another burst of wild laughter. "*Can* I die? Am I invincible? I mean, Stan lived, so I live, right? Maybe I could get hit by a car and walk away!"

"You can barely walk *now*," Rose points out.

I look at her over my shoulder, through blurry eyes. "Touché." That sends me into another fit of giggles.

Rose gives up on persuasion and marches onto the pavement, taking my arm. I let her lead me back off the road, where I collapse onto the grass, drained of all energy. "So," she says, "you don't get back."

"Nope."

"So the question is, what are you going to do now?"

I fight down another burst of laughter. "*Do?* I guess I'm going to turn into an angry, obsessive old man with no friends who never does anything with his life."

She shakes her head. "You're telling me what *he* did. I'm asking what *you* are going to do."

"Have you not been paying attention? He *is* me."

"No—he's Stan. He's the result of some *other* Justin who went into the past and never made it back. But that doesn't make him you. You can still do things differently than he did."

"Some other . . . Are you high? There's only one me."

"There are two of you in 2023."

"Yeah, but they're still both *me*. One's just older than the other."

"You don't know that they're *you* you. Maybe this keeps happening, and you keep going back into the past, but each time you do things a little differently. Maybe there are a bunch of alternate universes where you make different choices. Maybe in some of them, you *do* make it back. Maybe every version of you is a little bit different."

"So now, instead of two of me, you're saying there are, like, hundreds?"

"Maybe."

"Well, that's terrifying."

"Or it means you have free will, and your choices *do* matter, because this version of you has never existed before."

"But what if that's not how it works? What if this is just a loop, and there's just me and Stan, doing the same things over and over for infinity?"

Rose shrugs. "Then you have nothing to lose."

I frown. Much as I would like to believe that there's a way out of this, I just don't see it. I mean, look at the scar. I made all my choices leading up to that believing that I could change things, that I could make a difference, and I *still* did everything exactly the same way that Stan did, down to getting hit with a rock and falling at the precise angle and moment that would give me the exact same scar.

"I just don't see the point," I say wearily. "I've watched him try to solve this case my whole life. The fire happens tomorrow, and we still have no idea who does it. How am I going to do in twenty-four hours what *he* couldn't do in almost thirty-eight years?"

"Maybe he never got back because when he got to the point where you are now, where he realized that he is you, he gave up."

"But he *didn't* give up. I've seen the murder wall. It took over his whole life."

"Yeah, but he tried to solve it *after* the fire. I'm saying, what if he gave up trying to solve it *before?*"

"It doesn't matter. If there was anything else to do, I'm sure he would've thought of it."

"I'm not saying it's going to be easy or obvious. I'm just saying, you don't know for sure what he did once he reached this point. You only know what he did later. These next twenty-four hours are a big question mark. Maybe—"

"Just *stop,*" I say, unable to stomach another second of her relentless optimism. "Isn't it obvious by now? You were *wrong.* I don't matter; you don't matter; none of this matters. There isn't meaning in everything, there isn't some grand master plan, and the universe does not give a shit about either one of us. Maybe I'm not dead, but this *is* hell, and it's time we both just admitted it."

"Justin, you don't mean—"

"Shut *up.*" My face is hot, my eyes burning. "Don't tell me what I mean; don't tell me what to do; don't tell me *anything.* I should never have listened to you. I wish I'd never even *met* you."

Rose's mouth drops open, her face crumpling.

The instant the words leave my mouth, part of me wishes I could take them back. I'm stuck in this nightmare for the rest of my life, and I just torpedoed the one good thing about it.

But frustration and anger keep my lips pressed together, my eyes narrow. Maybe it's not fair, but I just need her to feel what I'm feeling for once. I need to not be alone in this fear and rage and despair. I need someone to share this absolutely shitty, hopeless feeling with me, because it's too much for me to handle by myself.

No wonder Stan was alone his whole life. We truly are the world's worst human.

"You know what?" she growls through gritted teeth. Her jaw works furiously as she straightens her shoulders. "I wish I'd never met you either. You've made it clear that caring about what happens to you is a waste of my time."

She starts toward her car, and abruptly, my need to push her away dissipates, replaced by a desperate need for her to stay. I wish I could wind back the last twenty seconds. Doesn't seem like a huge ask after accidentally winding back thirty-eight years, but time continues to march stubbornly forward. "Rose, wait—"

"No, *you* wait," she says, spinning so fast she sends me stumbling backward. "I don't *matter*? If it weren't for me, you'd probably have been in *jail* all week, or do you not recall how you nearly managed to get yourself arrested thirty seconds after arriving here? *I'm* the one who found you a place to stay. And *I'm* the one who's been here with you every single day trying to save your grandparents. Maybe it can't be done, but I'd rather try and fail than be like you."

I blink, stunned. I've never seen this version of Rose before. I didn't even know this version existed.

"You know what? Do what you want. I'm done with this." Rose throws up her hands in frustration as she stomps back to her car.

"Rose, I'm sorry." I trail behind her, giving her plenty of space in case she starts breathing fire again. Panic is beginning to bubble up inside me at the realization that I'm about to be abandoned to a life stuck in the past, all alone. And it's all my fault. "I didn't mean it," I plead. "I was just really upset."

Unbidden, Alyssa's voice pipes up in my head. *Sometimes even the most justifiable of excuses is still not an actual excuse.*

Oh god. Alyssa. I'd thought the worst thing about all this was the possibility of never seeing her again, but it turns out I was wrong. The worst thing is going to be seeing her again as *Stan.*

Rose turns to look at me as she reaches her car. "That's it? That's all you have to say to me?"

I spread my hands in bewilderment. "I said I'm sorry. I don't know what else you want from me."

"Never mind." She shakes her head, disgust evident on her face. "Don't call me again." She gets in and slams the door, and a second later, the engine growls to life.

I start to walk around to the passenger side, but she glares at me through the windshield and I stop.

Seriously, she's *leaving* me here? "How am I supposed to get back to Mrs. Hanley's?" I ask.

"Figure it out," she calls, her voice muffled by the windows.

And then she's gone.

I've spent a lot of time by myself since falling into 1985. I'm used to it. But this is different.

For the first time, I'm truly alone.

Chapter Fifty-Eight

ROSE

"Can we talk? In private?" The words were out of her mouth before she registered that Noah wasn't the only one standing in the doorway. Steph hovered behind him in an oversize sweatshirt that Rose recognized as one of Noah's. Steph had cut the neckline wide, so that it hung off one shoulder.

So she was wearing his clothes now. Awesome.

"Um," Noah said, his eyes flitting to the side, like he was trying to spin them around to the back of his head in order to gauge Steph's reaction to Rose's sudden presence on his doorstep. "Now's not a great time . . ."

"It's important," Rose insisted, not caring that she was being rude. She'd spent months walking on eggshells in order to not get in the way of his relationship with Steph. But he'd been *her* best friend first, and she was tired of feeling like last week's leftovers with every important person in her life. She mattered, no matter what Justin said.

"Please, Noah," she added quietly, unable to completely smooth out the slight quiver in her voice.

He stared at her for a second, looking conflicted, then turned to Steph. "I'm really sorry, but I need to go. Rain check?"

Rose pretended she didn't see the hurt expression flicker across Steph's face before she nodded. "Sure. No problem," she said with a too-bright smile. Her eyes shifted to Rose. "I hope everything's okay."

"It's not," Rose said impatiently, giving Noah an imploring look as he pulled on his shoes. She knew she should probably be nicer to Steph, but just then, she couldn't bring herself to put in the effort.

She looked away as Noah gave Steph a quick kiss goodbye—just a peck, she noticed—and led him to her car.

"Whoa," Noah exclaimed, his hand scrambling for the bar above the door as she pulled out of the driveway and into the street so fast the tires squealed against the pavement. He turned in his seat to look at her. "You were really rude back there."

She shrugged. "I'll apologize later."

He shook his head, frowning. "What is going *on* with you? And where are we going?"

That was a good question. She hadn't really thought that far ahead. Her only thought when she'd left Justin on the side of the road was that she was done wasting time. That led her to Noah's house. Beyond that, she wasn't sure.

She wound up driving them to the school parking lot, which was mostly empty, save a few cars clustered around the gym entrance. The sign in front of the school wished the football team luck in their away game, so the cars probably belonged to football players, cheerleaders, and band kids who had shown up earlier to load the buses. They wouldn't be back for hours.

Even so, Rose parked far away from the empty cars. No one would overhear them, but she still wanted to be as isolated as possible for this conversation.

The conversation that she had never intended on having. Until suddenly, she did.

"I have some things to tell you," she started, turning off the ignition and shifting in her seat so she was facing him. "They're going to sound a little . . . insane, but I just need you to believe me. Even though you're not going to want to. Okay?"

"Okay." His answer came without hesitation, despite his bemused expression.

Rose took a deep breath, steeling her nerves, and then the whole story came pouring out. How Justin wasn't really her pen pal, but someone she'd nearly run over the night of the bonfire. His insistence that he was from the future, and his knowledge about what was going to happen tomorrow. Her theory about why he was here. Their efforts to figure out who had started the fire at Mrs. Hanley's, and the discovery that it was Karl Derrin. Justin's realization that he was really Stan, a man he knew from his time as an angry surrogate-uncle figure, which meant he was destined to never make it back. Their fight over what to do with that information.

"That was right before I went to your house," Rose finished. "I felt like it was time you knew everything. I should've told you earlier. I'm sorry."

She'd been mostly staring out the windshield as she talked, too nervous to watch his face as he took in everything she was telling him. After the things Justin had said to her, she didn't think she could bear to watch someone else she cared about look at her like she was delusional.

Now she dared a peek, and wished she hadn't. He was staring at her with his brow furrowed and lips pursed, his body tensed like he was afraid she might suddenly attack him, or maybe rip out her hair and start howling at the moon.

"You think I'm crazy," she said, her heart sinking.

"No," he said without hesitation. "I would never think that. It's just . . ." His jaw moved far more than was necessary to form those few syllables. "This is a lot to process. I need a minute."

"Do you believe me, though?"

He hesitated before answering. "I believe that *you* believe you're telling me the truth," he said finally.

Her stomach tightened. "That's not the same thing."

He sighed. "I don't know what you expect me to say, Rose. I mean . . . *time travel?*"

"You *promised* you'd believe me."

"I thought you were going to tell me that, I don't know, your dad was working for the mafia or you'd started dealing drugs or something. Something that was far-fetched but at least *possible*. But this . . . Rose, time travel doesn't exist."

"You think I don't know that? I would've said that, too, a week ago. I'm not telling you this because I want to believe it. I'm telling you this because it's *true*."

Noah took off his glasses and placed them on the dashboard, pinching the bridge of his nose. "How can you know for sure, though? Did he like . . . predict anything to *prove* to you he's from the future?"

"He knew Michael McMillain was going to be fired."

"Who?"

"The janitor at school."

"He was fired?"

Rose opened and closed her mouth wordlessly. The truth was, she didn't know whether he'd been fired. Justin had said that would happen today and she hadn't seen McMillain at school, so she'd assumed he was right, but she realized she didn't know for sure. "I . . . think so," she said meekly.

"Rose," Noah said gently, "I know you love to believe the best about people, and that's an amazing thing about you, but isn't it more likely that he's just . . . really confused?"

Rose shook her head. "I know how it sounds," she said. "But I just . . . I *know* this is real. I can't explain why. I know it sounds impossible. And if someone else told me, I probably wouldn't believe it either. But this is *me*, Noah. And I'm telling you, this is real."

Noah sat for a moment, searching her face, then blew out a slow breath. "Okay."

"Okay?"

"If you believe it, I believe it."

331

"Really?" Relief flooded through her, and she realized she'd been braced for more doubt, more insistence that she didn't know what she was talking about. She'd been so ready for rejection, she hadn't truly considered acceptance. "Just like that?"

Noah smiled, his dark eyes warm and open. "I've always been able to trust you, Rose," he said softly. "I don't know why that would change now."

Tears of gratitude welled in her eyes as Rose reached across the seat and took his hand, something she'd wanted to do for months but had never been able to work up the nerve. Yet now, it had taken no courage at all. It was as natural as breathing. "Thank you," she whispered. She felt lighter, like she was floating. She hadn't realized how much this secret had been weighing her down. "I was so afraid you wouldn't believe me."

Noah squeezed her hand. "It's us, Rosie," he said. "I'll always be on your side."

She smiled, her lips quivering, and took a shaky breath. "That's good," she said, "because I need your help. Justin is convinced that there's nothing we can do, but I think he's wrong."

Part of her hated bringing their conversation back to Justin when she wanted nothing more than to just sit here, basking in the knowledge that she and Noah were a team, and always had been, even if she'd forgotten for a while. But she couldn't afford to do that. Not yet.

Noah sighed, staring at their interlocked hands. He was quiet, the only sounds in the car their soft breathing. Rose remembered how awkward she'd felt the first time she'd grabbed Justin's hand. How aware she was of where she ended, and he began. But somehow, with Noah, that didn't matter. Their hands were the point where they touched, but they'd always been connected. Why had she made it so complicated?

"Karl Derrin started Gran's fire?" Noah said finally.

Rose nodded. "He told Justin the whole thing. It was a freak accident. All those rags . . ."

"Yeah." He shook his head, letting out a slight chuckle. "So I guess it was kind of us after all."

"No, that's not what I—"

"It's okay. I'm okay," Noah said, squeezing her hand and giving her a small smile. "Gran will be glad to know what happened. Even if she'll never tell the insurance company. Or anyone else, for that matter."

"Yeah, that's what I thought." There was no way Mrs. Hanley would ever turn in a child, even if it was an accident.

Noah took a deep breath and blew it out in a slow, steady stream. "So this other fire is going to happen tomorrow night?"

"Right before the debate. Yeah."

"But you still don't know who will start it."

She shook her head. "McMillain is still our only suspect, and if he was fired today, he's got the motive, but . . . I don't know, he just doesn't feel like the guy to me. And Justin said Stan was always sure it wasn't him. But if it's not him, and it's not Robbie, then I have no idea who it could be." She looked into Noah's eyes, searching for truth. "You really believe all of this?"

He held her gaze, his brown eyes unwavering. "I believe in you," he said softly. "And I believe in us. If you ask me to help you, I'll always help."

Warm tears rolled down Rose's cheeks. "I believe in us, too," she said, her voice thick.

A smile tugged at the corners of Noah's mouth. He shifted his hand in hers, weaving their fingers together. "You know I love you, right?"

She smiled through her tears and nodded. "I know. I love you, too."

It wasn't the declaration she'd been agonizing over for months. Maybe this was how it would always be between them, or maybe one day, they would be something different to each other. She didn't know how the rest of their story would unfold, but just then, it didn't matter. That they loved each other wasn't a secret spilling out, or a scandal getting ready to ignite.

It was simply the unchanging truth they'd both always known, finally spoken out loud.

SATURDAY

Chapter Fifty-Nine

JUSTIN

I wake up while it's still dark, feeling like I'm going to vomit.

Saturday. October 5. 1985.

The day of the fire.

I roll over and bury my face in my pillow, trying to convince my body to go back to sleep, but it's no use. My knee throbs beneath the bandages, a constant reminder that I was always doomed to fail. Even the idea that I was dead or in a coma, and might someday just peacefully blip out of existence, has been taken away from me.

I'm going to be stuck here. Alone. For the rest of my miserable life.

And there was never anything I could do about it. It was stupid to think there was.

I toss and turn for a while, until the world outside the window begins to lighten with the hazy glow of dawn. Then I finally give up and get dressed, creeping downstairs as quietly as I can.

The house is quiet. Mrs. Hanley must still be asleep.

For the first time, I realize with a jolt that I'm going to have to figure out a place to live after this. And get a job. And some sort of ID. Staying with Mrs. Hanley was only supposed to be temporary, until I went back.

But I'm not going back. And I can't stay here forever.

The weight of all the years I have ahead of me comes crashing down all over again. A week ago, when I was waking up on Alyssa's couch, avoiding Stan, and dreading the bonfire, I thought I had no future. But that was nothing compared to this suffocating certainty that I'm going to spend the rest of my life alone and anonymous, destined only to hate myself.

I pass the kitchen window, averting my eyes from the house next door, which I thought held the solution to my problems just twenty-four hours ago. Robbie is definitely a monster, but chasing him won't do me any good. May as well leave him for the next monster hunter.

I slip out the back door, moving as silently as I can. I don't want to see Mrs. Hanley this morning, or eat the giant breakfast she's sure to insist on making. My stomach feels like it's filled with rocks.

The sun has almost finished rising when I step outside. It's a cool, crisp morning, with dew sparkling on the tips of the grass. My mom loves mornings like this.

The rocks in my stomach seem to double in size, and a few of them threaten to explode. God. My mom. Today is the day she loses her parents. The police report says she was in her car seat facing the school, all alone until the emergency vehicles started to arrive. I picture her sitting by herself, her little, round face washed orange in the glow of flames as she watches her parents burn.

Suddenly I realize, I can't do this. I can't be here when it happens, knowing there's nothing I can do to change it.

I have to get out of here.

Chapter Sixty

ROSE

Everything was loud that morning.

Veronica came over early, Millie in tow, to squeeze in some last-minute debate prep with Diane. The two babies took over the living room floor, surrounded by a wall of pillows, while their mothers sipped coffee on the couch and ran through talking points again and again.

Rose's dad bustled around the kitchen, clattering breakfast dishes. He'd baked up a storm the day before, preparing cinnamon rolls, monkey bread, and buttermilk biscuits, along with a breakfast casserole that was still in the oven. After all this stress baking, they wouldn't have to cook for weeks, provided they didn't mind living almost entirely on bread.

Lisa sat across from Rose at the kitchen table, both of them still in their pajamas. Other than exchanging murmured good-mornings over glasses of orange juice, neither of them said much. Lisa had been in bed by the time Rose arrived home from talking to Noah the night before, so she'd never learned what it was Lisa wanted to discuss.

Not that Rose had any energy to worry about that right now. Her mind was heavy with the weight of the day. Would Justin still try to do something to stop the fire? He ran so hot and cold all the time that it seemed just as likely that he'd stay in bed all day as show up to fight the fire with his bare hands.

Neither of which would be any help to her.

"Just a minute, Diane. I'll be right back," Veronica called from the living room. She rushed by the entrance to the kitchen, and a second later, Rose heard the bathroom door close, followed by the sound of retching.

Veronica must be nervous about the debate. Rose's stomach clenched. If Justin was right about what would happen tonight, Veronica would never even set foot at the debate. She'd be dead before it started.

But that wouldn't happen, Rose assured herself. She had Noah, who was ten times more reliable than Justin had ever been. Together, they could do this. They could change the future.

Chapter Sixty-One

LISA

Lisa sat at the kitchen table, drumming her electric-blue nails on its surface as she listened to water rush through the pipes in the ceiling. Rose had left to shower after breakfast, leaving her alone at the table. Lisa went through two cups of tea waiting for her to finish, hoping to settle her nerves, but if anything, she was more worked up now than she had been when she first woke up.

Today was going to be the day. Yesterday hadn't worked out, but today, she was determined to make it happen.

In front of her lay the newspaper, which she'd flipped over as soon as her stepfather had left the room. Today's front-page headline again lamented the dangers of the AIDS crisis, and she couldn't read it without feeling a little queasy.

Her heart jumped and strained against the walls of her chest like an anxious dog on a leash. She was scared, but also a little excited. Shawn had understood. Maybe Rose would, too. And once Rose knew, all the most important people in Lisa's life—well, except her mom, but that was a bridge Lisa wasn't ready to cross yet—would know who she really was. No more hiding and pretending, at least with a couple of people.

Lisa imagined holding Charlene's hand in a place where people could actually *see* them, and butterflies took flight in her stomach.

She heard the shower turn off, and sprang up from the table. Rushing past her mom and Veronica and the two squirming babies in the living room—"Careful!" her mom called out when Lisa skipped over a crawling Emmie—Lisa met Rose as she emerged from the bathroom at the top of the stairs, her hair wrapped in a purple towel. "Can we talk?" Lisa asked breathlessly.

"Oh," Rose said, seeming a little taken aback. "I was actually going to—"

"It's important," Lisa said. She was determined not to let another chance pass them by. "Please?"

Rose bit her lip, then nodded. After taking a minute to throw on a pair of sweats and a T-shirt, she walked into Lisa's room and closed the door. They perched facing one another on the edge of her bed, each with one leg pulled up and the other dangling toward the floor, like they had so many times over the years, even before they were living down the hall from each other.

Lisa took a deep breath, then told her everything. It was easier the second time, especially considering how well Shawn had taken it. The first time, it'd been terrifying, but also freeing. This time, that free feeling came earlier, outweighing the terror.

As she spoke, she watched Rose closely, trying to gauge her reaction. Was she surprised? Confused? Disgusted? The words came easier this time, but the heart-pounding anticipation was the same.

It didn't help that she couldn't read her sister's face. Rose sat motionless and expressionless, wet hair dripping onto her shirt.

When Lisa finished, she held her breath. For long seconds, no one spoke. "So," Lisa said hesitantly, "what do you think?"

"Do you care?" Rose's tone was icy.

"What?" Lisa blinked, confused. "Of course I do. That's why I told you. You're my sister."

"Yeah. I'm your *sister*. We always said we could tell each other anything. I always tell *you* everything. But you've been lying about this to me for how long? Months? Years?"

"That's not fair," Lisa said, heat creeping up her neck. Her fingers curled so her nails dug into her palms. She had just shown Rose the most vulnerable part of herself, a part practically no one else had ever seen, and *this* was her response? "You know this isn't like your crush on Noah or stealing earrings from the mall. I had to figure out a lot of stuff for myself first. And once I was ready, you're one of the first people I told. And one of the *only* people I plan on telling, at least for now. Which, I'll point out, is a lot more than you've been sharing with *me* lately."

"What's that supposed to mean?"

Lisa shook her head, her jaw hanging open incredulously. Was Rose even listening to herself right now? "Have any other *pen pals* that'll be dropping by this semester?"

"That is completely different."

"How? The way I see it, you don't get to be mad at *me* for not telling you absolutely everything going on in my life when you've had this whole secret boyfriend—"

"He is *not* my boyfriend."

"Does *he* know that? Guys don't typically just write letters or drop in for surprise visits to see girls they aren't into."

"Trust me, it's not like that."

Lisa stood, throwing up her hands. "Trust *you*? Rose, you've barely spoken to me all week. You never said one word about this guy to me until he was suddenly here. And yet you have the nerve to accuse *me* of keeping things from *you*?"

"It's not the same thing!"

Lisa was starting to get angry now. "Do you have any idea how hard this has been for me? How lonely? How scary? I have *agonized* over this for months, over what it meant for me and my life and my future. And I didn't have anyone I could talk to about it, except Charlene. You're allowed to have crushes that you obsess about and analyze to death and talk about all the time. I'm not. I can't say anything to anyone without risking *everything*. I didn't talk to you about it because I was scared. I

343

didn't know how you'd react." She crossed her arms. "I guess I was right. You don't get it."

"You didn't give me a *chance* to get it!" Rose was standing now, too, her face growing redder by the second. "I may not know how it feels to go through what you're going through, but I would've at least *tried*. Because I'm your sister. And I thought that meant something."

Lisa glared at her for a second, then grabbed her purse from her nightstand and stomped toward the door. But when her hand touched the knob, she hesitated. She couldn't let Rose have the last word. Not about this.

She whirled to face Rose, tears stinging her eyes. "You are one of the first people I told the biggest, scariest secret of my life. If that doesn't show that you're important to me, I don't know what does. But you have made it extremely clear that I am *obviously* not important to you."

With that, she stormed out of the room and down the stairs, running into the kitchen to yank the phone off the hook. *Please pick up, please pick up,* she chanted in her head as she counted rings.

Click. "Hello?"

"Hey, it's me. Can you come pick me up?"

"Is everything okay?"

"Yeah, I just . . . need to get out of here."

"Are you at home?"

"Yeah."

"Okay, give me ten minutes."

"Lisa?" her mom called, peering curiously at her from the living room, where she and Jim were getting Emmie's shoes on before heading to the community center to help set up for that evening. "Honey, where are you going? What's wrong?"

"Sorry, Mama," Lisa said, forcing back tears as she hung up the phone. "I know I said I'd help set up, but would it be okay if—"

"*Shhh*, baby, it's all right," Diane said, coming to her and folding her into her arms. "You want to tell me what's going on?"

Lisa shook her head, knowing she was getting wet spots on her mom's shirt. "Not yet," she said. "But maybe soon?"

"Of course, sweetheart. I'm here whenever you're ready," Diane said, stroking her back.

"I'll be there tonight for the debate," Lisa promised. "Is it okay if I go to Charlene's for a little while first? I know you asked me not to see her, but—"

"That's fine," her mom said, kissing the top of her head. "Never mind what I said. You go be with your friend. And you remember, I love you forever," she whispered into Lisa's hair.

Lisa nodded. "Thanks, Mama."

She closed the door and walked to the curb, wiping stray tears from her eyes with the back of her hand as she scanned the street. The seconds trudged by in a dismal parade as she waited for what felt like ages. With each one, she half expected to hear the front door open, and for Rose to come out and apologize. But the door remained stubbornly shut.

By the time Charlene's car pulled onto the street, slowing to a stop in front of her, Lisa was feeling mostly composed, although she was still mad at Rose. She yanked open the passenger door and flung herself inside.

"Lees? You okay?" Charlene reached tentatively across the seat to touch her hand.

Lisa had thought her crying was over, but as soon as Charlene's hand touched hers, the tears started to fall.

Chapter Sixty-Two

ROSE

Her conversation with Lisa had been playing on a loop in her head all morning as she joined the rest of her family at the community center to set up for the debate. Regret had enveloped her as soon as she heard the front door open and close. Why had she said those awful things?

The truth was that she wasn't nearly as shocked as she let on. It actually made a lot of sense. And despite how she'd reacted, she wasn't really mad that Lisa had waited to tell her.

She was mad at Justin. At the horrible things he'd said to her, and the impossible situation he'd put her in. And she'd taken it out on her sister at the worst possible time.

After returning home that afternoon, she tried calling Lisa at Charlene's a few times, but got the answering machine every time. It didn't seem right to leave an apology on the Derrins' answering machine, so Rose just hung up.

Her body hummed in anticipation of the evening, made all the worse by her guilt over Lisa. She and Noah had agreed to meet at her house tonight and head to the high school before the fire started. Rose figured that while she still may not know who would set it, they could at least prevent Bill and Veronica Warren from going into the building. Two entrances provided quick access to the guidance office: the main one at the front of the building, and another door around the side, near the office window. Rose and Noah planned to each stake out one of them and turn away the Warrens as soon as they arrived.

If they were successful, they could still get to the debate before it started, with everyone safe and no one the wiser.

She still had a few hours until she needed to meet Noah, though. Making up her mind, she grabbed the car keys off the table by the door and ran outside.

The drive to Charlene's felt like it was over in a matter of seconds. One moment Rose was pulling out of her driveway, and the next, she was working her way up the Derrins' winding drive. She still didn't have any idea what she wanted to say, only that she needed to fix what she'd broken that morning.

She rang the doorbell, shifting her weight nervously from one foot to the other as she listened to the muffled echo of the chimes inside the cavernous house. Charlene opened the door, her mouth set in a frown. "She doesn't want to see you."

"Can you please tell her I'm sorry? Please?"

Charlene looked conflicted, but didn't move from the doorway. "You really hurt her feelings, Rose," she said, lowering her voice.

"I know. I'm really, *really* sorry." Rose tried for a smile, although it felt tight. "Is she okay?"

Charlene tilted her head, her green eyes narrowing slightly. "Would you be?"

Rose wrung her hands, trying to think of anything she could say to make this better. "I shouldn't have said any of those things," she said, her voice shaking. "I didn't even mean them. I was mad about something else and I took it out on her, and that was a bitchy thing to do and I suck."

A small laugh escaped from Charlene. "I don't think I've ever heard you use the word *bitchy* before."

Rose shrugged. "Desperate times, I guess."

Charlene sighed, then turned to look behind her into the house, where Rose couldn't see. She ducked her face behind the door and whispered, and Rose realized with a jolt that Lisa must be standing right there, just out of sight.

A moment later, the door swung wide, revealing Lisa standing beside Charlene with her arms folded. Her expression was cold, her eyes rimmed in red as she stepped onto the porch. She didn't meet Rose's eyes as she stood in front of her, just glared at a spot on the ground, rocking slightly from side to side.

"I'm right here if you need me, okay?" Charlene said, looking at Lisa.

Lisa nodded, still not looking up. Charlene appeared uneasy but shut the door, leaving Lisa alone with Rose on the porch.

Rose took a deep breath. "Did . . . did you hear what I said to Charlene?"

A nod. Still no eye contact.

"I meant all of it. I am *so* sorry. I wish I could take it all back."

"Well, you can't," Lisa said, her voice sharp.

"I know." She ducked down, trying to get Lisa to look at her, but she still avoided her gaze. "I know that telling me was really hard for you. And scary. And different from anything I've ever told you. And I'm really sorry for acting like it wasn't."

Lisa's eyes flickered up. "I trusted you with a really big and vulnerable part of myself. And you made it about *you*."

"I shouldn't have done that."

"I mean, god, Rose, do you have any idea how scared I was to tell *anyone*? How scared I still am? I feel like I'm drowning. Every minute of every day, I'm worried that someone might find out. I read these . . . these stories . . ." Tears were beginning to trickle down Lisa's face, dripping from her chin down to the porch below. "People are dying, Rose. Every day. People like me, and they don't even have anyone, because the people they cared about stopped caring about them the second they found out who they were. And I just keep wondering, is that going to be me? Am I doomed to be alone?"

"You won't," Rose said, feeling tears pool in her own eyes. "I promise."

"You can't know that." Lisa sniffed. "I mean, Mom's campaign—"

"Diane loves you more than her campaign," Rose said without hesitation. "You know that."

"She loves me, but if she lost because of me, she'd always resent me for it."

"That's not true."

Lisa shrugged, spreading her hands helplessly. "No way to know for sure, though, right? I mean, I thought *you'd* be safe, and look how that turned out."

"Lisa." Rose grabbed her sister's hand and looked into her glistening eyes. Tears spilled freely down Rose's cheeks. "I messed up, and I am so, so sorry about that, and I'm sorry that your memory of that conversation will always include me being awful. All I can say is that I'm going to try my best to do better. I don't know what's going to happen. But I love you. You're my sister. You are one of the most important people in the whole world to me. And I swear, I will never, *ever* let you be alone."

"Well," Lisa choked through sobs, "maybe in the bathroom."

Rose let out a surprised laugh that came out like a bark. "Deal." She took a deep breath, squeezing Lisa's hand. "Can we start over? Please? Can you tell me again, and this time I'll react like your sister and not a monster?"

Lisa nodded. "I'm still kinda mad at you, though," she said, sniffing. "I forgive you, but I can't forget what you said. You *really* hurt me."

Rose swallowed hard, nodding. She deserved that. "I hope eventually I can make up for that."

"I hope so, too," Lisa said, giving her the faintest hint of a smile. She sighed heavily, wiping her eyes. "You have time to come in and talk for a little bit?"

Rose checked her watch—plenty of time until she needed to meet Noah—and smiled. "I do."

Chapter Sixty-Three

Justin

If it were possible to feel worse about myself than I already do, I'd feel really lousy about stealing from Mrs. Hanley.

I help myself to the cash that she keeps in the cookie jar on the kitchen counter, leaving the coins behind. Just a little under fifty dollars, mostly in ones and fives, although there's one twenty in there. It'll likely be days before she notices it's missing. By then I'll be long gone.

I try to tell myself that if she knew my situation, she'd give it to me anyway.

It doesn't make me feel better.

My plan is to go buy a bus ticket to Hawthorne, but I find myself taking a detour on the way to the bus station. My feet carry me to the community center, where the debate will be held tonight. I don't plan to go in. I just want to see them one last time before I leave.

Bill. Veronica.

Rose.

I don't see any of their cars yet, but I know they're all bound to show up here eventually. Rose told me earlier that the plan was for everyone to come here after breakfast to help set up, then return home to prepare for the event. I grab a newspaper and a hot chocolate—because there's no age limit on deliciousness—from a nearby diner, and settle in on a bench across the street to wait. Every few minutes, I raise my eyes and give the area a quick scan. Once I see them, I promise myself, I'll go.

I'm working through the Entertainment section, reading an ad for *Teen Wolf* ("A Howling Success!") when a shadow falls over me. I look up to see Deputy Kenny Gibson glaring down at me. "What are you doing here?"

What. The hell.

"Um, reading?" I say, holding up the paper.

He sits down beside me, propping a meaty arm across the back of the bench. If CrossFit existed in the '80s, this guy would be their god. "Interesting reading spot. Great view of the community center. Sure you're not waiting for someone?"

I shake my head, swallowing.

He narrows his eyes. "Not, perhaps, Rose Yin? Her mom's debating here tonight."

"Oh," I say, my voice sounding hoarse. "Yeah, I think I heard about that."

He shakes his head, his expression dark. "Listen, kid, I don't know who you are, but I know you were told to leave that girl alone. So if I were you, I'd go *read* somewhere else. Got it?"

Not knowing what else to do, I nod, clenching my teeth so hard my jaw hurts. All I wanted to do was see them one last time. I wasn't even going to say anything. And now I can't even have that much.

He pats my shoulder so hard my teeth rattle, then gets to his feet. "I'll be around all day. Don't let me see you here again," he says before heading into the community center, leaving me alone on the bench.

I want to scream, but instead I crumple the newspaper in my hands, my whole body trembling. Stupid Gibson. Stupid 1985. Stupid me, thinking I can do a single thing to make any of this more tolerable.

I get up from the bench and walk down the sidewalk, toward the bus station.

The ticket to Hawthorne is only a couple of bucks, but even with 1985's low prices, fifty dollars plus the last of Stan's Oreo money isn't going to last me long. I need a plan. I try to think back, remember whether Stan gave me any hints for what I'm supposed to do next, but I come up empty-handed. If he ever told me what he did to support himself in the years after leaving Stone Lake, I wasn't listening.

Stupid, stupid, stupid.

I don't get on the first bus, or the second, telling myself I have plenty of time. I'm not in a rush. I've got my whole life to be Stan, and I'm not quite ready to leave Justin behind yet.

To pass the time, I scan the job listings in the newspaper. They're all for Stone Lake, not Hawthorne, so they won't do me any good, but I tell myself it's helpful to know what sorts of opportunities are out there for a Dollar Tree–trained time traveler like me. Despite my lack of a high school diploma—in 1985 or otherwise—or any other credible documentation, it doesn't seem like it should be too hard to find a minimum-wage job, provided their background checks aren't very robust.

I guess I could eventually invest in the stock market. Get in on the ground floor of Apple or Google or Facebook or some other mega-bajillion-dollar tech company that will set me up for life. Maybe that's why Stan never worked. He always said he retired early, although I figured that was just code for "permanently unemployed." Now I wonder whether he actually had a lot more cash stuffed in his mattress than I previously thought.

But of course, becoming a stock-market millionaire still requires me to get enough money together to actually invest in the first place, and to tide me over for the years it will take for my knowledge of the future to actually become profitable. All the Google stock in the world won't do me any good if I starve to death before the internet becomes a thing.

Before too long, though, I toss the paper aside. Trying to plan out my lonely life of solitude is depressing as hell. Every time I focus on it too much, I get this awful, writhing feeling in my gut, like I've swallowed a snake. I've only ever loved three people in my life. And judging by Stan's completely nonexistent social life, that's the way it's going to stay.

Two of them I won't see again for decades, and when I do, I'll be someone else.

And the third is already done with me.

The thought is crushing. I can't hold it for long, or I'll forget how to breathe.

So I slump in my seat as morning bleeds into afternoon and buses continue to depart without me on them, trying to distract myself with the soap operas playing on the TV in the corner. They're the same ones I've been watching at Mrs. Hanley's, but I can't even get into them because I'm too distracted watching the clock.

Veronica's and Bill's faces keep flashing through my mind. They don't know that their time is almost up, and there's no way for me to warn them. Veronica already doesn't trust me. For all I know, if I tried to convince her and Bill to stay away from the school, it would turn out to be the very reason they go.

No matter how I look at it, saving them is a lost cause. In a couple of hours, they'll be gone.

Then why can't I let this go?

Why do I feel like I'm going to crawl out of my skin if I stay on this bench a second longer?

Can I really sit here watching soap operas, knowing what I know?

Can I really just get on a bus and leave?

I should. There's nothing I can do. My knee still throbs every time I put my full weight on my leg, a reminder that any attempt to change the past is pointless.

Rose doesn't want anything to do with me. That walking canker sore Gibson will probably throw my ass in jail if he sees me again.

There is nothing for me here. No one.

Except my mom.

Except her parents.

The family I never had. The family she *should* have had.

It's probably futile. It's most definitely stupid.

But I can't leave them. If there's even the smallest chance Rose is right, that there's still something I can do to save them, I have to try.

Shoving my bus ticket in my pocket, I head to the school. There's still some time left before the fire. I have no real plan, just the resolution to stop Bill and Veronica from getting trapped in that building in any way I can. If I fail, I fail. But I'm not ready to give up. Not yet.

It turns out Rose may have gotten under my skin after all.

I turn off the sidewalk to cut through the parking lot of the Food Mart and around the back of the store, taking a shortcut to the school.

I'm so busy thinking through how I might still save Bill and Veronica that I don't hear the footsteps coming up behind me until it's too late. "Now!" someone yells, and I turn just in time for the branch that was aimed at the back of my head to catch me between the neck and shoulder instead.

I fall to my knees, choking as I take in my attackers.

The monster and his minions. Robbie Reynolds and his two cronies. They stand over me grinning ghoulishly, looking extremely proud of themselves as I gasp for air. I want to wring their scrawny little necks, but my body is too preoccupied with trying to remember how to breathe after taking a tree branch to the trachea.

All I can do is paw feebly at them as they grab me by the arms and drag me behind a dumpster.

Chapter Sixty-Four

VERONICA

"Say that again?" Bill stared at her from across the bedroom, his face pale, the ends of his blue tie slipping forgotten from his fingers. Between them, Millie rolled around on the bed, entertaining herself in a pile of pillows and blankets.

"I'm pregnant," Veronica repeated, fastening her earrings in place. It felt a little more real every time she said the words.

She'd finally put the pieces together that morning when she'd gotten sick again at Diane's. After running to the bathroom, she'd checked her planner and confirmed her suspicion. She'd just been so busy lately, she hadn't realized how late she was.

"Are you sure?"

"I'll need to call the doctor's office on Monday to confirm, but it's been eight weeks, Bill. I'm never this late. And I've been feeling sick all week. I thought it was just nerves about the debate, but . . ." She shrugged, giving him a hopeful smile. "What do you think?"

Bill blinked at her uncomprehendingly for a moment, then shook his head, looking stunned. "I mean—well, what do *you* think? Are you, you know . . . okay with this? I know we weren't planning on it . . ." He trailed off, looking at her with what she recognized as his counselor expression: detached, empathetic, interested. But he couldn't hide the hope in his eyes.

She nodded. "I was really surprised at first. But after thinking about it all day, I think . . . I think I'm really excited."

Bill's expression lightened, a smile breaking across his face. "Me too," he admitted, then vaulted over the bed to sweep her up in a hug. "Babe, we're going to have another baby!"

Veronica laughed, feeling suddenly a hundred pounds lighter. "We are!"

"You're going to be a big sister, Millie!" Bill said, scooping Millie up off the bed and spinning her through the air. She squealed in surprised delight, uncertain why her daddy was flying her around the room, but happy to go along with it.

"Okay," Bill said breathlessly, setting Millie back down on the bed. "That means you'll be due . . . when, sometime in the summer?"

"End of May, I think," Veronica said. She'd done the math earlier, although of course she couldn't be sure until she saw her doctor.

Bill nodded to himself, and Veronica could almost see the gears in his head turning. "So school won't be done yet, but I've got some vacation time saved up that should be enough to get me through the end of the school year. And then—"

"Sweetheart," Veronica said, taking Bill's face in her hands. "I know you love to plan ahead, but we don't have to figure everything out tonight. We can slow down."

But that just seemed to remind him of something else, his eyes growing wide. "Oh, honey, the campaign! Are you going to be okay?"

She nodded. "I haven't told Diane yet, obviously—I wanted to wait until after I go to the doctor—but I should be fine. The election is in just a few weeks, so I'll still be pretty early and won't have to announce it yet. And then if she wins, she'd take office in January, so I'd have a few months to get everything set up and running smoothly before I have to leave." She'd been working it out in her head all morning. It would be a lot of work to do while pregnant, but she was sure she could manage it. Especially with a boss like Diane.

She shuddered to think of what this experience would be like if she were managing Gibson's campaign instead of Diane's. She'd probably have to keep her pregnancy hidden until the moment she gave birth. And then she doubted she'd have a job to come back to.

"Well, you know I'm here for whatever you need," Bill said, practically bouncing with excitement. "Trips to the store, foot rubs, extra time with Millie so you can take a nap . . ." He remembered the tie dangling around his neck and returned to the mirror, excitedly looping the fabric around itself into a quick, sloppy knot. He frowned, loosening it and starting over.

"Right now, I just need you to be cool for this debate," Veronica said, laughing as Bill made an exuberant mess of his tie yet again. "You're acting like a kid who ate all his Halloween candy at once."

"I *feel* like I just ate all the Halloween candy at once," Bill said, finally tying an acceptable Windsor knot. "But I can be cool. See? Look how cool I am. Cool as a cucumber." He moved around the bed doing a leisurely two-step, smiling as he took Veronica in his arms, continuing to dance to the sound of Millie babbling to herself in the bed.

"Very cool," she agreed, matching his steps.

He dipped her slowly back, then kissed her neck. "Congratulations," he said softly, his lips brushing her skin.

She straightened, draping her arms around his neck, and kissed him. "Congratulations."

He smiled against her lips, then released her suddenly, leaving her slightly off balance. "Oh, honey, do you mind if we run by the school real quick before the debate?" Bill asked. "I just need to get something from my office."

She sighed, glancing at the clock on her nightstand. "That's all the way in the opposite direction."

"I know, but if we leave soon, we'll have plenty of time to swing by and still make it to the debate early. It'll only take a minute."

"Okay," she agreed, smoothing her hands over the front of her skirt. She wondered how much longer she'd be able to fit into it before she'd have to pull her maternity clothes out of the attic. Wasn't it just yesterday that she'd packed them all away? "As long as it's fast."

"In and out," Bill said. "You'll barely even notice we stopped. I promise."

Chapter Sixty-Five

KARL

His fort didn't feel safe anymore.

After Robbie and his friends destroyed it, Karl considered going back to assess the damage, but couldn't bring himself to make the trek through the woods. After yesterday, he could barely force himself to set foot outside his room.

Not that inside the room was much better. His fort had been the safest place in the world. No one knew about it but him. If that wasn't true, then there was nowhere they couldn't find him. Nowhere they couldn't hurt him.

He hadn't slept last night, tossing and turning in his bed, seeing Robbie climbing through his window or popping out of his closet every time he closed his eyes. His house didn't even feel safe anymore. After all, everyone knew where he lived. He was easy to find. What was to stop Robbie from coming after him while his parents weren't home? Maybe the safest place to be was actually anywhere *but* home.

His parents had to head into town early to set up before the debate. They'd be manning a table in the lobby of the community center, passing out stickers and pamphlets rooting for Franklin Gibson. Karl had no interest in that, but he asked to accompany them into town anyway, thinking that as long as he stuck to public spaces, he'd be safe from Robbie.

He spent an hour playing *Donkey Kong* at the front of the Food Mart as shoppers milled in and out of the store. The large window gave him a good view of the parking lot, and he took comfort in the store's bright fluorescent lights, the low rumble of shopping cart wheels, the shuffling footsteps and benign questions of shoppers. It wasn't very busy tonight, but there was still always someone within earshot.

He was digging through his pocket for another quarter to feed to the game when he glanced outside to see Justin walking through the parking lot, his eyes trained on the ground in front of him. His hands were jammed deep into his jacket pockets and he appeared lost in thought, his head bowed, hair falling into his eyes. He was still wearing his torn jeans from the day before, his stride marked with a slight limp.

Karl started to raise his hand to wave—but then froze, the contents of his stomach congealing into a tight ball. Trailing behind Justin, keeping their distance but still obviously following him, were Robbie, Steve, and Kevin. They kept their eyes locked on him, none of them speaking. Steve leaned over to whisper something to Robbie, who grinned, nodding enthusiastically.

Karl stood still, heart pounding, the quarter clutched in his hand growing warm and sweaty. He watched the boys as they followed Justin around the back of the building, never glancing toward the store, where Karl belatedly realized he would've been fully visible, framed by the window. Swallowing, Karl looked around, hoping to see an adult who had noticed what he had and might intervene, but the people in the store continued to go about their business, maddeningly unaware of the situation outside.

"Can I help you with something?"

Karl spun to see a man in a red Food Mart vest blinking at him with polite interest, hugging a clipboard to his chest.

"I, um . . ." He glanced toward the front window again, suddenly second-guessing himself. None of the boys were visible anymore. For all he knew, they were all long gone by now.

Justin had scared them off twice before. He was probably fine.

Karl should at least check first, before asking for help.

"Everything okay?" The man peered at him over his clipboard.

Karl nodded. "Sorry," he mumbled, heat flooding his face as he turned and rushed from the store.

Once outside, he looked around the parking lot, but didn't see anything out of the ordinary. Tentatively, he crept around the side of the building in the direction Justin and the others had been headed, tiptoeing down the cracked delivery drive. As he approached the back of the building, he began to make out the low hum of voices punctuated by a series of dull thuds drifting from behind the dumpster.

Karl held his breath, venturing toward the edge of the drive, trying to catch a glimpse of the speakers without them noticing him. The outside of the lot was rimmed with spindly trees, and he stuck close to them, hoping to blend in with the tangles of branches.

Robbie, Steve, and Kevin were standing over someone on the ground, taking turns landing quick kicks on all parts of their body. Karl couldn't make out the face of their victim, but it had to be Justin. Of course they were mad at him for interfering in their torture of Karl. Twice. And Karl knew all too well how far Robbie could take things when he was mad instead of just bored.

He had to help him. But by the time he went back into the store to find help, it would be too late.

Karl looked around, searching for something he could use. About ten feet from where the boys huddled around Justin, a thick tree branch, about the length of a baseball bat, lay on the ground. Karl made his way toward it, crouching slightly, his arms stiff at his sides, his eyes glued to Robbie's back.

Beeeeep.

A car horn blasted from the lot behind him.

He'd covered only half the distance toward the branch, his fingers already outstretched to grab it. Robbie and his friends spun in surprise as Karl jumped, startled. For a second, their eyes locked in confusion, before Robbie's gaze darkened.

"Hey there, Derrin," he said, taking a step toward him.

Karl spun around and ran.

"Get him!" he heard Robbie yell behind him, followed a second later by the sounds of sneakers smacking against pavement.

Karl didn't bother to look back, knowing exactly what he'd see. Darting around a parked delivery truck, he cut through the trees that lined the edge of the parking lot, then skidded down a grassy bank and ducked into the storm drain, cold water soaking his sneakers as he ran. Hopefully, he had enough of a lead that the other boys hadn't seen him go this way and would assume he'd gone back around the front of the building, into the store. If he was lucky, he might gain a couple of precious minutes while they searched the aisles for him.

The drain came out near the school. Karl couldn't hear the others behind him and didn't want to stick around long enough for that to change. He started to move toward the school, but then realized it was probably locked on the weekends. Instead, he kept to the street, his eyes roaming frantically, searching for a hiding place.

Up ahead, a pickup truck stood parked alongside the curb. Karl peered over the edge of the bed to find a couple of shovels, a bundle of firewood, and a gas canister sitting on a folded blue tarp. No longer caring whether he made noise, Karl scrambled into the bed of the truck and pulled the tarp from under the gas can, shaking it out and pulling it over his head like a blanket.

He stayed there, huddled under the tarp, trying to move as little as possible. His breath rattled in his ears, his knees pulled up to his chest, as he waited for the threat to pass.

Interlude

Shawn, Five Months Ago

Shawn was beginning to panic. Finals were in just a couple of days, and he'd barely studied at all. It wasn't that he didn't enjoy all the impromptu activities Lisa suddenly wanted to do every time they got together to study—the mall, the movies, roller-skating—but if he didn't manage to ace his finals, there was no way he'd be in the running for the citizenship award. And he really needed that award.

Not that it was a sure thing even with the grades, but he thought he had a decent shot. It was also his *only* shot; his dad would never pay for him to go away for school—in Gabe Rothman's eyes, there was only one acceptable path for his son to follow, and that was directly in his footsteps.

So since the beginning of high school, he'd always made sure to play sports, join clubs, volunteer for committees, run for student council. All things the Buford County Citizenship Award selection committee would be looking for, in addition to the grades.

But he still needed the grades.

Lisa probably didn't realize how long it took him to prepare for tests; she had always been able to simply glance over the material the night before and earn perfect scores. He was sure she hadn't *meant* to make him fall so far behind. But now he had only a few precious hours left, and he wasn't sure it would be enough.

He balled his fingers in his hair as he paced around his backyard, trying to recite all the US presidents in chronological order. He kept getting hung up around Rutherford B. Hayes and having to start over. He was on his third attempt when he heard someone say his name.

"Shawn?"

He stopped pacing and blinked at Lisa, hugging her books on his back porch. "Oh, hey, babe," he said, forcing a smile. "I didn't expect to see you until five."

"It *is* five," she said, holding up her wrist to show him her watch.

"Are you serious?" Shawn exclaimed, his chest clenching. He'd thought he'd have finished studying for History and English by now and would be ready to move on to Precalculus with Lisa, but he was still on his first subject, with no end in sight.

He hurried over to his pile of textbooks and folders and notecards and riffled through them, as if maybe he'd discover he'd been mistaken about just how much work he had to do that afternoon, and he was actually almost done. But if anything, there was *more* here than he'd mentally accounted for.

"There is *no way* I'm going to get through all this in time," Shawn said, his voice coming out louder and higher than he'd intended.

"What's all this yelling out here? I can barely hear myself think," his father called sharply, sticking his head out the sliding door to the deck, his expression a thundercloud.

But then he spotted Lisa and his entire demeanor changed, his shoulders dropping and his face smoothing. In an instant, he was the Gabe Rothman people loved to invite over for Sunday dinners, the one who always kept Jolly Ranchers in his pockets for his clients' kids and shoveled the neighbors' driveways every time it snowed. "Oh, hi, sweetheart, I didn't know you were here. Can I get you a snack?"

"No thanks, Mr. Rothman, I'm good." Lisa smiled. "Just came over to study with Shawn."

"That's nice of you. Just don't let him drag you down," Gabe said with a wink. "He has a hard time staying on task."

"I think we'll be okay," Lisa said as Shawn's fingernails dug into his palms. Why did his dad *always* have to be like this? Everyone thought he was this great guy, yet when it came to his son, he was nothing but sharp edges and stinging barbs.

"Well, let me know if you need anything," Gabe said jovially, disappearing back into the kitchen.

Shawn looked at Lisa, his jaw quivering. "I'm sorry I yelled at you," he said softly.

"Listen," Lisa said, stepping into the yard and dropping her books on the wooden picnic table. "I know we need to study for Precalc, but you seem really stressed out. Maybe you need a break. It could be fun if we—"

"No, Lisa, no more *fun*." Shawn groaned. "Can't you see how behind I am? I don't have *time* for fun!"

"Sorry," Lisa said, looking slightly taken aback. "I was only trying to help."

"I know. I know you were, babe." Shawn scrubbed a hand down his face, heat pricking the backs of his eyes. "He just makes me so . . ." He trailed off, shaking his head.

He makes me like him, his mind whispered, but he shoved away the thought. He was *nothing* like his father. And that was how it was going to stay.

"What do you want to do?" Lisa asked.

"I want to go back in time and spend the past two weeks actually studying," Shawn said. "I love doing stuff with you, but saying yes to all the stuff you've wanted to do lately has put me so far behind, and I don't think . . . I'm not going to be able to . . ."

He swallowed, unable to voice out loud what he knew was true. He was out of time. He'd never get it now. "I just . . . I can't stay here with him," he said softly. "But if I don't get this scholarship, that's it. I'm stuck."

"No." Lisa shook her head, refusing to believe the truth that seemed so obvious to him. "No, there are still other ways. You can get a job or a loan or—"

"He'll never let me," Shawn insisted. "He'd always find some way to keep me here. You know he would. But I thought, if I've already got the money—if it's already *done* . . ." His eyes grew hot, then blurry. He wiped them on the shoulder of his shirt, hoping it looked like he was scratching an itch. "But that'll never happen now. I messed it all up."

"Shawn, I'm so sorry," Lisa said, looking horrified. "I didn't realize."

"It's not your fault," he said, his voice shaking, trying to keep from bursting into tears. "I should have said something."

"I shouldn't have put you in this position in the first place," she said, grabbing his hand and looking into his eyes. "I just kept suggesting stuff without thinking."

"I kept saying yes, even though I *knew*—"

"No, really, it was my fault. I just wasn't paying attention."

"It was *my* fault; I should've been more—"

"Okay, let's stop for a sec," Lisa interrupted, blowing out a breath. "We could go back and forth all afternoon about whose fault it was, but that doesn't help now. What can we do to make this better? Can I help you study? Quiz you? Help make flash cards? We've still got a couple days. You can still be ready."

Shawn dropped his eyes to the pile of school supplies on the picnic table. He thought through his mental study schedule, which he'd already completely blown. *It's too late,* his brain whispered. There wasn't enough time. He was totally screwed.

He took a shaky breath, then shook his head. "I think . . . maybe you should just go home," he said.

"What? No, Shawn, let me help—"

"You *can't* help, okay?" he snapped. "No one can. It's hopeless now, so you might as well not waste your time." He scooped up a stack of notebooks and walked across the deck to the large outdoor trash can. "I won't waste mine either," he said, lifting the lid.

366

"What are you *doing?*" Lisa asked, hurrying over to grab the notebooks away from him before he could toss them inside.

"I'm giving up," Shawn said. "Just like my dad always knew I would."

"Shawn, no. Don't say that." Lisa's eyes darted toward the house, and she bit her lip, her forehead creased.

"What?" Shawn asked after a minute of watching the gears behind her eyes turn. He'd known her long enough to recognize her thinking face.

"I have an idea . . . and it's probably a bad one," she said uncertainly.

"I told you, there's not enough *time* for—"

"There is for this. Barely. But it's a little . . . iffy," she said. "I heard about something, but I've never tried it. It could either help you, or it could go really, really wrong."

"Lisa, what on earth are you talking about?"

She shifted from one foot to the other, blowing out a long breath. "You have to know I wouldn't normally suggest this. Really, I shouldn't even *know* about it, but I overheard these kids talking and I was curious so I asked. And remember, you definitely don't have to do this if you don't want to, but I do feel like this is at least partially my fault, so—"

"Oh my god, will you *please* just tell me?"

She leaned closer to him. "If there was a way to . . . know *exactly* what to study . . . would that help?"

His heart sank. This was her big plan? Some sort of new study method? He shook his head miserably. "It won't make a difference. I already know which units will be covered in each test and—"

"No, Shawn, I mean like, *exactly*. Like . . . exactly exactly. If you want."

He narrowed his eyes slightly, tilting his head. Was she suggesting what he thought she was? Had she seen copies of the tests? Did she know what was on them?

He thought about it. He'd never cheated in his life. He wasn't one of those lazy jerks who assumed doors would swing open with nothing more than a look; no, he *worked* for his success. If he won the citizenship award next year, it would be because he'd *earned* it.

But if he didn't do well on his finals, his chances of winning the award would shrink to practically nothing. And along with them, his chances of getting out of Buford County, of escaping his dad, of carving out a life that *he* chose, no one else.

If he'd been able to study like he planned, he knew he would have done well. He always did. Did he really deserve to lose his whole future, just because he'd run out of time? Was that really fair, after working so hard for so long?

In a way, he wouldn't even really be cheating. He'd just be getting the grades he *should* have gotten anyway. The grades he deserved, to secure the future he had earned.

"Yes," he said finally. "I'll do anything."

Lisa took another deep breath, then lowered her voice. "Do you know about locker two forty-seven?"

Chapter Sixty-Six

SHAWN

His hands kneaded the steering wheel as he slowed his truck to a stop. Even though he'd picked a low-traffic street around the corner from the school, Shawn felt exposed, vulnerable. But no one was here tonight. It was Saturday, and besides, most of the town was getting ready to head to the debate. Which was where he would be soon, too. It would never occur to anyone that he'd made a stop first.

Plus, he was the citizenship-award winner. No one would suspect him.

That didn't keep his stomach from churning as he turned off the ignition and slid out of the driver's seat, his feet landing softly on the pavement. He winced at the sound of the door clicking shut, looking around to make sure no one had heard him.

But of course, there was no one around. The night was quiet. The school sat dark and still, the empty lot a sea of open spaces. Just as he'd planned.

Five minutes, he promised himself. Just a quick in and out. And then he'd never have to think about his stupid mistake ever again.

The doors to the school were locked, but Shawn had thought ahead. Friday afternoon, before he left, he'd stopped by the office, claiming he'd forgotten a book that morning. While he pretended to look for it, he unlatched a window, then moved a stack of trays in front of it so that no one would notice.

Pulling up the hood of his sweatshirt, he went around the side of the building and counted windows, picturing the inside of the office. The unlocked window was sluggish—these windows didn't get opened very often—but reluctantly conceded a few inches, then a few more. After some coaxing, he was able to open it wide enough to hoist himself up and in.

The office was nearly black. Shawn switched on the flashlight he carried in his back pocket, keeping it aimed low as he made his way toward Mr. Warren's office. Everything felt different in the dark. His sleeve brushed some papers hanging off the edge of a counter, sending them tumbling to the floor with a loud flutter. Shawn jumped, banging into a table, his heart racing in his throat as he tried not to scream. He stood there for a second, hand on his chest, his breaths coming in rapid gasps.

Just some papers. Not a person. Everything's fine.

Carefully, he crouched down, picked up the papers, and replaced them on the counter, hoping the order didn't matter.

He continued to the guidance office, keeping his elbows tucked close by his sides so he didn't knock into anything else. The door opened with a loud creak, causing him to grit his teeth. He wished he'd thought to bring some WD-40 with him.

Once he was inside, he shut it behind him with a soft *click. Almost there.*

Mr. Warren kept his desk well organized, making Shawn's task easy. The list was sitting in a wire tray labeled In Progress, tucked inside a manila folder. As McMillain had said, it was a list of locker numbers of every student who had patronized locker 247, beside which McMillain had penciled in dates and subjects. Someone else—Mr. Warren, probably—had started filling in names beside the locker numbers, starting at the top of the page. Shawn scanned quickly down the list, holding his breath, but was relieved to see the space beside his locker number was still blank.

He creased the paper down the center, preparing to fold it small enough to put in his pocket—later, he'd burn it, making sure the record was erased for good—when a pair of headlights swung into the parking lot, briefly washing Shawn with light.

He jumped, dropping the flashlight so it knocked over an open bottle that was sitting on the edge of the desk. The bottle fell to the floor, its contents splashing out onto the carpet as it rolled under the desk. The sharp smell of liquor hit his nostrils.

"Shit!" Shawn whispered through his teeth, bending down and fumbling in the dark. His hand closed around the neck of the bottle and he hurried to replace it on the desk but instead slammed the bottom of the bottle into the arm of Mr. Warren's desk chair, causing it to shatter. Liquid and shards of glass sprayed across the chair, the carpet, Shawn's pants.

"Shit!"

Crouched beside the desk, his nostrils burning with the smell of alcohol, Shawn switched off the flashlight as a car door opened and shut outside. A muffled voice drifted through the closed window. "We can talk about it more later, okay? Just give me a second."

Shawn's stomach sank. Mr. Warren? What was he doing here *now*? Shouldn't he already be at the debate?

He looked around the dark office, his heart hammering. There was nowhere to hide. He considered running out the main door of the guidance office and hiding somewhere in the school until Mr. Warren was gone, but before he could move, a light switched on in the main office.

Shawn dropped behind the desk, liquid soaking into the knees of his khakis, his breath coming in shallow gasps. Another light flipped on in the hall. Shawn could hear Mr. Warren humming softly to himself as he came closer and risked a glance around the side of the desk, through the doorway window.

Mr. Warren had paused by the mailboxes, a cigarette dangling from his lips as he flipped through a stack of papers. He opened a letter and scanned it, then sighed, breathing out a cloud of smoke.

Slowly, Shawn shifted from his knees to the balls of his feet, the muscles in his legs tensing to run. He adjusted the hood of his sweatshirt, pulling the drawstrings tight around his face. There was no way Mr. Warren wouldn't notice that someone had been in his office, so it didn't matter if Shawn was seen, as long as he wasn't recognized. If he could knock Mr. Warren over before he got a good look at him, he could probably get through the office and back to his truck unidentified.

As soon as Shawn heard the door to the office begin to creak open, he sprang forward. Tucking his head before Mr. Warren could reach for the light switch, he hit the guidance counselor at full speed, his shoulder colliding with the soft center of his body. Mr. Warren let out a surprised grunt as he flipped over Shawn's back and hit the floor of the dark office.

Shawn didn't look back; he just sprinted through the office toward the open window. He didn't think Mr. Warren had seen his face, and he couldn't risk changing that. Adrenaline roared through him as he pushed himself up onto the counter and outside, not caring anymore about the papers he knocked to the ground.

As soon as his feet hit the grass, he ran full tilt toward the side street where his truck was parked, his sneakers smacking the pavement in a frantic staccato.

"Hey! Hey, stop!"

Shawn glanced back to see Mrs. Warren's head leaning out the passenger side window of her idling car, peering toward him. Hurriedly, he turned away and kept his head down as he ran from the lot. Surely she couldn't have recognized him. Not in the dark.

It was only once he threw himself into the driver's seat of his truck that he noticed McMillain's list still crumpled in his fist. He tossed it onto the seat beside him and fumbled in his pocket for the keys, his fingers shaking as he turned the ignition. He glanced in the rearview mirror, bracing himself to see Mrs. Warren walking toward him, but the street behind him was still empty. Shawn pressed the pedal to the floor and drove off into the night.

Chapter Sixty-Seven

BILL

"We can talk about it more later, okay? Just give me a second."

He gave Veronica a quick kiss before stepping out of the car. They'd been discussing baby names the whole way here. It turned out that girl names were hard. Coming up with Millie's name had been easy—Millicent Esther, after Veronica's grandmother and mother—but now they weren't sure what they'd name a second girl. Boy names were easier; Veronica suggested Jonathan, after her father, and Bill was happy to go with that, since they both knew they wouldn't be using any of the names from his side of the family.

Bill reached into his shirt pocket as he walked toward the school, his mind whirring as he pulled out a cigarette and flicked open his lighter. His body moved automatically, holding the cigarette between his lips as he lit it, blowing out a cloud of smoke as he traded his lighter for his keys and unlocked the front door of the school. He'd already flipped on the light in the front office before his mind even registered that he was inside the building.

Another baby.

He was going to be a dad. Again.

Millie was going to be a big sister.

A smile spread across his face as he paused by the teacher mailboxes and pulled a stack of papers from his cubby. Cat Stevens lyrics ran through his head as he riffled through them, absently tossing aside college recruiting pamphlets and flyers for spirit nights and fundraisers.

An envelope caught his eye, his name scrawled across it in blue ink. He didn't recognize the handwriting.

Inside were two pages. One, a typewritten résumé, the top entry reading "Custodian, Stone Lake High School." The other, a short handwritten note. He scanned the latter.

Thanks for the opportunity. I won't let you down again. Sincerely, Michael McMillain

Bill sighed and pocketed the letter, hoping he hadn't lied to the guy when he'd said he might know of a place that would hire him. Tomorrow, he promised himself. Tomorrow he'd call his brother and ask him if he had—or could create—any entry-level openings at the Hawthorne office, just twenty minutes down the road. His parents may have effectively disowned him when he'd opted to counsel students in his wife's hometown instead of joining the family business, but he and Alan were still on decent terms. At least, he hoped they were.

But tonight was for celebrating.

He'd intended to wait until their anniversary next month to give Veronica the pendant he had asked Pat to make for her, but in light of the news about the baby, now seemed like the perfect time to surprise her. After he gave it to her, they'd head to the debate, and once Diane wiped the floor with Gibson—the pompous ass—he'd take Veronica home, put Millie to bed, and dust off his neglected record collection so that he could twirl his wife around the living room. They'd toast with the champagne that they'd been keeping in the top kitchen cabinet for a special occasion, then stay up late talking about the future, like they used to do before life slowly squeezed the energy out of them. He thought he'd read something recently about pregnant women being advised against drinking alcohol, but surely a few sips of celebratory champagne would be fine.

His mind already hours ahead of his next few tasks, Bill pushed open the door to his office, hand automatically reaching for the light switch.

Maybe if he hadn't been so distracted, he would've noticed the sharp smell of liquor cutting through the darkness, the rasp of stifled breathing.

Something rammed into his stomach, knocking the breath out of him, sending the cigarette flying out of his mouth. Bill's feet flipped up as his head dropped down, toppling over the body barreling out of his office. He didn't notice a face or shape or hair color. Just a broad shoulder, muscular arms, a low grunt of exertion. Nothing, really.

Bill's head struck the floor, the thin carpet doing nothing to cushion the blow. His thoughts blinked out as the darkness took him.

Chapter Sixty-Eight

VERONICA

Veronica stared at the entrance to the school, her heart thumping fast against her ribs. Who was that who had come running out of the school? He'd jumped out the window by Bill's office.

The light was still off. It shouldn't still be off.

And where was Bill?

In the back seat, Millie clutched her stuffed bear, murmuring gibberish into its chewed and tattered ear. She scooted forward on the bench seat to hold the bear up to Veronica.

"Mommy kiss."

Veronica twisted to kiss the top of the bear's raggedy head, and Millie grinned, hugging the bear tight. She lowered her voice, tucking her chin into her chest to do a bear voice. "Tank you, Mommy!"

Veronica looked toward the school again. The main office light was still on, but Bill's was off. She couldn't see him through the window.

She squinted, shielding her eyes with her hand as if that might somehow give her a better view, even though the sun had long since set. She stared at Bill's office window, waiting to see if she'd really seen what she thought she saw.

Yes, there! An orange flicker.

And was that . . . smoke?

Oh god.

Veronica jumped out of the car and flung open the back door. Scooping up Millie so fast that she dropped her bear, she plopped her back down in the seat and fastened her seat belt. She tightened it with shaking hands.

The quick motion had startled Millie, and she started to sniffle. Veronica picked the bear up from the floor of the car and pushed it into her arms. "Stay here with bear, baby," she said, hoping Millie didn't pick up on the tremble in her voice.

"Mama, hold you!" Millie was full-on sobbing now, stretching her arms toward her mother, her face scrunched up and red.

"Stay here," Veronica repeated, then closed the door, her heart pounding. Millie's muffled screams leaked through the window, but she would be safe. She didn't know how to undo the seat belt or open the door. At least, Veronica hoped she didn't.

The front door to the school was unlocked. Bill had his keys with him. Veronica threw the door open and ran inside.

The smell of smoke hit her right away, her ragged breathing pulling it into her lungs, which then worked to push it back out with equal force. Coughing, Veronica pulled open the door to the main office, covering her mouth with her sleeve.

The air was hazy, but she didn't see any fire yet. Her chest burning, Veronica moved through the office, her eyes scanning everywhere for Bill.

The door to his office was ajar. The lights were off, but she could still see inside, thanks to the dancing flames licking across the carpet, climbing up onto the desk.

Bill lay crumpled on his back, his arms splayed at his sides. He wasn't moving.

"Bill!" Veronica knew she shouldn't try to talk, but his name came out without thinking. Smoke took advantage of the moment to shove its way into her mouth, down her throat, into her lungs. Her eyes watered and dripped, her eyelashes fluttering frantically. Still, she couldn't help herself. "Bill, oh god, honey? Bill? Are you okay?"

She leaned down to press her ear to his chest, too frightened even to breathe. A comforting, steady thump sent relief sweeping through her. He was alive, just unconscious.

What happened?

There would be time for that later. Now, she had to get him out.

Veronica looped her arms under his, pulling with all her might. Her back strained and ached. He slid a little, but the process was agonizingly slow. Too slow.

Kicking off her heels and tossing aside the stifling red blazer she'd bought for the debate, Veronica hurried around Bill's prone body and grabbed his feet. Blinking sweat out of her eyes, she heaved his body around so his feet pointed toward the door, tucking each foot under her arms and gripping him tight at the ankles.

This was better. She shuffled backward, dragging him with her an inch at a time. Smoke stung her eyes and clogged her throat, but she kept going, determinedly placing one foot behind the other.

Her eyes streamed, so she closed them. It was a mostly straight shot to the door. She didn't need to see.

A fire was building in her chest, searing claws tearing through her with every breath. She ignored it as long as she could, trying to hold her breath, but she couldn't go more than a couple of steps before gasping for air, only to find none.

How far was the door? Surely she had to be almost there.

Step.

Step.

Step.

Veronica doubled over in a fit of coughing, straining for breath. Her head swam, her thoughts fuzzy. She stumbled, then realized she was on her hands and knees, gasping and hacking over her husband.

Get up, Veronica.

She braced her hands on Bill's stomach, one nylon-clad foot planting itself on the carpet and pushing upward. She was standing again!

But Bill. Where was Bill? She'd dropped his feet. She needed to find his feet.

She bent down, patting blindly along the floor, searching. *There!* Her hands closed around the rubber sole of his shoe, then his ankle. She couldn't find the other one, but one ankle was enough. She could work with one ankle.

She tried to get up again, to take him with her this time, but she couldn't. Her legs were no longer cooperating. Neither were her lungs. She knew what she needed to do, but she couldn't make her body do it.

The sound of the fire was growing louder. It cracked and spit, eating up everything in its path.

Soon, the office wouldn't contain it. It would spread to this room. And then beyond. The whole school, and whatever it could reach around it.

Whatever was nearby.

Millie. Millie!

A sob wrenched out of her as she dropped Bill's foot and turned to drag herself toward the door, leaving him behind. Her thoughts were little more than smoke-clogged sludge. She couldn't see anything. Everything hurt, like she was burning from the inside.

Inside her head, though, a clear picture:

Her daughter, crying. The fire inching its way toward the car.

She had to get to her. Her nails dug into the carpet, bending and breaking as she clawed her way forward.

It's okay, Millie, she imagined herself saying. *It's okay. Mama's here. It's okay. I'll fix it.*

She didn't notice when she stopped moving.

She didn't notice when her cheek came to rest against the carpet.

It's okay, baby. Everything's going to be just fine.

She didn't notice when she stopped breathing.

Chapter Sixty-Nine

JUSTIN

No wonder Karl is so afraid of these kids.

Winded, I can't do much more than curl into a ball and cover my head with my hands as they drive their sneakered feet into every part of me they can reach. I don't feel the tree branch again, but that's not much comfort when their shoes are smashing like hammers. My back, my ribs, my arms, everything screams for this to *stop, stop, stop*. But when I open my mouth to form the word, nothing comes out but a wet wheeze. My chest burns from the effort, and I picture my bones rattling around like nails in a jar, ripping and bruising from the inside out.

The boys' shouts mash together into a cacophonous jumble that births a high-pitched ringing in my ears. It grows steadily louder with each impact, piercing through the pain like rending metal.

Then, abruptly, it stops. The boys are talking, but my brain is too busy cataloging the damage to my body to make sense of what they're saying.

Move, my body begs me, and I try to obey, but none of my append-ages appear to be feeling particularly compliant at the moment. My skin feels like it's filled with congealed oatmeal that is also on fire, thick and gloopy and burning white hot. I attempt to crawl away, but only manage to flop from one crumpled pose into another, like a fish drowning on dry land.

You'd think that in all his attempts to prepare me for my predestined trip to 1985, Stan might have signed me up for a self-defense class or two. Or at least some cardio. Too focused on his murder board, I guess.

I wait for the onslaught to start again, making bets with myself on where the first blows will land, trying to position myself so that the most painful areas aren't presented as obvious targets.

But the attack doesn't come. Instead, the boys take off running, leaving me bruised and bloody on the ground like roadkill.

It takes more energy than it should to roll onto my back, and the uneven pavement pushes against my tender skin like eager fingers, every point of contact sending a fresh wave of pain shooting through me. Staring up at the gray sky, I work to slow my breathing and take stock of my injuries. Dark clouds are beginning to pile up, painted deep shades of red and orange by the setting sun, harbingers of the storms that will help keep the fire from devouring the entire school, but will arrive too late to save Bill and Veronica.

I'm their only hope.

Which means—somehow—I have to move.

Everything hurts, but nothing seems broken. I can feel bruises beginning to blossom all along my left side, my back, my legs. My knee feels hot and damp; the gash from yesterday must have reopened. Moving gingerly, I push myself into a sitting position, then close my eyes and wait for the world to stop spinning.

"Hey, man, are you okay?"

I blink a few times before the floating images of the person walking toward me solidify into one. The man is tall and lanky, with deep-brown skin, short black hair, and a thin pencil line of a mustache. His face seems familiar, but my brain refuses to give me any more context that might help with an ID. He stops when he reaches me and sets his paper bag of groceries down on the ground, extending a hand.

"Yeah, I think so," I say, grimacing as I reach up. He pulls me to my feet, where I teeter uncertainly for a few moments before regaining my balance.

"What happened?"

I shake my head, not in the mood to explain how I got waylaid by a trio of sadistic middle schoolers. "Just wrong place at the wrong time."

"I'll say." He frowns, his eyes scanning over me. "You should put some ice on that," he says, gesturing toward my face.

I touch my hand to my cheek and wince. Already, I can feel the side of my face puffing up, and although I can't see myself, I imagine the bruise will take the general shape of one of Robbie's sneakers.

But I don't have time to worry about myself right now. "I'm good," I lie, and force a smile—*ow*—turning away to limp toward the school. None of my injuries will matter if I can get there in time.

I haven't made it more than five steps before my bad knee—the one branded with Stan's scar—buckles underneath me, sending me sprawling. "God*dammit*," I growl as loose gravel claws its way into my palms.

His hand comes under my arm, helping me back up again. "Look, kid, why don't you let me give you a ride home? Or to the hospital? My car is right across the street." He points to the row of squat duplexes behind the Food Mart. "It's really no problem."

I shake my head, and immediately regret it. It feels like the inside of my skull is lined in barbed wire, and every little movement sends my brain sloshing up against it. "Thanks, but I've got something I need to do."

"Okay," he says, looking doubtful. "Well, if you change your mind, I'm in unit one-oh-three. Just come knock; I should be home all night."

"Thanks," I say again. Gingerly, I try putting weight on my bad knee. It hurts, but it holds.

"My name's Michael, by the way," he says.

Suddenly, it clicks why he looks familiar.

Michael McMillain, the man who will spend the next three decades in prison for starting the fire that kills my grandparents. I've seen his face countless times before, in a black-and-white mug shot on Stan's murder board.

No wonder he was always so convinced that Michael was innocent. Stan was his alibi.

For a second, I just stare at him, blinking dumbly as the gravity of what's about to happen falls on me like a sledgehammer. But there's nothing I can do to warn him, at least not without sounding completely insane. He'll never listen to me, some random stranger who just got beaten up outside the supermarket. The only way to save him is to save Bill and Veronica.

I stumble away from McMillain, my mind numb to the protests of my body. *If I can just get to the school in time,* I tell myself, *it'll be okay.* I can save him from his unjust fate. I can save them from their awful deaths. Maybe I can even save myself.

My injuries keep me from moving quickly, but I stubbornly press on. Already, I think I can smell faint traces of smoke, although it could be my mind playing tricks on me. I don't have a watch to know what time it is, but it feels like it has to be nearly six, maybe later. Am I already too late?

I come out from behind the Food Mart and make my way down the sidewalk, toward the school. I wish I could move faster, but my body is refusing to cooperate, sending signals of protest through me with every step.

"Justin?"

I look up from the ground, where my attention has been focused on dragging one foot in front of the other, to see Noah illuminated by the glow of the streetlights, peering at me from the other side of the street. He's wearing a button-down shirt and a tie, and a VOTE FOR DIANE pin. I wonder why he's here and not at the debate. I raise a hand in greeting. "Hey, Noah."

He jogs across the street toward me, his eyes widening when he gets close enough to appreciate the extent of my injuries. "Whoa."

"It's fine."

"You look like you got hit by a truck."

"It's really not that bad."

He shakes his head, frowning, but doesn't challenge me, probably because he doesn't care. "Have you seen Rose?"

"Isn't she at the debate?"

He shakes his head, hands in his pockets. "We were supposed to meet up at her house, but she wasn't there. I waited as long as I could, but then I thought maybe we were actually supposed to meet at the debate. I was just headed there now."

Something feels wrong about this. It's not like Rose to blow off plans. Maybe with me, since she hates me now, but not with perfect Noah.

"Did she say anything else about what she was doing today?"

He stares at me, a funny look on his face, but then shakes his head. "Nope. Just the debate."

His voice sounds weirdly hostile. Like a challenge.

I don't have time for this. I'm not sure what Noah's deal is, but I need to get moving again if I have a chance at making it in time. Whatever Rose and Noah were doing today that he's not telling me about, that's their business. She told me she was done with me, after all.

"Well, I hope you find her," I say, turning away from him to continue toward the school.

Noah lets out an irritated grunt, but doesn't push it any further. When I glance back, he's walking in the opposite direction, toward town.

I try to put Rose out of my head and focus on the task at hand, but my mind churns with each step I take, echoing with a chorus of insistent voices.

Noah: *She wasn't there.*

Why would Rose not be home when she said she would be? I've only known her for a week, but already I'm sure she's not the type to blow off plans with someone she cares about. She may have completely written me off, but I know she thinks Noah pisses rainbows.

Stan: *I was too late.*

Have I already missed the fire? He knew that by the time I got to this point, I'd know we're the same person. He knew I'd try anyway, even knowing he failed. He wanted me to know he didn't make it in time. That's why I'm hurrying now. But is that what I'm supposed to be doing? Or am I making the same wrong choices, all over again?

Rose: *There's meaning in everything.*

That's why I'm still in this armpit of a town, dragging my bruised ribs one agonizing step at a time toward a fire I have no chance of stopping, isn't it, Rose? Because despite everything, you've gotten under my skin with your infuriating insistence that this all has to *mean* something. Even if all the evidence so far points to the contrary.

Rose: *These next twenty-four hours are a big question mark.*

Except they're not. I know what happens. I've always known what happens, Rose. Fire, death, sadness. Wandering aimlessly for the next four decades. Rinse, repeat, second verse, same as the first. *You're* the one who wouldn't accept it, but I always have.

Noah: *She wasn't there.*

See, not even perfect Rose is reliable all the time. Tonight is your stepmom's debate, and where are you? Nowhere to be found.

Rose: *You can still do things differently.*

I can't, though. I tried for a week to make the very best decisions I could, believe in things I don't even believe, and still found myself in a well-worn Stan-shaped rut. There's no getting out of it. I was stupid to ever think there was.

Stan: *I was too late.*

So what am I even *doing* right now? Dragging myself toward a burning building to save two people I barely know from a death they can't avoid? I know I won't get there in time. Stan *told* me I won't. And even if I do, I have no guarantee that saving them will get me back home. That was always *your* thing, Rose, not mine. And even *you* bailed on me in the end, and apparently you've bailed on Noah, too, so why am I still working off your stupid theory?

Rose: *So the question is, what are you going to do now?*

Is there anything even left for me to do, Rose? I already tried everything I could think of. I believed in you, and you abandoned me. And then you abandoned Noah, which isn't like you. Where are you?

Where are you, Rose?

Stan: *Did you see the news? About the body. In the river.*

Alyssa: *Do you think it was someone he knew?*

Rose: *We need to figure out why you're here.*

I stop in my tracks, my breath hitching in my throat. "Oh *shit*."

Not here—1985.

There's meaning in everything.

Here, on the bridge.

I didn't just show up in 1985. I showed up in 1985 *on the bridge*. With Rose.

There's meaning in everything.

What are you going to do now?

I spin around, my voice bursting through the stillness of the evening. "Noah, wait!"

Chapter Seventy

ROSE

Lisa tossed her a little wave as she climbed into the passenger side of Charlene's car. Rose smiled, waving back. She dropped her head back against the headrest, closing her eyes for a moment as she listened to the engine of Charlene's car rumble awake. When she opened them, the car was shrinking as it wound away from her, back down the Derrins' long driveway.

Rose turned her own key in the ignition, listening to the Escort reluctantly cough to life. She felt a million pounds lighter after talking to Lisa. It had been hard, and their eyes were both puffy from crying, but she finally felt like she had her sister back. She hoped Lisa felt the same way.

The clock on the dashboard told her it was 5:52. She'd be a couple of minutes late meeting Noah at her house, but they'd still make it to the school well before 6:30.

She wondered what Justin was doing. Had he really given up, or would he still try to save them?

She supposed she'd find out soon enough.

Rose steered the car down the long drive and onto the road back toward town as the engine hiccupped and stuttered. Her dad was right;

it did sound like the irregularities were getting a little more frequent. It was a good thing he'd made an appointment with the mechanic.

Her mind turned to the night ahead, running over her plan yet again. After all the scheming and speculating she had done with Justin, it almost felt too simple. She and Noah would meet at her house first. Then they'd drive over to the school to intercept Bill and Veronica, who—if Justin's story turned out to be true—would be running late for the debate because they'd stopped by Bill's office.

Justin said the fire started around six thirty. So as long as they got there before then, they could stop the guidance counselor and his wife from going inside and make it back to the debate before the first question was asked. It would be like nothing ever happened.

Unless of course Veronica was at the debate already and Justin's story was completely wrong. That's what Noah was sure would happen. They'd go to the school, and no one would be there. Then they'd walk into the debate and Veronica would already be by Diane's side, and everything would be fine. The school wouldn't catch fire. No one would die or travel through time. Because Justin wasn't from the future; he was just crazy.

Part of Rose hoped he was right. That would certainly be the easier path.

But she couldn't shake her sense that Justin had been telling the truth all along. He was annoying and stubborn and immensely frustrating, but he wasn't a liar. Something in her was sure of it.

She'd told him that she didn't want anything to do with him anymore. That she didn't care what happened to him.

She guessed that was kind of true.

But that didn't mean she'd ever stopped believing him.

The car sputtered again as Rose turned toward the water, with the lights of Wilson Bridge just visible through the trees. A second later, the steering wheel began to shake, followed by the rest of the car.

Rose straightened in her seat, her fingers gripping the steering wheel as her dashboard clock blinked an uneven *6:04*, taunting her with just how little time she had left. "Please no, *please* not now, please, please, *please*," she chanted over and over as the car bucked and shook like it was experiencing convulsions.

In response, the car coughed one last time, belching up a black cloud of smoke before it died. Rose kept the accelerator pressed to the floor, leaning forward as though she might be able to make it the rest of the way fueled by sheer willpower. She stayed that way until the Escort rolled to a stop.

For a second, Rose just sat there, her hands clenched on the wheel. She tried turning the ignition off and back on, tried pumping the clutch and the gas in turn, tried shifting into every different gear in the hopes that one of them might magically coax the car back to life.

Nothing.

Grumbling under her breath, Rose climbed from the car, slamming the door extra hard, as if that would somehow ensure that the Escort would feel properly guilty for stranding her out here. She looked up and down the roadway, but no cars were coming in either direction. Lisa and Charlene were long gone. And no one else knew she was out here.

Above her, the dark sky began to growl with the promise of an approaching storm.

Justin had said it would be raining. She tried not to think about that.

Just in case, Rose pulled an umbrella out of the trunk. Then she began to walk.

Chapter Seventy-One

KARL

Karl whimpered as the truck rumbled to life. He curled his knees to his chest, squeezing his eyes shut as the vehicle rolled away from the curb and picked up speed. Stinging wind slapped against the tarp over his body, and he pressed himself against the side of the truck bed to try to shield himself as much as possible.

Just stay calm, he told himself. If this truck belonged to one of the students or teachers at the school, they probably lived nearby. All Karl had to do was stay small and quiet until the truck parked, then walk back to town.

Maybe this would actually be a good thing. This way, Robbie would really have no idea where to look for him.

It started to rain, first a gentle spray, then a downpour. The tarp fluttered around him, doing very little to protect him from the pummeling rain. Karl huddled even smaller as he bounced around the back of the truck, his clothing quickly soaked from the water leaking around the edges of the tarp and splashing up from the bed.

How far had they gone? He was starting to worry they were driving too far away, but he wasn't used to not being able to see anything. Maybe it was just his mind playing tricks on him. Maybe they hadn't gone that far after all.

The truck had turned a few times, but never slowed long enough for Karl to try to escape. His heart raced as he ran through worst-case scenarios in his head. What if the driver lived a hundred miles away? What if he got in an accident? What if he was a kidnapper and actually knew Karl was back here, and was taking him into the middle of nowhere to murder him?

That last thought spooked Karl enough to peek out from under the tarp, hoping to see something familiar. If he could figure out where they were, maybe it *would* be better to jump and run, as soon as the truck slowed down some. But rain sprayed into his eyes, making it impossible to identify anything in the dark.

He needed to sit up if he wanted a better view.

Holding tight to the edge of the bed, Karl pulled himself upright, looking around to get his bearings. To his surprise, he realized he actually *did* know where they were—the driver had just pulled onto Wilson Bridge, heading toward Karl's house. This was perfect. Once the driver reached the stop sign on the opposite side, that would be the perfect place for Karl to jump out.

Karl shifted into a crouch, still clutching the side of the truck bed. He didn't dare try to get to his feet yet, not at this speed, but he could at least get into a position that would allow him to move quickly when the time came.

His sneaker caught on one of the shovels as he adjusted his position, making him lose his balance. Karl let out a yelp as the shovels clattered under his feet. He grasped at the truck, suddenly terrified he might fall out.

He heard a muffled shout and turned his head toward the cab of the truck.

The driver looked back at him, his eyes wide in the rearview mirror.

Chapter Seventy-Two

SHAWN

The truck skidded down Clayton Road, away from the school.

Shawn blinked rapidly, pulling in deep breaths. Mr. Warren had hit the floor hard, but Shawn thought he would be okay. He had to be okay. All Shawn had wanted was to get that list of locker numbers. No one was supposed to be there. No one was supposed to get hurt.

He didn't think Mrs. Warren had gotten a good look at him in the parking lot.

And he didn't think anyone had seen his truck parked around the corner.

Everything would be okay.

He followed the curve of the road toward Wilson Bridge. He'd drive to the fishing lot on the other side—it would be empty tonight—and burn the list. No one would know. Then he'd head to the debate, and no one would be the wiser.

Of course, the liquor stains on his pants might be a problem. He didn't have time to stop at home for a change of clothes. Hmm. How was he going to explain that?

It started to rain, first a little, then a lot. Shawn turned the wipers as high as they would go, but they were still barely able to keep up with the rivers of water pouring onto the windshield.

Actually, this was good. If he parked down the street and walked the rest of the way to the community center, it would look like he just got caught in the rain. The stain on his pants would blend in with the rain. Problem solved.

As the truck passed under the steel arches of the bridge, something shifted in the bed of the truck. Shawn glanced in the rearview mirror, wondering whether something had fallen out, then squinted, trying to figure out what he was seeing.

A dark shape, moving around low in the bed. He couldn't make it out in the rain.

Then he realized what it was. "What the *hell*?"

There was a *person* in the back of his truck.

Shawn's eyes widened as whoever it was turned to look toward him. Their eyes met in the mirror as Shawn slammed on the brakes.

In his shock, he'd forgotten how hard it was raining.

The truck wheels locked, but the vehicle didn't stop moving. It skidded and skipped over the wet pavement, spinning toward the sidewalk on the opposite side of the road, where—

All the blood drained from Shawn's face.

Someone was standing on the sidewalk, her face shining in his headlights, her mouth hanging open in surprise.

He was going to hit her. And there was nothing he could do to stop it.

Then, suddenly, she was gone, replaced by someone else.

He didn't have time to see who it was before his tires hit the curb. The front of the car jumped into the air, Shawn pitched forward, and a body slammed against the windshield with sickening, deadly force.

Chapter Seventy-Three

ROSE

The bridge spooled out endlessly before her. Rose splashed through the puddles on the sidewalk, drenching the soft cream slacks she'd so carefully ironed that morning for the debate. But right now, her clothes were the last thing she cared about.

Too late too late too late, her feet seemed to pound out with every step. She tried to check her watch, but she knew what it would say. She'd left Charlene's house with plenty of time to drive, but not nearly enough to walk. Even if she were capable of morphing into a track star and sprinting the few miles to the school through the pouring rain, there was no way she would make it in time to save the Warrens.

Any minute now, the fire would start. Noah was probably still waiting for her at her house. And Justin . . . well, she knew better than to rely on him.

Her eyes grew hot, tears mixing with raindrops. She'd failed. After everything, all her work, all her determination. Nothing was going to change. It had all been for nothing.

The rain and the darkness pressed in on her, suffocating her, the river roaring angrily far below. She had never felt so alone.

Her steps slowed. Why was she even still trying?

A rending squeal screamed through the night, drowning out the rain. Like a hundred jagged fingernails being dragged over a chalkboard.

It triggered a memory that was not a memory. Another road, another car. A part of Rose that was not Rose, yet was half of her, taken too suddenly and too soon.

Was this what she heard, at the end, before hearing nothing at all?

Rose spun, her heart jumping into her throat.

She raised her hands in front of her, stomach clenched, knowing there was no protection from this. Like a single small flower digging in its roots to brace against an avalanche.

All at once, she was washed in light.

Interlude

Stan, September 30, 2023

By now, he's gone.

Or maybe I'm gone?

I've never actually understood how it works, this hellish loop that I'm in. Is the Justin I helped raise actually *me*—the same me who drove off that bridge thirty-eight years ago, or five minutes ago, depending on how you look at it—or some sort of alternate-universe version of me? If he succeeds where I failed, will I cease to exist? Will the world change around me? Will I remember?

Or will I just go on existing in this dull, gray world, living my dull, gray life?

The front door slams. "Stan? Justin? Anyone home?"

I stare at the mostly empty bottle of whiskey in my hand. Lissa can't see this. Can't know I ever had it in the house.

"I'm here," I call, rising slowly to my feet, my joints creaking and popping. The old scar tissue around my knee aches as I teeter to the door of my room and close it, then flip the lock. I glance around, then stow the bottle under a pile of dirty laundry. I'll get rid of it later, when Lissa's not here.

Funny, in the thirty-eight years I've had to think about what happened tonight, I've never really given much thought to what would happen to me—the me who is fifty-six years old, the me who has been here since 1985, the me who is Stan—after the Justin I used to be went off the bridge. Even as I traveled from city to city, bounced from job to job, changed my name, made up stories and toyed with the idea of ending it all, it somehow never occurred to me that after I left, I'd also still be stuck here, forced to watch my mother discover that her son is gone without a trace.

Of course, she doesn't know she's my mother. I could never tell her that. She'd think I was crazy, and maybe I am. Who else but a crazy person would spend thirty-eight years trying to solve a case that I *know* is unsolvable, because I remember watching Stan—watching *myself*—trying to solve it when I was a kid. And I remember him failing.

And yet, here I am. Who's that Greek guy who was constantly pushing the boulder up the hill, even though it kept rolling back down? King Sissy-something.

Well, that's me. Forever the King of the Sissy-somethings.

Will the police find my car? I always wondered if the car disappeared, too, or if it completed the drop down into the river. I wonder if that asshole Kenny Gibson will assume I drowned, or think I ran away from home.

I wonder if that's what Rose's family thought, when she disappeared. I wonder if they thought I had something to do with it.

I don't think I did. We weren't together that night, after all. I went to the school, hoping I might get there in time to stop it all from happening again, but of course I was too late.

The thing I didn't realize—or really, the thing I never bothered to pay attention to, since it's not like I didn't make sure to tell Justin this a hundred times—was that when they rebuilt the school, the layout changed. The offices moved to the opposite side of the building from the auditorium. I forgot about that, of course, until I was standing in the parking lot, looking at an entrance that was cold and dark, while from the opposite side of the school, smoke twisted into the night.

Everything was lit up by the time I got to the right entrance. I couldn't even get near the building. Their car was in the parking lot, with Millie crying inside. The keys were still in the ignition. I climbed into the driver's seat and drove away from the school, parking closer to the middle of the lot, far enough away that the fire couldn't reach us. We both stared at the leaping flames, held at bay by the rain, her screeching, me silent, until I heard sirens approaching.

Then I left, heading straight for the bus station, finally using the ticket I'd purchased that morning. The next time I set foot in Stone Lake was fifteen years later.

All those years, I'd assumed Rose was safe at her mom's debate. That our fight meant she was done with me, with this whole scheme of ours. That she was out there in the world somewhere living her life, and that it was better without me in it.

I never looked her up, not wanting to give myself the temptation of stepping back into her life and messing it up again. I knew Gibson had won the mayoral race, and that her family must have left town at some point, because a different family was living in her house when I came back. But I never asked where they went or why they left.

It wasn't that I didn't want to know. But I never belonged in her world, and if I found her, I knew I wouldn't be able to stay away. Leaving her alone felt like the best gift I could give her. The only way I could ensure I wouldn't screw up her life, the way I screw up everything else.

But yesterday, when the police pulled those bones out of the river—just like they did back when I was eighteen—I suddenly felt sick. I couldn't explain it, other than I knew something was very wrong. *I* had gotten something wrong.

In all the confusion of waking up in 1985 and meeting Rose and focusing on the fire, I'd forgotten about the body the police had pulled out of the river the day before I went off the bridge. In my anger at Stan for the things he'd said, I'd forgotten to consider the thing that set him off in the first place. In my obsession to figure out where I'd gone wrong in 1985, I'd forgotten that the answer was waiting for me in 2023.

Except, in all that time, I'd never *really* forgotten. It was always there. I just didn't want to see it, until it became impossible to ignore. Like I'd spent my whole life pretending I didn't notice a monster in the dark corner of my room, only for it to finally step into the light and tear me to shreds.

Today, once I knew the other me was gone, I finally let myself google her.

Rose Yin was officially declared dead in 1992, after no new evidence was discovered following her sudden disappearance in the fall of 1985. It turned out Gibson won the election only by default; Diane withdrew following the disappearance of her stepdaughter. Her name stayed on the ballot, but there was only one candidate actually in the race.

I have no idea why she wasn't where she was supposed to be that night. I have no idea how I was the one who drove off the bridge, yet somehow she was the one who wound up at the bottom of the river. I have no idea why I'm still here, and she's not.

All these years I spent trying to prevent that damn fire that killed two people I barely knew, and I never spent a single moment trying to discover what happened to the one person I actually cared about. Maybe if I had, I could've warned myself. Given myself some clues that would've allowed me to save her.

But I didn't look for Rose until it was too late. And now she's dead. She's been dead all this time, and will stay dead.

Because of me.

Chapter Seventy-Four

JUSTIN

The rain is coming down in a steady deluge by the time the bridge comes into view. Visibility through the windshield of Michael McMillain's car is basically nonexistent; he's slowed to a cautious crawl as we approach the bridge.

"I'll just get out here," I say, pushing open my door. Rain flings itself into the car, splattering the maroon fabric of the seat and instantly drenching the right side of my body.

"But—"

"Thanks for the ride," I say, cutting him off. Poor guy already seemed taken aback when I showed up on his doorstep asking him for a ride to the hospital—a route that just so happens to take us right by Wilson Bridge—just a few minutes after initially turning him down, but he grabbed his keys and helped me to his car, no questions asked. Now he blinks at me in bewilderment as I leap out of the still-moving car and slam the door, stumbling as I hit the pavement.

I can hear him calling after me through the closed car window, but after a few steps, the sound of the rain drowns him out. I would feel bad, but right now I have bigger things to worry about.

Calm washes through me like a tide as I step onto the bridge. My heart is racing, my breathing heavy, but in my mind, it is quiet. As soon as I decided to go to the bridge and not the school, it was like all my anxiety drained away.

Rose kept telling me how sure she was that we were on the right path. I never understood it. I feel like I've been fumbling in the dark since I got here.

But now I'm not fumbling anymore. It's like Thor's rainbow bridge just lit up right in front of me, and all I have to do is follow it.

It was never about the school. That was Stan's mistake. He always stayed focused on the school, because he was sure this was about us. About me. But it's not. I sent Noah to the school, hoping that if it's not me, maybe it can be him.

This is where I'm supposed to be. The bridge. I thought I kept coming back here because it was where it all started. But I think I was actually drawn here because this is where it's supposed to end.

It was always about the *where*, not just the when. This place. This time.

I don't worry anymore. I don't second-guess. I don't even think.

I just run. My knee throbs, threatening to buckle underneath me, but I know it will hold. It has to.

At first, I don't know what I'm looking for. I can barely see or hear anything through the rain, but I keep my eyes as wide as I can, trusting that I'll see what I need to.

There. A hazy figure on the sidewalk, hunched under an umbrella, moving toward me. Nearly invisible through the pouring rain, unless you were already looking.

If I had more time, I might wonder what she's doing here, where her car is, what's about to happen.

But my time here has always been borrowed, and I can feel it slipping away. My feet burn like I'm escaping a fire. I have to get to her, *now*.

"Rose!" I yell with as much volume as I can muster. I wave my arms. "Go back! Get off the bridge!"

It's no use. I'm too far away. She's not looking at me. My words are swallowed by the wind and the rain and the rush of the river.

There's no one here but us—not that I can see through the rain anyway—but I can't shake the feeling that this is wrong, this is dangerous, that being on this bridge tonight is death. I can't explain it, but I don't have to. I just need to trust it.

I push my legs faster, rocketing toward Rose, who's moving slowly up the sidewalk. The giant steel arches above me like an open mouth. It seems like it takes an agonizingly long time to get to her.

When I'm about ten yards away, I hear it.

An engine. Rumbling toward us.

I look back to see headlights pushing through the rain.

"Rose!" I call again. If not for the rain, she would almost definitely hear me, but her eyes stay downcast, focused on the sidewalk in front of her, her umbrella tipped forward like a shield.

The car is moving fast, far faster than Michael McMillain was willing to risk driving during this downpour. It'll catch up with us any second.

I break into a sprint. Rose should be safe on the sidewalk, but I somehow know that she isn't. *"Rose!"*

The car is close enough now that its headlights find us. Rose glances up, her eyes widening in alarm as the beams wash across her face.

"Move!" is all I can think to yell. Adrenaline floods my veins, and I push myself faster, faster, until I feel like I'm flying.

Don't let me be too late.

Everything happens in an instant.

I reach Rose as the car swerves wildly, reacting to some invisible obstacle. She glows in its headlights, her eyes as round as the moon overhead.

My hands lock onto her arms. I feel calm. Peaceful. Her terrified eyes jump from the car to my face. *It's okay,* I try to tell her with my eyes. *It's not your fault. This is why I'm here.*

I didn't understand it until this moment, but now I do. I wonder, is this what Rose has felt all this time? Is this faith?

I feel strong. Superhuman. Like I could lift a train.

I throw Rose out of the way. It's easy, as if she weighs nothing at all. She flies up, and back, and away, her arms spreading like wings. *Like a bird,* my mind suggests, except I know immediately that's not right.

No. Not a bird.

An angel.

I smile, and close my eyes.

When the car slams into me, I feel no pain.

Chapter Seventy-Five

JUSTIN

The first time I died, I didn't understand what had happened to me. I thought maybe I was still alive, or asleep. I thought I was a time traveler. And maybe I was.

This time, I recognize it for what it is. I don't wonder whether I might come back after this. I know I am finished. Maybe a version of me will exist, someday. A boy with my face and birthday and voice. But he won't be me.

My life ended the moment I fell from this bridge. It just took me a week to die.

They say that when you die, your life flashes before your eyes.

Turns out, that's only partially true.

I don't see my life. I see the people in it.

Flash.

Alyssa. She deserves so much more than what I've been able to give her. Maybe that future me, the one who will not be me, will be better for her. I hope he will.

Flash.

Stan. He was wrong about what I would have to do, but he did his best. Maybe he hated me because he knew I was doomed to fail. Maybe I hated him because, somehow, I knew he already had.

Stan won't exist now. No one will mourn him. I don't think he would mind.

Flash.

My mom. I don't think of her as I last saw her, passed out facedown on her bed. Instead, I think of Millie, smiling and laughing as she plays at her mother's feet. She loves, and knows she is loved. Maybe this time, she will get to hold on to that feeling as she grows up. Maybe she will be happy. I hope she gets to be happy.

Flash.

Bill and Veronica. My grandparents. I hope Noah saved them tonight. I never really knew them—even as I was trying to save them, I didn't *know* them. They are good people, though; I'm sure of that. Just as I'm sure that I was never here for them.

Flash.

That night on the bridge, the first time I died. I didn't recognize her then, but the memory is as clear now as looking through a window. A figure in my headlights, standing somewhere she was never meant to be.

Flash.

Rose.

It was always Rose.

Rose, who was so sure that I was here for a reason. Rose, who Stan spent his whole life missing. Rose, who was never supposed to die here tonight.

Rose, the girl the whole universe bent to save.

I told her that I didn't know if I believed in God. I told Mrs. Hanley the same thing.

Mrs. Hanley told me that maybe God believed in me. That never felt right. But maybe that's because it was never about me. Maybe I'm here because God—or the universe, or whatever it is—believes in Rose.

Chapter Seventy-Six

ROSE

What just happened?

Rose pressed a hand to her head, trying to still the ringing in her ears. She groaned as she slowly got to her feet. Justin had thrown her with a shocking amount of strength. She'd slammed back down like a crashing plane, skidding on her bare arms and leaving a good amount of skin embedded in the wet pavement.

Everything hurt.

But she was alive. If Justin hadn't pushed her out of the way—

Oh God, no.

Rose turned slowly, toward the truck balancing half-on, half-off the sidewalk. Abruptly, the rain slowed to a light drizzle, like it had served its purpose and was now ready to move on. The driver had gotten out—Shawn, she registered with dull surprise—and was staring at something on the ground with a horrified expression. His hands were fisted tight in his hair, like he wanted to pull it all from his head.

"Shawn?" Rose called. Her voice sounded like she'd swallowed razor blades.

His eyes met hers, wide and empty. *Like a corpse,* she thought with a sense of strange detachment.

"I didn't mean to," he said, his voice high and scared. "You have to believe me, Rose. I didn't mean to."

Rose didn't ask what he meant. She walked slowly around the truck, until she could get a good look at the boy on the ground.

This was the second time she'd stood over his body on this bridge.

As Rose looked at Justin's still face, her heart seemed to stop. Slowly, she knelt beside him but didn't touch him. There was no point. His eyes were wide and unblinking, his chest still. Blood was everywhere, spilling out of him like a cracked egg.

For a long moment, Rose just stared, her body numb.

Justin was dead. How could Justin be dead?

She closed her eyes, struggling to remember how to breathe. All around her, the world shattered into dust. Death wasn't supposed to win today. They were supposed to stop it.

She'd been so *sure*. But she'd been wrong.

It's okay, a voice whispered in her mind.

Not her voice. His.

"I'm sorry," she whispered, tears leaking from her closed eyelids.

It's not your fault.

"I should've tried harder."

This is why I was here.

Air filled her lungs. As she breathed in, she knew he was truly gone.

She opened her eyes, her heart aching. She was surprised to see Karl Derrin standing beside Shawn, face red and tear-streaked, eyes wide. Where had he come from? How long had he been here?

Shawn looked down at him, dazed. "It was you?"

"I'm sorry," Karl whimpered. "I-I was just trying to—"

Shawn shook his head wearily. "It doesn't matter." He sniffed, twisting his neck to wipe his nose on the shoulder of his sweatshirt. He dragged his gaze back to Justin's body. "We have to bury him," he said thickly.

"What?" Rose asked, incredulous. "We need to go to the *police*."

"What are they going to do?" He gestured to Justin's contorted body on the ground. "They can't help him now."

"That doesn't matter!"

Karl took a deep breath and straightened his shoulders, his limbs trembling. "I agree with Rose."

Shawn stared at him, seeming dazed. Then his expression shifted, and he slowly shook his head, his brow furrowed with something like— but not quite—concern. "Are you sure about that, buddy? I mean, if you hadn't distracted me, this wouldn't have happened."

"You think I'll get in trouble?" Karl whispered, his face going pale.

"Maybe. Do you know what manslaughter is?"

Karl shook his head vehemently. "I changed my mind. I don't want to go to the police."

Shawn patted him on the shoulder. "Good call, buddy. I'd hate for you to have to go to jail."

Rose couldn't believe what she was hearing. "Shawn, he's just a *kid*."

Shawn glared at her with a calculated coldness she'd never seen before. "So am I."

Rose's blood turned to ice in her veins. This wasn't the Shawn she knew. The one who had shown up to every fundraiser for Mrs. Hanley, the one who had dated her sister for a year and then hugged her when she finally told him the truth, the one who had tried to give her an awkward heart-to-heart about her nonexistent love life.

No, this was someone else. Someone she didn't recognize.

He looked at Karl, pasting a strange, determined smile on his face. "Time to be brave, buddy." He walked around the back of the truck and opened the tailgate. A few seconds later, he came back holding two shovels, and handed one to Karl.

Rose shook her head, horrified. She wondered if she might throw up. "You can't just throw him away!"

"We don't have a choice, Rose," Shawn said, his voice eerily void of expression. He unzipped his sweatshirt, swiping a sleeve across the damp hair on his forehead. Underneath, he wore a shirt and tie. He must've been headed to the debate.

Except . . . the community center was in the opposite direction. What was he doing out here on the bridge?

"Karl, grab that tarp out of the bed and bring it over here," Shawn said, walking slowly around Justin's body, his head tilted to one side. He nudged Justin's shoe with his toe, making Rose's stomach turn.

"Karl, stop," Rose said, beckoning to the younger boy. "Come here. You don't have to do this. We'll explain to the police what happened. You won't get in trouble."

"Don't listen to her, bud," Shawn said, his face still twisted into that unsettling smile. "She doesn't know what she's talking about."

"I know that you can't just bury people on riverbanks and get away with it." Rose could hardly believe she was having this conversation. Could hardly believe any of this was happening.

Did the Shawn she thought she knew even exist? Had she been wrong about him all this time?

Or was *this* Shawn the impostor? If she pushed hard enough, would she find her friend still inside?

Shawn spread his arms, gesturing at the empty bridge. "Who's going to find out? Does anyone else even know he was here? As long as we all agree not to say anything—"

"I'm not agreeing to that."

The smile fell from his face. "I thought you were my friend."

"I *am* your friend."

"Then help me!" Shawn's eyes were round and frantic. "Rose, this could destroy my whole life. I could go to *jail*. How could you do that to me?"

"I'm not doing anything to you!"

"Yes, you are. No one has to know. Unless you tell them."

"If you'd just *explain* to the police what happened—"

His head wagged stubbornly back and forth, hands buried in his hair again. "I can't. This is the only way. You have to help me, Rose. No one can know."

She tore her eyes away from Justin's unmoving body to look at her friend. His skin was pale in the light of the streetlamps, his eyes wide. He looked like a trapped animal. "Shawn," she said quietly, taking a step toward him. "It was an accident."

He stared at her, clutching the shovel. "Everything will be ruined," he whispered. "Please."

She knelt beside Justin, taking his limp hand in hers. It was still warm. She remembered the last time she'd held his hand, right before everything between them fell apart. Had that been only yesterday?

"He was my friend," she said, her voice hitching. She reached out to Justin's still face, and gently closed his eyes. "We can't pretend this didn't happen, Shawn. You know we can't."

Shawn was quiet for a while, and Rose gradually realized that he was crying, his breath coming in quick gasps. "I'm sorry, Rosie," he said finally, his voice barely more than a broken sob.

All she could do was nod, the lump in her throat bubbling up to her eyes, then spilling over.

He fell to his knees beside her, his shoulders shaking with sobs. "I didn't mean it," he repeated over and over, hugging his stomach as if to hold himself together.

She gathered him into her arms, rubbing his back. "I know," she said, her own face wet with tears. Shawn buried his face in her shoulder, his grief soaking into the thin fabric of her shirt.

Rose's eyes met Karl's over Shawn's head. "Run home," she said softly. "Call the police."

His eyes darted to Shawn. "Are you sure?"

"I'm sure."

Karl sprinted out of the glow of the headlights, his footsteps fading into the quiet night.

Rose knelt on the sidewalk as Shawn wept, trying not to think of Justin's broken body on the ground or the Warrens in the high school. By now, the fire, if there was a fire, would have already started. She was too late.

If Justin was right, they were gone, too.

But also—if Justin was right, he was Stan. If Justin was right, he should still be alive.

Yet he was dead.

Did that mean he'd changed things?

If he was dead, did that mean Bill and Veronica had lived?

Or if he was dead, had it all been for nothing?

She didn't want to answer that question. She didn't want any of this.

Rose knelt on the pavement until her knees ached and she heard sirens in the distance, holding Justin's killer until they were both washed in flashing red.

Chapter Seventy-Seven

Noah

Noah walked to the school, even though he was pretty sure he was wasting his time. He'd mostly agreed to it just to get Justin to stop speaking nonsense. "It can't be me," Justin had kept repeating, getting more and more agitated as he moved toward Noah in the street. "I'm not supposed to be there at all. I thought I was, but I was wrong. That was Stan's mistake. He thought it was supposed to be us, but it's not. We're here for something else. It has to be you."

Noah couldn't follow most of what Justin was talking about, but he didn't need to in order to understand what he wanted him to do. He wanted Noah to go to the school to try to save the Warrens from the fire he was convinced was about to happen. It was easy enough for Noah just to say yes.

Besides, maybe Rose was already there. They'd planned to go to the school anyway. Didn't hurt to check.

Rain was beginning to fall as he approached the school parking lot, the wind picking up to whip the trees that surrounded the lot into a frenzy, sending showers of wet leaves to the ground. Noah flipped up his collar, wishing he'd worn a coat with a hood, and walked around the corner of the building toward the main entrance, where the guidance office was.

Noah caught his breath, his stomach surging into his throat.

Parked in front of the school was an idling car. The headlights were still on.

Smoke swirled in the beams.

Noah crouched down as low as he could as he entered the lobby, pulling his shirt up over his mouth and nose. It looked like the fire had started in the office and was quickly spreading. Noah's heart pounded as he calculated how long he had until it consumed the whole building.

He pressed deeper into the smoke, coughing into his shirt. Thick black clouds burned his eyes, and tears ran freely down his cheeks. Somewhere in here, Bill and Veronica Warren were in trouble. In Justin's future, they were going to die.

Unless Noah could save them.

He couldn't see anything. He edged forward, one arm outstretched, sliding his feet along the floor tiles, navigating by memory. The office should be directly in front of him. Justin had said that's where their bodies were found, so that's where Noah needed to look.

His fingers bumped against something unyielding. A wall? His hands explored the surface before him, following the painted cinder blocks over until he found the open door.

"Hello?" Noah called. He tried to edge into the office, but his feet nudged something soft on the floor. He knelt down and rubbed his eyes, blinking in the smoke-clogged space. Veronica Warren lay sprawled on her stomach halfway out the door, one arm stretched in front of her. Bill lay a couple of yards behind her, his feet pointed toward the door.

Veronica must have been trying to drag him out, then given up only to quickly pass out herself. Noah fervently hoped he'd have better luck.

Rolling Veronica onto her back, Noah heaved her up over his shoulder, stumbling slightly under her weight. Picking her up pulled his shirt collar down, leaving his face open to the smoke.

Noah glanced down uneasily at Mr. Warren, unmoving on the floor. He hated leaving him here, but it was either save them one at a time, or not at all.

Holding his breath, Noah carried Veronica toward the doors of the school, praying he'd have enough time to come back.

THIRTY-EIGHT
YEARS LATER

Chapter Seventy-Eight

ROSE

Raising her bright-pink World's Best Grandma mug to her lips, Rose cautiously tasted her coffee, then grimaced. Cold, again.

What she really needed was one of those insulated mugs with a lid—the students were always selling them for one fundraiser or another—but Noah, bursting with pride, had given her this one on the day their first grandchild was born, and she didn't have the heart to tell him that it wasn't really practical for work. Being principal of Stone Lake High was an ever-lengthening to-do list of visiting classrooms, attending meetings, coordinating with staff, replying to emails, and making calls, and she could never manage more than a couple of sips in between tasks. One cup of coffee could easily last her the entire morning.

Maybe she should look into getting a microwave for her office. But then she'd probably just forget the coffee in there all day, instead of on her desk.

The secretary appeared in the doorway, rapping her knuckles on the doorframe. "Dr. Hanley, the Warrens are here."

Unbidden, her eyes filled with tears. She ripped a couple of tissues from the box on her desk and dabbed at the corners, blinking furiously. *Don't cry,* she ordered herself. It was just a scholarship meeting. That was all. She did a dozen of these at the end of every school year. Nothing to get worked up over.

But none of those other meetings had been for him.

"Thank you, Alice. They can come in."

She picked up her phone, tapped out a text. They're here.

The response came immediately. He must have been waiting for her message. Good luck. Love you.

Rose tucked her phone into her top desk drawer as her visitors entered the office, reminding herself to keep her smile reined in and her eyes appropriately principal-y. "Hello, Ms. Warren, Justin. Welcome," she said, shaking their hands.

Her voice didn't tremble. She was well practiced.

Justin and his mother seated themselves in the two upholstered armchairs in front of her desk. Rose had been aware of him, of course, as he'd risen through the ranks of Stone Lake High—the first time she'd spotted him in the halls as a gangly freshman, she'd had to excuse herself to her office, where she'd sobbed for a solid twenty minutes—but she hadn't had much opportunity to interact with him individually, until now.

Ever since the results had come in with this year's list of National Merit Finalists, she'd been looking forward to this meeting, and dreading it. It wasn't every day she got an opportunity to look at one of her students and know, for sure, that she'd influenced his life for the better.

But she couldn't tell him. He couldn't ever know what they'd been through together. That version of Justin had died in 1985. He existed now in only her memories.

The version in front of her smiled pleasantly, sitting up straight in his chair. His hair was blond, not the garish orange it had been when she'd first met him, although she still noticed a subtle line of black rimming his eyelids. He wore black jeans and sneakers—were they the same ones he'd been wearing the night they met? The night he died? She hated that she couldn't remember—and when he folded his hands in his lap, she could see an elaborate constellation of stars doodled in black marker along the inside of his arm.

He was so different. And yet, so familiar.

Rose cleared her throat, flipping through a folder on her desk, even though she'd had the contents memorized for days now. She smiled at him, unable to keep it from blossoming into a full, wide grin. "Well, congratulations, Justin. Being named a National Merit Finalist is a very impressive achievement. We're all so proud of you."

"Thank you, ma'am," he said politely, although she could tell from the flush in his cheeks that he was more excited than he let on.

"As you know," Rose went on, "many universities will likely offer you scholarships based on your status as a National Merit Finalist, but in addition to whatever they offer, you also qualify for a Stone Lake Academic Scholarship, in the amount of ten thousand dollars a year for up to four years, at the school of your choosing."

"Yes, ma'am." He nodded. "Thank you."

Millie Warren rolled her eyes at her son, nudging him with her elbow. "He doesn't want me to make a fuss, but it's not every day your kid is awarded forty thousand dollars just for being smart."

Justin shrugged, blushing.

"We called his grandparents," Millie went on, "and you could've heard them whooping all the way from New York, even without the phone."

Rose's chest grew warm at the mention of Bill and Veronica. Bill had still been at the high school when Rose started working there, although he'd left to take a university position in New York a few years later.

"How are Bill and Veronica doing?" Rose asked, hoping they didn't notice the slight quiver in her voice.

"They're good," Millie said. "My brother and his wife live just a few blocks away from them, so we get to see them all whenever we visit."

"Everyone still in good health?"

"Oh, totally." Justin chuckled. "Grandpa even said he'll teach me to water-ski this summer on my uncle Jonathan's boat."

"Really?" Rose laughed. She could picture Bill flying over the surface of the water, white hair swirling in the wind, as Veronica rested a manicured hand on the wheel of the boat.

Sometimes, when Bill had still been working with her, Rose had tried to picture the world that Justin had described—the one where he and Veronica were both gone, and Millie grew up an only child, hating herself—and found she couldn't do it. The tragedy was simply too great to fathom.

The name on Justin's school records now read Justin Jonathan Warren, his middle name chosen for the uncle he was always meant to have, instead of the one who was never supposed to exist.

"Yeah, he's been wanting to teach me for a while," Justin said, "but this time Alyssa's coming with me when I visit—oh, Alyssa's my girlfriend."

"I know," Rose said, smiling. She'd seen them in the halls, holding hands, laughing. It was strange, to see the boy who had once consumed her every thought, still young while she'd grown old, hand in hand with the girl he'd always regretted leaving behind.

She wasn't jealous, not exactly. He was still a boy, while she was a grandmother five times over. She'd had a wonderful life with a man she loved with her whole heart, and Justin's was still ahead of him.

But her chest still clenched at the sight of him with his beautiful, young girlfriend, and she doubted that feeling would ever fully go away. She wondered if anyone ever, in the history of the world, had experienced this feeling, or if it was just her. Plenty of girls had loved boys who'd died. But as far as she knew, she was the only one whose boy had come back decades later, raised in a world that he'd helped create, even though he had no memory of it.

It was an odd, lonely thought.

"Anyway, Alyssa really wants to learn, so I guess we're both learning," Justin finished with a smile. "We'll be there for two weeks in July, to give us time to pack before we head off to college."

"And where are you going to school?" She knew—it was right there in the file—but she wanted to hear him say it out loud.

"University of Pennsylvania," he said proudly. "It's where my grandparents met. They tried to pretend they didn't care where I went, but I could tell. Plus I'll be able to see them on the weekends and stuff. It's been weird, not having them here."

"I'm sure it has been," Rose said, a lump rising in her chest. Ducking her head, she made a show of adjusting her glasses before he could notice her watery eyes. *Get it together.* She cleared her throat, forcing a bright smile. "So let's talk about the details of this scholarship, shall we?"

She managed to get through the rest of the meeting without breaking down, shifting into autopilot as she delivered her standard speech about GPA requirements and distribution schedules, although she kept her eyes on her notes far more than she usually did. If she looked at him, she couldn't trust herself not to stare, searching for every difference, every similarity.

Finally, and too soon, her role was over, and she was shaking their hands, and then they were gone.

Rose waited until she heard the front door of the office click shut behind them before bracing both hands on her desk and taking a long, shuddering breath. She removed her glasses and rubbed her eyes, not caring whether she smudged her mascara. Not for the first time, she wished she kept something a little stronger than coffee in her office.

"Um, Dr. Hanley?"

Rose looked up, blinking rapidly. There he was, framed in her doorway, young and vibrant and alive in a way he'd never been when she'd known him.

"Yes?" She realized too late that she still had tears on her cheeks.

"I forgot my backpack," he said, edging into the room. Sure enough, there it was, slouched on the floor by his chair.

"Of course."

He shrugged the bag onto one shoulder but didn't leave right away. "Dr. Hanley?"

"Yes, Justin?" Even though she knew he never would, she wished he would call her by her first name, just once.

"I hope it's okay for me to ask, but . . . are you okay?"

Rose let out a little laugh, or maybe it was a tiny sob—she couldn't quite be sure. "I'm fine," she said quietly, wiping her tears with a fresh tissue.

"It's just that you seem a little upset and—"

"It's nothing." In her effort to keep from crying, her voice came out stiff, cold. It didn't even sound like her.

"Okay," he said uncertainly. "Well, bye."

He turned to leave, and her heart squeezed like it was being ripped from her chest. Suddenly, she knew she had to tell him, even if he wouldn't understand. "Actually," she said, her voice breaking, "I'm sorry, it's just that you . . . you remind me of someone I knew when I was your age."

He looked back at her, his bright-blue eyes staring into hers. For a second, she almost—she'd probably imagined it, but she *almost*—thought she saw a flicker of recognition.

"Who?" he said softly. As if he realized that this memory was delicate, and he didn't want to risk shattering it.

"A friend," she said. "He's been gone a long time, but when I look at you, I can still see his face so clearly."

"He died?"

She nodded. Tears were slipping freely down her cheeks now, and she didn't try to stop them. "He died a long time ago, and I never got to tell him . . ." She took a deep breath. This boy wasn't her Justin. She couldn't talk to him like he was. "Anyway, you look a lot like him, and it brought back a lot of memories. I'm sorry if I made you uncomfortable."

"It's all right," he said, giving her a shy, encouraging smile. "Were they good memories?"

"They were," she whispered.

"Then I'm glad." He hesitated, tilting his head. Just another reminder that this boy wasn't the one she'd known; her Justin rarely considered his words before he spoke. "Dr. Hanley, I'm not sure what happens when you die . . ."

Rose sucked in a sharp breath. How many times had she heard him start a thought just like that?

"But I think, if there was something you wanted to tell him, there's a chance he already knows. Or that you can still tell him, if you want." He shrugged, looking a little self-conscious. "I just think there's so much we don't know that we can't rule it out. Right?"

For the first time, Rose let herself truly look at him. Was her Justin in there somewhere? Was there a chance he could hear her? They'd always debated the meaning in his trip to the past, wondering whether some cosmic hand had picked him up in 2023 and placed him down in 1985, precisely where and when he needed to be. If people really could be put in specific places for specific moments, then could that mean that this Justin was here, right now, for her?

She took a deep breath, thinking through what she should say. She wanted to tell him all that had happened after he'd died. How Shawn had been sentenced to fifteen years in prison for second-degree arson and vehicular manslaughter, but had been released after seven for good behavior. After earning his college degree in prison, he'd gone to law school upon getting out, and now worked for the public defender's office.

One of his first clients was Robbie Reynolds, who had been in and out of prison for various offenses ever since he turned eighteen. Sometime later, Shawn confessed to Lisa—who had faithfully visited him in prison, and continued to keep in touch after he was released—that Robbie's was one of the rare cases he'd been happy to lose.

She wanted to tell him that Diane had won her race and served as mayor for the next eight years. Lisa had worked as an intern in her mother's office during college, which was where she'd met the wonderful woman who would eventually become her wife. After the birth of their second baby, Lisa had decided to follow in her mother's footsteps and run for public office, too. It turned out Lisa was even more of a natural than her mother.

She wanted to tell him that Charlene now ran Derrin Family Jams. She was divorced, but still lived with her oldest daughter and three grandchildren—all girls—in the big house across Wilson Bridge. Every fall, Rose and Charlene would find each other at the bonfire, still mostly unchanged after all these years.

Her brother, Karl, had moved out of Stone Lake right after graduating from high school, and rarely visited. Instead of joining the family business, he now made a living writing graphic novels in Chicago. Rose knew from Charlene that he had a son named Dave, although she didn't know how to ask whether he'd turned out better than the one Justin had known. She liked to think he had.

She wanted to tell him that Mrs. Hanley had died peacefully in her sleep eleven years ago, two weeks after casting her vote for Obama's second term as president and Lisa's first as a US senator.

She wanted to tell him that she and Noah had gotten married during their junior year of college—too young, some said, but by the time they finally got together, they both knew it was forever—and that they had three children and five beautiful grandchildren. She wanted to tell him that after Shawn lost the citizenship award, the county decided to grant it to Noah instead, thanks to his heroic actions the night of the fire. She wanted to tell him that Noah had used it to become a doctor, and that he now worked to save lives every day.

She wanted to tell him that she and Noah had named their oldest son Justin, after the boy who'd given up his future to save theirs.

She couldn't say any of that, of course. But she hoped, somewhere, he knew.

"I'd just want to tell him thank you," she finally said. "For everything. I'd want to make sure he knew that he was a hero. He made a difference. And . . ."

She hesitated, remembering a boy and a girl sitting across from each other on a flowered bedspread, turning up the radio as they made plans to change the future. "I'd tell him we were both right about the song."

She understood now. Death, but also love. The end of the world, but also hope for the future. All of it could be true at the same time.

"And it *was* a sign," she added, smiling to herself. "Even if he never believed me."

Justin—the 2023 version, the one who had two living grandparents who were going to teach him to water-ski, the one who was headed to college in the fall, the one who had never died even once, much less twice—grinned. "I think he heard you."

Rose smiled back. "I think he did, too."

ACKNOWLEDGMENTS

The road from "I think I may try writing a book" to publication has been a long one, and *I'll Stop the World* would never have made it out of my head and into your hands if not for all the people willing to travel it with me. Some walked alongside me, some led the way, and a cherished few tossed me over their shoulders and carried me when I felt like I couldn't take another step. I'll never be able to list every single person whose fingerprints are somewhere on this book, but to each and every person who helped me get here, thank you.

To my amazing agent, Holly Root, thank you for sticking with me, fighting for me, and never losing faith. I don't think either of us ever anticipated just how many twists this publishing path would throw at us when we first teamed up, and there are so many times when I might've given up had you not been there, cheering me on. Thank you for your steadfast confidence in my writing, for your patience and compassion during the hard times, for your incomparable expertise and razor-sharp instincts, and for helping me keep my feet under me when things got overwhelming. A big thanks, too, to Alyssa Maltese and the team at Root Literary for being such a well-oiled machine of consummate pros.

To the inimitable Mindy Kaling, thank you for seeing something special in this story and for believing in it enough to lend your name to it. I never dreamed when I wrote a book with a throwaway *Office* joke in it that Kelly Kapoor herself would be the one to publish it.

To my editor, Megha Parekh, thank you for seeing exactly what I was trying to do with this book and for your enthusiasm in helping shape it into the best version of itself.

To Emma Reh, Sarah Shaw, Jarrod Taylor, Carmen Johnson, Chrissy Penido, Ashley Vanicek, Lily Choi, Kellie Osborne, and the entire team at Mindy's Book Studio and Amazon Publishing, thank you for the countless hours of work you've put into this book and for how kind and supportive you've been during each step of the process.

To Megan Beatie and the team at Megan Beatie Communications, thank you for your enthusiasm for this book, and for your willingness to shout about it from the rooftops.

To Dave Andrews and the team at Brilliance Audio, thank you for your passion and vision in creating the best possible audio version of my book. And to the phenomenal cast who so perfectly embodied my characters: Michael Crouch, Natasha Tina Liu, Alaska Jackson, Brian Holden, Mark Sanderlin, Sarah Naughton, Scott Merriman, Marcus Stewart, and David De Vries, thank you for lending your incredible talents to this story, surpassing my wildest expectations.

To Heather Baror-Shapiro, thank you for championing this book literally around the world.

To my film agents, Jasmine Lake and Mirabel Michelson, thank you for seeing my characters as people you want to see brought to life. I hope we get to meet them someday.

To Sarah Brown, thank you for inexplicably saying yes all those years ago to an out-of-the-blue email from a stranger on the internet who was looking for a critique partner. I still have no idea what possessed either of us to venture out of our comfort zones and become friends, but I'm so glad we did. Thank you for the hundreds of hours spent talking about everything and nothing, for being undetectable to my introvert batteries, for reading nearly everything I've ever written and never getting sick of my stories, and for believing in me even when it became too hard to believe in myself.

To Ashley Herring Blake, MG Buehrlen, Paige Crutcher, Alisha Klapheke, and Myra McEntire, thank you for reading various iterations of this story and pushing me to make it better. You are all brilliant writers and friends, and your questions, suggestions, and insights were vital to making this book what it is today.

To all the friends who sat across from me in coffee shops, exchanged pages, passionately debated fictional scenarios, sent encouraging emails and texts, trekked through the woods, stayed up late laughing in hotel lounges, crammed into cars, and demolished innumerable orders of queso with me during the years I spent working toward publication: David Arnold, Carla Lafontaine, Erica Rodgers, Victoria Schwab, Ashley Schwartau, Court Stevens, and Kristin Tubb, a thousand thank-yous. I wouldn't have gotten here without you.

To the SHC, thank you for being a light in the darkness. Some of the conversations in this book may feel a little familiar to you. Thank you for being a safe space to process and heal.

To my parents, siblings, and all the extended family who have supported me throughout my life, thank you for your love and for helping me grow into the person I am today.

To all those who have encouraged me over the years, who have seen value in me and my writing, who have offered words of affirmation and support, thank you. It's amazing how even small acts of kindness can brighten a day.

To the readers who picked up this book, thank you for taking a chance on a debut author and for lending me your time, attention, and imagination for a little while.

To my family, thank you for never doubting that I could do this. Greg, thank you for building me desks and bookshelves, for watching the kids while I attended conferences and workshops and retreats, for spending countless evenings talking through character motivations and plot twists and backstories with me, and for always encouraging me to prioritize my writing even when I fretted that it might never go anywhere. You've been the best husband, partner, and friend I could ever have hoped for, and I am grateful for you every day.

And to my children, thank you for all the times you asked when my book launch would be, and whether there would be cake, as if eventually publishing a book was a foregone conclusion in your minds. Thank you for still wanting to spend time with me as you've grown up, for the huggie cuddles and laughter, and for sharing your passions and talents and worries and questions with me. It is a joy being your mom. I love you forever.

ABOUT THE AUTHOR

Lauren Thoman lives outside Nashville, Tennessee, with her husband, two children, and a rotating number of dogs and fish. Her pop culture writing has appeared in numerous online outlets, including *Parade*, *Vulture*, and *Collider*. For more information, visit www.laurenthomanwrites.com.